The Weight
of the City

Will Rhode

POCKET
BOOKS

LONDON • SYDNEY • NEW YORK • TORONTO

First published in Great Britain by Pocket Books, 2007
An imprint of Simon & Schuster UK Ltd
A CBS COMPANY

1 3 5 7 9 10 8 6 4 2

Simon & Schuster UK Ltd
Africa House
64–78 Kingsway
London WC2B 6AH

www.simonsays.co.uk

Simon & Schuster Australia
Sydney

A CIP catalogue record for this book
is available from the British Library

ISBN-13: 978-1-4165-0230-2
ISBN-10: 1-4165-0230-0

Typeset in Stone Serif by M Rules
Printed and bound in Great Britain by
Cox & Wyman Ltd, Reading Berks

To Pete, who gave me my first toolbox

Cooperative (adj.) **1** helpful by doing what one is asked to do. **2** involving acting or working together with another or others for a common purpose.
(n.) relating to a building with apartments owned by a corporation of tenants in which shares of expenses are calculated on the basis of the value of the tenant's apartment.

© Encarta

When Siddhartha listened attentively to this river, to this song of a thousand voices; when he did not bind his soul to any one particular voice and absorb it in his Self, but heard them all, the whole, the unity; then the great song of a thousand voices consisted of one word . . .

Hermann Hesse

The hem of her dress swam in the wind like an eel. It was delicately embroidered, with a simple, small flower design and an undulating cut made for dancing. I could see the tops of her knees. Her ankles were tenderly swollen and there was sinuous extra effort in her cream-stockinged calves. She was wearing dark-blue shoes, with small, smart heels. Her feet twisted in tiny circles as they talked, trying to kill time because they had arrived too early.

'Do you have everything?' she said.

'I think so. Christ, I hope so,' he replied, with a New England accent. 'It wasn't easy getting the application organized. They seem kinda strict in this building, if you ask me. I mean, who needs all this information? The thing weighs more than a ton. It looks like a Bible.'

'As long as we get the apartment, I don't care,' she replied.

'You're right,' he sighed. 'It's easily the best place we've seen, for the money.'

'I love you,' she said, one sole scraping sharply against the pavement as she moved.

There was the silence of an embrace. The wind kicked up white ripples on the river. A taxi careered against the cobblestones and through the wet behind them – *budapabudapabudapabudapapa fizzzzzzzzz.*

'Here goes nothing,' he said, as the faintest smell of her drifted down to me through the air grille like a butterfly uncertain in flight.

Anna-lise was staring at Morgan, full of frustration and fury. No one had stood up for her. No one had said anything to help. They were all openly relieved Morgan hadn't chosen them.

Anna-lise looked up, into the ceiling, to gather herself. She noticed a small knot in one of the exposed beams that ran the length of Morgan's apartment. It swirled like a tiny black tornado, a beauty spot on an already perfect, polished frame.

'Fine,' Anna-lise said eventually, feeling the ends of her sandy hair against her face as she looked back down into Morgan's darkness, noticing the faint bloodshot in her eyes. 'I'll do it.'

She pulled Ulysses in close to her chest so she could smell him.

'I'm glad because I wasn't actually asking,' Morgan replied, smiling as if it was a joke.

Anna-lise sank back into the sofa a little further.

'Will someone propose the motion, please?' Morgan continued.

Mike, who lived on the floor below, raised a thickly veined forearm. The bicep bulged against his skin-tight cotton T-shirt, making it stretch.

'Thank you, Mike,' Morgan said with an air of solidarity. 'Who will second the motion?'

'I will,' croaked Mrs Xhiu, the ancient Chinese lady who lived on the first floor. She was the hardest person in the building for me to read. She had religion and the television was always on in her flat – even when she wasn't there.

'All those in favour say aye.'

'Aye,' everyone said together, even Anna-lise, which was a bit stupid of her. She could be that way sometimes.

'Please make a note in the minutes, Frank,' Morgan said sharply. 'Anna-lise has been elected Building Treasurer.'

Ulysses went crazy when the bell rang, leaping out of Anna-lise's arms and running around and around in tiny circles of excitement, as he always did, yapping in a painful pitch. Morgan managed not to lose her temper; maybe because the last time she did that, the terrier had urinated on her floor.

Instead, she reached for the television remote so they could all observe the candidates on a special internal channel.

'Does everyone have copies of their application package?' Morgan asked.

There was a general murmur, which didn't give a straight answer either way, like kids in class.

'Interesting,' she said, as the screen came to life. 'Well, I hope you've all gone through it and have your questions prepared.' She reached for her intercom-linked walkie-talkie and said: 'Enter.'

The couple leant towards the camera to say thanks but Morgan cut them off with a long, loud electronic fart. The cogs in the lock gave way easily, which was a good sign. Once inside, Morgan had to buzz them again so they could pass through a second door. The corridor floorboards sang. They didn't say anything to one another as they waited for the elevator, and they didn't say anything to each other inside it either. Just before they reached Morgan's flat, though, she reached for his hand.

'Come through!' Morgan called as the elevator chimed.

'I hope we're not late,' the man said entering, his voice shaking slightly. Morgan sized him up from a distance. The couple moved like shadows into the living room.

'No, no, no,' Morgan said, willing them in impatiently.

'You must be Morgan.'

He extended his hand, trying to look at everyone at the same time in a sort of communal greeting. This meant he wasn't looking where he was going so he accidentally trod on Ulysses, who let out a tormented yelp.

In that instant, Morgan decided to approve their application.

'My poor baby!' Anna-lise cried, leaping to pick up the dog by the shoulders, its body splaying outwards.

'NOT LIKE THAT! NOT THAT! STOP!' Morgan shouted as Ulysses sprayed urine across the floor.

'My poor baby,' Anna-lise whimpered simply, pressing the dog's face to her own, kissing it openly on the mouth.

'My God, I am so sorry,' the candidate cried anxiously. 'Will he be all right?'

'He'll be fine,' Morgan said, throwing down readied paper towels with angry resignation and drilled efficiency. 'Can we get on? Please take a seat,' she said, motioning the couple towards the sofa. 'We haven't much time.' Then, as an afterthought: 'And you must be exhausted.'

'Thank you,' the woman replied, holding the base of her back with one inverted hand.

'This is a fantastic apartment.' The man tried to recover as Anna-lise curled into a ball on the sofa with the dog.

'Thank you,' Morgan said briskly. 'Now, shall I start with some introductions? You've just met Anna-lise and Ulysses. Next to you on the sofa is Frank. Frank is Secretary of the Board.'

Frank smiled flatly.

'On the uncomfortable-looking chair is Mike,' Morgan pressed on.

Mike nodded, his thick neck straining.

'Over there is Mrs Xhiu and over there . . . is Garry.'

'Hi,' Garry said with casual loping charm before sweeping a hand through shoulder-length brown hair, silver bangles on his wrist clinking together like coins in a purse.

The couple smiled at the room.

'As you may have gathered, my name is Morgan Honeysuckle. I am the President of the Board here at 444 VanVanVane Street, or 444 as we like to call it, and it is my honour to welcome you into the building. I wish you luck in your application and I hope that, even if you are unsuccessful in your bid to buy apartment G1, you enjoy your brief time here with us.'

The couple continued to smile.

'So, without further ado, and with the approval of the rest of the Board, I would like to proceed with some questions I have prepared in response to your, dare I say it, rather incomplete application.'

They stopped smiling.

Morgan paused to allow time for any possible objections before proceeding.

'Good,' she said, adjusting herself in her chair, picking up a clipboard and a new pen she'd bought especially for the purpose. 'Frank?'

'Yes, Morgan,' Frank sighed.

'Please take notes for the minutes.'

'Yes, Morgan.'

'Question one,' Morgan started, poising the pen in preparation for the answer, as if they were in an exam. 'You say that your name is Benjamin *B* . . . '

I had hoped it was the heating system.

It was November so it was just starting to kick in, making loud, sudden cracks like a hammer hitting metal. It wasn't meant to make these noises but the building was old and the pipes had settled over the years. Some of them were dead-set horizontal where there was meant to be a gradient. The water didn't drain back into the boiler properly. When the system fired up again and steam passed over the cold water trapped in the pipes it banged in a way that made me blink.

BANG!

Like that.

BANG! BANG!

It was hard to imagine it was just water expanding, it could be so loud and startling. It sounded more like something very strong snapping, like a rock or a slab of granite. I suppose, in some ways, it was something very strong in those pipes coming apart – liquid breaking. On the very cold days there would have been ice.

But the second time, I knew it wasn't the heating system. It couldn't have been. Because . . . it talked.

Not words. I didn't hear words. Not exactly. First there was a clicking noise – faint, persistent, rhythmic, difficult to pinpoint. It made my teeth ache.

Then there was a groan, or a long creak, like metal under pressure. Sometimes a heating-system crack was preceded by a groan. So I had hoped it was that – just another heating-system groan.

But then there was the talking sound.

Have you ever heard an audiotape when it gets chewed up in the machine? It was like that. It was like sound wound down – almost dreadful.

will rhode

It was then that I realized that I'd been tuning in.

Considering how easily sound carried in the building – in the heating pipes, through the walls, down the airshaft – I can see how I'd started again. I heard everything. The sounds of the building all got funnelled down to me in the basement.

I heard floorboards creaking, taps running, doors slamming, people talking, televisions tuning, envelopes tearing, eyes weeping, knives slicing, gas igniting, fabric whispering, rubber soles squeaking, lock works cleaving, drains sucking, joists shifting, bedheads hammering, air travelling . . .

Everything.

Sound came at me constantly. If I closed my eyes and really listened I could discern layers within the texture, the same way an architect might fathom a building, or a conductor hear his orchestra.

Some sounds belonged to certain layers, while other sounds moved across them. A steady sound with a constant volume and an even pitch, the whir in a thermostatic timer, for example – that had a layer. But a sound that swelled and faded, like a car passing in the street outside – that moved across layers. And some sounds moved but to a limited frequency, they oscillated within a layer. The sound of people talking in walls was like that.

Except for when they shouted.

Noise never stopped. There was no such thing as complete silence. Even in the dead of night, when everything was meant to be asleep, there was the neon in the street lights fizzing, or the thick bass of a nightclub pulsing, or the throaty, lost-voice roar of a distant highway.

And I was so close to everyone. I knew them. Long before I heard it, I knew what they did, what they liked, who they didn't like, where they liked to eat, what clothes they wore. When you live with people and see them day in, day out for years and years you get to know who they are, you get to know the way they think.

So I really should have expected it. Maybe I could have done more to stop myself. But I honestly thought I'd stopped. I didn't expect to start again. I hadn't tuned in for years when I took the job. This was meant to be a fresh start for me, a new beginning. I had been careful to set up my life differently from before. I didn't want to start again. I never wanted to go back to before. It terrified me to realize that, in spite of everything I'd been through and done, somehow I had slipped back.

And now it was too late to stop. Seeing them that night made me realize. It was like looking in a mirror, a mirror that looked back in time. The reflection made me see things for the way they were now. I felt as if I'd been caught in an old habit. I saw myself in the act. I'd let it happen. And now I was losing control. I couldn't stop it even if I wanted.

And besides, the signal had a quality that made me want to focus in. I found myself wanting to understand it, decipher it, locate it. Even though I was repulsed by it, there was a singularity to the new sound, a certain harmony. No signal had ever been like that before. Before, there had been chaos, a maddening cacophony. Now, even if it was ugly, there was unity, there was cooperation.

I know – I should have left it alone. I couldn't account for it, so I should have left it alone.

It was a bad transmission.

Cherry carefully selected another patch of scrotum to cover in rainbow masking tape. Harvey gasped slightly as she pressed it on.

'I don't think there's room for any more,' said Cherry, who was dressed in thigh-high latex boots and plastic red panties, the black lipstick on her round mouth moving.

'Try down there,' Harvey indicated with a nod.

'Where?' Cherry replied in her horizontal Brooklyn drawl.

'There,' Harvey said with gentle patience.

'Oh yeaaahhhh. Jeez, I nearly missed that bit.'

She tore another strip from the roll with her teeth. Harvey looked like he was about to cry as the heating pipe Cherry had tied his wrists to started to burn.

'Hey!' Cherry said, standing up straight, wobbling slightly on her nine-inch steel stilettos. 'It looks kinda pretty.' She giggled.

'Please,' Harvey whimpered at her, his shoulders straining forward. 'Don't make me wait.'

Cherry turned back into the camera and gave a look from out of the tops of her eyes as if to ask: *Well . . . should I?* The expression momentarily revealed her, the girl she used to be, the woman she was, under the Halloween costume. You could see the eyes behind the eyeliner, the trace of freckles across the bridge of her nose, the terracotta colour of her hair in the roots.

BANG!

The heating pipe rang violently through the apartment and shook in the old ceiling plasterboard, raining dust down onto Harvey's bald head.

'Please,' Harvey said again, twisting his wrists now. 'I want you to do it.'

Cherry manoeuvred herself at a forty-five-degree angle to the camera, legs apart, before tearing the strips off one by one. There were raw marks, one or two of the pieces even making small abrasions in the skin. Tears of ecstasy streamed down Harvey's fat face and his bottom lip quivered as she relieved him from the grip of all that glue.

'Cut!' Helmut said and immediately started laughing.

'Very funny,' Cherry said, walking across the empty apartment towards the kitchen sink. She turned on one of the taps. It groaned and shuddered and spluttered rusty water. 'Hey, Helmut, can't I get a glass of water?'

'They must have turned it off. Here,' he said, reaching into his bag and pulling out an Evian. 'Have some of mine.'

Cherry took three large gulps and leant against the kitchen counter, looking at Helmut. He was a tall man with frightening blue eyes and a thick fair beard that looked more like long stubble. The last time they'd slept together she'd noticed that he was developing a belly. His heavy bones would always keep him looking broad and strong, she supposed. She still found him attractive, which was good. How many girls could claim a steady gig *and* like the guy? Maybe it was just that Cherry knew the real reason Helmut shot porn, maybe that was why she liked him.

'Whose place is this anyway?' She sniffed, noticing the smell of baby talc.

'Daniel's,' Helmut said, his hands back in his bag.

'Who's Daniel?'

'Just a guy.'

'Where is he?'

'No one knows.'

'Whaddya mean?'

'He's missing.'

'I don't get it.'

'One day he was here, the next day he was gone. He just walked out the door and never came back.'

'He just vanished?'

'Ya.'

'He didn't tell anyone where he was going?'

'No.'

'That's freaky,' Cherry said, holding herself.

'What did the police say?' Harvey asked.

'They investigated but didn't come up with anything,' Helmut explained.

'They don't think he was murdered?'

'They said he could have been but until they find a body they have to treat it as a missing person's investigation.'

'I bet he was murdered,' Harvey said. 'What kind of guy just gets up one day and disappears without a trace?'

'All kinds,' said Cherry. 'He could have had debts. He could have had problems. Maybe he just decided to skip town. Christ knows I've thought about it.'

'He didn't pack,' Helmut said. 'He left the place just as it was. He didn't take anything with him. It was like he went out to go to work.'

'Never to return,' Harvey finished in a spooky voice. 'I bet you he was killed in here.'

'You're an asshole, Harvey,' Cherry said.

'So what happens to this apartment, then?' Harvey asked.

'It's for sale. The Board are interrogating candidates tonight.'

'They can do that?' Cherry asked. 'What if Daniel comes back?'

'He's been gone for over a year,' Helmut explained. 'He hasn't paid his bills, no one's seen or heard from him, so his life has officially ended. That's the law.'

'That's horrible,' Cherry said.

'I think it's kind of cool,' Harvey said quietly.

'Shut up, Harv,' Cherry snapped. 'I wish you'd said something, Helmut. This place is giving me the creeps now. Can't we go back to your place?'

'I'm sorry, baby,' Helmut said, looking directly at her. 'We've only got access because it's an open day. And we've started already. We'd have to re-shoot the entire sequence. Come, ya,' he added quickly before Cherry had the chance to get upset. 'Only one more scene. You like this one. This is where we get Harvey to really squeal.'

Helmut laughed and Cherry couldn't help herself softening.

'OK,' she said. 'But make it quick.'

'Great! Now stand back where you were.' Cherry walked along the room, her stilettos echoing across the wooden floor and against the empty walls and the trash-bag blacked-out windows. 'Good,' Helmut said, re-angling the spotlights slightly. 'OK,' he said, looking down into the camera briefly. 'Everyone ready?'

'I wonder how the killer did it,' Harvey said.

'Shut up,' said Cherry.

'He probably strangled him, less blood.'

'I'm warning you, Harvey.'

'The killer would have had to be strong. Otherwise there would have been signs of a struggle.'

'I'm not gonna tell you again.'

'I wonder how he got rid of the body. Maybe he used acid.'

Cherry threw her arms up in the air, exasperated. 'This is just great. This is fucking great.'

'OK, guys, enough,' Helmut said.

'Just for that, Harvey, I'm gonna make sure this really hurts you now,' Cherry said.

'Good,' Harvey replied, beaming.

I found myself thinking of Catherine, specifically the day I asked her to marry me. We'd threaded zeds through the grid system, following the WALK signals to the Empire State Building. She had something she wanted to show me. It was already one of those days, big and blue, the sky a million miles above, the faintest of webs in the ether.

And once we were on top of the Empire State Building – wow! The clarity of the day was so exaggerated. It was like standing on top of a rocket. I thought I could see stars in the brightness above. The air seemed thinner and more refined. I took in large gulps of it and let Catherine lead me through the knots of Korean and French tourists wearing flannel suits, to the south-east corner of the building.

'What do you see?' she asked me, pointing down into the noise coming off like steam from the streets below.

'Lots of buildings and people that look like ants.'

'What do you think it weighs?'

'The whole city?'

'Every brick, every person, every car and truck – count it all up.'

I laughed. 'A lot!'

'Can you be more specific?'

I looked at her. She had her teacher's face on, warm and understanding if a little strict. I think it had something to do with the way her forehead folded between her eyebrows sometimes. I could see lines forming there.

'Let me think for a moment.'

I considered what she was asking me. I started with the weight of people first. I knew the population of the city and multiplied it by two hundred to get a rough estimate in pounds.

I allocated one car to every five people and figured each one would weigh a ton. I started to get lost when I considered how much a truck might weigh and a little panicked when I realized I hadn't even started to consider the buildings, which were probably the most important part of the calculation.

'Do you want me to tell you?'

'No. Just give me a minute.'

'But you're taking too long.'

'Give me a chance, Catherine.'

'You're going about it the wrong way. I know, because it's taking you too long.'

'It's taking me so long because you keep talking. If you shut up for a second, I'll tell you.'

Catherine turned and looked out, over the city smoke, towards the bridges.

'Isn't it incredible that the island doesn't sink?' she said. 'Consider the rock the city's built on, how hard and strong it must be to take all this weight. It has to be heavier than all of this.'

She swept her hand across the horizon in a way that stopped me working on the problem and made me look out with her. I felt people taking photos beside us and realized with glee how corny it all was. And, from there, I found myself wanting to ask.

'Will you marry me, Catherine?'

She didn't say anything but I could feel her beaming. I turned to look at her and noticed that the sunlight had caught the line of her nose and was illuminating very fine and tiny hairs in a seam of gold. She threw her head round and said happily: 'No.'

I stared back at her, unsure of myself.

'Unless . . . ' she added slowly.

I felt my eyebrows floating. 'Unless I can tell you the weight of Manhattan.'

'To the nearest ton.'

'How generous.'

'You've got one minute.'

We spent that time looking at one another. I felt very happy, happier, perhaps, than at any other time in my life. I remember recognizing it at the time. It was extraordinary to know it, to know I felt that way in that moment. Until then, I'd only ever realized happiness by looking back. It was something that belonged to the past, which meant that it was something already gone, which made me feel nostalgically sad. Up to that day, happiness had usually been no more than an unpleasant paradox. But being with Catherine changed all that.

'Time's up,' she said eventually.

'So soon?'

'Yup. What's the answer?'

'I wrote it down,' I replied.

'Really?' She frowned. 'Where?'

'On a piece of paper.'

'Uh-huh?'

'In your pocket,' I said.

'Don't play games.'

'Take a look.'

I watched her reach into her jacket and pull out the receipt I'd written on earlier without knowing why. She unfolded it. She stared down into her hands, which were trembling slightly.

'It scares me sometimes,' she said, without looking up.

'I know,' I replied. 'It scares me too.'

She lifted her head. Her eyes had darkened.

'You'll never use it to hurt me, will you?'

Morgan Honeysuckle moved into 444 seven years ago. She bought the apartment on the top floor, a one-bedroom on the west side. But when the elderly couple who owned the flat across the corridor moved out she bought their place as well and converted the two apartments into a penthouse.

Strictly speaking, she wasn't allowed to do that since it meant she appropriated the building corridor as her own when really it was communal property, like the risers and the spaces between apartments.

But no one complained.

Her apartment was now the best in the building. It had panoramic views of the Hudson and New Jersey. There was five-inch solid-oak flooring throughout. It had its own private elevator entrance, and in the bathroom there was a free-standing cast-iron tub with power shower. Beams the size of trees ran across the ceiling and along the tops of exposed brick walls. There was a small fireplace. The kitchen was large with an island and a silver-green stone work surface. All the appliances were in brushed chrome. There was a four-poster bed in her bedroom with poplin sheets. The bedroom had its own walk-in closet as well as another smaller, en-suite bathroom with black-and-white art-deco-style tiles.

Morgan liked to keep the place spotless. A Haitian lady who spoke bad English came five times a week to clean and nothing was ever moved from its designated place.

Morgan also ran her life according to an immaculate schedule. After waking (6 a.m.), she did sixty-six minutes of yoga, stretching her long limbs across a special mat, watching herself in the mirror on the back of a closet door.

She had a beautiful body. As well as yoga, she used the gym

frequently. She had very elegant legs. She also had extremely long fingers. She kept her hair short, paying meticulous attention to a rough brushed look she paid two hundred dollars for each month.

When she washed, Morgan started with her feet and worked her way upwards, being sure to cover every inch. She used different products for different parts of her body and she kept these things in an orderly row on a small shelf on the wall nearest the bath.

She was very particular about her feet. There was a pair of nail clippers and an iron file and a pumice stone. Next to them was a lemon-and-sandalwood body wash which she used only for her legs and body. She had sensitive skin so she used a specially formulated scrub for her face.

Between the body wash and the facial scrub there was another pair of scissors, which she used to trim her pubic hairs. She used a rose-scented shampoo and a cream conditioner for her hair. She used a comb to scrape off excess water and dead skin before drying herself. Finally, she smothered herself in coconut butter.

After washing, Morgan got dressed. Most of her clothes were designed by Yarko Thomas and because of this she didn't have many. Yarko Thomas was expensive but very worth it. Everyone Morgan respected wore him. Morgan had two pairs of jeans, three skirts (one mini), one dress, four blouses, two pairs of smart shoes, seven pairs of tights, a black turtleneck jumper, a tracksuit, a pair of running shoes, a pair of shorts, three T-shirts and a favourite cardigan. She never wore anything for more than six months, donating cast-offs to Mrs Xhiu, who passed them on to a homeless charity. Clothes lost their shape after six months, she believed.

Her breakfast was muesli (in water). She drank black coffee. At the breakfast table, she read the newspaper and opened her post, which were mostly notices of direct debits from her bank account or paperwork concerning the building. She directed all other mail to her office.

After breakfast, Morgan took her medication. She kept these pills in a shoebox on a high shelf in her walk-in closet. They were mostly for anxiety but there were other pills too. She had problems sleeping. In a drawer next to her bed she kept earplugs and one of those blindfolds they give out on airplanes.

The last thing Morgan did before leaving for work was look at herself in the mirror. Her skin shone. Her nose was elegant and long. There was mathematical precision in the shape of her philtrum. Her mouth was round and small. It flashed a deep pink when she spoke. Her eyes were elliptical, Egyptian. Her ears were small. Her mother had once told her she was a descendant of pharaohs.

After Daniel went missing, cockroaches nested in G1. Everyone noticed there were more than usual, but they were clever. They didn't overrun the place. They infiltrated inconspicuously; as inconspicuously as three-inch, armour-plated, mandible-mouthed tanks crawling across the floor can be.

That was why I didn't consider it an infestation. They sent only the occasional scout, the odd spy, to foray and search for possible places of expansion, new sites in which to breed. They had their undiscovered hive, their headquarters, their collective. For the most part, they marched within perimeters.

Like a lot of people I simply assumed they were bad that year, something to do with the unusually hot summer. Morgan told me to cope with the isolated incidences, to lay down traps and poison in corners and under the cupboards of apartments whenever somebody complained. It never got bad enough to call in an exterminator.

In the end they didn't have time to colonize. A year after his disappearance, Daniel was officially declared missing and the Board were allowed to put his apartment up for sale.

I was given the job of clearing out the place. It was strange going in the first time. It was like someone had died but not been buried, their moment of departure from the world frozen in time.

I found a carton of milk and a small slab of cheese in the fridge as well as other items made indistinguishable by mould. I could see the shape of his body in the duvet on the bed. His laundry lay in a special bin in one corner of his bedroom – two pairs of underwear, a pair of socks and a shirt. There were three dirty dishes in the dishwasher and a coffee-stained mug. The smell was bad. It was broad and specied. It fed on itself.

Over the months I had collected his post from the mailbox in the building hall so there weren't any letters but there were pieces of paper around the place with reminders and notes from the past; yellow Post-its with his handwriting on them. I saw a letter written to him by his brother left open and lying on his small desk. The telephone company had disconnected the line so there weren't any messages but there was still his voice on the welcome. Listening to it was like communicating with the dead, a message-service medium. Everywhere there were pictures of smiling people: relatives, friends, loved ones, Sharon – all of them collecting dust.

When I turned the TV on, it was the Weather Channel, a ghost signal. The day he disappeared he'd wanted to know what the day would be like. Had he needed an umbrella? Medicines and hygiene products in the vanity cabinet were all exactly as he had left them, turned in particular and random ways, some labels showing, some not. There were some cartons closed, others left open. There was a single, empty brown bottle.

It still took me several days of clearing and cleaning to realize that there was a serious problem with the cockroaches. When I saw them around, in cupboards, climbing out of cereal packets, stamping down bathroom drains, I assumed the problem we'd had all over the house had naturally extended into G1. I never imagined they were originating from the apartment. I simply figured it was bound to be worse wherever there was leftover food and waste.

But after I'd cleared out the refrigerator and the kitchen cabinets, after I'd washed the floors and aired the rooms, after I'd scrubbed and cleaned and dusted, and still found five or six or seven of the monsters rummaging and roaming around every nook and cranny, I realized that something was up.

I decided to give the apartment one more thorough clean before calling in an exterminator. I still hoped that maybe I just hadn't managed to get into every corner. I vaguely imagined that maybe I was slowly beating them with the sprays and poisons I was using. This time, I told myself, I would leave no stone unturned. I would make absolutely sure. Wherever they were, I would find them.

It didn't take me long. The kitchen was the obvious place to start. I tried moving the refrigerator away from the wall. It was heavy and its rubber roller-feet were stuck in an impression on the floor, clogged with dust and dirt. I noticed a clicking sound when it first shifted, the sound of scampering feet and panicking teeth. I pulled on the fridge with all my body weight and, after a couple of seconds, the rollers gave way and a purple thundercloud erupted across the wall and over the ceiling.

It took four seconds for the whole apartment to turn black. Thousands, no, tens of thousands of cockroaches spread in a circular wave, sprinting with coordinated panic. The sound was terrifying – all that insect clicking multiplied and magnified. I thought they might leap at me and attack. I turned on my heels and ran out of there, slamming the door behind me with a bang.

I called the extermination company who told me I'd have to 'nuke' the place. They sent me a special canister that was set on a timer to explode poison throughout the apartment. No one would be allowed in for three days afterwards.

In the end, I had to bomb G1 three times to eliminate them. I must have been sweeping up dead cockroaches for days. One day, the first, I filled an entire trashcan.

After three weeks, I plucked up the courage to throw out the nest, which turned out to be a large roll of iron wire mesh caught between two of the coolant rods at the back of the fridge. There was still one extraordinarily large cockroach, four inches long, lying inside it, its legs upturned.

It must have been the queen.

Frank practised his scales. His voice rang in the airshaft and through closed windows. Most people in the block that formed 444 VanVanVane Street with 443 Hanover Street, which was the exact same shape and size as 444 and which dovetailed off the other side of the airshaft, could hear him. But no one complained. Pretty much everyone liked Frank. He knew most people in the area by name.

He needed to keep up his voice even though he'd given up going to auditions these past few months. He'd been too busy temping, trying to pay the bills. Today, he was starting a new job, a permanent job – public relations for a financial-software company. He still had to reassure himself that it was only temporary. It was too depressing to think of it any other way. He was only doing it because the money was good. Plus he got benefits. He swore to himself that he'd quit as soon as he'd paid off all of his maintenance debts.

'I'm leaving tooo-day . . . ' he started singing.

It had been Morgan's idea to introduce an escalating penalty scheme for anyone who fell behind on their monthly mainte-nance payments. She'd set a one-hundred dollar fine for the first month, two hundred for the second, three hundred for the third . . . all of it accruing. Three role rejections in six months and Frank had found himself more than five thousand dollars in debt.

The worst thing was he knew that if things got too out of hand, the Co-op Board ultimately had the power to revoke his lease and sell his apartment out from underneath him.

Frank loved his apartment – he'd bought it 'at a steal' in the early nineties, before the property boom and before the meat-packing district had become really hip. It was now worth nearly triple what he'd paid, but that wasn't the reason he loved it.

He loved it because it had a view; he could see the Hudson between two buildings from out of his west-facing window. Sometimes he sat on the fire escape and drank a glass of wine or watered his potted plants, watching the sun set over the industrial flats of New Jersey and the metallic line of the river, the colours in the sky phantasmagoric in the pollution, enormous over the western continent.

He loved it because even though his apartment was small, he'd managed to make the most of it to carve out two bedrooms and still leave enough space in the living room for a small desk. This he'd done with the help of his all-singing, all-dancing brother, who built a partition wall that turned his spacious double bedroom into two single rooms. Frank had little need for a double bed, he needed the rent more. He was still looking for someone to replace Jeff but it was hard to find sane people to live with in New York.

He loved it because of the area. He loved the disused warehouses and the village-like cobbled streets; the Frontier paradox in the vast urban emptiness and the intimacy within the developing neighbourhood. It was worth making friends with anyone you found here, if only for company's sake. There were now three delis, a video store, a liquor shop, a diner, a Mexican, a Chinese, an Indian and a photocopying place nearby. They'd even converted the old elevated freight railway into a park for kids.

Sometimes he saw famous tourists. He loved that he could see the Empire State Building. He loved that there wasn't a Fake! or a Manhattan Health World too close by. He loved that one of his best friends lived on the same block. He loved his exposed brick walls and working fireplace.

He loved his apartment because it was his.

The thought that he was at risk of losing all this made him angry. Maybe it was just that he was dreading the new job but he couldn't figure out why, when he had spent a hundred and ninety-two thousand dollars buying his apartment, he should find himself answerable to Morgan.

Before she had taken over as Board President no one else had cared if anyone fell behind on their maintenance. It was only on her insistence that the building get its accounts in order that everyone had agreed to the penalty scheme. It wasn't as if the building needed the money. It didn't have a mortgage and it was in relatively good order, there wasn't any major construction that needed doing. But the Board had agreed to it. Even he had voted for the motion, unaware of how dramatically it would ultimately affect him.

That was probably the thing Frank hated most about Morgan, the fact that she could get people to do what they didn't want to do. They might know this wasn't what they wanted or they might not, it didn't make much difference either way. In the end, she only ever got her way.

She commanded an arsenal of weapons to achieve this. She could alternate seamlessly between dry humour and stern disagreement. Her sweet smiles and sharp looks were like two sides of the same coin you never knew which way would fall. She was mentally incredible. When her mind was fixed on something, it was impossible to fight her. She never lost focus. She bullied intelligently, concentrating on the straight line that led her to what she wanted and then she meandered around it so everyone lost their thinking except for her. Before anyone knew what had happened, Morgan would have them saying the exact words she wanted. She always looked the person she was talking to in the eye so it was hard not to squirm, especially when she was being strict. But if she was being nice her concentration could be mesmerizing, it was like looking into the eyes of an upright cobra.

It was not until afterwards, away from her presence, that her spell was broken. Only when it was too late did Frank understand that Morgan was his enemy and he hated her. It was never clear whether this was because he could see her in the after-light for the snake that she was, or if it was simple resentment because, yet again, he found he'd let her win.

Frank caught sight of himself in the large round living-room mirror, its frame painted in imitation gold flake, mimicking the kind you might see in medieval religious portraits. It gave him the impression of looking at himself in a halo. He looked strange in an office outfit. His physique was more suited to the drama of costume. He was tall with a large operatic chest and thick tree-trunk legs – both of which conspired to make him look fatter than he really was. He had dark hair, which was thick and hard to control, and his face was young but filled with stern lines. They came from all his expressions and they were necessary. They were the lines that helped his face transform, under the lights and heavy make-up.

Dark hair, dark eyes – they were his template, a plain, elegant design, his father's looks. Despite his size, people rarely noticed Frank. Why would they? As an actor, Frank felt that his face was meant to be a blank. For it to be many things, it had to not be anything. Maybe that was why there was a martyred sadness in his reflection. As he was about to set off for a job he didn't want to do, Frank realized that no one ever saw him come alive these days.

He only ever did that on stage.

B en's fingers were slipping.
'Wait! Whu, whu, wai . . . Oh shit!'

'Don't worry, I've got it,' the superintendent said, sliding his knee beneath the box and propping it against the corridor wall.

The sinews in his forearms pulsed and he breathed calmly through his nose. He was old – his parted hair was white, there were veins meandering through his neck and brown rhomboids marked the backs of his hands – but he was very strong. He looked like the kind of man it was impossible to knock down. But that could also have been because he wasn't tall; he had a low centre of gravity. He carried boxes on his own that it had taken two to get out of their previous place. Ben had worried that the strain might attack his heart, but the man never stood around long enough for Ben to object. No sooner had Ben dragged something from the back of the U-Haul truck than the super had hoisted it from him and trotted into the building.

'Phew,' Ben said, piping a sigh up into his fringe. The sweat on his brow made some of the hairs stick. 'That was close. Mandy woulda killed me if I'd dropped this one. It's got all of Grandma's china.'

'Let's get it in,' the super said, smiling. He seemed like a very no-nonsense guy to Ben, something Ben liked. Maybe it was just that he was being so nice. Ben hadn't expected anyone to help him with the move, though he certainly needed it. Mandy was still in the hospital – a boy. People had been sweet. Someone had left a notice on the building blackboard congratulating them, and there were flowers in the apartment, the same kind as the ones Mandy got at the hospital. Ben had assumed they were from everyone.

Ben squeezed his fingers around the corners of the box and

the two men shuffled themselves down the corridor and through the door to G1, which they'd propped open with telephone directories.

'Just there, please,' Ben said, indicating a space on top of the kitchen counter with a nod of his head. 'That's awesome,' he sighed as they hoisted it up and laid it down. 'I don't know what I would have done without you.'

The superintendent didn't say anything. A single bead of sweat raced from his temple and drew a perfect line down the side of his face.

'Do you want some water?' Ben asked.

'Sure.'

'I don't know if we've got any bottled,' Ben said, quickly spinning around to open the fridge.

'No, no. Tap water's good for me. It's the best drinking water in the world, New York tap. Comes straight down from the Kensico reservoir. Contains plenty of fluoride. Excellent for the teeth.'

The super grinned without humour and tapped his two front teeth with a fingernail, demonstrating their integrity. Ben noticed, with some amusement, that the super's ears had started regrowing and were now disproportionately large compared to rest of his face. He looked like the Buddha.

'Really?' Ben replied, holding open the fridge door redundantly. A pale yellow light shone from inside. Apart from that and some shelves, it was completely empty. 'I didn't know that.'

'Excellent for the baby too,' the super added as an afterthought. There was a pause as he closed his mouth and licked his gums, his tongue rolling beneath his lips.

'Right, then,' Ben said, slamming the fridge door shut. 'All I gotta do is find you a glass.'

Ben started tearing open boxes as the super stepped out of his way and walked through the apartment, looking up and down its walls as if he were surveying it for the first time.

'You got a good space here,' he called out. 'Good for the family.'

'Yeah, Mandy and I are very excited,' Ben said, the sound of his voice getting swallowed by the paper rustling inside a cardboard box, like at Christmas. 'We didn't know what we would have done if we didn't get it. We were worried after the interview with the Board. They didn't call us for days. I was sure that they'd found somebody else. I wouldn't have blamed them. Seemed like I got everything wrong in our application, and you're never gonna believe this, but I actually trod on Annalise's dog during the interview. I felt like such an idiot.'

'She loves that dog.'

'I know. I felt bad.'

There was a pause. 'Do you mind if I smoke?' the super said eventually.

'No,' Ben replied, preoccupied. 'Go right ahead.'

'It won't hurt the baby?'

'They don't get back for two days yet,' Ben said distantly. Then: 'Aha!' He held up a glass, smiling triumphantly.

'Are you sure?'

'Sure I'm sure.'

'Thank you.'

The super pulled out a thin packet of rolling tobacco and some papers and started to weave a cigarette between his fingers over the kitchen counter.

It looked strange to watch strong hands perform so delicate a task. It made Ben want to have one. 'Do you think you could make me one of those?' he asked, flushing the tap.

The super looked at him from out of the tops of his eyes, mischievous and conspiratorial. 'You can have this one,' he said, pinching each end before passing it.

'Here,' Ben said, passing him a glass of water. They exchanged.

The super placed the glass to one side on the kitchen counter without drinking. He reached into his pocket and handed Ben a book of matches then rolled himself a cigarette. The two men smoked in silence. Ben occasionally picked the end of his tongue for loose strands of tobacco.

'It's been ages since I had one of these,' he said, savouring the rich, earthy flavour. 'They're good, aren't they?'

'I like them,' the super replied. 'Once in a while.'

'I don't really smoke but I feel like I'm allowed one, you know, after the birth and everything.'

'We'll call it a celebratory cigarette, then.'

'Yeah,' Ben said, laughing. 'I like the sound of that. To Billy.'

'To Billy,' the super said as they tapped cigarettes together, ash and embers raining appropriately like fireworks. 'May he live a long and prosperous life and bring you the happiness you deserve.'

They each took a long drag and exhaled blue clouds into the spotlight above.

'You got kids, Mr McMurphy?' Ben asked.

'No,' the super replied, looking away briefly, before turning back to smile gently. 'I don't. But I gotta say, this building's going to be a better place with the sound of a little one running around inside. I can hear the pitter-patter of feet in the corridor already.'

Ben snorted. 'Yeah, and the screams. I just hope he doesn't keep the whole block awake.'

'You don't need to worry about that. The main thing is you feel at home. You're very welcome here, sir, you and your family.'

'Thank you, that's very kind of you to say that. And please, call me Ben.'

'Mack,' the super replied, extending his hand and wincing a smile as smoke swam into his eyes.

'I gotta say I really appreciate you helping me move in like this, Mack.' Ben took his hand and grinned. 'It's been a pretty hectic week, what with the move *and* the baby.'

They shook, looking into one another's eyes.

'I can see that,' Mack replied. 'But it won't be long now before Mommy and baby are here and you'll be settled in. You must be excited, with it being your first home and all. These days don't come twice in a life, Ben. You gotta appreciate them while they're happening. Trust me, they're the good ones.'

Ben smiled. 'I'll try and remember to do that, Mack. Thanks.'

Mack picked up his glass of water, drained it, placed it down and dropped his cigarette into the bottom. There was a fizz and then brown smoke swirled heavily.

'Let's finish this job,' he said, his blue eyes, which were greying with age, dancing.

I was in my apartment the next time, getting ready for bed. I had the radio on – low. I liked to have the radio on in the evenings. It distracted me from all the other sounds and reminded me of where I was – New York City – which was something I could have forgotten.

I was in the bathroom, shaving. The reception went. The crash of the signal echoed down the length of my railroad apartment and made me jump. I stood still for a moment to see if I had imagined the distortion, then to see if the signal might fix itself. I even considered that it might have been part of the song.

But the angry hiss persisted. It sounded like a wave in a continual state of breaking. There were no troughs, no rhythm in the tide – just a stampede.

I wiped the remains of shaving foam from my face with a small towel and hung it around my neck. I was still dressed in my Dockers and boots and vest, which for some reason reassured me.

I turned to leave the bathroom to attend to the aerial and heard what sounded momentarily like a child crying. Then there was the sound of two men shouting. I heard a woman singing. Someone started panting, as if they were running. Another person started panting in time with the other and together they sounded as if they were having sex. A man's voice cut through and said the words: '*Caused by a mechanical defect.*' And finally, there was the sound of muttering.

I squinted. The words phased in and out within the background of the lost radio signal. They seemed to be coming very fast, like a nervous tic, or someone praying. The sentences tripped up on themselves and slowed to a standstill, at one point they even seemed to be going backwards. The effect reminded me of staring at the hubcap of a fast-moving car.

As I stumbled through my apartment I noticed that everything looked different. It didn't look like my place any more. All the things were there, everything was recognizable, but the narrowness of the room was exaggerated. It looked more scrunched up than it actually was, and more garishly coloured too. It looked like the bedroom in Arles Van Gogh painted: my simple bed, my bedside table, my single lamp, the desk and the small kitchen area to the left – an array of rich browns and rapeseed yellows. This shift in perspective didn't help my balance and I crashed my shin against the edge of the bed twice as I moved down the room, which seemed to be ever elongating, towards the radio.

I eventually reached the desk, and as I put my hand out towards the device I saw that I was shaking. I thought I wanted to turn it off but found myself trying to tune the signal instead. I felt the texture of the chrome-plated dial in my hand against the sweat in my palm. It felt immaculate and slippery, like a wet mirror.

I jerked too hard, and as the bar on the frequency strip skidded I heard what I thought was the same pastiche of sounds but this time they came too fast and I was unable to discern any differences within them. The only clear sound I could detect was the small bass thump you get when you flick through channels on FM frequency. There was a volley of them, a rhythmic assault, before I finally felt a bumping in my hand, and I knew I'd gone too far. I had to stop twisting the dial; I'd reached the end.

The radio fell quiet. There wasn't even a hiss. I saw the light inside the machine fade and then go out.

The gym was small. It was on the ground floor, next to the stairwell leading down into the basement.

There were two running machines, a rowing machine and three circuit weights – a Pec-Dec Press, a Phat-Lat Crunch and a Leg Lever for the thighs. There were also some free weights (mostly dumb-bells), a couple of brightly coloured foam mats and one large inflatable ball, which people used for abdominal exercises. There was a mirror against one wall so tenants could watch themselves working out.

By the door, there was a set of 'Gymnasium Rules' that Morgan had printed out on her computer and had had laminated at the photocopying shop.

1. The gym is for occupants of 444 only. No guests are permitted.
2. Observe the safety rules of all equipment before use. The building will not accept any liability for injuries.
3. During periods of heavy traffic, limit use on running machines to 20 minutes only.
4. No drinking in the gym, except water.
5. Wipe down equipment after use.
6. Do not expectorate into the water fountain.

The house was divided into three groups: those who used the gym in the morning, those who used it in the evening and those who didn't use it at all. Garry, Mike and Juan were morning users; Morgan, Henry, Frank, Anna-lise and Helmut were evening people. Mrs Xhiu was too old and Diva was too stoned to bother going at all.

Frank was on the running machine now, his cheeks puffing

out in small pockets against his jaw. He ran staring at a single spot on the wall. Sometimes he reached for a hand towel to wipe his brow. Sometimes he inhaled sharply through his nose to bring his breathing back into rhythm. The place had a strange odour, a combination of rubber and sweat and insoles and laundry powder. The smells happened all at once but never mixed. They came in varying orders depending on strength, like hands slapping on top of one another in a children's gang pact.

The running machine had buttons, which adjusted the speed and incline of the conveyor belt. There were also pre-pro-grammes that regulated the two, Random, Mountainous, Sprint, Competition, but he didn't use them. He preferred to run at a steady pace on a slight incline, like a mouse on the wheel in its cage.

Anna-lise and Henry were working out together on the cir-cuit weights. Anna-lise was dressed in white running shoes, ankle-less socks, tight black leggings and a black tank top. She'd used a band to tie back her short blonde hair, so that it stuck out sharply from the crown. Her broad forehead was accentuated this way and she knew that it made her look pretty. Sweat dark-ened her breastplate and the fleshy handfuls at the tops of her inner thighs. She kept her legs spread for Henry's benefit as he stood behind her, guiding her elbows through the motions on the Pec-Dec Press.

'It huuuurts, Henry,' Anna-lise squealed.

He grunted at her in encouragement. 'Come on, you can do it.'

Anna-lise worried that if she pushed herself too hard she risked screwing her face into an unflattering ball of lines and wrinkles and purple blood vessels. At the same time, she wanted to impress Henry. She knew that Henry – even if he did act like a literati liberal – was the kind of guy who was big on focus and competition (it was all a part of his secret upbringing) so she unwisely went for it. Halfway through the motion, through the blur of pain, she saw his expression change and she panicked. She U-turned at the last minute and released the weights with a terrific clang.

'That was lousy,' Henry said.

'You do it, then, Arnie,' she retorted.

'All right, then, I will,' he said, bending down to lower the pin and increase the resistance.

Anna-lise watched him take off his black tracksuit top. He was wearing a tight white ribbed wife-beater. She could see the muscles in his shoulders moving as he undressed. His black hair flopped forward as he took his keys out of his pocket and dropped them to the floor with his top, beside the machine. He swept it back as if he didn't care and it stayed in exactly the right place.

Like her, he too had a broad forehead, which made him look every bit as noble as he was. He also had creamy brown eyes, and pale, almost ghostly skin. There was a dimple in his chin and, to the right, a small smooth patch in his five o'clock shadow. His cheekbones were delicately carved, like the neck of a string instrument. Anna-lise knew that these looks weren't normal and she still didn't understand why Henry lived in 444.

As Henry started working out, Anna-lise noticed that Frank had slowed the running machine to a walk.

'How was your day, Frank?' Anna-lise said across to him.

Frank was breathing hard, his face red. He shook his head. 'Don't ask.'

'Tell me about it,' Anna-lise said, walking over. 'Maybe it's the moon. It's gonna be full tonight.'

'Yeah?'

'I do love it, though,' Anna-lise said. 'It's such a female time.' She stepped close so that Henry wouldn't hear. 'I always come on,' she added.

'Really?' Frank whispered back. 'Every full moon?'

'I'm like the tides,' Anna-lise replied.

'The Red Sea,' Frank giggled and Anna-lise laughed with him. Frank pressed the stop button and the running machine whirred to a halt. 'By the way, I've been meaning to say sorry about the other week. How are you taking to it?'

Anna-lise sighed and shook her head.

'That bad, huh? Oh well, maybe the new guy will take over,' Frank said. 'Did you see the way Morgan lit up when he said he was in banking? He'd make a perfect Building Treasurer.'

'I think he only said that because Morgan was giving him her speech about contributing to the running of the building. You know how much she loves that one.'

They both raised their eyebrows at each other.

'They seemed nice,' Anna-lise added.

'Yeah, bit Garmento, but fine,' Frank said, leaning against the safety barrier of the machine.

'Garmento?'

'You know, mid-town,' Frank explained.

Anna-lise's face screwed.

'Outta-town, middle America,' Frank explained. 'They're all over the place. Hanging around the Times Square mall and wearing chinos and doing things like marketing jobs in soap-stone skyscrapers in the garment district.'

'Oh,' Anna-lise replied. She paused before adding. 'Like you, then?'

'Shut up!' Frank said, gently jabbing at her arm with a finger. Anna-lise grinned. 'Anyway, poor souls don't know what they're letting themselves in for, moving into this place.'

'It's not so bad.'

'You're kidding, right?' Frank said, wiping his forehead. 'Garry can't play music any more because of the new "listening hours", Mrs Xhiu's toilet still leaks because Morgan refuses to pay for a plumber, Mike can't convert his bathroom because of the new construction rules, and now, because she's jealous about you and Henry, she's gone and made you Building Treasurer.'

'You think that?' Anna-lise whispered, aware that Henry was coming to the end of his routine. 'You think she made me Treasurer because of Henry?'

'Don't you?' Frank replied.

The door swung open and Morgan walked in. Anna-lise nearly screamed when she saw that she was wearing the same tracksuit as Henry. She even had on the same shoes. They gleamed with newness.

'Hi, guys,' Morgan said breezily, looking at Henry.

'Nice outfit, Morgan,' Frank teased. 'New?'

'Yes,' Morgan said, walking straight over to the Phat-Lat Crunch, next to Henry. 'Someone I know told me there was a sale on at Cartwright so I went down.'

Morgan smiled appreciatively at Henry in the mirror.

'Great,' Henry smiled back.

Anna-lise walked over and stood between them, simultaneously presenting her pubic area to Henry and her ass to Morgan, understanding the effect this would have on each of them.

'Shall we do some stretching?' she suggested with her hands on her hips, looking down at Henry while also happily noticing Morgan's revolted expression in the mirror.

Henry stood up and they moved to the mats in the corner just as Frank gathered his things and started towards the door.

'How are the minutes coming along, Frank?' Morgan called out as he crossed the room.

'I haven't had a chance to do them yet,' he replied, still walking.

'Going to work on them tonight?' Morgan said, pulling down the long, angled bar from above her head to under her chin.

'No. I was planning on going out tonight.'

'Interesting.' Morgan heaved, releasing the bar and breathing out heavily.

'Why?'

'Well,' Morgan sighed, 'what about this month's mainte-nance?'

'What about it?'

'How will you manage if you go out?' Morgan pulled down strenuously on the weights.

'Excuse me?' Frank said, feeling his cheeks burning.

Morgan released the bar back over and above her head. 'I thought things were tight for you at the moment,' she said, looking at him in the mirror. 'At least, that's what you told me last month.'

Frank hated himself as he felt a sudden lump jogging in his throat. He had to breathe very deeply to control himself. He'd sworn he wouldn't let Morgan reduce him to tears over the maintenance ever again. There had been a time when he'd been quick to cry, naively hoping that Morgan might melt, that he might be able to manipulate her with a sympathy stroke. Fat chance. Still, he found it hard to resist breaking down almost as part of the routine now. She was so much more powerful than he was.

'Not that it's any of your business,' he finally managed, hard-faced. 'But I'm only going to the cinema and, if you must know, I'm being treated.'

Morgan managed another heavy heave before releasing the bar so that the weights clunked dully.

'Oh that's nice, a date. Don't eat too much popcorn.'

'What?' Frank snapped, knowing that it was a mistake, know-ing that showing real emotion was to lose points in this game. But hadn't she just commented on his weight?

'Cinema food is so expensive,' Morgan said.

Frank stared and breathed.

'You're right,' Henry interjected as he pressed himself against Anna-lise's left leg, stretching her hamstring as she lay on her back on the mats looking up at him. 'I hate it when they try and get you to go for a large or a super size for twenty-five cents extra.'

'I spend the whole movie peeing,' Anna-lise added.

Morgan, Henry and Anna-lise all laughed happily together at this, just as if they were friends, which for a very small moment they thought they might be until they noticed the door swinging to loudly.

Frank had left.

Mrs Xhiu was watching the God Channel. The lights were out and the curtains were drawn. The TV flashed like a strobe in the darkness. It should have hurt her eyes but she was too engrossed to notice.

'Wail, lay-dees and gentle-main, we have a very, very, verily special guest with us tooo night.' Tamara Cassidy beamed, her huge platinum-blonde hair erupting and then curling across the top of her head like a wave breaking. Her reconstructed face barely moved as she talked, the numerous facelifts and Botox injections keeping her plum-lipstick grin tightly pinned across her cheeks. Her breasts were enormous under a pastel purple polo neck. She wore a matching skirt that stretched itself around her broad hips and all the way down to her ankles in what was supposed to be a show of church-going respect but which didn't happen because it was so easy to see her nipples.

Behind her, on the set, there was a makeshift altar, decorated garishly in a kind of Catholic reinterpretation of Puritanism. Those Catholics sure knew how to sell religion: bright colours and lots of gold. And this was Puritanism Hollywood-style. Even Mrs Xhiu could see this show for its evangelism – a sales take on America's austere religious roots, the theological equivalent of the American dream. Tamara Cassidy certainly looked like a glamorous actress, a porn star, maybe.

She was actually a musician. She'd started life as a Country and Western singer but after that failed she'd found God and managed to get herself onto Chucky Wagner's *Morning Glory* show. She played acoustic guitar and sang with the choir. After just two months, she and Chucky fell in love. They were immediately married and, six months later, she became co-host.

But when Chucky was discovered having sex with a minor

and charged with statutory rape and possession of an illegal substance, Tamara managed to convince the studio executives not to drop the show. In media interviews, she asked everyone to remember Chucky in their prayers, and the show was renamed *Tammy's Turn – a One on One with God*. It was also moved to an evening slot for the wider audience.

That was twelve years ago. The show was still running but numbers had been declining lately in favour of the more dynamic 'Mass Healing' shows, which were conducted in enormous stadiums with pop-star-status preachers working crowds into states of ecstasy. Cameramen in the aisles were told to focus in on the audience members who had perfected the art of hysterical weeping, instantaneous fainting and even the spectacular pulling out of their own hair.

By contrast, Tamara's show was outdated and dull. The lights glared too brightly now off her thick foundation, and the large cross that dominated the altar appeared to have been cast in plastic. The whole show looked as if it had been recorded in someone's garage, even though a lot of money had actually been spent on the set. It was just old.

Not that Mrs Xhiu noticed any of these things or, if she did, she didn't judge them. The only thing she was interested in was Reverend Jeremy. She didn't usually watch *One on One* but she adored Reverend Jeremy and he was the guest. Mrs Xhiu thought he had the most wonderful voice. At times it could be sublime and gentle and delicate as if he were wrapping her in a lovely, warm blanket; at other times, say when he was contemplating the wrath of God, a huge bass boomed from the cask of his chest and literally cast Satan back down into his hellish depths. He was also quite handsome.

'I know y'all gonna know him very well so I'm just gonna cut the enteroductions and get straight on right into the heart of the man. Rave Errand Jeremy, it sho' is a joy to have y'all on ma sho'.'

'Thank you,' Reverend Jeremy said deeply, making the speakers on Mrs Xhiu's old television rattle. *'Thank you for having me. I felt a very special need to come on your show today.'*

'Ray-eely,' Tamara cooed, shifting her large ass as best she could against the purple cushions with gold brocade and tassels that she'd found during her visit to the 'Vatican in Vegas Shopping Mall' three years previously. *'Pray do tell.'*

'It's just that I have an extremely important announcement to make, and I especially wanted all your viewers to hear it.'

Tamara shifted again, this time nervously.

'Yes,' he rumbled. *'I wanted it to come from me first, before anyone read about it in the newspapers.'*

Mrs Xhiu didn't know what to think. She could hear Diva moving into her bathroom above her. It was distracting. Every time Diva flushed her toilet, Mrs Xhiu's somehow overflowed. She'd asked the building to get it fixed but Morgan had told her it was an internal problem, that she was responsible for it. She couldn't see how.

In any case, she didn't have the money for a plumber. Morgan had suggested McMurphy take care of it, but Mrs Xhiu didn't like him coming into her apartment – she didn't like anyone coming into her apartment. Her apartment was her temple, her cave, her confession chamber. It was filled with abstinence. It bore the shame of self-flagellation. It harboured the physical manifestation of her love affair with Jesus. It was a secret place, a private and guarded world. If ever she had a visitor she opened the door in suspicious inches, the darkness looming behind her monastically. To let someone in would have been to stand naked before them, more than naked. It would have revealed her relationship with God.

She tuned back into the television.

'Why, Rave Errand, y'all teasing me now. Whatever could y'all be in the newspapers for?'

'Well, it's a little embarrassing, Tammy,' he replied.

Suddenly, there was a rumble in the walls and the sound of a pipe rattling violently. This was quickly followed by a long gurgling sound and then a high-pitched whine, like air squeezing its way out of the stretched neck of a balloon. Mrs Xhiu froze.

'I've been asked . . . '

'Yay-ess?'

'It seems that . . . '

A very loud sound of water erupting, gushing and then splashing came from Mrs Xhiu's bathroom. She tried to get up to see what was happening but she was too late. By the time she managed to get to her feet, her toilet had exploded, throwing what must have been several months of trapped waste into the air, across her bathroom floor, under the bathroom door, across the bedroom and living-room carpet until, finally, it seeped into the multiple electrical power point and exploded.

444 VanVanVane Street was thrown into an evil darkness.

They talked to each other. Down the stairwells, across corridors, through walls, out of windows, on the fire escape.

Hey, what happened, can't see a thing, the power's out, are you OK, it won't be long, is it just our building or the whole block, maybe it's a city power outage, no I can see next door's lights, can Mack fix it, maybe we should call in the electrician, somebody help, my fish is dying, who's got a flashlight, don't try and use the elevator . . .

In the dark, unable to see, they found that they could hear each other, that they could talk to one another – at least, they listened. The building sang.

It made me wonder if they were aware. They all seemed to know where to go to talk to one another, they all knew the sound spots, the wormholes that riddled the walls, the individual paths where sound travelled specifically. How did Garry know that the disused cold-water pipe that ran through his bedroom wall co-joined with Mrs Xhiu's kitchen waste two floors away?

'Are you OK, Mrs Xhiu?'

'Oh dear, oh dear, oh no . . . '

'What happened, Mrs Xhiu?'

'The television, Diva's bathroom, oh dear, oh no . . . '

'Don't worry, Mrs Xhiu. Just stay where you are. The power will come on again soon.'

Were they all listening?

I didn't know. Part of me was relieved. The burden wasn't entirely my own. Everyone knew. But another part of me was terrified. I felt as if they didn't need me. They already had each other.

But, as I listened, I realized that they only knew a part of the puzzle. They only understood the nature of *their* spaces. They couldn't see the whole picture.

Garry couldn't hear Frank on the landing with Mike. Morgan, Anna-lise and Henry thought they were cut off from everyone else in the gym. Ben was surprised to hear Diva talking to him through the radiator. He'd never even met her.

Sound was isolated for them. The apartments were linked but the connections were limited, two-dimensional. It was impossible for the tenants to hear everything.

I also understood something else. I could tell all their stories.

During their time, they had come to filter the sounds of others *out*. Garry wouldn't have wanted to listen to the sound of Mrs Xhiu's television if he was trying to sleep. He'd have learnt to block it out, relegate it to his subconscious. He probably always heard a hum, the dull tenor tones of muffled voices, but he'd never have heard the words, it would have become simple background noise, like the cracks of the heating system. Voices in the wall were something he'd had to get used to. It was a feature of his living in 444. Like everyone else, he'd absorbed it into his system – for the sake of comfort.

I wish I could have done that.

'MR MCMURPHY? MR MCMURPHY? CAN YOU HEAR ME?'

Morgan shouted down from the basement door. It was like a clanging bell, a screech of iron claws across a blackboard, a throbbing white noise. Her shouts rang in my mind and practically paralysed me. I felt like something nocturnal trapped in the headlights. There was too much input. The volume was too high, the colours were too loud.

'WILL YOU CHECK THE FUSE BOX? MR MCMURPHY? ARE YOU THERE?'

Somehow, I managed to make my way to the end of the basement, to the electrics. I reset the circuit-breaker. Power surged back into the building like a wave, the gentle, background hum of the electricity settling in with a long, meditative Ohm.

There were whoops of relief and excitement and thanks.

I listened to the building running smoothly again. I could hear all four cylinders, the pistons pumping, the cog teeth catching, the hum and rumble that, with the smallest press of the accelerator, could roar.

'Mr McMurphy,' Morgan said quietly now in the light, 'will you wait there, please? I want to come down and talk to you for a minute.'

M organ stepped gingerly down the rickety white wooden steps into the basement. She didn't like coming down here. There was the musky, damp smell of mud in the air, the smell of graves.

At the bottom of the stairs, there was a door to the left that led to a passageway that led in turn to the airshaft. The door had windows in it and a small embroidered curtain, which was drawn on a length of laundry cord. It was the kind of door you'd expect to see on the front of a picket-fenced prairie house, not in the basement of a New York building block.

Beside it, large industrial waste bins were stored. They were all black plastic now. The city had stopped recycling in 2002 so there was no longer a need to separate out the trash into different-coloured containers.

The floor was raw concrete, dotted periodically with elaborate wrought-iron drain covers. There were some storage areas that Mr McMurphy had fashioned out of chicken wire, corkboard and two-by-four. Tenants rented them from the building for a monthly fee. Morgan worried about them being a fire hazard. Should the city ever find out, she knew the building would face fines and probably have to rebuild them with safer materials. There was nothing she could do about it now, she told herself. Mr McMurphy had made them before she had moved in. There were more important places to concentrate the building's resources – much more important.

Along the white-painted brick walls, an assortment of safety notices in red said: EXIT, KEEP CLOSED, KEEP CLEAR. One door said BOILER ROOM. Towards the rear of the building, another said: B1. That was Mr McMurphy's place.

A maze of pipes, some bare copper, some painted, others

marked with metal dog tags with numbers and letters embossed on them, ran across the ceiling. Morgan noticed the points at which they'd been soldered. This pipe led to there, before turning to reach another. She saw the words COLD and HOT and suddenly understood why Helmut's hot-water supply had to be separated from the rest of the building's. It was like going down into the underbelly, getting under the skin of 444. The pipes ran like arteries. The foundation walls and pillars stood with skeletal strength. The boiler furnace roared like a beating heart. Morgan felt as if she could 'see' the building working down here.

She found Mr McMurphy standing by the security monitors. 'What's the story?'

'Everything's back online, 'cept the elevator,' he replied efficiently. 'Give it time. It runs on a separate circuit.'

This wasn't what Morgan had meant. She had been hoping to start a conversation on a more general, relaxed level.

'Interesting,' she managed.

Mr McMurphy was dressed in his blue overalls, smeared with oil and grease. His hands were covered with bright-orange brick dust and mud.

'Been working on that foundation wall again?' Morgan tried.

'It's still bleeding.'

'No flooding, though?'

'As long as I keep the drains clear.'

Morgan noticed how Mr McMurphy didn't look her in the eye; he talked across her shoulder. She could see that the man was short but somehow it felt . . . insubordinate?

'Maybe we'll have to get those guys in to seal it, after all,' Morgan said.

The super shrugged his shoulders. 'It's a big job . . . '

' . . . for not very much. I know, Mr McMurphy, thank you,' Morgan finished for him.

This was one of Mr McMurphy's famous sayings when it came to any sort of building work that required the help of contractors. The super didn't trust outside help. He said he could take care of most problems himself.

'In fact, that's sort of the reason I came down to talk to you.'

Mr McMurphy didn't say anything.

'You see, we're expecting to start some building work soon . . . It's quite a large project, actually.'

The super's gaze drifted into a mid-distance.

'The Board are hoping to develop the roof,' Morgan continued. 'We're to vote on it at the next meeting. Of course, it means there'll have to be another hike in maintenance.'

Mr McMurphy was definitely looking away from her now, as if someplace else entirely. Morgan found it very off-putting.

'Don't worry,' Morgan said, 'the hike won't apply to you. But it might mean that your wages are frozen for the year. All your other benefits will stay on as normal. We won't charge you rent, you'll have access to the gym and then there's always your Christmas bonus to look forward to.'

Morgan knew that these last two points were weak – Mr McMurphy never used the gym and they'd already told him what his bonus would be for the year – but she had to sell the story somehow. It was crucial that Morgan secure Mr McMurphy's approval before presenting the Board with her plan. Morgan knew that the super's rights would be the first thing those against the development would use. That was the lesson she'd learnt after finally getting everyone to agree that they should move Mr McMurphy into the basement so the building could rent out the first-floor apartment to Henry for extra income. The super's rights were like some tiresome aspect of the national constitution; people got very precious about them when faced with the clear and very desirable alternative of making simple money.

'Well, what do you say?' Morgan added, trying not to let her impatience with the man show, smiling treacly. 'Are you with me?'

It snowed the night before, just as Catherine had hoped, the December morning sky another big blue, scored only with silently thundering airplane trails and a lonely new moon. She'd wanted the ultimate white wedding, and as we took a taxi together through Central Park to the church, I could see why.

The cold sunlight winked playfully at us in the snowflakes as we travelled, showing off its spectrum in sparks. The empty trees' gnarled branches clawed at the air like witches' hands. I spotted the ice rink – low and emerald – like an eternal sleeping tomb.

And I'd never seen anyone as beautiful as my bride-to-be. All in white, save for some rose-red lipstick, she was Gothic horror. I was utterly entranced. I found it hard to take my eyes off her. She kept saying: 'Mrs Catherine McMurphy, Mrs Catherine McMurphy, Mrs Catherine McMurphy,' with varying emphases and looking back at me expectantly, waiting for an approval.

The fairy tale continued at St Bartholomew's on Fifth (she had it all figured out) with its pop-eyed gargoyles and dripping turrets and flying buttresses. Tourists stopped looking at the Christmas window displays and took pictures of us as we arrived. We skipped up the stairs over a weather-worn red carpet, embarrassed, and ran into the church, out of breath.

Our friends and families were already there waiting, looking back down the aisle at us in thin suits and crooked smiles. Catherine had been against the idea of being given away and she hated 'Here Comes the Bride' so we walked in silence together between the pews, our heels clicking on the stone floor, like the second hand of a clock descending.

I don't remember much of the ceremony. It passed in a blur.

I had a sudden attack of nerves and couldn't seem to focus on anything but the priest's mouth. I didn't like standing up in front of a crowd, especially one that knew me. I do remember him saying that I should probably look at my bride, not him, as I swore my oath. Unless, of course, I liked him more. People had laughed at that and afterwards they remembered the wedding for it.

There were rice and bells and pictures outside. I heard a passer-by say that they thought we might be famous. The car service we'd arranged never showed and, after the initial flurry of excitement had worn off, there was an uncomfortable twenty minutes as we hurried to organize taxis to ferry everyone on to the reception. Everyday churchgoers squeezed past us on the steps to attend midday mass and Catherine got frantic. There was a feeling that we had overstayed our welcome.

But that all dissolved in the first glass of champagne. We borrowed a photographer friend's studio, which dwarfed our modest gathering and made our conversations echo. We couldn't afford to feed everyone lunch but we were determined to get them drunk, so we arranged for plenty of alcohol. There were canapés to keep them going. Friends in a band played and people danced the boogaloo and kids ran around as fast as they could until one of them cut their knee and then they were told to calm down. Catherine's grandma got so drunk she fell over and thought she was paralysed but it turned out that her pantyhose had just slipped down over her knees.

I was forced to give an impromptu speech, which descended into an expletive-peppered list of thank-yous. I looked at everyone and remember feeling astonished that so many people had turned up. They seemed genuinely happy for us. I realized then that it was the best day of my life and I would have said so if the moment hadn't passed so quickly. I imagine, when I die, that image of all those people smiling warmly at me like that will flash before my eyes.

Eventually, someone ordered pizzas so the party could continue into the night. Catherine and I managed to stay until our jaws ached from smiling. It was snowing again when we left but our apartment was close by so we walked. I asked her what she thought had been the best bit and she said watching me dance, so I threw her over my shoulder and carried her home, screaming.

She forgave me after we crossed the threshold and she saw the flowers – white lilies, of course, to keep with the macabre theme. I knew that Catherine would enjoy the joke. I'd arranged with our florist friend to strew them across the bed and fill the bathtub and the sink and cover the living-room floor. We ruined our clothes as we made love, scarring my suit and her perfect white dress with rusty stamen stains. Well, she said, she'd never wear it again, would she?

We fell asleep, naked in each other's arms, warm in our bed of wet stems and shredded petals.

Ben and Mandy were having a flat-warming party. They had invited everyone with a message on the building blackboard.

COME AND WET THE BABY'S HEAD!
ALL WELCOME.
TUESDAY, 7.30 p.m., G1.

Morgan had also left a notice:

NEXT BOARD MEETING: 7 p.m.
Wednesday, 11 December, #F2
Important new business, concerns all.
Notify if unable to attend.
M

Outside, snowflakes fell like feathers. The city was quiet. Only the occasional taxi persisted. They didn't get any business. People preferred to walk when it was like this, before it got muddy and slushy, before enormous tar-bottomed lakes guarded the street corners. It was as if the city were being wrapped in a soft blanket, comforted with the cold. Lights from skyscrapers filled the clouds, the Empire State alternating red, white and blue. There was something magical about it, the same magic people see in snow globes. New York was a life-sized snow globe that night.

Mandy was in the baby's room showing Billy off to Anna-lise and Frank. The baby was on its back, swaddled in a blanket from the hospital, the words St Vincent's sewn in sky-blue lettering along one side. Only his round face and one arm were showing, the arm resting above his head in devoted submission.

Mandy still didn't understand many of the emotions she felt as she looked at the child. The only one she really recognized was fear; fear that something was wrong with the baby, that something might happen to it. The sense of responsibility was overwhelming. Every time the baby cried, she felt phantom sensations in her belly, the same way amputees feel a lost limb. The baby was a part of her that had been physically removed and now she had a whole new reality to deal with.

'He's gorgeous!' Frank and Anna-lise whispered one after the other in the dim light.

'He is just tooooooo cute,' Anna-lise continued. 'Look at those cheeks. It makes you wanna eat him, doesn't it, Frank?'

'Yeah,' Frank said, gazing down calmly.

They watched his tiny chest slowly rising and falling.

'Come on, let's go,' Frank said. 'I'm scared we're gonna wake him.'

'It's OK,' Mandy said, trying to seem as relaxed as possible.

'No, come on,' Frank said, leading Anna-lise away.

'I want to eat him!' Anna-lise said again before they stepped into the brightness of the galley kitchen, which extended out into the small living room.

Morgan sat on her own on a stool by the breakfast counter, picking at a bowl of olives. She'd hardly drunk any of her beer. Ben was busy trying to make the music system work as Garry scanned his CD collection. Henry was talking with two of Mandy's friends, expertly letting the better-looking of the two know that he had noticed her, without offending anyone.

'Oh, Henry,' Anna-lise said, sliding Ulysses out from his arms. 'You've got to go and take a look at little Billy. He's adorable.'

'I saw him in the corridor just as Mommy got back from hospital,' Henry replied. 'You're right. He's totally cute,' he added, looking at Mandy.

Mandy smiled back uncomfortably. She felt so ugly and fat.

The music started and there was a knock on the door. Mandy

excused herself. It was Mike and Juan. She tried to take their coats but they stopped her.

'We've only come for a quick drink,' Mike explained.

'I hope this fits him,' Juan said, handing Mandy a small box. 'Three to six months. That's right, isn't it? So he can grow into it.'

Mandy thanked them and kissed them and said she was sure it would be perfect. She led them into the apartment and Morgan arrived to kiss the two men on the lips.

'It's snowing out,' Mike said flatly.

'We'll never get a taxi,' Juan added.

'But the show starts at nine,' Morgan replied.

'I love it when it snows,' Mandy said, smiling brilliantly. 'It's so romantic.'

'I know,' Mike said. 'But it's awful for my shoes. They're brand new.'

'Gucci,' Juan said, rolling his eyes.

'You didn't,' Morgan cried.

'He did!' Juan exclaimed.

'How much, Michael?' Henry asked.

'Honestly, Henry!' Juan said, sliding quickly over to him. 'You really mustn't ask such personal questions.'

'I'm sorry,' Henry said, smiling. 'I didn't know he was so sensitive.'

Juan smacked Anna-lise's wrist. 'This man is an outrageous flirt!' he exclaimed. 'If you're not careful, Anna-lise, some floozy is going to swan in and steal him from you.'

Anna-lise grinned back. 'I don't care, I've got Ulysses.'

She pressed the dog to her face and kissed it. Morgan screwed her face into a ball.

'How revolting,' she said.

'Who needs a man when his best friend will do?' Anna-lise continued, laughing, ignoring Morgan. 'That's what I always say.'

'Hear, hear,' the better-looking of Mandy's friends said, glancing at Henry meaningfully.

'I mean, what can a man give you that a dog can't?' Anna-lise pressed.

'Sex?' Mandy said.

'Don't be so sure, sweetie,' Juan said.

'I definitely wouldn't put it past Anna-lise and Ulysses,' Morgan added.

'That's gross,' Mandy's friend said, laughing.

'Ha, ha, Morgan,' Anna-lise said, pretending to be offended. 'Anyway, I'd rather be loved by a dog than fucked by a man. Any day.'

There was a talk-show hum of approval at this provocative comment. The party hadn't even really started, and already there was a doorway debate.

'And what do you say to that, Henry?' Mike asked.

Henry snorted. 'I'd say we still have our uses.'

'Like?' Anna-lise said, turning to look at him defiantly.

Henry looked at his audience.

'Well, what about Billy? Men can give women babies.'

'Touché,' Juan said.

'That doesn't count,' Anna-lise said. 'There isn't a man in this city that will commit to having kids.' She turned to Mandy. 'Ben being the rare exception, of course.'

'And he still accuses me of tricking him into it,' Mandy replied.

'Well, I want to have children,' Henry said. 'One day.'

'Yeah, right,' Anna-lise said.

'I do. Just not right now.'

'Trust me,' said Mandy. 'There's no hurry.'

'There is for Anna-lise,' Morgan said.

'What!'

'Don't pay any attention to her, darling,' Juan said. 'She's being foul.'

'Well, no one's getting any younger, are they?' Morgan said.

'You're being rude now, Morgan,' Mike said.

'OK, then, think of it this way,' Morgan countered. 'How long have you two been seeing each other?'

'Only a year,' Henry replied.

'Fourteen months!' Anna-lise cried.

'Sorry, fourteen months.'

'I'd say that was long enough to know if you want to be with someone, wouldn't you? If you're going to commit to one another you should stop wasting time.'

'Stop pressuring them, Morgan,' Mandy said. 'Having children is a big deal.'

'Yes, Morgan, leave them alone,' Mike added.

'I don't know if I even want babies,' Anna-lise said, with vague nonchalance.

'*Oh, Henry, you've got to go and take a look at little Billy. He's soooo adorable,*' Morgan squealed in a fairly accurate impersonation.

There was a scatter of nervous laughter, like pebbles being sprayed across a lake, momentarily breaking the surface tension, but still making waves.

'I'm going to wait until I'm at least thirty,' Mandy's good-looking friend said.

'Anna-lise is thirty-six,' Morgan said flatly.

'Jesus, Morgan,' Mike said. 'What is it with you tonight?'

'It's not like it's a secret, Mike.'

'You could always freeze some eggs, darling,' Henry said. When he saw the look on everyone's faces, he added quietly, 'Or something.'

Enormous, delicate tears brimmed quickly at the edges of Anna-lise's eyes and then tumbled catastrophically down her face. She stared at Henry for a moment, before running with a small wail into the bathroom where she flicked the light on, locked the door and crumbled onto the toilet so she could sob into Ulysses' coat.

Everyone looked at Henry.

'What?' he said to them, holding his palms open. 'I meant that in a good way! I want to have kids. I said that. Didn't I just say that?'

Morgan beamed at him. Henry, looking very anxious, started moving towards the bathroom. Mandy pressed a hand against his forearm and mouthed: 'I'll go.'

'It's not your fault, Henry,' Morgan whispered. 'You're much younger than her. It's easy to forget that.'

'I guess,' Henry said quietly, looking very lost.

'Maybe we should go,' Mike whispered to Juan.

'Yes,' Morgan said. 'Let's.'

'Bye, bye, gorgeous,' Juan said, kissing Henry on one cheek.

'Bye,' Henry replied in a daze.

In a flurry of sudden activity, like a swirl in the snowstorm outside, the threesome collectively bundled their way out of G1 with waves and effusive goodbyes, finally falling over themselves into the street in each other's arms, laughing. More guests arrived and rang the doorbell. Mandy shouted at Ben to get it, but Henry offered to do so instead. Slowly and eventually, Anna-lise wiped her eyes, unlocked the bathroom door and let Mandy in.

Diva's drug dealer, Jonathan, was trying to convince her to try his latest product.

'It's DMT in a pill form,' he said, passing her a 'fortune cookie'. A traffic-signal-coloured shoulder bag full of Chinese-food delivery cartons, each with different drugs in them, sat by his feet. He even had a Chinese-style food menu, the pharmaceuticals listed alphabetically. Everything from acid to Zanax was available, delivery on demand. All Diva had to do was text Jonathan her account number and he arrived at the front door within thirty minutes.

Diva loved the cleaned-up New York. The police had successfully pushed drugs off the streets and into the privacy of people's apartments with the efficiency of, well, a drug pusher. It was more expensive these days but there was better quality assurance and it was much more civilized.

'What's DMT?' Diva replied, placing the 'fortune cookie' on the arm of her La-Z-Boy and pulling out a pack of large Bambus.

Jonathan gave away 'fortune cookies' to his favoured customers though Diva was only interested in dope now. She'd done most drugs already and she'd pretty much done them to excess. There hadn't been anything she hadn't been willing to try, there hadn't been anything she didn't like. She was a born addict.

And she'd been made to pay for it. There was always a price. Diva had discovered that the downs were pretty much in direct proportion to the highs. Her husband was dead and her daughter didn't talk to her, which was why Diva opted for dope now. She only had the stomach for mild lows. She couldn't afford to get too high, she couldn't afford to suffer any more than she already had. One day she'd give it all up. One day.

'Dimethyltryptamine. They say the brain releases it when we die. It gives you visions. It's not orally active unless used in combination with a monoamine oxidase inhibitor. You had to either smoke it, or inject it, or drink it with ayahuasca, like the South American tribesmen.'

'I remember hearing about those guys,' Diva said. 'Didn't they like find the only vine in the whole Amazon to get off?'

'The *Banisteriopsis caapi* vine,' Jonathan said, excited. 'They added it with viridis leaves to get high. Without the vine, the leaves did nothing because amino acids in the stomach broke down the DMT. But the vine blocked the body's defences and gave them some of the most profound psychedelic experiences.'

'How did they figure that out?'

'The gods showed them how to do it.'

'Yeah, right.'

'The chances of them figuring it out by themselves were about ten hundred billion to one. They wouldn't have known that viridis leaves contained DMT or had any hallucinatory potential. On top of that, they managed to find the only frickin' vine in the whole jungle that *would* make it work. Even if they went through the entire Amazon testing different combinations of plants by trial and error, it would have taken them about three thousand years to find the right mix. Considering half the plants are poisonous in the first place, I doubt they would have survived the experiment without the help of the gods.'

'I'll take your word for it,' Diva said. 'So, what does it do again?'

'This pill is the start of a new revolution,' Jonathan said, holding up a fortune cookie between thumb and forefinger. 'Once everyone starts taking DMT, it'll accelerate evolution so we can emerge from the muddy lake of individual existence and flower into the sky-blue world of One Thought. You know, just like the Buddha and the lotus flower. We'll all tune into the collective consciousness.'

'What's collective consciousness?'

'OK, right, yeah, right on. Collective consciousness – not to be confused with Jung's collective unconscious, OK?' Jonathan paused to give Diva the chance to acknowledge the clarification. She nodded vaguely at him, not having the slightest clue what he was talking about. 'Collective consciousness is a theory that says humans will one day evolve to a higher conscious state where we're able to tune into the collective thought of mankind. With DMT, everyone's going to start thinking beyond the death plane. We're gonna start communicating telepathically. Eventually, we'll lose our mouths . . . ' Diva's face screwed with revulsion. 'Maybe,' Jonathan added wistfully.

'Like the Borg in *Star Trek*, you mean?' Diva said.

'Yeah!'

'But they're scary, Jonathan. I'm not sure I want to be assimilated into a collective hive just so as I can take orders telepathically from some evil queen. I don't want to be a drone.'

'Not that way.'

'What way, then?'

'That's just a sci-fi script some TV people came up with. I'm talking about something real. I'm talking about something that already exists and is beautiful.'

'How do you mean?'

'We've all encountered collective consciousness at one time or another, it's just most of us don't realize it. Like at a rave party. I'm talking about spiritually connecting with the rest of humanity, entering the very same space of mind and thought. I've been to parties and been high and been dancing and I've felt myself going into a state where I'm out of my body, I'm out of my mind and I'm tuning in to all the other beings around me – feeling their energy and their collective love and the ecstasy of existence shooting through all of us at the same time. It was probably the same at some of the festivals you used to go to, right?'

'I guess,' Diva replied, realizing she couldn't actually remember.

'And you know it can happen when a crowd is cheering its team on, or if there's a political march where everyone is supporting the same cause, or even when two people have sex. When people make love they connect in a way they never do otherwise.'

Jonathan looked at Diva directly when he said this. He seemed to genuinely enjoy Diva's company, which attracted her to him. He had a habit of saying stupid things that he thought would impress her, like what a wild night he'd had, how he'd 'triple dipped' before he'd 'flipped'. Even though she didn't have the faintest idea what he was talking about half the time, she was flattered that he might think she did. When the moment arose, she always tried to respond in her lexicon of old-school cool. Her sixties phrases struck the right chord with him, as if they had somehow since become 'classics' in the world of drug talk. He'd definitely picked up the word 'cat' from her.

Diva wondered if she wanted to sleep with him. He wasn't a good-looking boy necessarily but he had such an open look in his eyes, they seemed just that little bit wider than most people's, as if he was ready to take the whole world in. His cheeks were still rosy from the cold outside, which made him appear even more vital.

But she quickly decided she couldn't be bothered. She'd done men, like she'd done drugs. Even though she was still an attractive woman – in a Svengali sense, she had very pale Siberian Blue eyes – she never made the effort any more. She only ever wore the same old tracksuit and T-shirt now, hiding her tall, lithe body beneath baggy clothes. Her hair dye was going too, the last of a henna hazelnut whirl fading into white roots with lollipop two-tone. She never put on make-up.

'Oh, shucks, Jonathan,' she said, breaking the spell. 'I'm still not sure I'm interested in a drug that will make me lose my mouth.'

She reached for her 'crispy wonton soup' and picked out a long, fat, fluorescent-green bud of hydroponically cultured marijuana. She could see the THC crystals glistening across it like diamond dust and dark veins of dried leaf coursing across its surface. The rank, intense smell was delectable, practically solid. It was like a morsel of rare cuisine; so rich it could only be consumed in small quantities. She savoured the aroma.

'I said maybe,' Jonathan persisted. 'In any case, that wouldn't happen for decades, even with the drug's acceleratory effects. The important thing is that we start thinking collectively as the human race. It's time we moved beyond limiting concepts like race, nationality, ego. We're all essentially the same, and until we start understanding that and tapping into the unifying conscious state we'll never realize our full potential as a species. We'll just be trapped the way we are now, obsessed with our own pathetic individual existences, limited because we can't achieve anything on our own. It's only if we come together that we'll amount to something, become a real force in the universe.'

'It's an interesting idea, Jonathan,' Diva drawled patiently. She picked at the bud. 'But you know,' she said slowly, 'I don't really do these kinda things any more. I've still got all the other cookies you've given me over the years. They're in a jar somewhere.'

'I know, Diva, but this is different. I swear to God, this stuff is the shit.'

'If it's so good then everyone will want to do it, won't they? You don't need me.'

'People are cautious these days, they don't like to experiment. They're only interested in coke and crystal meth. I need customers that are prepared to try anything, get the word of mouth going.'

Diva knew all about this. She'd gone out with a recreational chemist for a short period in the late eighties, before she'd decided to get herself together. Underground drug makers were all looking for the Next Big Thing, like publishers searching for the new bestseller, the zeitgeist drug that would capture the collective imagination of a generation. Secretly, every drug maker pined for the intelligence and financial resources of the legitimate biochemists. They were the ones at the real cutting edge of pharmaceuticals. They were the ones with the real power to alter the path of mankind, with manufacturing companies behind them throwing billions into research and marketing and legislative approval, changing the human future for ever.

'Well, I won't be any use, then,' Diva said. 'I hardly ever talk to anyone.'

'But you still go to meetings, right?'

'Only AA. I had to stop NA.'

'Why?'

'They made me secretary for a month and gave me the mobile-phone helpline. When people called up I told them where they could score. It seemed like the easiest answer to their problems.'

Jonathan laughed.

'They had to change the number in the end, the line was inundated,' Diva added, smiling.

'That's exactly why you'd be perfect for this job.'

'They'll kick me out, if they find out.'

'Those guys could do with this kind of help. You'll be advancing the human race, remember.'

Diva looked at Jonathan. For some reason she wanted to believe. So what if she'd spent a lifetime learning that drug-ups had their drug-downs? Maybe Jonathan was right. Maybe this was different. After all, humans were nothing more than an extremely complex biochemical reaction. With the proper drug, the right combination, humans could find utopia. Theoretically, drugs could change the world. That's what everyone knew. There could be everlasting happiness, no war, love. And the professional chemists weren't working on it. No NYSE-listed firm would finance a positive endeavour. Where was the profit control in that? So it was up to the beats. The lesser-qualified, lesser-resourced, recreational chemists. They were Man's only hope, God help us all.

'Give me a couple more, then,' she said. 'I'll tell you what I think next time I see you.'

'You're the greatest, Diva.'

'I know.'

She tap-danced up the metal stairs to the front door, childishly sexual, with OTT make-up and bright sleazy clothes under a puffa jacket: pink miniskirt, rose halter-top, ruby shoes – as tarty as bougainvillaea in bloom.

She pressed the intercom nipple with the finger-pad of a flat hand. Her nails caught the sun and shone in translucent, fleshy tones, like small tide-shaped seashells. She waited with her hands held solemnly in front of her, holding the strap of a turquoise box purse, her shoulders pinned back, standing to mannequin attention.

'Ya!' The intercom speaker crackled.

'It's me!'

The buzzer sounded. She pushed her way through the front door and waited for it to close behind her. She waited for the second buzz, and then pushed her way into the corridor. She walked briskly to G2 and rapped lightly by the spyhole. There was the sound of sniffing and something falling over before the door opened lazily and caught Helmut on his shoulder.

'What time is it?' he asked.

'Seven thirty,' she said, throwing an arm around his neck, pulling herself up on tiptoes, kissing him on the lips and sliding past into the apartment.

Helmut mouthed the time to himself in disbelief and rubbed his eyes with the heels of his hands, before allowing the door to fall to.

'I wasn't expecting you so early,' he said, pulling the white towel he had on tighter around his waist, noticing there was a larger overhang than he would have liked.

'Got any coffee?'

'I'll make some.'

She perched herself on the edge of an armchair as Helmut padded his way towards the kitchen. She glanced over the apartment. Silver foil was taped to the walls and floor at the end of the sitting room. There was a bare mattress on the floor and beside it an empty easel. A canvas covered in Pollock flicks was propped against one of its legs. A camera tripod mirrored the easel in miniature on the other side of the room. There wasn't anything else in the place she hadn't seen before: the odd framed picture, the random bookcase and CD shelf, the video-editing suite, the half-assembled music system and the mountain of boxes.

'How's school?'

'Fine,' she huffed, pulling a pack of cigarettes out of her purse, lighting one, crossing her legs, brushing lint off her thigh, blowing out smoke with professional distaste.

Helmut danced with the coffee percolator.

'How's business?' she asked.

'Fine,' he huffed back.

Helmut stepped towards her and reached across for the cigarettes.

'You need a shower,' she said.

'Thanks,' Helmut replied, wincing as he lit up and took the first drag. The action seemed to spark his mind and he walked with direction across to the bookcase, bending down to reach inside. 'Here,' he said, turning and handing her a pink-wrapped soft parcel. 'I got you something. Happy Birthday.'

She stabbed her cigarette out cruelly. 'What is it?'

'Something no fifteen-year-old should be without.'

'Tell me,' she whined.

'Open it and see.'

He watched her open the package and felt himself waking up. The beauty of youth; it was so intoxicating. Just being near her made Helmut feel alive. Maybe it was the way the young shared their youth. They gave it away like indestructible monsters. The more they gave, the younger they remained.

And when she took out the new CBX video mobile phone and beamed up at him with perfect cherry lips and green eyes shining like sunlight off the sea, her puppy-fat cheeks dimpling, Helmut thought he might pick her up and swing her around the room in his arms till they fell over onto the mattress and stayed there for the rest of the day.

'Awesome!' she yelled, jumping up to kiss him. 'Thanks, Dad!'

Helmut held her and closed his eyes.

'Everyone is getting these,' she said, breaking away.

'I know,' Helmut said, turning to pour the coffee. A vanilla aroma spread across the room, cloyingly. Helmut threw in sugar and milk and passed her a cup.

'No one looks after me like you,' she said.

'That's what I'm here for.'

'Wait a second,' she said, putting her mug down. 'What's this?'

'What?'

'There's something else in the box. Is it a card?'

'I don't know. Take a look.'

Helmut watched her neck bend like a swan's.

'Oh,' she said.

'What?'

She looked up, holding a square of bills between thumb and forefinger. 'What's this?' she said, smiling.

'Just some pocket money.'

'Helmut,' she said admonishingly. 'This is too much.'

'Nothing's too much for my angel.'

'I bet you say that to all the girls.'

Helmut laughed.

'Drink your coffee,' he said, walking around her, feeling happy, taking a seat. 'Tell me your news. I want to hear everything before you go.'

I remembered. I *had* picked up a signal like this one before. Not in the same way, not in the building, but outside.

That was probably why I'd never put the two together, up *until* then. The transmission I'd heard in the pipes and later when the radio reception went – they had seemed to come from *inside*, they had seemed to be a part of the building, or at least something to do with the building, a part of its airwave traffic, a specific signal like a TV frequency or a ray in its energy field.

I was outside when I made the connection, shovelling snow from the sidewalk, throwing salt and grit onto the metal steps, chipping away at the plates of ice, my breath making clouds in the blue air, the ends of my fingers cold inside my gloves, wetness seeping into the calves of my trousers where the top of my boots and the snowline met.

The realization struck me quickly and I thought to myself: how could I have missed that?

The only answer I've come up with since is that it was the building that put me off, set me on the wrong track. Maybe it was because the heating pipes were going off at the time, or maybe it was because I was constantly aware of the building – I was tuned into it.

Maybe that was what threw me. I was thinking about where exactly in the building the signal could be coming from, or how it might have found its way to the basement and to me, or why it had started in this particular building, of all the buildings in the city. I couldn't see the transmission in any other context. I had heard it in the building so I had simply assumed it had come *from* the building.

Which was a mistake – a mistake that prevented me from *understanding*. I had been like a man trying to find a word on the tip of his tongue. The longer I looked for it by concentrating on the residual clue, the taste of it, the longer the answer escaped me.

All I ever found, again and again and again, was the mere hint of the word but never the truth, because the building didn't hold it.

The signal I heard was a part of the building's sound system but it wasn't the only place it could come from. Signals of that nature had other sources too. And the longer I tried to find the source of it in the pipes, the more lost I would become. Because it didn't always come from inside. Sometimes it came from *outside* – from the city, from the world.

It was the horn that reminded me.

'NNNNNGGGGGG! NNNNNNNGGGGGG!'

The red fire engine had blown its trumpet like an old giant clearing catarrh from the back of his throat; long and grinding and persistent. The sound grated and flew through the air behind me so violently that, even though I'd heard its loud sirens already wailing from the end of street, this sudden noise as the vehicle passed made me jump.

'NNNNNGGGG! NNNNNNNGGGGGG!'

I turned to watch. Several others did too. There was still a respect for the fire service in the city. There was the kind of respect that should have previously existed. The type of respect that, before, had only come from those who'd known what it was to be saved. It was respect born out of gratitude. Traffic moved out the way.

I remembered the day – the sirens and the screams and the signal.

The way the three had interlaced, echoing each other. The more the world screamed, the more the sirens wailed, the sharper the signal became. The sirens screamed that they were coming, help was on its way, there would be a rescue. Just hold on, just hold on.

But the screams didn't stop. The screams went on. Even the ones that started as screams for help. They mutated. The screams for help became screams of terror, screams of pain, screams of death.

So many people died.

And it was in the screams that I picked up a signal. When the whole city was concentrated and charged on that point at the end of the island: everyone thinking the same thing, the mental mass of New York's humanity centred on those two towers, fearing. Every eye turned, every thought directed, every media radio wave oscillating to the same message.

And the towers themselves . . . pulsing like beacons at the centre of it all, answering the call as clear as the sky had been that day, as clear as the day when I remembered.

They stood so that everyone could see:

Red flames licking, black smoke barrelling. Fuselages fused with building bones. A plane tail jutting from what had been an elegant face of sheer chrome. The images of how they got there. Replaying over and over and over in everyone's mind and on every television screen. The way they had angled. And then struck. The people jumping.

It went on for a long time. If the real world had been quiet, anyone could have tuned in. You wouldn't have needed to be telepathic, even.

The transmission camouflaged itself in the echoes that rang down the empty, road-blocked avenues. It whispered in the blades of the television helicopters that circled the towers. It hummed in the silences and the looks people trapped within the buildings gave each other as they waited.

In the midst, there was the voice. Not so much a human voice as . . . the voice of humankind. It didn't sound like a single person. More like many people making the same sound. It wasn't all in line, there wasn't complete harmony. Some parts overlapped, some moments began just as others were ending.

There were brief instances when all the voices united and the volume stepped up a pitch. There were moments of relative quiet. There was also quite a lot of scratching and distortion. Maybe that came from the individuals still operating. I had thought that maybe these were the stray, selfish considerations, the egotistical indulgences. I couldn't honestly be sure. I understood so little about it.

But one thing I did comprehend. There was a message in it.

It was Frank's turn to host the Board meeting and, right from the get go, it was clear that there was going to be an argument.

Maybe it had been the way that Mrs Xhiu had turned up unusually early, perching herself on the edge of Frank's sofa, drumming her fingers in front of her and refusing every one of the refreshments Frank had prepared. It was as if she were poising herself to unleash the barrage of thought she was busy typing out in invisible print on her knees.

Or maybe it had been the way that Garry had come in, also unusually early and even more unusually flustered, having had what he described as 'one helluva bad day at work'. Frank didn't even know he had a job, he thought he was a DJ, which wasn't exactly work in his opinion.

Or maybe it had been the way that Anna-lise, the newly elected Treasurer, had strolled in empty-handed and somehow managed to completely ignore the look that Morgan had given her as she called the meeting to order.

'Right, everyone,' Morgan started. 'I want to keep the meeting brief tonight because I have a dinner appointment. First, does anyone have any amendments to make to the minutes for last month's meeting?'

The Board scanned the stapled pages Frank had given them and didn't say anything.

'No one?' Morgan asked. 'Interesting. Well, I have three changes I would like to make. According to my notes, the meeting was in fact called to order at 7.58 p.m. not eight o'clock.' She took a red marker pen to the careful print. 'There should be an apostrophe for the "its" in the third paragraph, fourth line, and you've misspelled "appointment" – there should be two Ps.'

'Anything else?' Frank said.

'No. But might I suggest you use your spell check in future so we don't have to waste time on these silly errors?'

'I find it doesn't work very well,' Frank replied.

'What do you mean?'

'Just that it's often wrong. It tells me things like a sentence is too long or that a sentence would read better if it were rearranged back to front. Some of the time it suggests complete nonsense. And to be honest, I don't really like using it because I think it's making me lazy. I'm getting worse at English because I'm relying on a computer to do it for me, just like everyone relies on calculators to do the most basic math. I think we should make the effort to check our grammar ourselves. I mean, come on, people! Let's bring back the dictionary.'

Morgan looked at him through half-eyes. 'Thanks for that, Frank,' she said drily. 'Shall we move on?'

'Fine by me,' Frank said, smiling at her, finding that he was in an inexplicably happy mood for a Board meeting.

'Treasurer?' Morgan said, turning to Anna-lise.

'Yes?'

'Can we have this month's Treasury report?'

Mrs Xhiu raised an arm.

'Yes, Mrs Xhiu,' Morgan sighed.

'What about my bathroom?'

'We'll be dealing with that during our discussion of new business.'

Mrs Xhiu squinted before returning to her train-of-thought typing.

'Right, Anna-lise,' Morgan said, turning towards her again.

'Yes?' she replied.

'The Treasury report, please.'

'Everything's all there, the bank wasn't robbed, everything is fine.'

Frank and Garry made eye contact and raised their eyebrows

with small smiles at one another. Morgan breathed through her nose.

'Is that it?' Morgan said.

'What else do you want to know?'

'Well, have you prepared an income statement for the quarter?'

'No,' Anna-lise said, looking back at her.

'Why not?'

'Because I've been Treasurer for only a month, I can't be expected to account for the previous quarter.'

'But I gave you all the records,' Morgan replied. 'You had all the information you needed to prepare the statement.'

'How do I know it's correct?' Anna-lise said calmly.

'Because I said so,' Morgan frowned. 'I prepared the figures myself.'

'Well, I'm sorry, Morgan,' Anna-lise said, her back very straight, 'but I've been told that since you are responsible for two of the three months, then it should be you who prepares the quarterly accounts. I can't sign off on figures I haven't prepared myself. That wouldn't be proper procedure.'

There was a small snigger at this hijacking of Morgan's catchphrase but Morgan ignored it.

'Who told you that?' Morgan asked.

'A little dickie bird,' Anna-lise replied.

Morgan paused.

'Fine,' she said with exhaustion. 'I suppose it makes no difference that *I* will be unable to verify *your* figures but in this instance I suppose we'll just have to make do. Please be sure to give me the laundry receipts, an account of the monthly maintenance payments, all the bills you've paid and any bank statements for the last month so that I can do the report next week.'

'No problem,' Anna-lise replied.

'Let's move on to old business now,' Morgan said.

'What about my bathroom?' Mrs Xhiu said again.

'I've told you, Mrs Xhiu,' Morgan snapped before gathering herself. 'We'll be dealing with it in the discussion of new business.'

'When will that be?'

'After old business. Please be patient.'

Mrs Xhiu squinted again before resuming her furious typing.

'Right,' Morgan continued looking at her notepad. 'I have two items of old business to deal with. The first is in response to Garry's proposed motion that the "Sound after Hours" rule, which the Board drew up and ratified in June of this year, should be amended so that there be a one-hour extension for those wanting to listen to music during weekends. As you may recall, we deferred the vote until this meeting because we had to interview the new tenants last month and were short of time. I will assume, however, that Garry wishes to proceed with the proposal. Is that correct, Garry?'

Garry nodded his head.

'Have you drawn up a formal proposal for us to consider?'

Garry shook his head and looked suddenly worried.

Morgan tutted. 'Well, I suppose it won't matter, but, Frank, will you please be sure to pay careful attention for the minutes? You will only have your own record of Garry's proposal to go by. Garry, when you're ready, please proceed.'

'It's not that complicated,' Garry started, addressing the group. 'I just feel that since people aren't working on the weekends, there should be an extension to the sound hours on Friday and Saturday nights.'

'Some people work on Saturdays,' Morgan countered. 'Mike, for example, he works.'

'I have to be up at seven on Saturdays,' Mike confirmed.

'Well, OK, then,' Garry conceded. 'How about just on Saturday nights? I'm only asking that I be able to listen to music until ten in the evening. Surely that's not too much to ask?'

'I sing with the Harlem Gospel choir at seven on Sundays

which means I have to be up by four,' Mrs Xhiu said, momentarily stopping her fingers.

'And you have to remember Garry that Ben and Mandy have a small baby,' Morgan said. 'That's a 24/7 job.'

'But they live on the ground floor and I'm on the third,' Garry replied. 'They wouldn't hear a thing.'

'Yes, but we are considering a new rule for the whole building not just for you and, as such, we have to consider everyone's rights and not just your own particular demands,' Morgan said.

'I'll be able to hear you,' Mrs Xhiu said.

Garry looked at everyone with disbelief. 'I don't believe this,' he said, getting irritated. 'All I'm asking for is one lousy hour on a Saturday night. It's my work too, you know. It's not like I'm just doing it for fun. I have to listen to my records before I can DJ, I have to practise my mixing.'

'Why can't you do that in the mornings?' Mike asked.

'I'm not in during the day, at least, I'm often, you know, sleeping or something.'

'Sleeping!'

'Yes, Mike, sleeping. A lot of gigs don't end till late. I have to sleep.'

'Just like the rest of us mortals, then,' Morgan said.

'No one's asleep at ten o'clock on a Saturday night,' Garry protested.

'I am,' Mrs Xhiu said.

'I think we're going around in circles here,' Morgan said.

'You could always use headphones,' Mike suggested.

Garry looked at him acidly.

'Is that the end of your proposal, Garry?' Morgan asked.

Garry turned and looked blankly at Morgan.

'Right, then, will you propose it, please?'

With an exasperated voice of defeat Garry said slowly, 'I propose a motion to extend listening hours until ten o'clock on Saturdays.'

'And who will second the motion?' Morgan asked.

Frank raised his arm.

'All those in favour say aye.'

'Aye,' Garry said.

'Aye,' Anna-lise said.

'Aye,' Frank said.

'And against?'

'Aye,' Mrs Xhiu said.

'Aye,' Mike said.

'Aye,' Morgan said. 'Which means that, again, we have a hung vote. As you know, in these cases the President of the Board's vote counts for two, meaning Garry's proposal to extend listening hours has been rejected by a margin of four votes to three. Frank, please make a note in the minutes. Right, on to the next item on the agenda.'

'You always do that,' Garry said.

'I'm sorry, Garry?' Morgan said, looking at him.

'You always make your vote count twice.'

'I don't know what you mean. It is the President of the Board's vote that counts twice, not mine.'

'And who puts herself up as President, year in, year out?'

'You are welcome to bid for the position at the next AGM if you wish to take over, Garry,' Morgan said matter-of-factly.

Garry swallowed at this challenge knowing that he, like everyone else in the building, wouldn't be able to bear being President, especially with someone like Morgan looking over his shoulder the whole time. He also knew the building wouldn't vote for him anyway. Morgan might have been unpopular but everyone agreed she got the job done.

'I suspected as much,' Morgan said. 'Now, if we can move on to the second item of old business.'

'What about my—' Mrs Xhiu tried.

'We're still on old business, Mrs Xhiu!' Morgan cut her off.

The typing resumed.

'As agreed at the last meeting, the Board would prefer to give Mr McMurphy a gift rather than money for his Christmas bonus this year since he seems to appreciate it much more. There is a computer at my office that I barely use and which I think would be a good way to get Mr McMurphy connected to the Net. It is relatively new and I've never had any problems with it so, even though it is worth substantially more than the five hundred dollars we usually allocate for the super's bonus, I am prepared to accept this amount as payment. Does anyone have any problems with this suggestion?'

'So will you be taking Mack's bonus for yourself, then? Is that what you are saying?' Frank asked.

'No, Frank, that's not what I am saying. I do wish you would listen,' Morgan replied. 'I am offering the building the opportunity to buy a computer from my firm at a discounted rate so that we can give Mr McMurphy a good gift for Christmas. If you object, however, I am perfectly willing to let you find a computer for him on eBay for five hundred dollars.'

'What kind of computer is it?' Garry asked.

'An Apple.'

'What year?' Frank said.

'I don't remember.'

'Apples are pretty good, Frank,' Garry said, shrugging his shoulders.

'It seems like a sensible arrangement to me,' Mike said softly. 'As long as you're sure Mack will like it.'

'Well, I can't guarantee *that*, can I, Mike? But I'd be surprised if he wasn't pleased,' Morgan said, visibly annoyed.

Mike pursed his lips apologetically at Morgan. 'I'm sure it's a good idea,' he said, before adding with an innocent grin, diplomatically trying to lighten the mood, 'Hey, we could tell him we'd decided to give him an Apple Mac for Christmas. Get it? An Apple *Mack*.'

Mrs Xhiu laughed but in a way that was clear she didn't get

the joke. Anna-lise smiled kindly. Morgan glanced at the floor briefly and then around the room, sighing heavily.

'Anyone else got any other thoughts?' she asked eventually. Everyone shrugged their shoulders.

'Right, good,' Morgan said. 'That settles it, then. I'll bring it home next week.' She sucked on her teeth before continuing. 'OK, let's move on to new business. First on the agenda is a very important proposal concerning the condition of the building's roof and future development of the top floor.'

'What about my bathroom?' Mrs Xhiu said.

'Oh yes, I'm sorry, Mrs Xhiu,' Morgan said, looking at her manly watch. 'I've just realized that the question of your bathroom is probably a matter for old business, since it has been a subject of ongoing concern for some time now.'

'But you said . . . '

'Yes, I know what I said but we are already short of time and the Board has to deal with this new matter before next month's annual general meeting. I suggest we try and squeeze in the question of your bathroom at the end of tonight's meeting and, failing that, we'll deal with it as part of the old-business schedule next month.'

'Why can't we deal with it as part of the old business for this month?' Frank said.

'Because we've just concluded old business,' Morgan said without the slightest trace of shame. 'If you'd been paying attention to the minutes you should know that. We're on to new business now.'

'But you said it was a matter for new business,' Mrs Xhiu said.

'I know I did, Mrs Xhiu, which is why I am being lenient now and suggesting we try and fit it in at the end of the new-business session this month. Failing that, please bear in mind that it is a matter for old business in next month's meeting. Now, we must get on. The more time we spend discussing this, the less likely it will be that there will be time to address it at the end of tonight's meeting.'

Mrs Xhiu didn't even have the energy to resume typing.

'Right, now, as I was saying. It has come to my attention that the roof of the building is in a bad condition. Cracks are appearing and there is the possibility that leaks could start at any minute. I am afraid that construction work is urgently required.'

A general groan span through the room.

'How bad is it?'

'When did you find out?'

'Will it cost much to repair?'

'How long will construction go on for?'

'Why has it suddenly started now?'

'OK, guys, one at a time,' Morgan said, revelling in the general panic. 'I'll start at the beginning and hopefully that should answer most of your questions. It was me who discovered the problem. I noticed a hairline crack in the plasterboard between the beams and asked an expert to come and look. He said that, for some reason, the roof is currently being supported by my living-room ceiling, which is why it is cracking.'

'How much will it cost to fix?' Frank said again.

'Well, I'm afraid that's the bad news.' Morgan paused to allow the tension to take hold. 'The guy I spoke to said we should probably replace the whole roof.'

'The whole roof?' Mike gasped. 'Are you sure? That's a massive job. Can't Mack just patch it up?'

'Well, he could I suppose but we'd only be delaying the problem for a year or two. We've pushed our luck for too long already. It could collapse if we don't act soon.'

'How much will it cost, Morgan?' Frank said for a third time.

'Depending on the roof we go for, anywhere between thirty-five and sixty thousand dollars.'

There were several very long gasps. Mrs Xhiu threw her hands up to cover her mouth as she whispered, 'Oh my Lord.'

'Sixty thousand dollars!' Frank panicked. 'How much do we have in the bank?'

'Treasurer?' Morgan said, looking at Anna-lise.

A scared-looking Anna-lise could only manage a pleading look in reply.

'As far as I can remember,' Morgan said for her, 'the building has ten thousand dollars in the current account and twenty-eight thousand dollars in CDs, which came mainly from the flip-tax profit the building made on the sale of G1. We should be grateful, if we hadn't agreed to increase the maintenance as we have over the last few years then we wouldn't even have that much.'

'Where on earth are we going to get the money from?' Garry said.

'We'll have to borrow it from the bank,' Mike said.

'What, and pay outrageous interest to those corporate thieves?' Garry snapped.

'Interest rates are still low, Garry,' Mike said.

'I don't care. I don't want anything to do with the KKK.'

'What?' Mike asked.

'Kapitalist Korporate Kulture,' Garry explained.

'Well, it doesn't look like we've got much choice,' Mike said.

Morgan oversaw the discussion with regal calm.

'You said that a new roof could cost anywhere between thirty-five and sixty thousand dollars,' Mrs Xhiu said.

'Yes,' Morgan said.

'Well, which is it? Thirty-five or sixty?'

'It depends on the type of roof we go for. If we choose to replace the old one as is, it'll cost us anywhere between fifty-five and sixty thousand dollars, but if we convert it and go for an extension with a simple flat roof, then the cost comes down.'

'Why is that?' Mrs Xhiu said.

'Mainly because roof-conversion companies compete for business. They do the restructuring as part of their work anyway, so it makes no difference to them if they have to stabi-lize the roof in the process. The main thing they're worried about is securing the conversion contract. Straightforward re-roofing companies, on the other hand, charge more to rebuild roofs, especially old ones like ours.'

'Well, let's just do that, then. It's obvious,' Anna-lise said. 'Isn't it?'

'Maybe,' Morgan replied. 'That's what we're here to decide. Of course, the final decision rests with the Co-op, which was why I wanted to discuss this before the AGM, so we can elimi-nate some of the options first.'

'Can the foundations take another storey?' Mike asked.

'Of course. We all know what Manhattan's made of.'

'And what would we use it for, the additional level?' Garry said.

'We could turn it into a roof garden,' Anna-lise said.

'Maybe we could expand the gym,' Mike suggested.

'How about a cinema!' Frank giggled.

'Or a chapel.' Mrs Xhiu smiled.

'Hold on, hold on,' Morgan said. 'I'm afraid you're all miss-ing the point.'

Everyone looked at her.

'No one else in the building can gain access to the roof, except in cases of emergency, without my permission,' Morgan said flatly.

'What?' the whole room said together.

'Anyone trying to get to the roof has to pass through my apartment first and, no offence, but I don't particularly want the rest of the building tramping through my corridor to get to a roof garden or a gym or a cinema, or a chapel for that matter.'

'If the rest of the building can't gain access to the roof, what are we going to use the extension for?' Frank asked.

'Well, I was thinking that, since I have sole access to the roof, the thing that would make the most sense would be for me to turn it into an additional bedroom and bathroom for my apartment.'

'What?' they echoed.

'Well, it's either that or we opt to have the more expensive, original roof replaced,' Morgan said.

'Morgan, I can't believe you're not going to let us use the new roof extension,' Mike said.

'If all this means that you're going to get to expand your apartment then I don't see why we should have to pay for it,' Frank added. 'If you want another floor, then you can pay for it.'

'Yeah,' Anna-lise and Garry said together.

'No, in fact you're wrong,' Morgan said. 'If you look in the shareholders' agreement you'll find that the roof is a communal liability and therefore everyone has to pay.'

'But if it's communal liability then it's communal property,' Garry argued. 'We must have access.'

'Well, I'm afraid you can't. I own the top floor and I say you can't and that's that.'

'Fine,' Frank said quickly. 'If you want to play it that way then I vote we go for the more expensive roof and forget the extension idea.'

'Yeah!' Anna-lise said.

'That's perfectly all right for the Board to consider that but, of course, I don't need to remind you, Frank, that, as Mike mentioned, we will have to finance this project with a bank loan, which will mean, even with interest rates being where they are, the building will have to increase maintenance, perhaps by as much as forty per cent by the end of next year. Anyone who fails to keep up their maintenance payments will face possible repossession of their property. The more money we borrow, the harder it will be to keep maintenance levels low.'

The room fell silent.

Eventually, quietly, it was Mike who spoke up.

'How urgent is the job?'

'The man I spoke to said we should start work in the spring,' Morgan replied. 'My suggestion would be that we present the case at the AGM next month and, subject to their approval, we put the job out for tender as soon as possible.'

'And what happens if we do nothing?' Anna-lise asked.

'The roof could collapse and costs could escalate to more than a hundred thousand dollars, not including damage to my apartment, compensation for which I would obviously be entitled to.'

'I don't believe this,' Garry sighed.

Anna-lise looked as if she was about to start crying. She fumbled with her hands searching for Ulysses but found she only had herself to hold on to. Henry was dog-sitting.

'I think we should adjourn the meeting now,' Morgan said softly. 'There has been a lot for everyone to take in and, as I said earlier, I have a dinner appointment.' She turned to Mrs Xhiu. 'Mrs Xhiu?'

'Yes.'

'I think it would be better if we left the issue of your bathroom until the next meeting, don't you?'

Mrs Xhiu simply nodded.

'Frank, I would like to see a draft of the minutes for this meeting early next week, please, and, Anna-lise, if you could drop those Treasury reports off to me in the morning, I can get on with the quarterly statement.'

They didn't reply. Everyone except them stood up to leave the room. Slowly, silently, single file, the Board started walking towards the door.

'Morgan?' Frank suddenly called out.

Everyone stopped.

'Yes, Frank,' she replied, turning.

'Why didn't you say something before?' he beseeched. 'Why didn't you warn us?'

Morgan looked at him and, for a second, Frank thought he detected a small smile in the corners of her mouth.

She shrugged her shoulders at him and said simply: 'I only just found out myself.'

'**B**onjour!' Nicolette said breezily as she entered.

'*Bonjour!*' Juan replied, leaning over to kiss her on both cheeks before turning to lead her down the long thin corridor that stretched its way through the apartment.

'It is a very beautiful day today,' Nicolette said in her heavy Haitian accent as they stepped into the east-facing living room, sunlight pouring through the shutters.

'I'm afraid the apartment is very dusty, Nicolette. Will you pay special attention to the shelves?'

'Of course,' she said, undressing. 'I always do.'

Juan watched her slip out of her pencil skirt and blouse and put on her overalls. She was a small woman, with a slim figure. There were few signs that she'd had two kids – one was a policeman like Mike and the other was a checkout girl at Dino's. Nicolette lived in the Bronx and came once a week to clean their place as well as Morgan's. As she reached for a pair of ankle-less socks from her backpack, Juan caught a trace of expensive designer perfume.

'Nicolette, you have to be the world's most glamorous cleaning lady,' Juan said, smiling at her.

'And you, *monsieur*, are a very kind man.' She smiled back.

Juan reached for a stiff cardboard bag that was standing on the coffee table. 'Here, I got you something.'

'Oh no!' said Nicolette, taking it. 'You should not have! Why did you?'

'It's just something they sent me at the magazine. A freebie.'

'Thank you!' Nicolette exclaimed, pulling out the miniskirt. 'It's DCG.'

Nicolette pressed the skirt against her waist and immediately went to kiss Juan again on both cheeks. '*Tu es très gentil*,' she said. 'Thank you, thank you.'

'You're welcome,' Juan said, looking into her freckled face. She reminded him so much of his mother. He felt a surge of emotion and had to swallow hard to stifle it. 'MIKE! Are you ready?' he called, turning quickly to look down the corridor.

'Coming,' came the muffled reply from the bedroom.

Nicolette turned, put the miniskirt carefully in her back-pack and pulled out a pair of bright-pink rubber gloves. She slapped them against her thigh and blew air into them so the fingers popped out one by one. She wriggled her hands into them.

'I will start in the bathroom,' she said.

Mike emerged from the bedroom, tucking a shirt into his jeans.

'Oh hi, Nicolette,' he said. 'How are you today?'

'*Fantastique*,' she beamed back at him. '*Merci, monsieur.*'

'Have you called Morgan?' Juan asked as Mike took him by the shoulders. They kissed.

'No answer. Besides, do you feel like seeing her today?' Mike said after they broke.

'She'll be hurt if we don't.'

'We don't have to invite her every week, do we?'

'She doesn't have anyone else, Michael,' Juan stressed. He always used Mike's full name to make a point. It was usually a sign that they were having an argument or, worse, that they were about to have one.

'And whose fault is that?'

'What does that mean?' Juan said.

'I dunno,' Mike said, walking away and into the kitchen. He opened the freezer and reached for the coffee.

Juan didn't say anything. He watched Mike fill the Italian percolator with water and coffee, screw it together and place it on the stove. Even with his physique, Mike seemed to do these sorts of things feebly.

'Here,' Juan said, reaching for the percolator before Mike

ignited the gas. 'You haven't screwed it on tight enough. It might explode.'

The two men found themselves in each other's space and looked at one another. Mike turned the gas on and pressed a button. There were three steady clicks before the stove lit with a whoosh.

'I don't think you should be angry with Morgan because of the roof,' Juan said.

'I'm not,' Mike replied.

Juan frowned knowingly at him.

'Honestly, I'm not. I don't even want to convert the bathroom any more.'

'Yes,' Juan said. 'And Morgan is our friend.'

'I know,' Mike said. 'It's just that . . . '

'What?'

'I'm fed up with the way she does everything with us. Even when I think it's going to be just the two of us she's there. We never seem to spend any time alone.'

'What about last night?' Juan said, slipping a small hand into Mike's shirt.

'Yes, there was last night,' Mike said, turning.

The two men embraced and kissed again, closing their eyes. There was a loud rapping on the window.

'YOO HOO!' Morgan cried through the glass, waving excitedly from the fire escape.

Juan felt Mike slump in his arms before turning to wave.

'See what I mean?' Mike muttered under his breath.

Juan jabbed a finger into his steel abdominals. 'Be nice,' he said, before moving to open the window.

'I was in the shower when you called so I thought I'd just come down and get you,' Morgan said as Juan slid the window open. She climbed into the apartment. 'I hope I wasn't interrupting.'

'Of course not,' Juan said, helping her over the window sill. 'We were just making some coffee.'

'Thank you, I'd love a cup,' Morgan grinned, throwing herself into a chair by the kitchen table. 'It'll give me a chance to show you the plans I've had drawn up for the roof.'

'Isn't that a bit premature?' Mike asked.

'Of course not, Mike, don't be stupid,' Morgan replied, unfolding a large piece of paper as the percolator started to rasp. 'Honestly,' she added, throwing a conspiratorial look at Juan as if to say: 'How do we cope with his lesser mind?'

Mike watched with irritation as Juan rested a forearm on Morgan's shoulder and leant over her to inspect the plans.

'Mike, come and look at this,' Juan said. 'I love the spiral staircase.'

'I designed that myself.'

'It looks great, Morgan,' Juan cooed. 'Your place is going to be worth a fortune when it's done.'

'I know, but don't tell the others, OK?' Morgan said. 'I don't want them thinking that.'

'But it will be of no use to anyone else.'

'That's not the point. The extension belongs to the building, even if I am the only person with access.'

'I can't see what difference it makes. If you're the only tenant with access, it's effectively yours. It must belong to your apartment.'

'Reading between the lines, a buyer will know that. But there's no need to rub people's noses in it. The last thing I need is for other tenants to start getting jealous.'

'Do you think that's avoidable?' Mike asked, bringing over the coffees. Juan took one.

'Maybe not,' Morgan replied. 'But people should remember I'm doing them a favour. These plans are saving the building thousands of dollars.'

'That's true,' Juan said.

'You know how people can be,' Mike said. 'Personally, I'm on your side, but I can see how someone could get upset.'

'Which is exactly why I want you to keep this our little secret,' Morgan replied.

The sound of the shower came from the bathroom.

'Who's that?' Morgan jumped.

'Just Nicolette,' Juan replied.

'Oh,' Morgan said, visibly relaxing. Then she frowned. 'Why's she here on a Sunday?'

'Monday nights don't work for us any more,' Mike said. 'We've joined a reading group and they come here every other week.'

'When did you start doing that?'

'Not long ago,' Juan said. 'Do you want to join?'

Mike stiffened.

'Sure,' Morgan replied. 'What are you reading?'

'*Another Country* by James Baldwin.'

'I'll order it off the Internet today.'

'Great,' Mike said, smiling tightly.

'Shall we go?' Morgan said. 'I'm starving.'

'I've just got to get my laundry,' Juan said.

'OK,' Morgan said. 'That'll give me a chance to talk with Nicolette. Did you know she actually used lemon cleaner on my work surface? It's burnt right through the seal and now there are marks everywhere. It feels like my kitchen has caught a disease.'

'I'm sure she didn't mean to,' Juan said.

'That doesn't mean I have to tolerate it. I'm going to take the bill for resealing the surface off her wages.'

'You can't do that,' Mike said.

'Why not?' Morgan said, getting up from the table.

'Oh, Morgan,' Juan said. 'Just leave it. It's lovely outside and we've got the whole day ahead of us. Life's too short for these little arguments.'

'Ah, you see,' Morgan said, visibly steeling herself. 'That's where you're wrong, Juan. Life's all about these "little arguments", as you call them. There're no handouts in New York, you of all people should know that. If Nicolette's not prepared to do my apartment properly, then I'm sure I can find someone else who will.'

'Fine,' Juan said, walking away. 'Do what you like, Morgan, but not today. If you want to tell Nicolette off then you can do it on your own time. She's too busy to talk to you right now.'

Mike watched Juan swing his hips towards the bedroom and smiled with pride as Morgan turned to face him.

'Has he got his period or something?' Morgan said, slightly exasperated.

'Yes, Morgan,' Mike said, picking up the coffee cups and walking towards the sink. 'Or something.'

I feared I might have missed them when I heard Mandy call from the front door but then I heard her say they'd forgotten something. I managed to jump up the basement stairs, catch my breath, and step nonchalantly into the corridor just as Ben was on his way back to G1.

'Oh hi, Mack. How's it going? We're just off out for a walk.'

'Do you need a hand?'

'I'll say. It's taken us three-quarters of an hour just to get out the apartment, there's so much stuff to remember.'

'What can I do?'

'Would you mind helping Mandy get the stroller out the front door? I've just got to get Billy's hat.'

'Sure.'

I looked down the corridor and saw her.

She was just as I imagined. She had the same dark features and long nose and satin skin, though I noticed a streak of metallic white in her hair. I liked it. It was the sort of thing Catherine might have done. She was also wearing the same sort of clothes. A long dark overcoat, with big round buttons, that cut into the waist and reached her knees but was a little short now on the arms. She had a black wool hat that touched her ears and pressed her combed hair down to the sides of her face. She was wearing a blue T-shirt and a V-neck jumper and jeans and loosely laced sneakers. She looked serene, especially with the light behind her, coming in through the door the way it was. Maybe it was the way she held herself as she bent down to check the baby.

Time seemed to stretch as I walked towards her. I watched her smiling into the buggy, her cheeks shining, the crinkled edges of her eyes gleaming. I felt a surge of happiness. Her ears were identical! I had to catch myself from falling for a moment of déjà vu as she saw me coming and stood up straight and turned to greet me, face to face. I so wanted to go back to that place, though I knew it had never existed, at least not this way.

'You must be Mr McMurphy,' she said simply. 'Ben's told me how great you were, helping him with the move.'

It was all I could do to return her smile.

'We really appreciate it. Thank you.'

'No trouble.'

'Mandy,' she said, throwing me a hand.

I held it.

Catherine.

'Joe,' I replied instinctively, wincing at the slip. It was the first time in years I'd said the name. It felt strange on the tongue. She didn't take any notice. 'And this is the little guy?' I added quickly.

'It sure is. But not so little. Nine pounds and ten ounces of pure trouble.'

'Nine pounds!'

'I ate a lot of yoghurt raisins.'

'Do you mind if I take a look?'

'Of course.'

She stepped aside and I squeezed alongside the buggy. I told myself to take it slow, that I shouldn't expect too much. But when I looked down and saw him there, staring up at me with prototype blue eyes, wide alive, I was stunned. It was uncanny. He had the exact same light, the one that I had marvelled at all those years ago; the one that said he had seen something we have all forgotten, that he had just come from a place we can't remember; the universal void. How does so much come from nothing? It seemed impossible. Impossible! It amazed me as much this time around. It was enlightenment. I hated the idea that he would lose it. Hunger, touch, smell, sight – senses were already starting to take over, distracting him, destroying him. I

could see him trying to focus on me. I wanted to tell him: Stop!
Don't! Step back! Stay where you are! He was starting to forget.
Just like the rest of us. It seemed unfair. I found it hard not to
despair. It was just like being there, with him again, the two of
us, me learning all the things he had to show me. I needed
more time to understand, more time. Where was he now? Was
being dead the same as being unborn? Can we go back after
consciousness? I didn't think so.

'Do you mind if I hold him?'

'Oh you know, I wouldn't, but we're just on our way out
and . . . '

I heard the door to G1 slamming shut and Ben's footsteps in
the corridor.

'You're right,' I managed, somehow tearing myself away. I
looked at her for one last enchanted glance. 'Let me help you
outside.'

'Next time, OK?'

I nodded with a smile.

'Did you find it?' she said, turning.

Ben waved the hat victoriously, like the flag of a little king-
dom.

'Are we finally ready to go out now?'

'As ready as we'll ever be.'

'Mack, would you mind getting the door?'

'Sure thing.'

I watched them bang and bundle and shuffle their way into
the outside, catching ankles and gripping the buggy too tightly.
As the door swung to, I watched them gather themselves on the
sidewalk, making sure they had everything, that they were prepared for every eventuality. Ben waved silently at me through
the glass and then the three of them were off, walking with
final, forward purpose into the beyond.

I sure hoped they would be OK out there.

Sunlight streamed through the windows of 1999 making the yolks in eggs look very yellow and the icing sugar on doormats of French toast sparkle. There was the sweet smell of maple syrup. Coffee steamed and strands of orange rind clung to the insides of glasses. Waiters rushed and cutlery chattered and the snap of Sunday brunch rang routinely.

Frank was looking with worry at Anna-lise across the table in their red-vinyl booth. Her eyes were swollen and raw, her mouth trembled, her nose ran mercilessly. He thought it would only be a matter of time before she started sobbing loudly again but, as it turned out, it wasn't.

'Hey, hey, hey,' Frank said, sliding quickly out of his side and crossing over to take Anna-lise in his arms. 'It's gonna be OK, Anna-lise. Ssssh, sssssh.'

The mothering made Anna-lise wail. A small voice inside Frank's head panicked that she was having a breakdown.

'You don't know that,' Anna-lise cried. 'How can you say that? You don't know that.'

Frank could feel Anna-lise's misery making his sweater wet. He decided to change tack.

'Now you listen to me, Anna-lise,' he said, pulling her away sternly by the shoulders. Anna-lise's head stayed slumped. 'I've had enough of this. He's just one guy, OK? One lousy, stupid guy. And you – look at you – you are one hot chick. You're gonna find someone and you're gonna get married and you're gonna have lots of kids and you're gonna live happily ever after. So stop giving me this trash about the tragedy of it and never being happy. Anna-lise, you have to believe me when I tell you: this will pass, OK? You're gonna get over Henry, I swear.'

Anna-lise nodded into her chest, her breasts pressed tightly under an army-green T-shirt that said: China White. They'd been talking for two hours already, Anna-lise giving him the break-up in wretched detail. The worst thing was how nice Henry had been about it.

'I'm not going to lie to you, Anna-lise,' Frank continued in a gruff voice. 'You're gonna have some rough times, there's gonna be more lows. But it will get a little easier each time. The best thing you can do right now is stay as far away from him as possible. Take time out for yourself. Get yourself well again, that's what counts.'

Anna-lise looked up, crow's feet clawing at her temples. She snivelled enormously. 'He . . . he says he's going to go away. Give me some space.' She wiped the back of her hand across her dog-wet red nose.

'That's good,' Frank enthused. 'That's really good. Are you gonna go away for the holidays?'

'To my parents.' Anna-lise shivered.

'It will be good for you to get out of the city.'

Anna-lise nodded weakly. They looked at each other and, for a brief instant, Frank believed with dread some of the things he'd said, and worried that, while Anna-lise *was* an attractive woman who would get her guy, Frank wasn't an attractive man and he wouldn't find his girl. Then he nearly felt like crying himself.

But Anna-lise beat him to it.

'I thought he was the One,' Anna-lise said, breaking down completely again, falling into self-pity as if the respite of the previous moment had simply been an illusion, the floating instant a cartoon character has before plummeting. 'It's the tragedy of it that kills me,' she sobbed. 'I know we're meant to be together and now we're not. It's just so goddamned sad.'

Frank, who couldn't bear the prospect of his sweater getting any wetter, reached simply for Anna-lise's hand and let her cry some more. Part of him believed Anna-lise needed to do it, another part knew that Frank wouldn't be able to stop her even if he wanted.

But then something happened.

A realization spread quickly across Anna-lise's face and burnt in her cheeks and evaporated her tears and dried her nose. She looked up at Frank in a way that was both heartening and terrifying, her eyes glowing with a sudden, sinister new strength.

'Morgan,' Anna-lise stated simply, the word turning the thoughts in her mind.

'What?'

'Morgan. That time, at the party in G1. Morgan told Henry I wanted babies.'

'So?'

'Don't you see?' Anna-lise said. 'I told you, right? During the break-up, I kept asking Henry why he wanted to end it and he said it was because he thought I was looking for something serious and I couldn't figure out why he should think that because I'd never said anything to him about getting serious but seeing as he'd brought it up yes I was and he said that he'd known that and that he'd been able to tell but I couldn't figure out how because I . . . because, because . . . Goddamn it, Frank, it was Morgan! Morgan freaked Henry out at that party by saying I wanted babies. It's her fault! Don't you remember?'

Frank shook his head. 'I'm sure there must have been other reasons besides.'

'No!' Anna-lise snapped. 'There weren't. I'm telling you there weren't. Everything had been great up until then. I never did anything to scare Henry off. I've been out with enough guys to know how not to do that. But that night, I couldn't help myself, Billy made my heart melt and Morgan just had to go and say something. Christ, I can't believe it. Henry split up with me because of Morgan.'

Frank looked at Anna-lise and thought carefully before

saying what he wanted to say. For some reason, the words made him nervous. They seemed dangerous. But he decided to say them anyway.

'You might be right.'

Garry was having the perfect Sunday, working a triangle of record stores in Chelsea. He'd started with a fair in an industrial-warehouse art gallery on Eleventh Avenue, between 22nd and 23rd. It was a small event, tucked in between a lighting installation called 'Brilliant' and a disorientating display of video art. One guy there had a good selection of funk but Garry found he already owned a lot of the records. Still, he picked up a mint-condition original of *The Soul Providers*, which he decided might come in handy as a spare.

He ambled down to Chelsea Market listening to the *Across 110th Street* show and noticed a couple of new 45s he'd never heard before. At the market, he bought some rucola for Stacey, a girl he'd met at Rooski's.

From there he cut back across to Eighth and stopped by his favourite diner, a Cuban joint with lipstick-red swivel seats, steamed-up windows and a fantastically fat man behind the bar. He ordered a Cuban sandwich filled with ham, pork, cheese and pickles, grilled to flat, mouth-sized perfection, the length of a child's arm. He had a double espresso and read an especially dull edition of the *New York Times* to help digestion.

After lunch he walked north and stopped by the spice store to pick up some jalapeño peppers before braving his way past Pot Luck, the sofa-filled coffee house. The whole avenue smelled of flour: pancakes, waffles, tortillas, French toast, burritos, bagels, pretzels, heroes, tacos, nan bread, chapattis, burger buns, hot-dog rolls . . . it was carbohydrate heaven. At 23rd, Garry crossed over the avenue and bought himself a tub of Frauleines and Queens from Häagen-Dazs.

Back across the avenue he found that his favourite hairdresser, a Jew from Tajikistan, had an opening, so Garry decided to get his long black hair trimmed so it wouldn't look so grey. In the seat next to him, a black kid from the projects across the street was having his crew cut clipped to immaculate detail. On the wall there was a sign warning customers that the store would be closed at weekends. The hairdresser told him it was because he and his brother were becoming more religious. Garry noticed that there was a new strip of pink lights along the walls and a section of the store was now dedicated to nails.

Feeling fresh after this dose of pampering, Garry turned onto 29th and went to his favourite store, the Second Hand Record Center. It was one of those places that only those 'in the know' could find since it wasn't advertised and was obscurely located on the eighth floor of an office block.

'It's open,' the woman said down the intercom, buzzing him in.

Garry entered the building lobby with a growing sense of anticipation. He often managed to find the most incredible stuff at this store. Music no one even knew existed which, in an age of CDs and music downloads, was what vinyl offered real music lovers and DJs like him – the lost and the rare and the beautiful.

How sweet was the irony of that! The music industry, in its greed, had phased out vinyl in favour of the cheaper, lighter and lower-quality CD format only to find that now, in an age of the Internet and music downloads, it was vinyl that was surviving and not the CD. A lot of old music was being reissued on vinyl and even new music was again being produced on records.

By contrast, mega music companies that produced only CDs were having their ridiculous profits squeezed because they'd so cheapened the musical product. No one wanted to own a CD! They were small, plastic and shit. You couldn't even play them once they got scratched. People only bought them because, for a long time, they were conned into believing they were better, and then, for a while, they were the only way to listen to music. Not any more.

With the introduction of CDs, the music industry had turned their product into a simple commodity, a song and nothing more. And a song wasn't enough. People didn't want to own songs, they were content to borrow them.

Small and judicious wonder, then, that the music industry should suffer now. If they'd made it so that people didn't want to own the music any more, if they'd distilled it down into just the song, a mere series of ones and zeroes, then they had only themselves to blame for the downloading.

A record offered something else entirely. Records gave Garry an entire package. When Garry bought a record he devoured its every aspect. He held it and turned it over in his hands, appreciating the gatefold seam and the intricacies of the cover art. He read the liner notes with avid interest. He took the vinyl out and enjoyed its size, weight and texture. When Garry bought a record he felt he was actually getting something for his money, and this was before he'd even listened to the music.

In fact, by the time it came to placing the record on the turntable and allowing the needle to fall into the groove with a brief, tantalizing crackle – an existential pleasure in itself, far superior to any techno laser-light experience a CD player might offer – Garry was usually in such a state of excitement he was practically climaxing. If the music was good, he would. But just like good sex, that satisfaction came only with a build-up. Records offered Garry the foreplay, the kisses, the tenderness and the love that are needed for real pleasure. CDs – well, they only ever delivered the come shot.

But sadly, after nearly an hour in the store – spent methodically flipping through the rows and aisles, the rare sections and the new arrivals – Garry found that apart from this crucial new understanding of the dynamic undercurrents of the music industry (he thought he might submit it as a piece to *DJ Week*), he had just eight dusty fingers to show for his time. A far cry from the orgasm he'd been searching for.

'I don't suppose you've got *Sleeping Beauty* by Sun Ra, have you?' Garry asked the owner on his way out.

'I sold a copy on Wednesday,' the woman replied without any hint of emotion as she changed the Alice Coltrane record that was playing on her finely balanced Riga.

'No way,' Garry replied. 'I've been looking for that for ages. Do you remember how much you sold it for?'

'Forty bucks,' she replied.

Garry's heart collapsed. 'That sucks,' he groaned.

'Sorry.'

How many times had that happened to Garry? It was a hazard of the passion, he guessed. He left the store feeling empty and decided to take a taxi down to the record fair around the corner from Basin and Bubbles.

He slid himself across the navy-grey plastic seats behind the driver, whose name he noticed on the badge in the bullet-proof Perspex divider that no one ever closed any more: Sultan Kamran. They travelled in silence, the taxi bouncing over manholes and through cross-street junctions like a fat kid with a lazy, streetwise gait. Garry gave him a one-dollar tip.

The second record fair was much larger and Garry didn't know where to start when he first walked in. There were rows and rows of stalls, men with bad body odour standing behind them, inspecting their customers with folded arms and impatient eyes. He saw one stall busy with young Japanese men and decided to try there. One of them had a small portable turntable and was playing a punk 45 on it through tinny speakers. Garry watched the man pay three hundred and seventy-five dollars after a few seconds of listening and a brief inspection. This stall was out of Garry's league.

He decided to try elsewhere for bargains. It was a long and emotional process. Garry found himself selecting piles of 'wants' out of some stalls only to decide, after discovering the enormous total, not to buy any of them. He couldn't make up his mind which ones to leave behind. At other stalls he found records that interested him but he walked away because he wanted to see if he could find something better, only to return five minutes later and discover they'd been sold. It was slow and frustrating but it was also exciting. It was like looking for treasure.

After three and a half hours of steady trawling – his hands covered in dust, his mouth tasting like the inside of a vacuum cleaner, his clothes as stiff as cardboard – Garry finally found a small stall specializing in the Chicago-based Argo and Cadet record label: Charles Stepney, Minnie Ripperton, Ramsey Lewis, Etta James, Rotary Connection, Dorothy Ashby, Marlena Shaw, Frank Foster, Lorez Alexandria.

Also looking through the stall was a boy with inch-thick glasses, a harelip and a furry, vole-like moustache. Garry couldn't figure out what the boy's problem was but he seemed to select records blindly, fingering through the pile while staring into mid-air, rubbing the edges as if checking for general thickness and wear. With uncanny consistency, the boy would pull out the rarest and most expensive record from the collection and press it close to his face, millimetres from his nose, gently rubbing the corners and edging the seam through the soft pads of his fingers. He actually seemed to be sniffing out the record he wanted.

Garry watched this from out of the corner of his eye until, eventually, out of nowhere and with complete inconsistency to the rest of the collection, the boy pulled out a mint original of Marvin Gaye's *What's Going On* – signed!

Garry's heart stopped. As the boy sniffed and snorted, Garry prayed for him to put it back. He didn't know if he'd be able to bear to see someone, quite literally, buy this from under his nose. It was difficult to not let this fear show; record collectors had a knack of knowing when the person next to them wanted what they held in their hands.

'Hey, enough with the sniffing already,' the cardigan-wearing proprietor of the stall said. 'That's a rare item you've got there.'

'How much?' the boy asked.

'Three hundred.'

The boy grunted at the man with disgust and started poring over the texture of the label.

'Hey, I told ya that's enough,' the cardigan said again. 'I don't need you drooling all over it, pal.'

With this comment the boy thrust the record back into the box and walked off muttering something that sounded like: 'It's only worth two hundred.'

'I'll buy it.' Garry immediately stepped in after the boy had left, picking the record out and feeling himself buzz with excitement to hold it in his hands.

'That'll be three hundred bucks.'

Garry pulled out the money from his wallet.

'You wanna check it for scratches?' the man asked.

'Sure,' Garry replied, pulling it out of its sleeve and holding it expertly between thumb and middle finger without touching the surface of the vinyl. 'I'm so damned excited to find this I can't tell you. A signed original! Unreal.'

'It's a great record,' the man said.

'Why you selling it?' Garry asked.

'I've got three more at home.'

'That looks great,' Garry said, after inspecting it. 'Have you got a bag?'

'Somewhere,' the man said, looking in between boxes.

'My girlfriend's gonna kill me when she finds out I bought this,' Garry said.

'Why?'

'Oh you know, she doesn't get it. She says I'm addicted.'

'Well, at least you're not addicted to crack,' the man replied. 'You should tell her that. She should be grateful.'

Garry looked at him as he took the bag and considered this wisdom.

'I'll be sure to mention it,' he lied.

Instead of taking the subway, as he should have, Garry decided to get another taxi. He couldn't wait to get home. Manoosh Subramaniam drove. He didn't dare take the record out of the bag.

Garry tumbled through the doors of 444 and into the elevator up to the third floor. He threw open the door to his apartment, tore off his gloves and hat and walked straight to his sound system without taking his coat off. He picked the needle off carefully and placed it with a snap, crackle and pop into the first groove.

Mother, mother
The music rolled down the heating pipe.
There's too many of you crying
It was like water to a fire.
Brother, brother, brother
A balm to my raw ears.
There's far too many of you dying
The red transmission was silenced.
You know we've got to find a way
The discord was muted by harmony.
To bring some lovin' here today
I found myself smiling.
Father, father
I felt calm.
We don't need to escalate
I closed my eyes and swam in the relief.
War is not the answer
I nodded in time with the rhythm.
For only love can conquer hate
I felt the hairs on the back of my neck.
You know we've got to find a way
My heart soared with the strings.
To bring some lovin' here today
I was being lifted up on angel's wings.
Picket lines and picket signs
I was free!
Don't punish me with brutality
I could see that we were all free.
Talk to me, so you can see
I wanted to shout it to the world:
Oh what's going on,
What's going on,
What's going on.

There was a sharp thud-dud. It came from Mike and Juan's. Garry looked at his watch. 5.42 p.m. More than two hours left of listening time. He ignored it and let Marvin Gaye take him higher. He held his hands up in the air and sang with the music. Tingles rushed down his spine and nerves exploded across the back of his head.

There was another bump and the muffled sound of Morgan's voice from above.

'Turn it down, Garry.'

Garry reached for the stereo remote, hiked the volume up a notch and shouted at the ceiling, pointing one defiant finger towards the plasterboard.

Who are they to judge us
Just because our hair is long

He closed his eyes and let the music take over again. There was no beating this feeling. It was joy. It was wisdom. It was truth. It was light. Garry couldn't help himself smiling. He just had to share it. *This* needed to be shared. People needed to hear this song. The world needed to hear this song. It was quite possibly the best song ever written. Was there a person on the face of this planet who couldn't feel this?

'We're trying to watch a movie,' Morgan's muted voice shouted.

Garry snorted. Of course. There was *one* person. Not even her place, he mouthed aloud before pumping up the volume. If Morgan refused to listen then Garry was going to make her. Marvin Gaye was a prophet for our times, a genius, a Buddha. He spread the message. He spread peace. He inspired belief. Who was Morgan compared to that?

Immediately, there was a very loud bang on the ceiling that

made one of the lamps on Garry's bookcase rattle and a book from a shelf above the turntable slip. Garry pressed the volume three times and said in a normal voice:

'Fuck you, Morgan.'

Morgan pounded harder. Listening to one of the greatest odes to peace had somehow inspired war. Garry saw the book. The book was falling. Garry suddenly remembered that Marvin Gaye had been shot. He tried to move but he was too late. Shot by his own father. The book tumbled and splayed and fluttered its leaves. A reverend who killed his own son! It caught the arm of the turntable. How evil was that? The diamond stylus careered across the vinyl. The speakers screeched. Garry thought he was going to vomit. The world was sick. He threw a hand to his mouth.

Duh-dum, duh-dum, duh-dum . . .

The stylus limped across the paper circle in the centre of the record. Garry stepped over to the record player and turned it off. He picked up the arm and saw that the stylus was crushed. He lifted the record. A thick white scar shuddered across its surface.

The front door banged.

'I've written up a complaint in the log book,' Morgan said, through the door. 'That's your third one this week, Garry, and you know what that means. Pay the fine to Anna-lise by Thursday.'

Garry felt a rush of fury. He threw the record onto a side table and strode with intention to the door. Morgan was turning away, just as Garry hurled it open into the wall.

'WHO THE FUCK DO YOU THINK YOU ARE?' Garry shouted.

Morgan stopped and stood for a second with her back still turned before slowly looking over her shoulder at Garry. Garry found himself having to stare up at her.

'YOU JUST RUINED THAT LP! IT COST ME THREE HUN-DRED BUCKS.'

Garry could feel his nostrils flaring as he breathed. He wanted to attack her, he wanted to tear her eyes out, rip her apart limb from limb. He hated this woman. He was full of violence. Could he kill her?

Morgan rotated slowly on her heels and turned to face him. She took a step forward and said, 'Yes, Garry?'

'My record,' Garry said quietly. 'You broke it.'

Morgan looked at him.

'When you banged on the floor,' Garry explained meekly. 'You made a book fall.'

Morgan's face remained impassive.

'It hit the turntable,' Garry said, his voice failing him.

Several snail-paced seconds passed. They looked at each other, like soldiers at the battle lines. Garry eventually capitulated, letting his gaze fall to the floor.

'Thursday,' Morgan said again finally before turning towards the elevator.

'. . . did it say?'

'I don't remember.'

'You don't remember!'

'Sorry, I didn't mean to do it.'

'"Sorry" isn't going to help me, Mandy.'

'I'm know, I'm sorry.'

'CHRIST!'

'She'll call back, won't she?'

'What do you think?'

A pause.

'And you definitely don't remember the name of the firm?'

Another silence.

'Was it Jacob and Stevenson?'

'No.'

'Largent?'

'I didn't really listen to it. At least, I didn't take it in. All I know is a woman called about an interview.'

'Fuck, Mandy. Four buttons. Four lousy buttons, that's it! PLAY, SAVE, RECORD, ERASE. I know it's an old machine but how hard can it be? You can be so stupid sometimes. I mean, what goes on in your head? Ever since . . . '

'Go on, say it.'

'Fine! I don't care. I will say it. It's not like it's a big secret between us. Ever since Billy arrived you've been gone. I don't know where you are but you're not here, that's for sure. You're not living on earth with the rest of us. I mean last night you nearly dropped him, for Christ's sakes!'

'This is so unfair of you.'

'Is it, Mandy? Is it really unfair? I'm worried. I mean, this funk you're in the whole time, it's driving me nuts. It was you who wanted *the goddamned baby, insisted we go ahead with it, told me to trust you, and now you're the one who's fucking depressed. Er, TOO LATE TO BE DEPRESSED! We have a baby now! If you didn't want one you should have thought about that before. It's too late to go changing your mind. So just snap out of it, woman. Get a frickin' grip.'*

'I'm just tired.'

'Tired? Tired? How can you be tired? I'm the one who gets up in the middle of the goddamned night to bottle-feed the baby. I'm the one who can't get back to sleep for two hours afterwards. I'm the one who has to go to work the next day. What do you have to do except sit on your fat ass and watch daytime television?'

'Fuck you.'

'No, Mandy, fuck you.'

'This wouldn't matter if you hadn't got sacked.'

'Redundant. I was made redundant.'

'So you keep saying.'

'What's that supposed to mean?'

'You shouldn't have had that fight with Steve.'

'Oh, so now it's my fault. You erase the goddamned answer-machine message with a job offer and now I'm to blame for everything. This is great, just great.'

'Look, darling, we're on the same side.'

'I know, Mandy, that's the whole point. Don't you see, we won't be able to keep up the mortgage on this place if I don't get another job soon.'

'Are you serious?'

'Deadly.'

'Jesus, Ben. What are we gonna do?'

'I dunno, Mandy. I think maybe we should start by . . . '

BEEP!

Morgan put the phone down. She'd decided not to leave a message.

'From Tadasana, inhale, and into Utkatasana, exhale, and breathe . . . '

Henry was working well. Too well. So far he hadn't even tried to check out the new recruits in his yoga class, which was strange considering it was the reason he'd come.

'Back up into Tadasana, now Uttanasana, don't forget to breathe . . . '

Yoga was by far the best way to pick up beautiful women in New York. Classes at the Purple Love Bud Yoga Center on the Lower East Side, particularly, were full of aspiring models. And the combination of sauna heat, scanty clothing and dim, natural light seemed to constitute the perfect conditions for sexual thinking.

'Keep your back straight and lift your sacrum . . . '

It was much more straightforward and less expensive than picking someone up in a bar. There were no games or fronting. Yoga cut straight to the chase. Women got their clothes off and themselves worked up. They were always relaxed and horny after. Somehow yoga broke the ice, it put women in the mood. One of Henry's previous yoga lovers had explained it was because the postures echoed the female sexual experience; all that sweat and stretching and heavy breathing.

'Breathe . . . '

It was easy to make eye contact or start a conversation after class. Maybe it was the disarming way yoga made participants push their asses in the air. Or maybe women just felt like they'd already had sex with you, or an approximation of it, so going back home to fuck was a logical progression. Yoga was stimulating simulation. Or maybe it was just a sexy spiritual Indian thing.

'And inhale, back into Tadasana . . . '

Even if Henry failed to get himself invited back to someone's apartment for herbal tea, he always took great pleasure watching (carefully, of course) lithe beauties bending themselves in front of full-length mirrors. When else would he enjoy a woman's body this way? When else would they do it? It rarely happened in bed. Why people even bothered with porn, striptease or live sex shows, Henry would never understand. Yoga was far more erotic.

'Exhale, into Uttanasana again . . . '

But, hard as he tried, things just weren't happening on that front. He didn't even respond when the woman in front of him – six foot, blonde, Scandinavian, hand-width waist and fake breasts – floated down in front of him with agonizing ease and winked at him from between her knees, the egg of her vagina described in pink Lycra, moments away from his face.

'Long deep breaths, Pranayama . . . '

He missed Anna-lise.

The yoga teacher came up behind him and pressed into Henry's lower back with firm but gentle hands.

'Breathe,' she hissed into his ear.

This was very unlike him. He figured he'd be over her by now. It had been nearly three weeks and he still hadn't slept with someone else. It wasn't as if he didn't have options. He'd always had options. Maybe he should just bite the bullet and sleep with this woman in front of him. Even though he didn't want to, maybe it was the best way forward. He had to start somewhere. He had to get back into the bachelor swing of things, remind himself of what it was to be a single man in New York, remind himself that there was always someone else out there; someone better-looking, more intelligent, funnier than the person he'd just been with. That was how he used to operate, back in the old days, his days as the nomad with gonads.

'And inhale, into Tadasana . . . '

Henry gazed across the long, hall-like room, with its parquet floor and skylight frame, its wall-to-floor mirrors multiplying people and space, the wind-chime music tinkling through cube speakers, the rows and lines of purple and pink and black body mats, the people positioned like mannequins in a play, the faint odour of floor polish in the air, the taste of hunger in his throat, the sensation of the ground pushing up through his feet, his spine, the crown of his head, into the space above him: aware of it all but not holding on to any of it. He tuned into his being and understood completely: he just didn't want to sleep with Scandinavia.

'Prepare for Parsva Uttanasana. Inhale and stretch up through the spine . . . '

Why the hell not? She was better-looking than Anna-lise, she had a much harder body. Not that that was the point. Henry wasn't completely shallow. Not so much any more, at any rate. After sleeping with a lot of beautiful women, Henry had learnt that beautiful women weren't necessarily up to much, he didn't always want them around in the morning. He didn't necessarily want them around in the night either. But there never seemed much point dating and then not having sex. And Henry didn't believe you had to like the person to sleep with them. Some of the best sex he'd ever had, had been with women who irritated and bored him intensely. In fact, for a while it had become a rule of his to sleep only with the most distressing dates. Not only was there no risk of becoming emotionally involved but there was also a certain freedom to the sex, an intensity – perhaps because he knew he'd never see or talk to or want to be anywhere near the person ever again. Nightmare dates helped him shed his inhibitions.

'Place your hands in the Prayer pose behind your back . . . '

The trouble was that he liked Anna-lise. He really liked her. She was talented and independent and smart; some people didn't think Anna-lise was smart because she played ditsy but

Henry knew that that was just a trick. Look at how she manoeu-vred herself out of the Treasury job. She was probably the only person in the whole building who'd actually managed to get the better of Morgan. Coming up with that excuse about the quar-terly reports had been all her.

A spray of sunlight laser-rayed through the skylight and hit Henry square in the face. He closed his eyes and bathed in it.

'Inhale and stretch up into the upper back bend . . . '

And they were good together. They liked all the same stuff, the same movies, the same designers, the same food, the same places. She made him laugh. Better still, she laughed at his jokes. It was great going places with her and laughing together, at people, things, situations, themselves.

A cloud edged into the sunlight enough for Henry to open his eyes again. There was a magnificent gilt to it.

'Now bend forward from your hips, exhaling, spine extended . . . '

Henry told himself he'd already considered all this. The simple fact remained: Anna-lise wanted serious commitment and Henry wasn't in a position to provide it. Well, it wasn't that he wasn't in a position, he just didn't want, well, not exactly not want . . . OK, he was scared! There. He'd admitted it to him-self. He was scared. What difference did that make? Knowing that he was scared didn't make him any more inclined to commit. The thing he had to do was move on. He was only making things harder on himself this way. It was time to get over her. He had to stop coating her in crystal. He had to stop martyring her; turning her into the one that got away. Anna-lise was not that special. She was not that great. She was not the only woman in the world for Henry to fall in love with. There were a million women out there to fall in love with. It was up to him to decide when and with whom he wanted to fall in love. What he had to do was start fucking again. It was that simple. That was the way forward.

'Keep your spine extended for as long as possible before rounding it to bring your head towards your leg . . . '

But what if he wasn't deluding himself? What if Anna-lise was special? What if she was the One? What if there really was such a thing as the One? Was he throwing away his only chance at true love in life? What if he was making a mistake, the biggest mistake of his life? Was he really coating Anna-lise in crystal? What if he'd burnt through her layers? What if he'd seen her soul and found the true meaning of beauty, of life, of love? What if he'd been caught in a trap, a trap of nature that bound him to her? What if he wasn't able to fall in love with anyone ever again? What if he went through the rest of his life never wanting to fuck another woman? Christ!

'And inhaling, return to Tadasana . . . '

Henry knew one thing. He'd found someone who loved him. Anna-lise definitely loved *him*. Not Henry James Bartholomew III as so many other women would have. She loved Henry, just Henry. He knew that much because she didn't know his secret. He could believe in her love. She loved him for who he really was, not for the money. And that totally blew him away. Anna-lise didn't know the first thing about Henry and where he came from and the inheritance, yet she still loved him. She Loved Him! It was a miracle. It was an honour. He couldn't get over that. It was an amazing thing, to be truly loved. The most amazing thing possibly in all of life, to know that someone wants you: just you.

'Relax into Samasthiti, breathe, relax . . . '

So what if she wanted to get married? So what if she wanted to have babies? That was fair enough. That was her biological prerogative. She was entitled to feel that way, she was entitled to make her demands. What was he so scared of anyhow? Now that he knew that she loved him and that he loved her, what was the problem? Was it just the fear of making a mistake? What if not being with Anna-lise was the mistake? Which of the two mistakes would be worse?

'Breathe deeply . . . '

It could be the ultimate New York love story – if it was true. He knew that the newspapers would lap it up: 'In Search Of Truth, Trust Fund Runaway Finds Love'. He should be sure. He couldn't be wrong about this. Too much hinged on it, there was his family to consider. He couldn't embarrass them. Not again. But most of all, it wouldn't be fair to go back to her unless it was for good. Not on either of them. He didn't need to put her through another break-up. They'd both shed enough tears already. Next time, if there was going to be a next time, had to be the last time. It had to be the only time, it had to be for real and for good. And before he could know that, for absolute sure, he needed to think. He needed to take time. He needed some space. He needed to meditate.

'Om.'

Diva was just beginning to brace herself for the rush of paranoia that always followed quickly on the heels of her first smoke of the day and made her wonder why she even did it, when the door snapped with a loud, formal knock.

The word COPS flashed instantly in front of her eyes.

She had to get her shit together, and fast. Already primed – her heart pounding in her chest, hot sweat greasing her temples – she hauled herself dizzily to her feet and scrambled around for her materials: papers, pipes, clipper lighter, the big bag of grass.

She found a drawer and threw them inside.

Thinking better of this idea, she then took them out and searched the room with her eyes. She tried to squeeze them behind some books but that was no good, three whole novels stuck out proud. Hurriedly, she rushed to the bathroom and briefly contemplated flushing everything down the toilet.

But the mere sight of all those beautiful buds was enough to stop her.

She told herself to take it easy, take a deep breath, stay calm. There had to be a rational answer for who could be at her front door at this time of day. Only then did she consider how the police could have made it inside the building without being buzzed.

Maybe she should go take a look through the spyhole, she thought to herself. Blind panic was slowly giving way to logical thought again.

At least, Diva believed that to be the case until another aggressive rap on the door made her realize she'd actually just been spacing out for two long minutes in front of the bathroom mirror.

She span the drugs up on top of the vanity cabinet and raced out into the living room to open a window. She fanned the air with a magazine and tried to sort her hair out.

All in all it was a shambolic display – in her dealing days they used to have these evasive measures drilled to military perfection. She felt thoroughly ashamed of herself now.

Morgan's voice came through the door: 'Diva? Are you in there?'

It was even worse than she thought. The cops Diva could handle, Morgan was altogether a larger problem, one that didn't just go away. Instinctively, Diva found herself crouching down towards the ground, trying to fly below the radar vision of her voice, or the chance that she might somehow be looking into her apartment through the keyhole, or something . . .

'Diva, there is a very powerful aroma coming from your apartment. Will you open the door, please?'

Crap! She was totally busted. She should have known better than to start smoking before everyone had left for work. She wasn't usually awake this early. Even so, she could usually count on Morgan and the rest of the building passing her apartment corridor via the elevator. How come she'd ended up taking the stairs?

As if reading her mind Morgan added: 'There's a problem with the elevator so I happened to be walking past. Is that marijuana I can smell?'

Diva's mind tore through all the possible responses – ranging from burning an incense stick to hurling herself out of the window – and somehow managed, in her frozen, crashing condition, to find the best response of all, which was to do nothing.

Morgan beseeched her through the walls.

'I know you're in there, Diva, there's no point hiding. Open the door so we can talk about this. I won't tolerate drugs in the building, Diva. Diva? Diva? Open this door immediately . . . Damn it, I'm going to be late. OK, Diva, you've got away with it this time but I'm *warning you, if I ever smell marijuana coming from your apartment again I will call the police. I'm only being lenient now because I know you've been in the building for a long time and things used to be different round here. But this is the last time, Diva. The last time!'*

Diva waited for the sound of her footsteps to shrink and die before finally she timidly tiptoed up to the door and checked the spyhole. When she was quite sure that it was safe she ran straight to the bathroom and rolled herself another joint.

It was going to take a strong smoke or three just to recover.

Mandy was stressed. She was trying to fix a plug onto a lamp Ben's mother had given them as a birthing/house-warming gift. She was determined to prove that she wasn't totally useless at these sorts of things.

But the plug was winning. It had said on the pack: 'Snap and fit, it's that simple', but Mandy just couldn't get it to snap. It was really fiddly. Her fingers ached from pressing too hard on the plastic edge. Who the hell gave lamps as birthing presents, anyway? What about a nice Babygro for Billy instead?

She took a deep breath and concentrated. This was her only chance to do this. Billy would wake up any minute. And then she'd be chained to the sofa for an hour and a half feeding because it was impossible keeping him awake on the breast. She'd tried everything: rubbing his cheeks, tickling his feet, putting a wet flannel on his tummy, pinching him – a little too hard once. Thankfully, Ben never noticed the wound – a nasty blood blister on the back of his calf. God, how she hated herself for that.

Of course, if she put him down again, he woke up and screamed. It was a Catch-22 situation. They went around in these never-ending circles, on and on and on. Ten minutes of feeding, asleep, five more, asleep, another five, asleep . . . God, she hated it! Why couldn't the kid just eat and sleep and give her some peace?

She'd thought about quitting. Her breasts ached. Even after expressing, her nipples were raw and chapped from his chewing. She often leaked. She'd wake up in the night in a pool of milk. She found it humiliating to not be able to control her own body. It was like wetting the bed. And she was so sick of the smell. It followed her everywhere, that tangy, sour, off-milk smell. It got into everything, even with the diaper-like breast pads she degraded herself to wear. All her clothes were ruined.

And the poor child was starving. That was why he screamed so much, not because of colic, but because he was hungry. She knew, because he was quiet after a bottle. She was just torturing him this way. It was her inability to provide nourishment for her son that was causing him so much distress. It was all her fault. She was a useless mother. She wasn't equipped. She was no good at it. She should have known. She should never have had him. It had all been a big mistake. She was killing her child with her own inadequacy. She was a useless, worthless, vile human being.

Ben was pressuring her to stop. He said there was no point in her feeling this way, beating herself up over it. If Billy was hungry they should just give him formula. But Mandy feared mastitis. And, she knew, the guilt would be unbearable. Once she stopped, she wouldn't be able to go back to it. She would have severed the umbilical bond completely. The baby was barely a month old and already she wanted to cut him loose.

It was official: she was the world's worst and most evil mother.

And she was a lousy wife too. Ben was right. Just look at her.

She was ugly. She had gruesome milk spots that looked like small meteors had smashed against her face, exploding her skin.

She was boring. Mandy had only one thing on her mind, there was only one thing she seemed capable of talking about these days: the baby. Baby this, baby that, baby boring, boring, boring. No wonder none of her friends called. At first she had thought it was them. That they were too young, or too single, or too jealous to take an interest. But now she knew. It was just her.

She was a zombie. She had no energy. She hardly went out. She told Ben it was because it was too difficult on her own with the diapers and the change of clothes and the stroller and her purse and ... but they were just excuses. The truth was, she couldn't be bothered. She was just too tired. She didn't want to go wandering around the park in the freezing cold, negotiating taxis and stairs and manic people furiously racing to go their own way, to get their own way, screaming at her to get out of their way. She'd do anything for a solid night's sleep. Anything.

It was torture. When she did sleep it didn't feel like sleep because she slept with one eye open. If the baby so much as twitched his nose, Mandy was up. She spent night after night just listening to him breathing, terrified every ten seconds that he'd stopped.

And she hated sex. She couldn't think of anything she wanted less than sex. When Ben reached across in the night and touched her breasts it made her want to hit him. Couldn't he see? They weren't *for that* any more. They'd changed. They weren't sexy. They were just feeding machines, milk pumps. And they hurt like hell. What did he think he was going to do with them? Kiss them, suck them, knead them? Ha! How would he like a kick in the balls? That's about how sexy her breasts felt, that's about how sexy she felt. She still hadn't said yes. She'd even lied, telling him the doctor had said she couldn't.

Poor Ben. Would she ever want to sleep with him again?

That morning she'd forgotten about the teats she was sterilizing and they'd melted in the pan. Ben had just looked at her. The night before she put the video they'd rented in the dishwasher. He didn't know about that yet. It was the reason she wanted to get this lamp going. She had to do one thing, just one thing, so that he could be pleased with her. She had to give him a reason to want to stick around for all this because, to be brutally honest, if the shoe were on the other foot, if she didn't have to, if she wasn't physically condemned to, Mandy couldn't be absolutely sure that she would stay. If she were Ben, she'd probably just leave.

'Come on, you!' she said, squeezing the wires in with one last push. She heaved and squeezed and something snapped. She thought, with fear, that she'd broken a nail and that the pain was about to sear through her arm. But then she saw it was the plastic from the plug, her only one. She wished it had been a nail. 'Goddamnit.'

And there it was. She couldn't do it. She couldn't even put this stupid plug on this stupid lamp from his stupid (but oh-so-capable-and-brilliant-and-perfect-and-wonderfully-natural) mother. All Mandy was good for was being an ugly, boring, sex-hating zombie that violently molested (and secretly hated) her baby. Oh, and sitting on her fat ass all day watching TV as well, of course. How could she have forgotten that?

'Oh shit!'

She suddenly remembered the laundry. Ben's shirts. His interview. They wouldn't be dry in time.

'Shit, shit, shit, shit.'

She quickly checked Billy and risked leaving him to go to the basement. She would be two minutes. Two minutes. She slid herself out of the front door into the corridor, through the basement door and down the stairs. When she got there she found Joe, taking Ben's clothes carefully out of the machine.

'I'm sorry, Mandy,' he said. 'But Diva wanted to use the laundry. She'll be back in a minute.'

'It's me that should be sorry. The cycle finished two hours ago.'

'I know. And, er, I'm afraid that maybe . . . '

'Oh no,' Mandy said, quickly stepping forward and taking the shirt from Joe's hands. 'Oh God, please no.' She held it up. 'Are they all like this?'

'I'm afraid so.'

'Why? I can't believe it. What did I . . . '

Joe held up the little red jeans she'd bought for Billy from Fake! on Eighth the previous weekend.

'How did that get in there? It's not possible. I separated. I know I, I, I . . . '

Mandy felt herself cracking up. She couldn't hold on much longer.

'I think there's some Vanish some place—' Joe started but before he had a chance to finish, Mandy was sobbing wretchedly into his chest, clutching Ben's new tie-dye office wear to her face, desperately trying to hide her shame.

I didn't know what to do. It had been a long time since a woman had cried in my arms. For a few moments I felt bad because I couldn't raise my embrace. I wanted to hold her, I just didn't feel that it was my place. So I just stood there, my arms pinned to my sides, a little terrified as she leant into me and bawled. Shouldn't her husband be here to take care of this, I thought to myself, vaguely aware that Diva could walk down and find us this way.

But then I realized; I could help. In fact, when I thought about it, it was help that Mandy needed more than anything right now, even more than comfort. I could do more for her than just hold her. I could solve her problems. I could take away her worries. Wouldn't that be better than comfort?

It was time this poor lady stopped doing everything by herself. No one could be expected to do all this alone. Where was this girl's mother? Why wasn't she here? Families were meant to come together in times like this. They were meant to be there to support one another. Young mothers weren't meant to mother alone, they needed their mothers to help them, and their aunts and uncles and anyone else around too.

Because a baby was too big of a job for one person. It took at least three to bring a child into the world. That was how it used to work in the old days. A mother and father could rely on the second generation to help look after the children. It was the logical way because it was the mother and father who were fit to earn. Traditionally, taking care of kids was a job for the elders, not the young. It was never meant to work the way they make you think it's meant to work these days. These days they expected people to be independent, to manage all on their own. They derided you if you did anything less. The world was so selfish, people didn't dare ask for help. Women were expected to bring up their kids, keep house, even work.

It just wasn't realistic. Women weren't superheroes. Mothers needed help. Everyone had to pitch in, share the load. That was how to make young families work, that was how to keep them together. People wondered why there was so much divorce, they wondered why families were breaking up the whole time and they couldn't see it was because we were all to blame. We weren't contributing to the collective.

B en opened the door, wet with snow, fed up and tired. It had been a bad day. The interviews weren't going anywhere. Hiring freezes, layoffs and cost cuts dominated the world. The fact that the holidays were coming up didn't help. People told him he was lucky to even get a foot in the door for their 'advice'.

Ben wasn't so sure. They only painted a grim view and Ben had enough realism in his life already.

But there wasn't time to moan. He had another interview in an hour. He just wanted to shower and change. The only thing he could possibly hope to expect, and which would make him happy, would be if Mandy hadn't burnt down the building. So far, at least, things were looking good on that front.

'Hi, honey, I'm home,' he called out.

Silence. Ben frowned, opened his umbrella to dry by the door and took off his coat. He stepped slowly into the apartment.

'Honey?' He stopped. Something was wrong. The apartment looked . . . tidy? And that lamp – where had that come from? And the shutters were fixed. And the spotlights were *working*? And the kitchen cabinet had been painted. And the sofa had been moved. It made the room look much bigger.

'Mandy?' Ben called, walking with purpose. 'Mandy?'

As he stepped towards their bedroom he heard laughter. Loud, happy, throaty laughter – Mandy's. It sounded strange to hear it, he hadn't heard it in a while. He opened the door.

'Mandy?'

She turned with a big smile. 'Hi, darling!'

The baby was on their bed, gurgling on a brightly coloured quilt, looking up in wonder at plastic shapes hanging from a fabric arch. They were shaking and there was a bell that jingled, and a man's hand.

'Mack?' Ben said.

Mandy met him quickly with a kiss. She threw her arms around his neck and squeezed him for too long. It was as if she hadn't seen him in weeks. Ben didn't know how to respond. He saw that the super was embarrassed. They both were.

'What's going on?'

'Wait, just wait, you've got to come and see this,' Mandy said, breaking and pulling him into the room by the hand. 'Go on, Joe, show him.'

Ben watched as Mack snapped the toys to the left and then to the right and then left again so that the shapes shook quickly and the bell sounded as if it were about to ring off its mount. Little Billy immediately responded by throwing his arms and legs into the air and gurgling a spittle sound that was frighteningly close to a giggle. There was a broad, toothless, open grin across his face to go with it. Ben's heart instantaneously folded in half.

'Hey there, little guy,' he said, leaning over into Billy's air space, wanting to share in the moment. 'Is that funny? Do you like that?'

The baby gazed for a second in confusion at this shift in shades before Mack shook the toy again and he was off, flinging his limbs and choking on laughter. And it wasn't long before Ben and Mandy had joined in as well and the whole room was filled with flailing baby faces and happy distraction each time the super shook the toy. They were all kids at the show, thrilled and enthralled whenever the puppeteer pulled the strings.

'Again!' Ben said. 'Do it again! Again, Mack! Again!'

He didn't even notice the family pictures and paintings and mirrors that had been hung on the walls, or the assembly of toys and mobiles in Billy's bedroom, or the fixed toaster, even the disassembled video cassette that, just possibly, with a bit of luck, could still yet work well enough to be returned to the store.

But he would. Eventually.

The building had the feeling of people leaving. The sound of slamming doors, the thump of feet on the floors, suitcases banging against the walls of corridors. Everyone was in a hurry – to catch a flight, to catch a taxi, to take a train, to beat themselves out of the front door. Passport, tickets, money: check! There was so much purpose. Everyone had somewhere to go, somewhere to be . . . everyone but me.

Bye, Mack!

Bye, Soup!

See you later!

Have a good one!

Those were their last words before they left. I was their last thought, their final consideration before they climbed into the vehicle that took them away. It was because I was the one to help them: suitcases in the trunk, a smile for a goodbye. They all shouted my name and waved to me, to the building. They were dynamic. I was static.

On the day they left, the sun was blotted by a blanket of cloud. I watched it through empty apartment windows. It was like looking at a dim bulb through fabric. It was just a thumbprint, a mere impression of its brilliant self. Someone had drawn the blinds on the world and I was left in an empty white room. I felt lonely. It wasn't nice to be the one who got left behind.

A nna-lise was working in Morgan's apartment. She'd lent
her a spare set of keys so she could use the photo-editing
software on her computer while she was out of town.

At least, Anna-lise was telling herself she was working. This
was what she had determined to do to take her mind off Henry.
To work. Work, work, work – the whole way through the holidays. It was either that or talking to Mom and she knew that
that would only make things worse. She still planned on going
home but she would take some negatives with her. She could tie
up all her money jobs – wedding work, mainly – and there was
her exhibition portfolio to work on. Anna-lise had plenty of
work. Plenty and plenty of work.

Henry hadn't said goodbye. She hadn't expected him to. She
hadn't wanted him to. She wanted to hate him. She was trying
to hate him. She was trying to think of a way to hurt him. She
was thinking of a way to get her revenge. She was trying to
think of a way of getting him back.

And then there was Morgan. Bitch. Cunt. Anna-lise had lots
of bad words for Morgan. She made long lists of them in her
head. Morgan, above Henry, was who she wanted to hurt the
most, even if she was doing her small software favours like
these. Anna-lise wanted to hurt Morgan as much as she had
hurt her. She wanted to punch her in the breasts. Many times.
In a row. Over and over. Until she begged her to stop. And then
she'd have carried on.

She found herself occasionally scanning the apartment to
see if she could do damage that she wouldn't be blamed for
later. But no good ideas came.

Slowly, seeping through the air, Anna-lise heard noises. She
stopped for a moment and listened, taking the chance to also

look at Ulysses, who was asleep, as cute as ever, on the floor by her feet. There were moans. It sounded like somebody in pain. There was a sudden shout of ecstasy and Anna-lise realized she was listening to sex.

She groaned. This was all she needed. Trying to work, trying not to think about Henry, and now someone was having sex in the walls. She went back to her negatives with fresh, hard concentration – the beaming bride looking stunning in her black dress – but the noise went on. Was this some sort of misery conspiracy? Thoughts of Henry, wedding work, the sound of sex coming through the walls . . .

It took a while for the penny to drop but when the woman managed to roll from one orgasm to another for twenty minutes straight, Anna-lise eventually realized she wasn't listening to sex, she was listening to porn.

She concentrated harder, looking at the walls and windows, trying to pinpoint the source. Then she realized. It was coming from the stairwell.

Helmut.

A strange and random thought occurred to her and Anna-lise found herself taking off her glasses and looking at the computer screen contemplating it. She laughed out loud. It was too ridiculous.

She listened to the long sighs and the muted, shouted demands for a moment longer before her anger at the situation finally got the better of her. She threw back her chair and marched to the door. She was going to complain. In fact, she was going to do a hell of a lot more than that. It was time to give Helmut a piece of her mind.

She stamped down the length of Morgan's apartment and threw open the entrance to the stairwell as quickly and violently as possible. It was as she did so that she remembered she was dressed only in a long silk kimono. She had a pair of panties on underneath but that was it.

And she was in no way prepared for the vision of the scrawny-looking woman being roughly treated by a short man in thick spectacles on the stairs. She froze. They, on the other hand, didn't skip a beat. Helmut, who was standing on the landing below, glanced up from his camera.

'Ahna?'

'What . . . what the hell do you think you're doing?' Anna-lise eventually managed to blurt out as the couple copulated just below her. It was hard not to stare at them. They looked so animal-like – their bodies reflex jerking, tongues lolling, tails wagging.

'Ahna?' Helmut repeated slowly.

'I'm working in here,' Anna-lise said, realizing that that was only half a complaint. The other half was an explanation for her being in Morgan's apartment.

'I thought no one was in the apartment,' Helmut said as the loud cries bounced in the stairwell between them.

'Well there is. Me.' Anna-lise said.

Helmut sighed apologetically. 'OK. Sorry.'

'Please can you go and do . . . ' Anna-lise tried to throw a severe look. '*That* somewhere else.'

'Ya sure. Ya. OK. Cut, guys, cut. I'm sorry.'

Anna-lise slammed the door and turned on her heels to go back to work, feeling strangely unsatisfied. Forty minutes later, just as she had recovered enough to get back to work, a knock came from the stairwell door.

'Who is it?' Anna-lise called out, already knowing the answer.

'It's me, Helmut. I've come to apologize.'

Anna-lise contemplated telling him to go away before eventually softening. She wasn't the kind to reject an apology. Besides, it wasn't that big of a deal. Part of her, the part that wasn't furious with her life, had even found it funny. She'd giggled a little to herself about it, after the initial anger had subsided. She walked to the door and opened it slowly. A very contrite-looking Helmut stood directly below her on the stairs, giving the impression of being on his knees, holding out a bottle of red wine.

'Forgive me?' he said.

She saw him glance into the V of her breastplate, which was directly in his line of sight, and at the edges of her breasts.

'No,' she replied, smiling with her lips pressed together.

'What can I do to make you happy?' he asked, looking quickly back up into her eyes.

'To make me not tell Morgan, you mean.'

'That as well,' Helmut replied without smiling.

'Look, Helmut, don't worry about it, I'm not going to say anything,' Anna-lise explained a little impatiently. 'It's just that I'm trying to work. I really do have a lot to do.'

She motioned as if to shut the door.

'Wait,' Helmut said, reaching out to touch her arm. 'What is it? Are you OK?'

'Yes,' she said, a little stunned by the question. 'Why wouldn't I be?'

'I don't know,' Helmut replied. 'You look sad.'

'Really?' Anna-lise said, feeling the sudden weight of her depression. 'I'm not sad.'

'I saw Henry leaving today. Why didn't you go with him?'

'I'm leaving tomorrow, to stay with my parents,' Anna-lise said quietly.

'Me also. I go to Hawaii.'

'That's nice,' Anna-lise said, realizing that somewhere in the conversation Helmut had moved up a step and now they were standing very close.

'We are the last ones to leave,' Helmut said.

'It feels like the whole city is empty,' Anna-lise agreed.

Helmut looked at her.

'Can't I come in?' he asked.

'Haven't you got company?'

'No, they've gone.'

Anna-lise nodded slowly.

'Come on,' Helmut said. 'Let's have a drink.'

Anna-lise looked at him and took a second to consider. It *was* the holidays.

'OK, sure,' she sighed. 'Why not?'

Two and a half hours later and they were both drunk. Anna-lise was sitting sideways on Morgan's leather sofa, her legs draped over the high arching armrest, her dressing gown slipping down her thighs. She was forgetting herself in laughter. Helmut was much funnier than she had known. He wasn't afraid to be politically incorrect, in fact he played up to it, almost to the point of being offensive. They'd talked about the opposite sex a lot. Helmut was currently confessing his fetish for 'Nubian beauties'. He said he 'couldn't help himself' from stopping them in the street for their telephone numbers.

'Why not?' he shouted. 'If I was a big handsome black bastard with an enormous dick no one would blink an eyelid. They swagger around and whistle and suck their lips at any woman they like. Just because I'm white I'm not allowed to do that, I'm not allowed to worship these incredible women? Fuck that, I want to love them! I need to love them!'

'But, Helmut!' Anna-lise laughed. 'You can't love a woman just for her skin colour.'

Helmut turned to Morgan's stereo and inserted a CD he'd fetched from his apartment. A bass-heavy song with a lilting guitar riff trotted out of the speakers.

'This is what Nubian women like to fuck to,' Helmut shouted over the music just as a set of triumphant horns blared. 'Fela Kuti. What a guy! You know him?'

Anna-lise shook her head.

Helmut started to dance in the middle of Morgan's living room.

'This guy was a god! He had more lovers than you can count.'

Helmut hurled the CD cover at Anna-lise. 'You see all those women, all those beauties in his band?'

'Yeah.'

'They were all his wives.'

'There's thirteen of them!'

'I know. And look how beautiful they are!'

'There must have been a lot of jealous politics.'

'Of course not. Fela made all of them happy. He was a sex god. His penis was fucking enormous.'

'He's very handsome.'

'Come ya! Dance! You cannot listen to Fela without dancing!'

Anna-lise giggled and got up. Helmut took her hands and rocked on the balls of his feet, nodding in time with the rhythm. Anna-lise awkwardly swung her hips and grinned.

'You're right!' she shouted. 'It's great music.'

'It's even better live,' Helmut replied.

'He's still playing?'

'No, he was murdered. But his son, Femi Kuti, he plays. I saw him at Summer Stage.'

'Murdered? Why?'

'He wrote a lot of songs against the military government in Nigeria. They smashed his genitals with the butt of a rifle and then they poisoned him with AIDS.'

'Jesus!' Anna-lise said. 'That's horrible. But . . .'

Anna-lise now held her hips against Helmut's, his hands resting on her waist.

'Don't you think that his having AIDS might have had something to do with fucking hundreds of women, Helmut?'

Helmut shrugged. 'Maybe.'

The music throbbed between them and Anna-lise could feel Helmut drawing closer. She wanted him to.

'Isn't that something you ever think about?' she suddenly found herself asking.

'What?'

'You know, AIDS.'

'Why?'

'Oh, come on, Helmut.'

'We test.'

'Do you?'

'Of course,' Helmut replied. 'I love to fuck but I don't want to die because of it.'

'Is that why you shoot porn, then – because you love to fuck?'

Helmut stopped dancing and pulled away from Anna-lise. He looked down at her.

'What did I say?' Anna-lise said.

Helmut smiled slowly and moved to turn the music down. He reached for their third bottle of wine sitting on the table and filled their glasses.

'Happy holidays!' he said, toasting.

'Helmut, I'm sorry. I didn't mean to offend you.'

'It's OK. You didn't offend me.'

'Then why have we stopped dancing? I was enjoying myself.'

'Because you asked why I do what I do and I want to tell you. But first, we need a drink.'

'Oh,' Anna-lise said, sitting back down in the armchair. 'OK, then.'

'I had a girlfriend once who was in the business.'

'What was her name?'

'Leticia. Her real name was Helen but she never let anyone call her that.' Helmut seemed to lose himself for a moment. 'She was a very beautiful, very good woman.'

'What happened to her?'

'She was killed in a car accident.'

'That's horrible. I'm sorry, Helmut.'

'It's OK, it happened a long time ago. Anyway, that was how I got into the industry. After she died, I adopted her daughter, so I had a lot of bills. Porn was a good way to make fast money. It was also my ode to Leticia. She loved the business.'

'Where is she now? Leticia's daughter, I mean.'

'Upstate, in a very expensive school.'

'How old is she?'

'She just turned fifteen. She wants to go to NYU to study politics,' Helmut said proudly.

'How come I've never seen her?'

'She visits. But you're on the third floor. We usually go away during holidays. My apartment is too small for the two of us.'

'Is she going to Hawaii with you?'

'Just for Christmas and New Year. She's going on a school skiing trip in Canada first.'

'Wow, Helmut. I never knew you had a daughter.'

'You just thought I was a dirty old man, I know.'

'No, of course not.'

'It's OK, I don't mind.'

'Helmut, if I thought that's all you were, I never would have let you in here.'

She glanced flirtatiously at him.

Helmut looked hard at her. 'Anna-lise, you're drunk. There's Henry, remember.'

Anna-lise let out a hard laugh. 'I'd rather not, thanks.'

'I'm sorry it didn't work out.'

'Me too. *C'est la vie*, hey?'

'Why did you break up?'

'You want it in one word?'

He nodded.

'Morgan.'

'Morgan?'

'She told Henry I wanted babies. Henry got scared, the rest is history. It's the same old boring New York story. I want marriage and children, Henry is terrified of commitment. I hate myself for being such a cliché.'

And so cued the tears, wretched never-ending streams welling from a bountiful spring of self-pity and despair. At least, they would have never ended had Helmut not said, handing her tissues:

'Tell me, Anna-lise, what would you like?'

Anna-lise snivelled.

'Apart from having Henry back, you mean?'

'Ya. Apart from that.'

'Killing Morgan, of course.'

'Killing?'

'OK, maybe not killing. Hurting. Badly. I don't know. Some sort of revenge.'

'For telling Henry you wanted babies?'

'Not just that. Revenge for everything, revenge for everyone. Revenge for the way she treats Mrs Xhiu, always talking down to her just because she's old, making out like she's senile or stupid or something. Revenge for the way she winds Frank up, making unsubtle hints about his weight. Revenge for the way she pretends to be Mike's friend when she's not, she just uses him because she needs an ally sometimes. Revenge for the way she treats everyone, the whole world. The woman deserves something really horrible to happen to her.'

'Exactly.'

Anna-lise levelled her look.

'What do you propose?'

'You know, I like to use the building for my films. It's a theme, the storyline. I like to pretend it's what really goes on in this building.'

'OK,' Anna-lise said slowly.

'I think it would be good to shoot a scene in here, don't you?'

Anna-lise stared at Helmut. 'What, with me?'

'Why not?'

Anna-lise laughed. 'You wouldn't catch me dead in one of your films, Helmut.'

'You might like it.'

'Yeah, I might. And the rest of the world with me. What would everyone in the building say? What would my mother say? I'm flattered, Helmut, but no thanks.'

'It was just an idea.'

Anna-lise carried on laughing quietly to herself. Hadn't this been what she'd had in mind when she first heard them in the stairwell? Hadn't this been her ludicrous notion, not Helmut's?

After a pause, she restarted, 'Just out of interest, what kind of thing did you have in mind?'

I set to work early. It was a big job but I was hoping to have it finished in a couple of days, three at the outside.

I'd done a lot of preparation. I'd taken a good look at both Diva's and Mrs Xhiu's bathrooms and considered my strategy. I'd assessed my point of entry, where I thought the problem lay, and doubled my time estimates in allowance for headless screws and worn threads.

The previous weekend, I'd ventured out to Hank's for tools and supplies. I had to admit I liked it in there. I liked the tight enclosed aisles and the chaos of loose washers and screws. I liked that Hank didn't suffer fools lightly and deliberately avoided helping people if he could. He was a fat, scarred Latin man (I've no idea how he could have gotten the name Hank) who spent most of his day wedged in behind the cashier counter. There were stickers of the Twin Towers burning and Osama bin Laden being eaten by an American eagle. He flew the Stars and Stripes outside. He issued a handwritten receipt for everything. He insisted on it, even for a screw that cost only ten cents. It was all a part of his old-school ways.

I bought six metres of four-inch piping, ten right-angle joins, ten T-pipes, two rolls of plumbing tape, a bag of assorted washers, a fresh box of screws and wall plugs, a bag of assorted nails, a bag of plaster, two tubes of filler, three tubes of grout, a new hammer, two new drill bits (a sixteenth and an eighth with titanium tips).

I also hired a stopcock wrench, a drain snake and a pump. I took a rain check on the twelve-inch piping. There didn't seem any point in my buying that until I knew the extent of the problem. There was a chance I wouldn't even have to replace a section of the main drain, as long it wasn't cracked or rusted out too bad.

The bill came to $79.58.

If anything, I might have over-prepared for the situation. I didn't sleep much the night before, just thinking about the job. I wasn't daunted. Generally speaking, plumbing is easy. People make more of it than it is. Ninety per cent of plumbing is simply a matter of connecting one tube to another. It's even easier nowadays with modern plastic piping. There's no soldering and less risk of leakages compared to copper. It's just plug and play, as easy as Meccano, a kid could do it.

I was just excited. I hadn't had a chance to do a job as big as this in a long time.

I started upstairs in Diva's because I figured it would be easier to work down on the problem rather than up from underneath it. I also figured that the problem had to start someplace near Diva's since Mrs Xhiu's toilet only overflowed when Diva flushed. If there had been a blockage in the main drain then Mrs Xhiu's would have overflowed when anyone above her flushed, not just Diva.

I spent the first forty minutes preparing my workspace; carefully clearing the area, taping down dustsheets, plugging in the wireless and setting the volume to low to fill the background and reduce the risk of distraction. I set my toolbox, my drill and my supplies in the bath where I could easily find them, remembering to put the plug in the drain so nothing slipped down.

I started by cutting away sections of plasterboard and cork lino behind and around Diva's toilet with a Stanley knife. I found the labour instantly meditative. I concentrated on it completely. As I was cutting away at the plasterboard I was aware that I was thinking of nothing else. My eyes were looking at the line I had drawn with the pencil and the angle of the Stanley knife as I cut.

I didn't hear the radio or take in sound of any kind. I didn't think about Catherine. I wasn't scared or anxious or worried, I didn't feel emotion of any kind. The closest I came to feeling anything was contentment. There was nothing I needed or desired. I was aware of my own condition, aware of my hand aching or if I was getting hungry, but I didn't dwell on it. I simply accepted my state of being for what it was in that moment. It was existence without thought; simple, satisfactory industry.

I was cutting a hole in the wall.

That was all I was thinking about. And that made me happy. This was my work. This was part of the reason I had become a superintendent in the first place: for the happy simplicity of life while doing a task. Manual labour stopped me from thinking and helped me to just be. It stopped me from dwelling in my melancholy. It stopped me from thinking too much about things I had no power over. It took me away from the dark thoughts and the self-doubts and the fears and my pain and brought me closer towards the truth, back into the light.

It showed me that a nine-inch nail will do what a six-inch nail can't. It showed me that there is a result after action, that work leads to something real, that a certain number of screws and a certain amount of wood and the right tools and the right labour and the right time will make something: a table or a chair or a storage area. It taught me the principle of cause and effect.

When I saw a screw drilled in tight to a wall and considered the impossibility of removing it with my fingers, I understood how I had been going wrong in my life. And when I saw how easy it was to remove the screw using a drill and the right Phillips head, I realized how to set myself right.

Labour showed me that I was in control of my own destiny. Given the right tools, I could do anything. It gave me the confidence to know that I was in charge of some things, such as my actions and myself.

This was how I managed to move on after Catherine. This was how I pulled my life back together again.

Laying down on my side, a slight numbness swelling in my hips, I peered with my flashlight into the hole I had made.

Straining inside further, I was able to reach my head in far enough to see down into the slice-shaped world that existed between the two apartments, below Diva's floor and above Mrs Xhiu's ceiling. I could see the network of pipes, I could see the dusty joists, I could see the imperfections in the plaster. When I cast the light away, shedding darkness again, I could see how light shone through from Mrs Xhiu's. It didn't surprise me that sound travelled so easily through the building. The distance between the two apartments was only about ten inches and there was no insulation to speak of.

Finding the problem was easy. For some reason, there was an additional waste pipe that teed away from the main vertical drain below Diva's toilet. I guessed immediately that it was this additional section that had become blocked and was causing Mrs Xhiu's toilet to overflow whenever Diva flushed. It had to rejoin the main drain on or around Mrs Xhiu's level. Diva and Mrs Xhiu were operating on their own separate sewage system while waste from the rest of the building plummeted past, as it should have done, down the main drain.

I couldn't understand why there might be this detour.

The simplest and most straightforward solution would have been to pour drain clearer down Diva's toilet. But there was no guarantee it would have funnelled down the diversion. It was lethal stuff. If it got trapped in the pipe for too long, the acid would burn right through and instead of solving one problem I would have created fifteen new ones. I faced the same conundrum with the drain snake. How could I be sure I could channel it down the relevant section of pipe?

A little frustrated, I gave Diva's toilet another vigorous pump with the plunger but it didn't work. I couldn't create the suction required to clear the blockage, since the main drain breathed life out of the vacuum. And I was starting to suspect that the blockage was further down the pipe anyway, perhaps closer to Mrs Xhiu's level.

I'd have to go down and take a look.

I took a break and ate an early lunch. I had a meatball sandwich delivered from the deli. Tomato and basil sauce poured between my fingers while I ate. The meat and Italian bread filled my cheeks. I washed it down with gulps of sweet Sprite. I ate too quickly, still working the problem in my mind, not wanting to let go of it. The food exhausted me. I stared into the toilet as I sat on the edge of Diva's bath and lost myself momentarily, drifting into a daydream place that was empty and hard to snap out of. It was a little like blacking out but with my eyes open. I could see but I wasn't registering what was in front of my eyes. It was just an image, as featureless and meaningless and without landmarks as black space. Eventually, I came to, startled, without knowing where I was. It passed. I gathered my bearings again and collected my thoughts.

I couldn't resist throwing open the curtains in Mrs Xhiu's apartment. Dust rained down on me in a sunlit squall. I opened the windows too, letting the cold December air snap life back into the place, clearing the cobwebs and marshalling the pockets of trapped heat out into the open. It was a liberty but I figured it was one I could afford since Mrs Xhiu was away and wouldn't be back for another ten days. By the time she returned, the musk would have set back in.

Indeed, it was only because she was away that I'd been allowed access. She'd clearly anticipated an intrusion. With the exception of a single crucifix, the walls were empty. There were rectangular sections of the old floral wallpaper that stood in clean contrast to the rest of the room and that were marked out and exaggerated by thick, yellowy-brown borders. The chests and cabinets and drawers were all locked, small brass padlocks hanging and shining from them with incongruous newness. The television had been unplugged and turned to face the wall. The bed had been stripped and the linen draped over the furniture. The smell of old wok oil, which had been fried into the walls and the ceiling over the years, poured down on me in thick rivulets, staining my overalls.

Inside her bathroom I could see rust from the flood still spreading itself across her tiles. I was glad to see that the temporary silicone patch I'd used to stop the leak was still holding. It was a wonder there was a toilet bowl left at all.

I got an idea.

If I removed the two toilets and used the pump at Mrs Xhiu's end and channelled the snake drain down from Diva's, I could probably shift the cause of the blockage and force it either into the pump or down the vertical main.

I set to work immediately, leaping down to the basement to turn off the mains at the stopcock before jogging back up to Mrs Xhiu's. The job went well and within minutes I was looking into her gaping waste pipe, a pool of brown water hovering ominously at the brim. I then went up to Diva's and did the same. When I removed her toilet the sewage pipe burped an obscene smell from the depths of the New York sewage system.

It took me several minutes to recover.

From there, though, it was easy to guide the snake down the right drain. I threaded ten feet through, then went downstairs to turn on the pump. It ate something immediately and ground to a halt with a metal-on-metal screech. I switched off the pump and unplugged it. I opened the filter cap. Nothing. I dismantled the pump from the pipe. There was a thick multicoloured amalgam sticking out of the machine, caught and disfigured in the Saniflow blades.

At first I couldn't tell what it was. But when I pulled on it and watched it slowly twist between the props, a single small piece tore loose and revealed the whole by reshaping to its original fluorescent-yellow spongy form.

It was an earplug.

I liked my new computer. I could hear the disk inside it spinning, whirring like my brain. I noticed it took a long time to shut down. It didn't have enough memory, the capacity, to process information quickly. There was too much to get through before it could stop. So I kept it on all the time. It seemed easier. I wasn't sleeping much either.

Garry had helped me get connected to the Internet, the World Wide Web. He explained to me that it was all the computers of the world linking, all their information connecting, everyone talking in the same language: a series of ones and zeroes.

I liked that idea.

11100011010010000111110000001100100100010000001111
11100100110000100000100101100010001000001001111110
00100100100100100000111100101000001111111110001001 1
0010010010001010 = Health.

11001001001001000000111111001010001010011111110010
10010101000010100010111111100100100001001001001111 1
11010010100100110100101000100101001011111111001010 0
10101010101010111010101010010101001010100101010101 0
010101010100101010101 = Wealth.

10001010101000000011010100101001001001001001001 11
10100101001000100001010101010101010100101010100101010
10101010100100101010010101110010100101001010101010 1
01001010111110000101001010010100100100101001001001
000010100101010101010101100111111111111000100100100
10010100101 = Pornography.

11111100100100101010100100100100100100010100000000000
000011010100101010010010100100100100000101010100101
01101001010010101001001010101000101001100101010 0101

148   will rhode

```
010101010100101010010101001010101000101001010100000
000111111111111111111111111111111111111111111111101
100100100100100000011111100101000101001111110010100
101010000101000101111111001001000010010010011111110
100101001001101001010001001010010111111110010100101
010101010101110101010100101010010101001010101010010
101010100101010101111111001001001010101001001001001
001010000000000000011010100101010010010100100010010
000010101010010101101001010010101001001010101000101
001100101010010101010101010010101001010100101010100
010100101010000000011111111111111111111111111111111
111111111111101100100100100100000011111100101000010
100111111001010010101000010100010111111100100100001
001001001111111010010100100110100101000100101001011
111111001010010101010101010101110101010100101010010
100101010101001010101010010101010101111111100100100101
010100100100100100101000000000000000011010100101010100
100101001001001000001010101001010110100101001010100
100101010100010100110010101001010101010101001010100
101010010101010001010010101000000001111111111111111
111111111111111111111111111111011001001001001000000
111111001010001010011111100101001010100000101000101 1
111110010010000100100100111111101001010010011010010
100010010100101111111100101001010101010101011101010
101001010100101010010101010100101010101001010101011
111110010010010101010010010010010010100000000000000
011010100101010010010100100100100000101010100101011
010010100101111111001001001010101001001001001001010
000000000000001101010010101010010010100100100100000010
101010010101101001010010101001001010101000101001100
101010010101010101010010101001010100101010100010100
101010000000011111111111111111111111111111111111111
111111011001001001001000000111111001010001010100111
111001010010101000010100010111111110010010000100100 1
```

001111111010010100100110100101000100101001011111111
001010010101010101010101110101010100101010010101010101
010101001010101010010101010101111111001001001010101010
100100100100101000000000000000011010100101010100100101
001001001000001010101001010110100101001010100100101
010100010100110010101001010101010101010010101010101010
010101010001010010101000000000111111111111111111111
111111111111111111111111110110010010010010000000111111
001010001010011111100101001010100000101000101111111110
010010000100100100111111101001010010011010010100010
010100101111111100101001010101010101011101010101001
010100101010010101010101001010101010010101010101111110
010010010101010010010010010010100000000000000011010
100101010010010100100100100000101010100101011010010
100101010010010101010001010011001010100101010101010
100101010010101001010101000101001010100000000111111
1111111111111111111111111111111111111101100100100
100100000011111100101000101001111110010100101010000
101000101111111001001000010010010011111110100101001
001101001010001001010010111111110010100101010101010
101110101010100101010010101010010101010101001010101010100
101010101111111001001001010101001001001001001010000
000000000001101010010101001001010010010010000001010101
010010101101001010010111111100100100101010100100100
100100101000000000000000011010100101010100100101001001
001000001010101001010110100101001010100100101010100
010100110010101001010101010101010010101001010100010101
010001010010101000000000111111111111111111111111111111
111111111111111101100100100100100000011111001010
001010011111100101001010100000101000101111111001001001
0001001001001111111010010100100110100101000100100100
101111111100101001010101010101011101010101001010100
101010010101010100101010101010010101010101111111001001001
010101010010010010010010100000000000000011010100101

```
010010010100100100100000101010100101011010010100101
001010100100101001001001000001010101001010110100101
001010100100101010100010100110010101001010101010101
001010100101010010101010001010010101000000001111111
11111111111111111111111111111111111111111011001001001
001000000111111001010001010011111100101001010100001
010001011111110010010000100100100111111101001010010
011010010100010010100101111111100101001010101010101
011101010101001010100101010010101010100101010101001
010101011111110010010010101010010010010010010100000
000000000011010100101010010010100100100100000101010
100101011010010100101111111001001001010101001001001
001001010000000000000011010100101010010010100100010
010000010101010010101101001010010101001001010101000
101001100101010010101010101010010101001010100101010
100010100101010000000001111111111111111111111111111
11111111111111111011001001001001000000111110010100
010100111110010100101010000101000101111111100100100
001001001001111111010010100100110100101000100101001
011111111001010010101010101010111010101010010101001
010100101010101001010101010100101010101011111110010 0100
101010100100100100100101000000000000000110101001010
100100101001001001000001010101001010110100101001011
111110010010010101010010010010010010100000000000000
011010100101010010010100100100100000101010100101011
010010100101010010010101010001010011001010100101010
101010100101010010101001010101000101001010100000000
11111111111111111111111111111111111111111111111101100
100100100100000011111100101
```

Can you hear me?

On Christmas Day, the telephones rang. Rang and rang and rang. I listened to the answer machines all over the building click and talk and whirr and then rewind. But there was never any message. I started to think that maybe they were trying to reach me. I don't know why I thought that. It was a stupid thing to think. I had a telephone in my place. If they'd wanted to get hold of me they could call me there.

I happened to be in Mike and Juan's fixing some loose shelving in their kitchen when I decided to pick up. I was terrified of doing it. I didn't know what I expected to hear. I left it for four rings, knowing that on the fifth the answer machine would take the call, but at the last second I snapped the phone from its cradle and held it in the air of my face. There was a silence. Slowly I drew the phone closer. I pushed it to my ear. There was a clicking, a very irritating, unidentifiable clicking. I listened harder. Then, loudly:

'Good day! This is Leonard Barnes from ElectroCert just putting in a courtesy call to see that you are satisfied with the service we have been providing you and to see if you could take a few minutes to check whether your existing power provider competes with our deregulated rates. Please don't mind the automated service, if you simply press the appropriate keys on your handset in response to the prompts then, before you know it, you'll be speaking to an operator who will be able to assist you further. Now, let me just start by asking . . . '

The building started screaming. The whole place shuddered and yelled and erupted. I dropped the telephone but I was paralysed, rooted to the spot. I didn't know what to do. My mind was frozen. What was happening? Eventually I managed to find my feet and I sprinted down the stairs. As I descended, the sound shifted. I could hear the rush of water.

By the time I got to the basement, the floor was three inches under. By the time I called the emergency services, it was four. I raced to cut the power supply and shut down the boiler. There was nothing I could do to save the laundry machines. The same went for property in the storage bins. By the time the workmen arrived the basement had flooded completely.

Water started seeping into the building corridor. It even washed out through the front door. When it was over, as the emergency services left, I saw that the flood had created a frozen lake in the street. An old picture of Catherine was among the debris. I could see her looking up at me, frozen in the tarmac, kids in mittens skating across her face.

I spent the night in little Billy's room. There was a spare single bed near his cot. I'd had to go into G1 to clear the water anyway, so I didn't feel like I was intruding. Besides, where else was I going to sleep? Everything I had was gone.

Still, it was a mistake. I shouldn't have chosen his room. I should have gone into Ben and Mandy's bed or, better still, Helmut's. But I thought that it would have been rude. I thought it would be better to sleep in a guest bed, a vacant bed. I wish I hadn't been so considerate.

I was awake the whole night. I don't remember ever feeling so cold. I dressed myself in layers of Ben's clothes and I piled as many blankets as I could find on top of me, but somehow the blizzard that was raging outside managed to find its way – under the doors, between the cracks in the window frames, through the brickwork – into the bed.

I shivered in the dark. I didn't have a flashlight to see by. Mine had been in the basement. Everything I had was gone. I couldn't find another anywhere else. Hank's was closed for the holidays. I found some candles but they lasted only a couple of hours. Then they went out and there was just an intense purple darkness. I couldn't even see my hands when I put them up in front of my face.

The building was silent. The city was completely still. There wasn't even the sound of sirens. All I could hear was the whistle of the wind and the lash of snow against the windows. There were no doors opening and closing. No creaking floorboards. No voices through the walls. Not even the groan of the heating system.

'Be careful what you wish for,' I said out loud and my voice boomed and bounced and echoed in the room as if I were in a long, dark tunnel. It reverberated and took a long time to finally fade. I heard the sentence repeating itself over and over and over. I was glad when it eventually stopped.

But then I was alone again, in the dark, lost. There were no bearings for me to go by. Everything I had was gone. I couldn't hear anything to help me see. For the first time in as long as I could remember, I was blind.

The world was so black. It felt like my body was disappearing into the void and there was nothing to ground me. I felt as if I were falling in the darkness, that my mind was separating from the physical and was drifting into nothingness.

This was how I feared death to be. I was going out of myself and away to float for an eternity as a body-less consciousness, alone and lost, through an indifferent, cold, empty space.

I kept having to catch myself from going there. I spent the night alarmed and disorientated. I repeatedly came to my senses in the midst of a nosedive into emptiness, pulling myself out of it at the very last second.

It reminded me of being in the mountains with Catherine and being too scared to fall asleep because each time I drifted off my breathing slowed and I choked on the thin air. It felt like someone was suffocating me. As the tender touch of slumber wrapped itself around me I found myself jolting violently awake with a surge of life-threatened adrenalin.

And the really scary thing was knowing – in those breathless, sweating moments of apnoea, my heart beating fast and hard in my chest – just how rapidly I had been falling, how close to unconsciousness I had been and how close I had come to letting go and sinking into it and being gone, for ever.

Frightened, I pulled my knees up close to my chest and leant against a wall for support and reassurance, drawing the blankets in close. There must have been something of Billy's among them because, out of nowhere, I could suddenly smell him – that indescribable baby smell, the one that comes from the crown of the head – and I was instantly teleported away from the darkness and back into a past where I was standing in the light again, in those bright important lights, and I was holding him, just the two of us together.

And then he was gone. He simply vanished, ripped away from me by some whimsical passing breeze, just as he had been before by some whimsical passing God, and I was thrown back into the dark again, alone and cold and blind in that empty room in that empty building in that empty black world.

I seized the blankets and turned them quickly in my fingers, desperately searching out the source, that spot of scent, so I could focus in on it and be taken back, back to my heaven, away from this hell.

And I found it. I pressed the blankets to my nose and drew in the smell and I was there again, I could see him now, I could feel him in my arms. I was close to tears it felt so good, the joy was immense, I was so happy . . . and then he was gone. I'd lost him again.

And then I found him . . .

And then I lost him . . .

And then I found him . . .

And so I spent the night: teleporting between heaven and hell on a smell. It went on for hours, with me alternating violently between anguish and relief, suffering and happiness. I became so quickly addicted to it that I was unable to see what was happening to me, the trickery and deception I was under.

It was only with the late, low, slow dawn – so poor in light I couldn't even call it a morning, it was just a lesser night, a very vague day – that I started to see, that I started to realize. The two worlds I'd been travelling between were not as they had seemed.

The place I had thought was hell wasn't hell at all, but my home. I had spent the night in Apartment G1, 444 VanVanVane Street, New York, NY 10111.

This was where I lived. This was where I worked. This was my reality. This was my life. This was what I had created after they left. This was what I knew now. The silence hadn't taken it away. The light was returning. Sound was coming back. People would come home again. I wasn't alone. I wasn't lost. I was still here. This was my place. I didn't need to be scared. I could be at peace. There had been a time, once, when I had been at peace in this place.

I needed to remember that.

Because the heaven I thought I had found in the night wasn't heaven. It was an illusion. I could never hold it. If I went there I'd become trapped again, just as I was before I took this job, like Tantalus in Hades. My joy would evade me. The smell would always drift from my grasp, it would recede the moment I tried to possess it.

For this was my hell. To have him in my arms for a few brief moments, only to lose him, see him taken away. I couldn't hold on to that smell, because he was gone.

But I was still here. I wasn't dead. The night was over. It was a new day. It was time to put away the blanket. I was back in my building and there was a lot of work to do.

IMPORTANT INFORMATION!

LETTER CONCERNS ALL.

TAKE ONE ONLY.

M

3 January 2010

BASEMENT FLOODING

Dear Tenant,

Welcome back and Happy New Year.

Regretfully, courtesy of the State Water Board, there was a serious accident over the holidays and the entire basement was flooded. There has been substantial damage to the electrics, the boiler, the laundry machines and to property kept in storage bins.

Mr McMurphy has been worst hit by the flood, losing everything in his apartment. If it hadn't been for his quick thinking in turning off the power and shutting down the boiler, overall damage to the building could have been much worse. We all owe him our gratitude.

Attached is a form to be filled in, listing personal items damaged by the flood. The forms should be handed in to me so that I may forward them to the Water Board. They have agreed to replace, where possible, damaged property and to reimburse individuals otherwise. Reimbursement for damaged goods will not include anything of non-commercial value, such as photos and other memorabilia, so please do not include them on your list. Instead, the Board has agreed to compensate the building with a single lump sum for inconvenience and distress caused by the damage.

Jay Bruck, our lawyer, is handling the matter.

In the meantime, your patience and understanding would be very much appreciated. While the laundry rental company have told me they expect to provide new machines to the building within the week, we can still expect minor interruptions to the power supply and the heating as final repairs are still ongoing. I am unable at this stage to tell you when these repairs will be completed so please don't ask. Once again, thanks to Mr McMurphy's quick action, a lot of the essential drying and cleaning work got done before the New Year and we are doing all we can to remedy the situation as quickly as possible.

If anyone has any suggestions or would like to volunteer to help in the clearing and reorganization of the basement area, please come to see me. There is a lot of work still to be done, most especially in the replacement of important building documents, which were kept in a filing cabinet in the basement and were severely damaged by the flood.

Let us all hope that 2010 improves from here, it would be hard-pressed to get much worse.

Yours sincerely,

Morgan Honeysuckle
President, 444 VanVanVane Street,
New York, NY 10111.

The basement buzzed.

The electrician was testing and resetting circuits and replacing damaged fuses. The plumber was re-servicing the boiler and stress-testing the gas supply. Mike and Ben were helping to shift boxes and trunks and junk from the storage bins back to their respective owners' apartments. Helmut was helping me repair the storage bins. Diva painted. Mrs Xhiu, Anna-lise and Juan were going through the files, though Anna-lise and Juan spent a lot of time giggling. Records that needed to be reprinted or retyped went up to Frank in his apartment.

People came to me with questions. They looked to me for answers. They seemed to think that I should be the one in control. Maybe they just felt that way because they were in the basement, in my territory.

We all ate lunch together. Mandy ordered a bunch of stuff from the deli and there was a sort of picnic by the bike rack. She even brought forties of beer. People talked about their holidays, joked, fooled around. They seemed to be enjoying themselves even though it was a Saturday. No one wanted to be anywhere else that weekend. They wanted to be here.

They wanted to know about the flood. Everyone was very sympathetic. The previous week, Mrs Xhiu had arranged with a charity to replace my most necessary items, like my mattress and my linen, even my wireless, to keep me going until the settlement went through. She said she was grateful to me for fixing her toilet. Her appreciation made me swell with satisfaction, I'll admit.

After lunch Frank came down from his apartment with flasks full of coffee. He brought up the subject of the roof. Looking back on things, with everyone all together like that, I probably should have been more careful.

But I felt puffed up. I was so happy to see everyone home, not just home, but happy and working together to make the building strong again. Pride got the better of me. I found that I wanted to tell them what I thought. I wanted them to make a stand.

I shouldn't have got involved. It wasn't my place. I wasn't a shareholder. I was there to help out, that was all. Just because I observed, didn't mean I had the right to contribute. All my interference achieved was to increase the signal, make things worse.

It was another mistake.

Morgan stepped into the shower and turned it on. The water fizzed down. She screamed silently and was momentarily paralysed. Eventually, she managed to gasp and hop out of the way of the freezing spray. She grabbed a towel and threw it around herself, rubbing vigorously.

She finally plucked up the courage to reach in and adjust the temperature control. She tested the water again. It slowly travelled from freezing to cold.

'Interesting.' She frowned, turning the tap off.

She threw on some trousers and a top and a pair of flip-flops and headed for the elevator. In the basement she called out for Mr McMurphy but there was no reply from his apartment. She slapped her way towards the boiler and found the temperature regulator for the water supply.

'Interesting,' she said again when she saw the setting.

After looking over her shoulder briefly, she flicked the dial and waited for the boiler to roar, before going back upstairs to resume her day.

Diva was late getting up, as usual. She padded towards the bathroom, put the plug in the bath, turned the taps on full, sat on the toilet, lit the end of a joint she still had in her fingers from the night before and let nature take its course.

Ten minutes later and she was ready for her Churchillian morning soak, which could take anywhere between half an hour and an hour. It depended on whether she fell back to sleep again in the bath or not. She made sure not to look at herself in the mirror before plunging a lazy leg deep into the tub.

'ARRRRRRGGGGHHH!'

She threw herself back and lost her balance, crashing through the bathroom door behind her into the living room, over a pair of trousers she'd left on the floor and flat onto her back.

'Jesus!' she said, holding her leg, which looked like it had just been boiled in blood. 'What in the hell?'

Morgan pushed her crisp rectangular glasses onto the bridge of her nose with her middle finger. She pressed the small of her back into the hard wooden dining chair and sat up straight, pulling her shoulder blades down. She crossed her legs, forcing the denim miniskirt she was wearing to ride high and show off her shapely, muscled thighs. Her files were on a small table to the left of her, her pens and some miscellaneous building paraphernalia (a spare key to the boiler room, a tin of paint from the corridor on the third floor, the extra stencil for the front door lettering) were on her right. She had arranged the sofa and some chairs in a small semicircle.

She checked her nails and tsk'd when she noticed that the Korean girl hadn't filed her left little finger properly. She thought about going to the bathroom and doing it herself but when she looked up and saw that the clock on the wall read two minutes to eight she realized she didn't have time.

Helmut and Diva were the first to arrive, Helmut's loud laugh audible through the elevator doors before they'd even opened.

'OH WOW, THIS IS GREAT, FANTASTIC. COME, DIVA, LOOK, YA.'

They appeared from around the corner. Helmut's arm was wrapped around Diva's waist. Together, they looked tall and elegant, they could have been a couple.

'MORGAN!' Helmut shouted, releasing his arm and throwing both hands in the air as he walked through the corridor. 'PLEASE, I LOVE YOUR PLACE. IT IS INCREDIBLE.'

'You've never been in here before, Helmut?' Morgan said, getting up from her chair and beaming a broad smile.

'Christ, no!' Helmut exclaimed as he moved to embrace Morgan in a bear hug. Morgan found herself flapping her arms

the weight of the city   **167**

upwards, weak and childlike. Helmut threw Morgan out of his grasp and held her away, gripping her by the shoulders. 'I want to film in here,' he said, looking Morgan in the eyes.

'No chance,' Morgan grinned.

'Why not?' Helmut said, seemingly stunned. 'The light is fantastic. We will be in and out, BOOM BOOM,' he shouted, smacking a fist into a palm. 'You won't even notice we were here.'

'Oh, I'm sure that I would,' Morgan continued, unable to stop beaming. 'And besides, Helmut, you know the rules.'

'Ya, ya sure. No filming on private property, access areas only. I know.'

'Best to keep things out in the open, don't you think?' Morgan replied as if the whole conversation was a joke. 'We wouldn't want anything inappropriate, would we?'

'No,' Helmut replied, straight as an arrow. 'Absolutely. You're right.'

Morgan was still smiling as she turned to Diva, moving to kiss her on the cheek. 'Happy New Year, Diva,' Morgan said.

'If you can say that,' she replied as Morgan's face pressed against hers.

'I know,' Morgan said, breaking. 'The flood.'

'That and the fact that someone keeps changing the temperature control on the boiler.'

'Oh yes, that's me,' Morgan replied.

'You!' Diva said, pointing an angry finger at her chest, trying hard to be menacing, hoping she wouldn't bring up the marijuana episode. Diva figured that as long as she stayed on the attack Morgan wouldn't get a chance to remember. 'I've been looking for you. My hot-water supply has started running at a hundred degrees. I practically burnt my leg off the other day trying to get into my bath.'

'Well, my showers are running cold. Can't you just fill your baths with more cold water?'

'I've had to start, haven't I? But my taps are too hot to even touch now. I use a flannel to turn them on because they're scalding. Do you have to turn the central control on so high?'

'My shower has its own temperature regulator and if it doesn't get enough hot water to it, it only runs warm.'

'What's wrong with warm?'

'It isn't hot.'

'So I'm meant to burn so you can have a hot shower?'

'Something must have happened since the boiler got reset. I'll get Mr McMurphy to look into it. There has to be a logical reason for why this has started now.'

'Yeah, there is a logical reason,' Diva said. 'You keep fucking with the controls.'

Morgan looked at her sharply. 'There's no need for that kind of language, Diva. Please refrain from it.'

Diva snorted. 'I'll talk how I like, thank you.'

'Not in my apartment, you won't.'

'What are you going to do? Throw me out?'

Morgan took a deep breath. 'If I were in your apartment, Diva, I would respect your wishes. I would appreciate it if you extended the same courtesy to me.'

'Whatever, dude,' Diva said, realizing it was just the kind of thing Jonathan might have said.

The elevator chimed and Anna-lise, Ulysses, Frank, Garry, Mike and Juan all arrived together. Diva took a seat on the sofa, muttering something about how if Morgan respected her apartment then she wouldn't screw with its water supply the whole time.

There were more helloes and smiles. People looked refreshed and happy from their holidays, even though they'd been back a week already. Morgan poured out soda but she hadn't arranged any food. Garry wanted a coffee so Morgan put the kettle on. The elevator chimed again and Ulysses went crazy, reminding Morgan to give Anna-lise her present.

'Here,' she said under the general buzz. 'I've bought a little something for Ulysses.'

Anna-lise looked at Morgan with a slightly bemused expression before tearing away the wrapping paper. It was a dog bed in dark-blue towelling.

'It's washable,' Morgan explained.

'Gee, thanks, Morgan,' Anna-lise replied.

'Well, shall we see if he likes it?' Morgan suggested as Mrs Xhiu entered the living room. Helmut leapt up from the sofa with an elaborate gesture and offered her his seat.

Anna-lise put the bed on the floor and beckoned Ulysses, who was busy sniffing and licking Juan's ankles.

'Come on, Ulysses, come to Mommy. Look at your new bed, darling,' Anna-lise tried.

'He's tickling me!' Juan shrieked.

Mike picked up the dog and carried him over to the bed but, as soon as he put him down, Ulysses tried to run away. Anna-lise made three half-hearted attempts to keep him on the bed but finally let him escape between Morgan's legs.

'I'm sorry, Morgan,' Anna-lise said. 'I don't think he likes it.'

'Don't worry,' Morgan replied, nonplussed. 'He will.'

Morgan scooped the dog from the floor, picked up the bed and carried it into a corner, away from the rest of the room. She dropped the bed and pressed the dog into it, holding him down.

'Now you listen to me, Ulysses,' Morgan hissed, feeling Anna-lise behind her looking on anxiously. 'You stay in this bed like a good doggie, got it!' She thrust a long finger into its face. 'I'm warning you.'

The dog sat, stunned, and looked up at Morgan and then at Anna-lise with large doey eyes.

'Good boy,' Morgan said, standing up and turning to face Anna-lise. 'He'll be fine there, Anna-lise, I promise.'

Anna-lise let herself be led away into a chair and given a

glass of water. Ulysses started whimpering faintly in the background.

'Has anyone seen Ben and Mandy?' Morgan said to the room, noticing that it was ten past.

The elevator chimed.

'I'm sorry,' Ben called out, holding Billy in his arms. Mandy walked behind him. 'We couldn't get him down.'

'That's OK,' Morgan said. 'Come in and take a seat. We should get started.'

The room cooed and ah-ed and craned their necks to see the baby as the family trod carefully through the chairs.

'Right, then, if that's everyone,' Morgan started.

'Hang on a second, Morgan,' Frank interrupted.

Morgan turned to look at him.

'Yes, Frank.'

'We're still waiting for one more.'

Morgan frowned. Then, thinking she understood, quickly explained, 'Oh that's OK, Frank, Henry doesn't need to be here because he's not a shareholder. Besides, I think he's still in Thailand.'

'No,' Garry replied. 'Not Henry.'

'Who, then?' Morgan asked.

'We have asked Mack to come,' Helmut said.

Morgan looked around the room and noticed for the first time that everyone was looking at her with an understanding in their eyes, an understanding that she wasn't privy to. She set her gaze on Juan and Mike, who were both looking a little sheepish, and realized what was happening.

'Interesting,' she muttered to herself as the elevator rang.

'Good idea,' Morgan recovered quickly, staring at the super. 'Good idea, guys. Mr McMurphy, will you take a seat?'

Morgan watched the super look momentarily lost because there wasn't a seat spare. He hovered uncomfortably for a few moments before Frank and Anna-lise tried to make space for him on the sofa. In the end, he just shook his head and leant against the nearest wall.

'Suit yourself,' Morgan said. 'OK, let's get started. You're quite right to have Mr McMurphy come up. It's probably a good idea that we deal with any outstanding issues left by the flood, though I must say, I'm extremely impressed at how quickly we have managed to get things back on track. I was expecting some very unpleasant interruptions with the heating and power supply but, as it is, there haven't been any.'

Diva coughed loudly. 'Hardly any,' Morgan corrected herself.

'Aren't you going to call the meeting to order?' Frank suggested.

Morgan looked at him. 'Yes, all right.'

Then she paused.

'In fact, no,' she restarted. 'No. I'm not going to do that.'

'Why not?' Frank asked.

'Because the AGM is for shareholders only. I think the important thing is that we hear from Mr McMurphy how things stand and then we'll take the meeting from there.'

'What about the roof development?' Garry asked.

The muscles in Morgan's jaws jerked.

'What about it?'

'Won't Soup have a say in that?'

Morgan frowned as if genuinely confused.

'Er, no. Why would he?'

'What Garry means is – ' Frank interrupted. Morgan darted her gaze at him, quickly understanding that he was the leader of this insurrection. ' – shouldn't we consult Mack about the roof as well? It would help to have as much information as possible, wouldn't it?'

'I don't understand,' Morgan said.

'Let me put it for you more simply,' Frank said, unable to help himself. 'We have asked Mack for his opinion on the roof and he says he can't see a problem. In fact, he says he doesn't see a need to do anything other than minor, remedial work, if that.'

'That isn't what he said to me,' Morgan replied.

'What do you mean?' Frank asked.

'I've already consulted Mr McMurphy with regard to the roof.' Morgan watched Frank's expression falter. 'Didn't he tell you?'

Frank turned to look at the super. 'Er, no. As a matter of fact, he didn't.'

'Oh yes,' Morgan said. 'He agrees entirely with everything I have proposed. Isn't that right, Mr McMurphy?'

The superintendent felt the whole room looking at him, he could feel all their thoughts and energies concentrating.

'You did come and talk to me about it, yes.'

Everyone's body visibly floundered in a collective and exhausted sigh. Only Frank persisted.

'And what do you think, Mack? What is your opinion?'

'I can tell you that when it comes to dealing with the matter during the AGM,' Morgan said.

'I want to hear it from him, thank you, Morgan,' Frank replied, sitting up.

'Well, then you can do that after the meeting and in your own free time,' Morgan said. 'Right now we have a lot to get through, so if you don't mind—'

'But I want to hear it from him now,' Frank stated.

'And I said it will have to wait.'

'I don't care what you said. Mack has told the rest of us that the roof is fine and I want to hear it from him if he told you different.'

His voice was shaking and his face was red and he was staring at Morgan, anger and frustration seared into his brow.

'As President of the Board . . . '

'I DON'T CARE IF YOU'RE PRESIDENT OF THE GOD-DAMNED COUNTRY,' Frank shouted. 'I WANT TO HEAR WHAT MACK HAS TO SAY!'

There was a stunned silence. The baby didn't even cry.

'Mack,' Frank said, trying to control his breathing, 'just tell everyone what you told me.' The super looked at him. 'It'll be fine,' his eyes said.

He believed them.

'As far as I can see the roof of this building is sound,' the super said, under Frank's gaze.

Frank darted his expression away and broke the spell, throwing his 'told you so' face at anyone who cared to look.

'There are two hairline cracks in Ms Honeysuckle's ceiling caused by pressure from the roof, but support can easily be reinforced on this load-bearing wall to relieve it,' he said, pointing to his left. 'I could have the job done in a week.'

'So do you think the roof needs to be rebuilt?'

He fell back into Frank's look. 'No.'

Frank turned back towards the room. Unable to contain his excitement, he settled his eyes on Morgan.

'Before the AGM starts I would like to officially announce my candidacy for President of the Board,' he said heavily. 'I believe that, while Morgan has done a good job of improving the running of the corporation, her current proposal to develop the roof so that she can expand her own apartment at cost to everyone else in the building is both unfair and unwarranted. If you vote for me, I will abandon all plans to develop the roof and save the corporation tens of thousands of dollars. I will place a freeze on all maintenance increases and remove the system of fines for late payments. In addition I . . .'

He stopped as Morgan stood up and reached for the files on the table beside her chair. Starting with Mrs Xhiu, she moved in a circle around the room, handing one to everybody.

'Please don't let me stop you, Frank,' Morgan said, as she passed a file to Garry. 'I was enjoying that.'

'What's this?' Garry said, looking up at Morgan who seemed to tower over him.

'This?' Morgan asked, shrugging her shoulders. 'Oh it's just a bit of reading material.'

'Reading material?' Anna-lise asked as Morgan smiled down at her across the long length of paperwork.

'Well, it's more of a dossier really.'

'What kind of a dossier?' Frank asked.

'Why don't you read it?' Morgan said.

Frank, along with the rest of the room, opened the file and started turning pages.

'I'm afraid I didn't prepare one for you, Mr McMurphy,' Morgan said, glancing dismissively in his direction. 'If I'd known you were coming to the AGM I would have made sure, especially seeing as you're such an expert on structural engineering.'

'What are all these diagrams?' Diva asked.

'This looks like gibberish,' Garry said.

'These are diagrams detailing load distribution in 444 drawn up by Ashton and Ashton, a well-known engineering firm in the city,' Morgan said, retaking her seat. 'There is a long letter from them explaining in detail what the drawings mean and the problems we face. In addition, there are proposals from three roof-development firms which—'

'Hang on a second,' Frank interrupted. 'When did you do all this?'

'I don't see how that's relevant,' Morgan replied.

'Well, how did you pay for it? Who authorized you to have a structural engineer come in and survey the building?'

'The law,' Morgan replied.

'I'm sorry?'

'By law, Assisted Housing Corporation buildings are obliged to take professional advice as soon as they become aware of any structural problems. If something had happened and I hadn't done anything, we might have been liable.'

'Shouldn't you have at least consulted the Board first?'

'It wouldn't have made any difference either way, we had to get it done,' Morgan said.

'Well, we might have had some say in which firm you used,' Frank continued.

'HOLY SHIT YA!' Helmut suddenly yelled.

Mrs Xhiu made the sign of the cross.

'It says here that the woof is going to collapse within one year!' Helmut said. His r's slipped when surprised.

'One of these proposals is for ninety-five thousand dollars!' Diva exclaimed.

'I don't see how we can trust this information—' Frank said.

'Oh, come on, Frank,' Mike interrupted. 'Morgan's hardly going to make it up, is she?'

'She might,' Frank tried, staring back at him.

'Are you even reading this?' Anna-lise said. 'I think you should read this, Frank.'

Morgan glanced over at Ulysses and noticed with glee that he was asleep.

Frank slammed his folder closed. 'This is bullshit. Can't you see what she's doing?'

No one listened to him, they were all staring pale-faced into their folders.

'Thank you, Frank,' Morgan said slowly, crossing her legs. 'Now,' she sighed, 'it would probably be best if all of you went through this information in your own time so that you can properly digest it. Of course, if Frank wants to have another independent survey carried out then he, should he be voted President, can take care of that. Suffice to say that I believe everyone here is by now aware that Mr McMurphy's opinion, valued as it is, is no longer relevant to our situation.'

She paused, turned to the super and smiled hatefully at him.

'And since you are not a shareholder of this corporation and since this is a shareholders' meeting in which many important matters have to be discussed, including, among other things, your tenure, I'm afraid you are going to have to leave and attend to your usual duties, Mr McMurphy. We will deal with the flooding situation in more detail later and I will let you know how the Board has decided to proceed. Thank you.'

The super looked at the room.

No one looked back.

'Goodbye,' Morgan said, her eyes as cold as night.

I collapsed in the elevator. It was the signal. It struck me hard this time. I hadn't picked up on it for a while. Maybe I'd dared to believe it had gone away. I panicked. It seemed so much stronger than before. And it was wretched, so wretched. It hit me between the eyes and made me clamp my ears with my hands. It thundered in the cavernous elevator shaft. It rang through the walls. It splintered in the bells and the chimes and through the spyholes in everyone's front door like white light refracting. I fell to my knees. I cried out for it to stop. But it got stronger.

I saw the floor of the elevator fall away. I stared into the abyss. Down into the basement. Deeper. Below into the foundations. Further into the hard black, solid granite rock of Manhattan. Into the burning sulphur, the liquid molten lava, the moving epicentre of Earth. I felt myself falling.

All the time, the transmission filled me and screamed.

'Please, it's not my fault, I tried to help, I couldn't, you don't understand, it won't work, it won't help, it's not my fault, you mustn't, please don't, you mustn't.'

I was on the floor. I was writhing on my back. My body was twisting and convulsing, muscles spasming, I yelled. I could see my incarcerated body from above. I could see myself being tortured. The signal pierced me like a many-weaponed, many-headed demon, a visible blue form, thrusting stakes into me, twisting my ribs and breaking my back and tearing. I tried to jerk myself away from the attacks, as if I were trying to escape, wrapped in a straitjacket of sound that I wanted to contort myself out of but each time I moved the pain struck me from an opposite place until one direct hit to the solar plexus from a very powerful vibration made me vomit white liquid.

There was momentary relief in that small mercy. The violence abated just long enough for me to see where I was, to know that the elevator had stopped, that I was on the ground floor and that the doors were open for me. I slid myself across the corridor to the basement door. I managed to creep my fingers into the small proud gap left by the latch, and open the door wide enough for my body to crawl through. I tumbled down the broken stairs; the first set, to one small landing, and then down the second into the hard concrete of the basement floor.

I knew that it would only be a matter of time before it started again. The meeting wouldn't be over for a good two hours. In that time, their collective fear would continue to come at me – snapping and biting and thrusting like an electrical cable torn loose, lashing out wildly in unpredictable snake-like shapes.

I had to get back to my apartment. I could see the heating pipes starting to shake with excitement, building to a new crescendo on the wave of anger swelling within Morgan's walls. And I was caught in the surf. I had survived one and surfaced, but now I could see another looming, imminent, bigger – all the time their feelings pooling, collecting, rolling at me, ready to crash.

How long would this last? What would happen after the meeting? Would I survive? There were always going to be more waves. My arms felt exhausted.

I managed to pull myself into bed. The reception refined itself, slow and sure, deep and ominous. I waited for it to tune. I knew it was going to hurt me badly this time. There was real black malice in it – genuine hatred and anger and hurt and fear. There was nothing I could do to stave it off.

The Westchester sat opposite Central Park. It was snowing gently. There were horse-drawn carriages with men from New Jersey calling out to tourists. There was still an elaborate Christmas display in the window of Profigliano's but it looked January-tired now.

Henry watched his breath make thick clouds and took a final drag on his cigarette. He hadn't felt this nervous since the last time they'd met. Eventually, knowing that he was late and hoping that this would make the man angry, he threw the cigarette to the ground and stamped on it. Why was he even bothering?

The doorman held the door open and Henry marched anonymously across the thinly veined marble floors, his heels clicking, and then into the library with its dark leather sofas, his heels falling mute against the lush carpet, and finally past the bar with the candles and clouds of whiskey-tainted breath. In one corner, by a large log fire, he could see a long private area and an old hand falling, full of violence, to one side of a seat. A man in a black suit with a gun on his chest nodded deferentially at Henry as he approached.

'Sir,' he said simply, stepping to one side.

Henry walked past and stopped behind the chair. The two men hesitated within each other's space, knowing that the other was there but not knowing what to do. Eventually, it was Henry's father who managed to grumble and cough and stutter excitedly, 'My boy, my boy, my only son, thank God.' He coughed again as he managed himself to his feet.

Henry could see that there was moisture in his eyes as his father leant heavily on the armchair to stand, but that could have been the effort of standing or his condition.

'Please, quickly, come quickly,' his father beckoned him. 'I want to embrace you.'

Henry let himself be drawn towards him and taken into the large arms that had never grown smaller since his childhood even though Henry was himself now a tall, well-built man. He felt his father's belly against his, navel to navel. He could feel the weight in the man, the inability to support himself. He did seem worse.

'Now tell me,' his father said, pushing Henry away and looking at him. 'Why have you dragged me to this hole of a hotel?'

'Happy New Year, Father,' Henry said, passing him a large envelope.

'What the hell is this?' his father exclaimed, taking it.

'It's nothing, a gift. Open it later.'

'I will,' his father replied. 'I will. I know I will.'

There was a pause.

'Sit down now. What will you drink? The whiskey is disgusting.'

'I'll take a vodka gimlet.'

The man in the dark suit nodded, someone else moved and the drink arrived.

'My God, look at you, Henry. You look so well, so wonderful. Have you grown?'

Henry didn't say anything. There was a long pause and both men looked into the fire.

'Your mother sends her love.'

Henry smiled.

'She misses you. We all do.'

Henry didn't say anything.

Eventually, his father sighed. 'There's still time. If you want to, if you need to come back.'

'I can't, Father, you know that.'

'I don't understand it.'

'Let's not go into all this again.'

The old man looked at Henry with the fire burning in his eyes.

'Yes, you're right. Tell me, then. What have you been doing?'

'I've been away. Thailand.'

His father nodded in comprehension only, the approval still not there.

'And living? Where do you live now?'

Henry smiled. 'Nice try, Dad.'

He shrugged. 'Hell, boy, if I can't find you then I figured I may as well just come right out with it and ask.'

'You nearly did once.'

'Yes, that place in the Lower East Side. Henry, you can't honestly tell me that you're happy, can you? How can you be?'

Henry shrugged.

'Do you have money?'

'Yes.'

There was another long pause.

'I've retired from the Board.'

'I know, Father,' Henry replied. 'I read about it in the paper.'

The two men looked at each other.

'I'm dying.'

'I know.'

Henry watched the old man draw the emotion from his lips and physically suck up the pain, the fear.

'And you still won't come back?'

'I can't.'

'Then why did you come, boy?' The old man grumbled and coughed and spluttered his way back into the depths of his tall chair, encased in it, entombing himself in its shadows. He angrily waved away the man in the dark suit, who had turned.

'I wanted to tell you,' Henry started. 'I've met somebody. At least, I think I have.'

His father looked at him. 'A woman?'

'Yes, Father,' Henry sighed.

'Well, that's something at least. Who is she?'

'No one. I mean, not no one, just . . . well, you wouldn't know her.'

'Do you love her?'

'Yes. I wasn't sure at first but I found, while I was abroad, I couldn't stop thinking about her.'

'Will you marry?'

'I haven't asked her yet. I wanted to speak to you first.'

'I can't think why.'

'She loves me, Father.'

'It isn't hard for women to love men like us, Henry.'

'That's just it. She doesn't know yet.'

His father squinted at him. 'I see.' He paused. 'Well, can we meet her?'

'I'd like you to,' Henry said.

'When?'

'Soon.'

'Don't wait too long.'

'I won't.'

There was a pause.

'I'm happy for you, son.'

'Thank you.'

'And don't worry,' his father sighed, glancing at the package Henry had given him, 'I'm sure your mother will enjoy your book. She can tell me all about it when she's done.'

'Yeah,' Henry replied. 'I figured she might.'

Fifteen-dollar mignon steaks, dyed pink and tenderized, sat blood-stuffed on the chopping board, black pepper and rosemary rubbed coarsely into their flesh. There was a fresh spinach salad with walnuts and squares of blue cheese in a large china bowl with sky-blue glazing. Three bottles of California Syrah lay in the wine rack. The glass table had been laid, candles burnt. The spotlights were low, everything was ready, the potatoes were baking. Mandy was smoking a cigarette, perched on a stool by the kitchen counter watching as Ben opened the wine.

'You don't think you've gone a bit overboard?' Mandy said, sucking hard and inhaling with half-open eyes and a half-open mouth as if temporarily intoxicated, shuddering slightly on the smoke.

'No,' Ben replied, giving her a look.

Mandy ignored it and took another drag. 'I just don't see why you had to invite Morgan.'

'Isn't it obvious?'

'Not to me, not after the way she treated Joe at the AGM.'

'What do you mean?'

'Oh, come on, Ben, you saw what she did. Joe was just trying to help. Morgan made out as if he didn't have a clue. She humiliated him. Couldn't you see how embarrassed he was?'

'I don't know, maybe,' Ben said, pouring wine into their glasses. 'But I'm not sure that was Morgan's fault. If anything it was Frank making him feel uncomfortable. He should never have insisted Mack come to the AGM. Morgan was right. If he wasn't a shareholder, he shouldn't have been there.'

'You've been working in those banks for too long,' Mandy replied, taking a glass from Ben. 'They've brainwashed you with all that corporate nonsense. Don't you think Joe should have a say in the running of the building? After all, he's the one who keeps the place standing.'

'You've changed your tune.'

'What's that supposed to mean?'

'Just that you're very appreciative of the superintendent all of a sudden. When we first got here you said you thought he was creepy. Now it's Joe this and Joe that. Where did you get the idea to call him Joe, anyway? Everyone else calls him Mack.'

'He just looks like a Joe to me. Besides, it is his name.' Mandy took a sip of her wine and raised her eyebrows appreciatively. 'But you're right. I have changed my mind about him. I think he's great.'

'Don't you think you should trust your first impressions?' Ben sighed, turning the cork over in his fingers.

'Why? Don't you like Joe?'

'It's not that I don't like him. He's really helped us out since we got here. And he's great with Billy. I just, I don't know, I can't put my finger on it but there's something about a guy living in the basement that freaks me out a little.'

'I can see that,' Mandy said, gently crushing her cigarette out in the ashtray. 'But, you know, since moving in, Joe's been there for me, for all of us, in so many ways I can't even count. He is a truly good man. I really feel as if he has our best interests at heart. I feel as if he's looking after us.'

Ben looked at his wife and felt a surge of love. Sometimes, she said things that made the world seem beautiful. Only she had the power to make him feel that way.

Just then the doorbell rang, making him jump.

'Maybe this wasn't such a good idea,' he said quickly, looking worried.

'Don't worry,' Mandy said, smiling and walking to him, trailing an arm tenderly across his back. 'Everything's going to be fine. You're gonna do great.'

He listened to his wife greeting his new boss through the intercom.

'Oh, hi, Susannah, great, buzz again as you come in . . . '

There was a rap on the door. Ben listened to Mandy open it.

'Talk about timing . . . '

Morgan's voice swelled from the corridor into the apartment and then into the kitchen as she strode in.

'I'm afraid I can't stay too late,' she said brusquely. 'I've got a terrible cold.'

Ben turned to face her and noticed that she hadn't brought any wine.

'It's great that you could come at all, Morgan,' he said, motioning to kiss her on the cheek. Morgan swerved out the way.

'Careful. My cold, remember.'

'Oh, yeah. Right.'

The buzzer went again and there was the sound of footsteps in the corridor.

'Hi, you must be Mandy . . . '

'Can I get you anything?' Ben asked Morgan.

'Just a glass of water.'

'Are you sure?' Ben said, trying to hide his disappointment. 'We've got a great Syrah.'

'No,' Morgan replied tersely.

'Are you sure I can't tempt you?' Ben tried again.

Morgan shook her head as Mandy led Susannah into the apartment.

' . . . I love the neighbourhood,' Susannah said in a nasal voice. 'It's so Bohemian.'

Ben bent down to kiss her. She was a tiny woman, with clipped brown hair and chipmunk features. She was wearing dark lipstick and a dark jumper with long sleeves to cover a withered right hand.

'I'm so pleased you're here,' Ben said as she passed him a box.

'Something for dessert.'

'You shouldn't have,' Ben said, then turned to introduce Morgan. 'Susannah, this is Morgan. I think I've mentioned her to you before, she's the President of the Co-op Board here at 444.'

Morgan extended her hand and said, 'Nothing bad, I hope.'

Susannah laughed and moved to shake her hand. 'Not that I can recall.'

Ben watched as Morgan took Susannah's limp fingers deftly and shook without showing any trace of surprise. For a second he dared to believe that the evening might even be a success.

'So what exactly do you do, Morgan?' Susannah asked, taking her glass of wine.

'Me? Oh not much,' Morgan replied. 'Try and keep this house standing, mainly.'

'Why don't we go into the living room?' Mandy suggested. 'Ben can start cooking the steaks.'

'Surely, being a co-op president doesn't take up all your time?' Susannah continued as they took their seats on the sofas.

'Actually, it takes up most of it,' Morgan said. 'But I do run my own business. A small interior-design firm.'

'Really? Does it do well?' Susannah said, taking a large gulp.

There was a loud hiss as Ben threw the steaks into the frying pan. Smoke billowed into his eyes.

'Going by Ben's current account, about half as well as investment banking.'

'Hey, how do you know about Ben's current account?' Mandy cried, half-jokingly.

'From your application. You gave us three months of bank statements, remember?'

'I didn't think you actually scrutinized them.'

'Are you kidding? That's half the fun.'

Susannah laughed and threw the rest of her wine down her throat. 'Well, interior design may not earn as much but it's three times more interesting, I'll bet,' she replied.

Mandy took Susannah's glass and moved to refill it.

'Oh, I don't know,' Morgan said. 'I know that Ben was very happy to get the job with you guys.'

'And we're thrilled to have him. He was a very strong acquisition. You wouldn't believe the lengths we had to go to, to poach him from Maverick and Marshall's.'

'Poach?'

'Hmm-mm,' Susannah smiled.

The smoke detector suddenly went off, making everybody jump.

'Ben, the baby!' Mandy hissed.

'What kind of lengths?' Morgan said over the ear-piecing alarm.

'What?' Susannah half-shouted.

'Lengths? You said you went to lengths to convince Ben to leave M&M. What kind of lengths?'

The baby was screaming now. Mandy went to attend. Ben climbed onto a stool to take the battery out of the smoke detector but when he couldn't release the mechanism from its casing he rashly smashed it with the back of his hand, splintering the cream plastic into shards, one of which pierced his wrist.

'Shit!'

Blood poured into the cuff of his shirt. Mandy came out of the bedroom holding Billy, his face purple with exhausted fear and rage. Ben climbed down from the stool and pushed his hand into the sink, blood surging.

'What happened?' Mandy said, the baby writhing in her arms.

'It's nothing,' Ben replied.

'Is everything OK?' Susannah asked.

'Everything's fine,' he called out. 'I've cut myself, that's all.'

'Do you want me to do anything?' Susannah asked.

'No, no,' Mandy said, rocking the baby in her arms. 'Please just pour yourself some more wine and relax.'

'Sure?'

'Yup.'

Mandy saw that Morgan hadn't moved from her seat.

'Darling, will you be OK?' she asked. 'I'm going to try and settle him.'

'Yeah, go ahead. Good luck.'

'I think they've got everything under control in there,' Susannah said returning with a full glass of wine to the sofa opposite Morgan. There was the faint sound of the baby's cries being muffled into a warm breast in the room beyond the wall. Calm seemed to momentarily descend.

There was a pause. Morgan smiled at Susannah. She smiled back then glanced away, trying to find something to look at on a wall.

'Have you got your answer machine fixed yet, Ben?' Morgan eventually called out casually.

'What?' Ben said from behind the kitchen counter where he was busy looking for a bandage.

'I called up the other day and it seemed to go on to speaker-phone or something. I could hear every word you and Mandy were saying. You seemed to be arguing.'

'What?' Ben said again, emerging, frowning. His face slowly changed as he slotted the pieces together. The blood drained from his cheeks. 'Oh, that!' He felt himself fumbling for the right words. 'Er, yeah, we did, thanks.' He looked at Susannah. 'We had some problems with the answer machine and, wow, you're never gonna believe this, but while Mandy and I were talking I stupidly pressed the Record button for the greeting message. We had it on there for days.'

'How embarrassing!' Susannah said.

'I'll say,' Morgan said, looking at Ben. 'You really should get voicemail.'

'It was only when I noticed that no one was leaving any messages that I checked the machine and realized what had happened.'

'Well, I'm glad I telephoned you while you were in,' Susannah said.

'Me too,' Ben replied.

'BEN!' Morgan called out. 'The steaks!'

'What?' Ben said dreamily.

'They're burning!'

'Oh no!' Ben said spinning round. He immediately grabbed the frying pan with his good hand and squealed. 'OW!'

He dropped the pan onto the counter but it caught the edge and quickly flipped, throwing the steaks and smoking oil across the kitchen floor. Ben pressed his face into his hands. He could see light splintering between his fingers. 'This is bad,' he whispered to himself.

Susannah quickly came to help, rescuing the steaks, while telling Ben to rinse his burnt hand under a cold tap. Morgan also stood up but only to inspect the catastrophe and remark: 'Those will have to be thrown away.'

'No, no,' Susannah replied. 'We can just rinse them off, they'll be fine.'

'They're burnt to a crisp,' Morgan said.

Susannah didn't say anything but Ben could tell that she agreed as she quietly slid the steaks onto a plate and placed them in a discreet corner of the kitchen.

'Is your hand OK, Ben?' Susannah asked.

'I'll be fine,' he replied.

'I'll get you some ice,' Morgan said, jettisoning into action.

'Thanks, Morgan,' Ben said. 'There's some in the cooler.'

Mandy emerged, tiptoeing from the bedroom. She smiled with pursed lips and sighed quietly: 'Finally.' Then she frowned. 'Hey, what's with all the smoke?'

'A mini-disaster,' Susannah slurred.

'We could do with a window open,' Morgan said.

'I've burnt the steaks,' Ben said despondently.

'And he's burnt his hand,' Morgan added, pulling out the ice tray.

'Oh, darling, are you all right?' Mandy said, stepping quickly across the room.

'Yeah, I'm fine,' Ben managed. 'I just need a Band-Aid to stop this damn cut.'

'I'll go and get one,' Mandy replied.

'Where's your bathroom, Mandy?' Susannah whispered.

'Come, I'll show you.'

'OK.' Susannah beamed.

'Morgan, I don't suppose you could pour me a glass of wine, could you?' Ben sighed, taking the dishcloth full of ice Morgan had prepared.

'Sure,' Morgan replied sympathetically. As she picked up the wine and poured she said, 'Well, Ben, I guess this is as good a time as any to tell you the good news.'

'Good news?'

'I want you to take over as Building Treasurer next month.'

Ben looked up at her. 'What? So soon?'

'Yup,' Morgan replied.

'But we haven't been in the building a year yet. I thought we had to be here a year before we could take office.'

'No, you just have to be on the Board. It was one of the main reasons I wanted the building to vote you in at the AGM, though of course it also solved the hung-vote problem we had last year.'

'I see,' Ben replied slowly.

'Yes, I'd like to announce it at the next Board meeting, if you're willing,' Morgan said, passing Ben his glass. 'Which hand?' She grinned.

Ben held out the burnt one and took the glass. 'Er, gee, Morgan, what can I say? I'm honoured. But, well, it's just that . . . do you mind if I think about it? Now's not the best time for me, what with the new job and the baby and just moving in and everything. I'm pretty snowed.'

Morgan looked at him with flat eyes and said sternly, 'Please don't tell me that I have to remind you, Ben, that when you applied to buy shares in this building you accepted the responsibility of contributing to the running of it.'

'No, of course not, of course you don't have to remind me,' Ben replied quickly. 'And I want to help. It's just that . . . hell, I'm trying to cook you a nice dinner here, Morgan. Can't we just relax and talk about this another time?'

Morgan smiled at him. 'You're right. I'm sorry. I've said it now; we don't need to go into it.'

'Thanks.' Ben sighed.

Morgan's smile grew as Susannah sailed back into the room.

'Your wife has told me to give you these,' she said to Ben, holding out a tube of burn cream and a Band-Aid. Morgan looked at her as she handed them across the kitchen counter.

'Sooo, Susannah,' Morgan cooed. 'You never did tell me exactly how you managed to poach Ben from M&M.'

'Hmm?'

Ben stared at Morgan.

'Oh yes, I want to know all the gory details,' Morgan said, ignoring him.

'Well, I gotta tell you it was darned hard to convince him to leave,' Susannah said. 'Ben was in real demand.'

'That *is* interesting.'

'I don't think it was any one thing we did. I think we were just the right outfit. I think that's why Ben came to us, he knew he'd found a good home,' Susannah said, smiling warmly at him now.

Ben smiled back stiffly.

'Yes, all the pieces were there,' Susannah continued. 'We make a terrific fit. It was a no-brainer, looking back.'

'Quite,' Morgan replied.

'Oh shucks,' Susannah slurred, sliding over to Ben and snaking an arm too low around his waist, resting her withered hand on his ass, making the hair on Ben's spine bristle. He was thankful that Mandy was still in the bathroom. 'We were just damn lucky to get the guy, that's all I know. I don't know what we'd do without him.'

There was a long pause as the three of them basked in Susannah's warm, drunken glow. Morgan turned slowly to look at Ben and smiled. Ben stared back at her, powerless.

'I know exactly how you feel,' Morgan said slowly, taking a strong hold of Ben's gaze.

Mrs Xhiu looked at herself in the mirror, her naked body nicotine-yellow under the single pale bulb hanging in the bathroom. A tap was running. There was another mirror on the wall behind her, sending her reflection into infinity. It was there to make the bathroom look bigger but Mrs Xhiu wished it wasn't there. It made her feel like she'd been opened up. She could see her spine, creased like a well-read book's; there were weather-worn, dog-eared pages of flesh turned across her ribs and, across them, thin veins etched like lines from an old story that no one wanted to hear. She felt tired and quiet.

She turned the tap off and immediately heard the sound of Reverend Jeremy coming through the wall, his new channel, his new religion, blaring. People said it was occult, the work of the Devil, that he'd left the Lord. Mrs Xhiu didn't know what to think. She believed that he was a good man. But she couldn't make sense of his change.

'We have to harness the power, the true power that Jesus has given us. Abandon yourselves. Listen for the thought. Can you hear it? Do you feel it? We are all as one. Each of us is united in His common body. There is no I, there is only Him, Us. We must listen to Him, what He is saying. We as Christians have been victims of our divided consciousness and Jesus won't come back until we unite ourselves to His singular truth and attune our minds to His, not the mind of man. Through our unconscious we share in the mind of Christ. We have to merge simultaneously in prayer. Hear it now. Abandon all things that define you as individuals: religion, race, nationality. We are all the same. Listen to Him. He is within us all. Amen!'

Mrs Xhiu sank into her bath, watching the water distort her body shape. Her amulets, the heavy silver cross with Jesus in agony and the two saints on pendants, hung from her neck. She lifted them and gazed at them and kissed them. Christ's wet face, his body, his feet. She could feel the cold and melded metal on her thin lips.

'If schizophrenia were treated by a method that affirmed His truth, the drugs prescribed to suppress the prophetic hearing of voices would not be necessary.'

There was the sound of the stadium crowd coming, a low-pitched, swaying hum, like some heathen, hedonistic rite, a brainwashing, mind-controlling vibration that slowly filled the water. Over the top of it Reverend Jeremy talked of sporting fans and marching crowds.

'When people think the same, when people cry for joy together, when there is celebration or mourning, wherever there is oneness, there is God. Look at the people screaming, look at what they can do. We are here to change the world. Scream with me!'

So she did.

Juan woke with a start and sat up immediately in the bed. He was terrified but he didn't know why. He'd heard something, something terrible, but by the time he'd woken up it wasn't there any more and he couldn't be sure if he'd heard it at all, even if he knew what 'it' had been. He told himself he must have been dreaming. Mike stirred beside him.

'Michael?' Juan whispered in the darkness. 'Michael! Did you hear that?'

'What?' Mike said groggily.

'Did you hear . . . '

Just then, there was a scream.

'SOMEBODY HELP! THERE'S A MAN! HE'S COMING THROUGH MY WINDOW. PLEASE! CALL THE POLICE!'

Now Mike sat upright, his large body causing the bed covers to quickly slide to one side and slip slowly off the edge and onto the floor.

'I'll get my gun,' he said, getting up quickly.

'Holy Mary mother of God,' Juan said, pulling up the bed-covers from the floor to cover his slim bronzed body. He sucked on a corner of the fabric.

There was another scream, this time very long and toe-curling.

'HE'S GOT A KNIFE! HE'S GETTING IN! SOMEBODY HELP ME, PLEASE!'

Juan whimpered into his bed sheets and Mike started punching the numbers on the phone.

Ben turned on the lights in his apartment so that Mandy could check on the baby while he called the police.

Mrs Xhiu was on her knees in her bathroom reciting an urgent prayer.

Garry rummaged through his wardrobe looking for a flash-light.

Anna-lise was in her living room squeezing Ulysses into her chest.

Helmut threw on a pair of jeans and ran to his bathroom window with his camera.

Diva failed to wake up.

Morgan put in her earplugs.

The beams from two flashlights now swung with erratic panic through the airshaft, desperately searching the back wall of 443 Hanover Street for signs of the intruder. Frank was hold-ing one of them. He managed to find a fat man in a string vest hanging out of one window; he was busy shouting out to another window below and to the left of him that gaped openly in the wall.

'HEY, FUCK FACE, I'VE CALLED THE COPS!' he was shouting into the airshaft. 'I'VE CALLED THE COPS, YOU'VE GOT NO CHANCE!'

'HEY, CARLO!' Frank shouted across to him. 'DID YOU SEE ANYTHING?'

'I THINK HE'S IN THE AIRSHAFT!'

Frank swung his flashlight down into the darkness but he couldn't see anyone. He scanned the rest of the block opposite and noticed for the first time the other apartments and their activity. Some had their lights on, three or four windows had heads hanging out of them, the others were all darkness, pre-sumably empty. One apartment remained dark but Frank could see the glow of a cigarette moving slowly within it.

'IS SHE OK, CARLO?' Frank said, pointing the light quickly now at the intruded window, which hung ominously open, like a terrified mouth trapped in a silent scream.

'I'M GONNA CHECK!' Carlo replied, manoeuvring his pasta-filled frame out of his window and into the bright light of his apartment.

'Hey, Frank!' Garry called from the right. 'What happened?'

'Some asshole just tried to break into next door,' he replied, turning his head to peer along the brickwork wall. 'I think it might have been Hazel's place.'

'Is she OK?'

'I dunno.' Frank turned and yelled. 'HAZEL? YOU OK? HAZEL? DON'T WORRY, THE COPS ARE ON THE WAY. EVERYTHING'S GONNA BE OK. HAZEL? HAZEL?'

Then he heard the commotion below.

He had a very young face, beautiful in its own way. Acne scarred and scared eyes, but fresh and full of strength. He couldn't have been more than eighteen, nineteen max.

I hadn't expected to run into him, not really. I suppose I was hoping to head him off but I figured if he'd made his way into Hazel's apartment then he'd probably have just gone on to escape through her front door. There didn't seem much point in his dropping back down into the airshaft. Unless Carlo managed to head him off.

All I know is, almost as soon as I'd clambered up the thin, steep stairs from the basement up through the fire-escape hatch – the triangular coal-chute kind – and into the airshaft, he was in front of me. We looked at each other for a second and that was when he had shouted. I didn't get the words, something Hispanic.

His hand was quick. Maybe he could see that I wasn't about to yield, that I was strong, that I would fight. Or maybe he just panicked.

I didn't see the knife. There was a flash of something and I somehow knew that something had happened to me. It took a few moments for the pain but in that time I was paralysed, the shock took hold. My brain couldn't register what had happened. I stood and watched as he stared into my chest. I watched his eyes digest what he had done and then wheel with panic, looking for an exit. He eventually threw himself past me, our bodies meeting hotly for a brief, intimate, violent moment, like two wrestlers. We were both full of breath and I heard him panting as we came together.

I crashed to the ground and felt my head hit the white concrete, just as the pain in my chest ignited.

'Quickly, somebody get down there,' Frank cried out, his voice shaking and weak, in shock from the sight of it. 'Mack's been hurt.'

'I'M GOING, I'LL DO IT,' Garry shouted.

'ME ALSO,' Helmut said, from below

'Wait, wait, how do we get in there?' Garry asked.

'There are stairs from the basement,' Frank replied. 'They lead to the airshaft.'

'DON'T MOVE!' Mike shouted. 'The intruder could still be down there.'

'Yes,' Anna-lise cried. 'Please don't go, it's too dangerous.' She pointed to the helicopter that was hovering above and beaming its spotlight down. 'The police are here now. Let them take care of it.'

Garry and Helmut, emboldened by adrenalin, didn't listen. Garry was already jumping down the building stairs two, three at a time, the sound of his feet crashing through the corridors. Helmut waited for him in the corridor by the door to the basement, armed with a lamp. Mike tried to catch up to them but he made the mistake of taking the elevator.

'EVERYBODY STAY CALM,' a police loudspeaker hailed from beyond the walls. 'STAY WHERE YOU ARE! PLEASE REMAIN IN YOUR APARTMENTS AND LOCK THE DOORS.'

'Mack? Mack? MACK!' Frank cried down the airshaft. 'Are you OK? An ambulance is on its way. Mack? CHRIST! SOMEBODY HELP HIM!'

Very white, bright lights in my eyes. They were incandescent, like burning magnesium, painful to watch, blinding.

More cries, disjointed and hard to place, difficult to string together.

I'M GONNA NEED THAT ADRENALIN ... NOW, GODDAMNIT ... WHERE IS THAT RESPIRATOR? ... HAVE YOU MANAGED TO GET THAT STRETCHER THROUGH YET? ... OK, GIVE ME A VEIN ... WHAT'S THIS GUY'S NAME? ... NO, THEY DIDN'T CATCH HIM ... WHAT? WHAT DID YOU SAY? ... DOES HE HAVE ANY RELATIVES? ... SHIT! I THINK WE'RE LOSING HIM .... MR McMURPHY? JOE McMURPHY? HANG IN THERE, BUDDY ...

Maybe it was the panic in the words that put me off. Maybe it was the burning in my chest. Someone was twisting a red-hot iron into me. The pain distorted the sounds, made it hard to hear. There was the thump of helicopter blades. I heard them in slow motion. They were such a distinct sound. I could make out the spidery silhouette of the machine hovering above, through the brightness, beyond my closed eyes, through my eyelashes, above the building, beaming its spotlight down.

I tried to stay focused, I tried not to let the whiteness, the glare of the night, overwhelm me even though I could feel it growing, even though I could see it coming in from all around, seeping through, in from the edges of my mind, starting to envelop my mind. I tried to stay focused, I tried to listen, but the sounds were getting fainter, more and more difficult to discern. It was the pain.

I saw Catherine.

Her back was turned to me, she was sitting on the grass, leaning on one hand, her legs folding to the right. She was wearing blue jeans, turned up, with pink embroidered socks and pointing white shoes.

I looked at how her body flowed from flesh to slenderness like some lyrical composition; the outward curve of her buttocks into the curl of her waist, the round edge of a breast just visible.

Above the cut of her blouse I could see the line of her shoulder blades and her collarbones, the muscles moving gently as she shifted her weight. An edge quickly slipped to reveal a whole shoulder, eggshell-shaped and eggshell-coloured, framed by the straps of a black bra and a pink slip she was wearing underneath.

She didn't move the fabric back. She just sat there, exposing herself. It was innocent enough – unless you knew her.

Around her neck she wore a dark silk scarf that mirrored her hair. I loved the way it fell and folded loosely; and the way she was able to rearrange it without care and yet still have it look new and exciting and lush.

I studied her fingers. They were long and refined and white.

I could sense the darkness and the heat in her groin, her thighs pressing over it, forbiddingly inviting.

She turned away from the book she was reading to look up at me – pink pressed lips and jasmine skin, a sculpted nose and darkly drawn eyebrows, her bright-green eyes flecked fantastically with sparks of black matter; her noble forehead, her round ears.

There was a strange spring light above her. The sun was

shielded behind heavy black and white clouds but it was shining brightly above and through a brilliant dark-blue sky. The contrast was dramatic.

As she looked at me, the sunlight suddenly caught the blossom in a cherry tree so that it blazed, like sex. The fire flickered fiercely from the branches, momentarily threatening to engulf us in a ball of fury, before dying out just as suddenly, and fading.

The flowers didn't fall but the passion in the blossom burnt out on itself so there were only faded husks sheltered within the brittle shells of brown leaves and the skeletal tips of black branches.

'What are you thinking?' I heard her ask.

'Nothing,' I replied.

I woke up in hospital with a nurse tucking the sheets in at the end of my bed. She was a large African-American with ironed hair tied back stiffly in a bun, and wobbling arms that stretched and tested the cut-off sleeves of a perfectly white, starch-stiff uniform.

'Nice to have you with us,' she said, her head still down, into her bosom, busy at the final corner.

'War—' was all I could manage before she turned to a table that was on wheels behind her.

'I'll be surprised if you manage to get this down.'

I heard her Southern accent through the hollow of her body. She poured from a rectangular plastic jug.

'They had to burn the outside of your lung so as it would go raw and stick to your chest cavity to re-inflate. You probably won't be able to swallow.'

I tried to shift myself up onto one elbow but the pain slammed itself across my body as soon as I moved and I was pressed back down into the bed. My eyes closed tightly.

'Hey there, Rocky!' she said, beside me. 'You gotta be a fool to move. Here . . . ' I heard the sound of mechanics whirring and felt my torso being elevated. 'Let me get you set, OK?'

I lay there with my eyes still closed, waiting for the pain to subside, feeling myself slowly rising. I tried to breathe but found I could manage only shallow, lopsided gasps. Eventually I opened my eyes and saw her face.

The sight of her startled me. It was like seeing a ghost, or experiencing déjà vu. She was looking down at me with those doey eyes and that large smile with the gap between the two front teeth, just as she had done all those years before. I scanned her chest, looking for the nametag, searching confirmation. And then I found it.

That was impossible.

I believe in angels. They're here, among us, working in the neo-natal clinics of hospitals all around the world.

They don't look like angels – at least, not in the conventional sense. No white wings and bone-china skin. In fact, most of the angels I saw in the neo-natal clinic at St Martin's were African-American women who handled sick babies like semi-inflated footballs – slinging them over their shoulders to wind, resting them tenderly on their bed-like breasts to sleep, singing lullabies to them in melodic, mantric whispers.

They were so graceful. I loved to watch them. It was like being let in on some big secret to see that there were these people in the world – simple, ordinary-looking people – who travelled on the subway and took the bus and who you'd never guess were anything other than nothing, coming to work in bleeping grottos like these, nurturing tiny lives into existence and helping the weakest through death.

I watched them resuscitating beings no bigger than a hand several times in a single day. 'Come now,' they would coo, rubbing still ribs and pressing firmly on tiny diaphragm cups. 'Wake up now, honey. The party ain't over yet.'

Often there would be movement again. Sometimes there wasn't.

Life and death were the currencies of their working day. A good day at work would see a patient discharged, a bad day would see a baby die. And it was almost always them who told the parents, delivered God's message.

Sure, the doctors did their bit, but they tended to not get as involved. The nurses, though, the guardian angels – they were the ones who got to know the parents. They knew the child, even loved the baby; having bathed and fed and understood everything that had happened in its tiny, entire existence.

They were there in the beginning and they were there for the middle and they were there for the end. They watched over a being's whole life, so neatly and tragically wrapped up in a nutshell, just like the acorn bodies they briefly occupied.

Jimmy was born on 18 October 1981, ten weeks premature.

Catherine never got the chance to hold him before they took him away and I had to leave her weeping in the recovery room to go with the doctors and the nurses to intensive care. In the elevator I'd watched him, swaddled on a thin mattress inside a Perspex container that sat on top of a trolley. He was trying so hard to breathe it made me proud.

I'd already been prepped for the Caesarean so I hadn't needed to scrub up or put on a gown or plastic blue socks over my shoes as I saw another man doing when we raced through the thick flexi-plex double doors with the words NEO-NATAL CLINIC written across them.

I remember feeling vaguely superior because of that.

I jogged and the doctors walked briskly straight to BED NUMBER 10 and, again, I remember feeling pleased to see that there were people there, waiting especially for us.

Looking back, I know now that it was the adrenalin.

Catherine and I had spent so many hours in the hospital, being ignored, getting frustrated, because the doctors had thought she was just having Braxton Hicks.

Then there had been a sudden rush to operate and get the baby to intensive care and in a strange way that had been a relief because at least it seemed like things were finally happening, that people were actually attending to our crisis.

Funny how the mind can play tricks on you like that.

They un-swaddled Jimmy and transferred him to the bed, which was bathed in a deep-orange light from a heat lamp. A lot of his body was still blue, especially his lips and his fingers, which were actually purple.

Already, I could see Catherine's face in his.

A sharp plastic tube was threaded into his mouth and down his throat and a respirator was pressed against his face while a nurse flicked at a wrist and started jabbing with a needle, trying to find a vein. He didn't move, but his inhumanly small body somehow arched gently away from the bed beneath him.

Three injections were made and black blood was taken before a drip was attached at another point in the joint of his elbow. Round white sensors were unpeeled like playtime stickers and attached to his chest, his arms, his legs. A machine started bleeping.

They rolled him onto his side and inserted an impossibly large needle into his spine. I watched them draw fluid.

The room tipped heavily to one side, like a boat listing, before pitching up and over me in a startling swarm of sickening lights.

The next thing I knew, I was opening my eyes and a woman's face was coming into focus in front of mine. There was the taste of ammonia burning in the bridge of my nose.

'Well, now, you sure do know how to get everyone worked up real good,' she said. 'Honestly! A grown man like you fainting in the neo-natal ward, setting off all kinds of panic. You really should be more considerate, Mr McMurphy, there's chilluns sick in there, don't you know?'

'Jimmy? Where is he . . . I've gotta . . . '

'He's fine,' she said, pressing me back into the armchair with a soft hand. 'We're in a room right next door to the clinic. You can go see him in just a moment. Rest now, you've been out for a while. Here,' she said, passing me a plastic cup. 'Take a sip of water.'

I took the cup and drank. We sat together in silence. The room was quiet and hot, stuffed with cushioned chairs the mottled colour of cigarette filters. There were some magazines on a wooden table. I could hear myself breathing.

Eventually, I recovered enough to say, 'Thank you, Miss . . . '

'Joan.'

'Thank you, Joan. I'm sorry for the trouble.'

'It's OK. I understand. It's a terrible thing to see your child come to a place like this. But you must believe me, Mr McMurphy, your son is getting the best attention available. We are doing all that we can for him. It's important you don't move too fast. Try to take things one step at a time.'

I listened to her words and, seemingly from nowhere, with shocking immediacy and painful clarity, the situation suddenly hit me. I saw where I was and what was happening. My wife was upstairs in a hospital ward recovering from a serious operation. She'd lost a lot of blood and was very weak. Our child – our perfect baby boy . . . he wasn't going to make it. He only had days, hours, moments to live. We'd never know him.

My son was going to die.

I can't remember at what point in the realization I started to weep. I don't think Joan even noticed at first. My face didn't screw into a ball. My chin didn't judder. My lips didn't tremble. My body didn't shake. My head remained unbowed. I didn't choke with emotion. I didn't sob. I didn't wail. I didn't even blink.

The tears arrived simply, like water coming quickly to the boil in a pot, spilling out of my eyes, the overflow of all my emotions. And because of their abruptness, because their silent arrival was without announcement or melodrama, I caught a terrifying glimpse of just how much crying there was for me to do. There were no thoughts of self-pity or agonizing physical symptoms to take me away from the insight. I could just see it: my Truth. I had a whole pot of sorrow inside of me.

And these tears . . . they were just the bubbling excess, the merest of beginnings, the early tears.

Yet, how they flowed.

As I convalesced over the following weeks, we talked. A lot. Sometimes we talked into the night – before her shift started – as the winter darkness climbed in early through those tall, iron-meshed windows. Sometimes we talked during the day. We usually kept a bedside lamp on for comfort, even in the daytime.

I told Joan everything – about Catherine, about me. I explained how things got out of control after Jimmy died, how I lost my job, how we broke, how I had to go away and why I couldn't see Catherine again.

'I don't get it,' she said. 'You guys were doing OK. Losing Jimmy didn't mean you had to lose your whole life. What happened?'

When she spoke I liked to look up into the vaulted ceiling of the Gothic hospital and let the sound of her voice wash over me, transport me back to the neo-natal clinic where I could see her sitting with Catherine and me, holding our hands while we stared numbly at Jimmy and his machines. Sometimes I barely noticed the horror of the architecture or even the dreadful screams of the people recovering for the first time from their operations in the amputee ward just next door.

'It's hard to explain.'

'Try.'

Joan had already told me how I'd ended up in St Martin's because of bed shortages at other hospitals. She was still working in the neo-natal unit and had seen my name in the newspaper – GOTHAM *SUPER*-HERO STABBED – so she'd come to see me, out of interest, see if it was the same Joe McMurphy. She didn't think it would be, but it wasn't any trouble to her to travel a couple of wards. I couldn't understand how it was she hadn't aged.

'Where do I begin?'

'Same place as everybody else, Joe; at the beginning.'

She was sat three rows up, in an aisle seat, facing me, against the direction of the train. We were the last ones in the carriage, heading towards the end of the line.

She was reading a book. I was marking papers. Outside, Long Island was melting into the Atlantic. Trees and soil and verges were shifting into sand bars and saltwater plains and long, sharp grasses. I could see boat masts, a difference in the shapes of houses, snapshots of the sunlit ocean.

The Tannoy told us we were coming in. 'Montauk. This is Montauk. Last stop. This service terminates here. Montauk.'

We both looked up from what we were doing and caught each other's eyes but dropped them again quickly. I concentrated on putting my papers away. I'd spread myself over a couple of seats and I didn't want to lose my place. It was important I kept what I'd done in order.

I had my back turned when she said from behind me, 'Hi.'

I turned too quickly and the papers I'd been working on fell and scattered across the compartment floor like doves out of a cage.

'Shit.'

'Here, let me help,' she said moving.

'No,' I said too quickly. She froze and frowned. 'I mean, no thank you. It's OK, I've got it.'

The train brakes squealed and the station platform swelled like a snowball in the corner of my eye. I watched her steady herself against the seat and avoid my look. I tried smiling – unsuccessfully.

'I'm sorry,' she said. 'I didn't mean to bother you. It's just that, well, aren't you staying up at Sarah and Jimmy Field's place, near the cliff?'

'Er, yes.'

'I'm at the Hermitage. Just down the road from you.'

'Really?' I said, as if I didn't already know.

'I was just thinking, seeing as we're both so close to one another, why don't we share a cab?'

The train pulled up and sighed as it sank down on its weight on the tracks.

'I'm sorry, but a friend is picking me up.'

She exhaled with a small, knowing smile.

'OK, then.'

'We could give you a lift, if you like.'

'No,' she said, still smiling. 'Thanks. You have a great weekend.'

'You too,' I replied.

She turned and left.

I climbed down onto my hands and knees and started the slow process of gathering each piece of paper. It took a while. Some had managed to travel several rows, one had even ventured across the aisle.

When I finally stepped down and out of the carriage, I was hot. The evening summer sun and sharp sea air blasted my face. I wasn't used to the wide-open spaces that I could sense coming in at me from all directions and I had to concentrate as I walked down the platform. It was like walking the plank. I was in pirate territory.

I found her still waiting in the car park, her small bag set down beside her, slumped pitifully in the dust. A crow was laughing at her.

'No luck?' I said.

She turned and smiled. 'There's one on the way. I just telephoned.'

I scanned the barren bowl.

'Your friend is late,' she said.

'Hmm.'

'Maybe you should call.'

'I don't have the number.'

She raised her eyebrows at me. 'Are you sure she's gonna show?'

I laughed, taking no notice of the hint.

'I hope so. I don't have a key.'

'No number. No key. Sounds like a risky mission, man.'

'Yeah,' I said, frowning.

'That's the last train back to the city,' she said, nodding in the direction of the chiselled brick engine breathing oil. 'If you miss it, you'll have no place to stay.'

'That would be a problem.'

There was a pause as we both looked out over the empty, rising circle of the car park, the road beyond it teasing us with rare, racing vehicles.

'A buck,' she said, suddenly turning to face me with a glint in her eye.

'Excuse me?'

'A buck says she doesn't show.'

She held out her hand.

I didn't take it.

'I don't think so.'

'Why not? You chicken?'

'No. I just think that if you're right, I'm going to need all the money I've got for a motel.'

A blue Chevy winked from the horizon.

'That's sensible.'

It buzzed brightly across the thin grey line of tarmac, catching the glaring reflection of the sun in its windows.

'Thanks.'

'But hey, if you lose you could always crash at ours.'

I didn't dare reply.

'There's plenty of room.'

I could see the slow orange blip of the indicator, too early for the turning.

'I know what.' She sighed. 'I think you should just accept defeat right now, give me my buck and get in the cab with me. It would save us both a lot of time, don't you think?'

I laughed. 'Sounds to me like you're angling for a free ride.'

'No,' she grinned. 'Not exactly free. I am offering you a sofa in return. And let's face it, you're not exactly in a position to be picky.'

'Have you run out of money or something?'

'Me?' she said with mock shock. 'Run out of money? No chance.'

The car leant to as it started to make the turn into the station drive.

'Tell you what,' she started. 'You don't need to decide. Let's just leave it to fate. If this car is your friend, then it's farewell. But if it's the cab, you come with me.'

'And pay for the ride, of course.'

'All you gotta do is get in the next car,' she said, flabbergasted. 'Is that so hard?'

I laughed. 'Are you being serious?'

'C'mon, I know you don't love her.'

'What?'

'You want to but you can't.'

'What makes you think that?'

The car kicked up dust as it bundled and rolled into the car park, veering wide, ready to sweep broadside.

'I can read minds,' she replied.

'Gee!' Joan said, taking a pillow out from under me so she could fluff it. 'Kinda pushy, huh? I never would have thought that of her.'

'I know. She was actually very timid.'

'So what happened next? Did you get in the cab?'

Joan pressed me onto one side so she could squeeze the pillow in underneath. Already, I was much more mobile.

'Of course not. My girlfriend would have killed me. But I did do something I shouldn't have.'

'What was that?'

'I showed her,' I said.

'You showed her?'

'It was stupid of me. It went against everything I'd ever learnt and promised myself about my powers. But she'd got under my skin. I think I wanted to put her in her place, or show off, or something. That last comment had really riled me. It was as if she knew already and was teasing me about it. Maybe I wanted to give her a taste of her own medicine. I don't know exactly what. I told myself I was being stupid right before I did it but then I went ahead and did it anyway.'

'What happened?'

'I helped her with her bag into the cab and opened the door for her. I think it was clear by then that I wasn't going to go with her. She was pretty embarrassed. She wouldn't look at me until I shut the door and leant in through the window to say goodbye. I remember how she glanced at me with flat eyes and I saw her cold beauty. Her face was very striking. Anyway, I started out by saying thanks for the offer and maybe I'd see her around, and she was smiling and nodding and I could hear her dying inside and wanting to get as far away from me as possible, and I felt bad that she should think this way about me so I just said: "So long, my beautiful Catherine. I'll always love you."'

'Get out.'

'I know.'

'What did she say?'

'Nothing. I slapped the roof of the cab and it sped off.'

'She didn't stop it?'

'Didn't even turn around. I could hear her head spinning, though, right up to the road, then she fell out of range.'

'Hey! You!'

I felt a sharp pain on one side where she jabbed me hard in the kidney and then knocked my elbow so I ended up spilling my beer across the bar. It quickly flooded the counter and the drunk next to me, who had bulging eyes and a swollen look like a fish out of water, spun violently and unsteadily towards me. He looked as if he might swing a punch but the force of his turn sent him clear past me and in sight of Catherine. He double-took when he saw her and, in a slurred instant, the colour of his aggression shifted.

'What?' he tried.

'I wasn't talking to you,' Catherine replied.

I turned my head around slowly but remained facing the bar. I didn't want to lose my place, especially seeing as I was going to have to order another beer.

She was wearing a purple dress and a cleavage. There were two diamond studs in one ear. I noticed for the first time how short her hair was. It was bobbed at the back like the hull of a boat.

'I was talking to him,' she said, giving me another jab, this time in the ribs.

'Ow!' I said. 'Stop that.'

The drunk wasn't having any of it. He looked like a man who'd been out at sea for too long and needed this catch. This was one fish he was going to reel in, whether she liked it or not.

He wasn't the only one. The place was filled with thirsty eyes all fighting for the same trickle of city women. It was the only bar in Montauk open late, so everyone came here, fishermen and city weekenders all.

Nylon fishing nets and broken boat parts and fibreglass

sculptures of marlin hung from wood-panelled walls in a low green navigation light. There was a pool table and a jukebox. Legends about semen were written in the washroom. It couldn't be long before a fight broke out. The tension was already tighter than a fishing line drawing in tuna.

'Let's dance, darling!' the drunk said, suddenly picking Catherine up and swinging her around on her heels as two men cheered from their bar stools. I didn't relish the idea of saving her so I turned to the bartender, a startlingly orange woman with a freckled neck, to order another beer. Suddenly there was a squeal which made the jukebox stop so I, along with everyone else, turned to see what was going on.

'Touch me like that again, Patrick O'Reilly,' Catherine said, holding the drunk's nose so tight between two nails that he was bent double, 'and I'll do worse things than just scar your fat ugly horn. Got it?'

O'Reilly nodded submissively and Catherine let go, revealing two throbbing crescents of raw blood. As the music swelled back into the room and the whoops of laughter rang out to the chatter of pool balls in the rack, she levelled her look at me and said: 'I want an explanation.'

'What for?'

'Very funny. How the fuck do you know my name?'

I shrugged. 'Do I know your name?'

'Don't play games. I want to know and I want to know right now how you know my name. Unless, of course, you fancy a nose job like Patrick's.'

God, I thought to myself in that instant, as the light came through her hair from behind, her pale Irish cheekbones glowing, her green eyes firing, her tender lips trembling – you are so beautiful!

'Oh, it's easy,' I said mockingly. 'I can read minds.'

'Listen, I've had enough of your shit for one day. Now, I'm not going ask you again. How do you know my name? Did

Tommy send you? Did he tell you to say that to me? Is this some kind of sick joke or do you usually spend your Saturdays playing mind games with helpless women you meet on the train?'

'Helpless?' I said, looking at Patrick O'Reilly, who was nursing his nose in the corner with ice from someone else's Jack Daniel's.

'Don't change the subject.'

'Don't worry, I won't,' I said, starting to move.

I squeezed my way through hot bodies to the door. The air outside was clean and cold and salty. I could hear the bells of boats and the thump of hulls against the wharf. My head cleared enough for me to breathe again.

Then, just as I thought I was clear of the fog and smoke, I heard a foamy head of bar sounds rush me from behind. I was about to turn round to defend myself when it suddenly stopped, just short of me, with an abrupt bang of the door.

'Where the fuck are you going?'

'None of your business,' I replied, without turning, still walking.

'Back home to your girlfriend?'

I didn't take the bait. Footsteps danced against the tarmac and then I felt the tight pull of her hand in the crook of my elbow. She span herself in front of me.

'Why are you running away from me?'

'I just want to be left alone.'

'No, you don't.'

'How do you know? Are you reading my mind again?' I said, with a drunken sneer.

'Why did you say what you did?'

'When?'

'You know goddamned well when. At the station. After I got in the cab.'

'I don't know.' I sighed. 'It just came into my head. I'm sorry. I didn't mean to offend you.'

I could see her jaw working hard against the emotion. 'Why are you doing this to me?'

'Doing what?'

'Just when I thought I was over him. Just when I thought I could move again. Jesus, you're the first guy I've had the guts to go up to since he left and you had to go and say a thing like that. Why would you do that? Why would you throw that in my face? Is it something the whole town knows? I mean, Christ . . . '

I watched her claw her hands through her hair and realized with horror what I had done. In my moment of arrogance, in my moment of egotistical stupidity, I had cast this.

Without thinking, without any consideration for why I might be hearing those specific words, her lover's last, I had simply spat them at her, like some ruthless, evil reflection that wasn't fair, that wasn't kind, just unflinching in its stare.

Those words, so old and yet they still rang so loudly, echoing and vibrating their way through her essence, her being, her mind. They were all I could hear when I tuned in.

How long had I been aware of its power? And yet here I was, looking at the damage it could cause. I saw her tearing herself apart all over again. I saw her going back, way back to the beginning of her nightmare, and reliving all its misery.

All because of me. I had done this. It was my fault.

'Come on,' I said quietly, taking her arm. 'I'll walk you home.'

'**S**o it was love at first sight, then?'
'Sound. Love at first sound.'

'Yeah, I can see that.' Joan smiled.

She was doing her nails, resting a wrist against my sun-soaked thigh, arching her fingers into each custard-yellow brushstroke.

'And it wasn't exactly the first time. I'd kind of had my eye on her all summer.'

'But it was the first time the two of you talked, wasn't it?'

'Yeah,' I said quietly. 'It was.'

'So there you go. But tell me, Joe, didn't you feel like you were picking up where the last guy left off? Sounds to me like she was still in love with . . . what was his name again?'

'David.'

'Yeah, David,' she said absent-mindedly before hissing: 'Damn!'

She reached for the nail-polish remover on the bedside table and shook it like someone with a physical handicap. She couldn't unscrew it.

'Here, can you do this?'

'Isn't that the way for a lot of people?' I said, taking the bottle from her. I was already much better.

'Sometimes. I'm just wondering, wouldn't it have been better to let her love you for just you? Maybe let her get to know you first, and then let her in on your secret.'

'What difference would that have made?' I said, handing her back the bottle.

'Thanks,' she said, dabbing remover on the infected scar across her knuckle. 'I dunno, Joe. I'm just asking.' She took a tissue and wiped the wound clean away. 'Aren't we trying to figure out why things didn't work out between you two after Jimmy died?'

'I thought we were talking about everything that happened after Jimmy died. Catherine was only a part of it.'

'A big part.'

'OK, a big part but there was other stuff besides.'

'Like what?'

'Like my job.'

'OK, then. Why did they fire you?'

'They didn't fire me.'

'Sorry. Extended leave. Why did they give you extended leave?'

'Well, things started happening.'

'What kind of things?'

'Bad things. After Jimmy, I lost control. I couldn't stop it. I couldn't turn it off. I couldn't filter. Everything started to come at me all at once. Everyone's head inside mine. Anyone I came within fifty metres of, I could hear. The noise was unbearable. It took over. I couldn't move for the headaches. Going outside became impossible. Work was out of the question. The only place I got any relief was in the bath, underwater, away from everyone. I just had to stay away from people. It was the only way.'

'Is that why you drove Catherine away?'

'Don't you see? I didn't have a choice. She was inside my head all the time. I could hear everything. I knew everything. I knew how she blamed me for Jimmy. I knew how she hated me. She thought I'd done it, that somehow I was to blame. She hated herself for choosing me. She hated me for taking away the one thing that could make her truly happy. It was like you said; she never really loved me. I was just the guy picking up the love scraps David left behind. You only fall in love once. After you've crashed, you're so damaged you never really soar again, not truly, not innocently, not with the real abandon of that first time. There's only one true love in any person's life and it's the first. David was hers. She was mine. I let go when I met her. But she'd already flown. While I was rocketing, she was limping along behind me. I saw it, I saw it all. Everything that went on in her mind – from the numb silences to the black rages. I just couldn't get her out of my head.'

'Joe? Joe? Please, Joe, don't do this. Please, will you let me in? Just for a minute. Please, Joe. I swear I won't touch you. Please. Just let me help you. I want to help. Joe?'

'Go. A. Fucking. WAAYYYYYYYY!'

How am I here? I can't take this much longer. He hates me. I can't bear the way we're trapped in this house. What is this . . .

I took another deep breath and plunged under the water. I felt it fill my ears.

Glug, glug, glug . . .

I lay still in the warmth and the wet. I could feel my eyelids pruning. My body slipped and slimed within the enamel bowl. I was a pale, tender, marinated slab of flesh, suspended in my flotation tank, the only place I was safe.

I could feel sleep coming, my body slowly letting go and my mind falling not quite silent but much muted. I could hear only the tone of her in here but thankfully not the words. If she went away like I asked her to then I could have real peace.

But she was stubborn. She wouldn't let go. She wouldn't let me sleep. She was worried I might drown. I had to admit, it was a possibility. Would that really be so bad?

There was the sound of my gasp and then air filling my lungs and the splash of water against the grey stone tiles of the bathroom floor . . .

. . . his tiny toes. The nails even grew. I clipped them that one time. He survived long enough for that. God, how my body aches for him. I just want to hold him again. Just one last time. Please, Jimmy. Come back. Don't leave me here, all alone with this. I can't do it.

Glug, glug, glug . . .

This time I would try. All I had to do was suck in the water. I opened my eyes. The world was a blur. I tried through my nose first. A small tester. I felt the water burn in the bridge and down the back of my throat but I seized up quicker than a clam.

That wasn't going to work.

I would have to do it fast. One short, sharp inhalation. I was already running out of breath. Was the fear eating up my air? My heart was thumping. Do it! Just do it. Go on. Take a breath. Take it in. I opened my mouth. One, two, three . . .

I vomited myself out of the water. The force of life surged up from my gut and threw me out and over the edge of the bath, my arms flailing against the sides. I caught myself, retching and coughing and crying.

'JOE! WHAT'S GOING ON IN THERE? JOE? ANSWER ME!'

Oh my God, what's he done? He's killing himself. Jesus Christ. Get a grip. Catherine! 911. OK. Quick. Telephone. Where is it? 911, 911, 911, 9 . . . 1 . . .

She faded away. At long last. My headache thumped louder than ever. I don't think my mind could take that final assault. It wasn't the kind of head that could starve itself of oxygen. It was the kind of head that needed to be smashed in.

Yes. I could see that now. My brain had an ulcer. It needed a hot iron driven through. It needed to be cauterized. It felt the same way an ulcer on the gum feels. It needed to be burnt, burst, ripped out. The throbbing sore needed the pain. That was the only way to exorcize it.

I could drive something into it. Something hard and sharp to get through, into the matter. It could enter through the temple.

I looked around the bathroom. I saw the bathrobe hanging. I saw the chrome hook. It was beautiful. I climbed out of the bath. I took the bathrobe down.

Too high.

I looked at the toilet. If I steadied one foot against it and one foot against the edge of the bath, I could probably get the angle I needed.

'Joe? Darling? Are you all right? I've called for an ambulance. They're on their way.'

The sound of her slammed into my chest and threw me back into the bathroom mirror. It smashed and splintered into my back. I felt a shard slice me. The pain. In my head. I couldn't move. I fell to my knees. Please go away, Catherine. Please go away. I can't take this.

'Please.'

'My, you sure were one sick puppy.'

'Hmm.'

'No wonder they took you away. Men in white coats, huh? Poor Joe.'

'Yup.'

It was quiet in the amputee ward that night, for a change. Joan had told me why. They'd cut out a guy's throat. Cancer.

'What was it like?'

'What?'

'The asylum.'

'Nice and quiet. They gave me my very own padded cell. It was perfect.'

I could see nurses' hats through the ward doors, moving in the lights.

'Did they know about your hearing?'

'Not at first. They just thought I was some guy trying to smash his own head in.'

'Did they find out?'

'Eventually.'

'Then what happened?'

'They treated me for schizophrenia.'

'They thought you were imagining it?'

'They said I'd suffered a breakdown after the death of my son. In a way, I think they were right. I think the emotional strain of losing Jimmy made me lose control of my hearing.'

'Didn't you try and prove it to them? Why didn't you show them – like you showed Catherine?'

'They gave me a lot of drugs to stop it. They said the voices would go in time.'

'And did they?'

'Yes. Eventually, I lost my ability.'

'How did that make you feel?'

'Sleepy. Those drugs were strong.'

'And Catherine? What about her?'

I turned and tried to look for Joan but it was dark that night, her brown skin had melted into the blue. Where was the bedside light?

'We decided it was best not to see each other any more. She went away.'

'Where to?'

'I don't know. I didn't ask.'

'Don't you miss her?'

'Every second of every day.'

'You never thought about trying to find her, after you got out?'

'No. We tore each other apart in those months after Jimmy died. My breakdown was just the last of it. We were finished.'

'So how did you come to take the job as a super?'

'They had us doing DIY workshops at the hospital. I got good. When the city charities came round looking to recruit patients ready for reintegration I applied for handyman positions. After a few months they placed me at 444.'

'You didn't consider going back to your old job?'

'No. There wasn't a point to my ambition any more. I just wanted a simple life. I didn't want the nice car, the nice house, the bills. I didn't have anyone to look after except myself and I didn't need much. Besides, I'd lost my hearing. I wouldn't have been much use to them.'

'But what about a new family? What about meeting someone else? Didn't you want to try again for that kind of life? Being a super – gee, it sounds . . . lonely.'

I thought it was funny for Joan to say that, considering all the visits I'd got from folks in the building. Nearly all of them had come, even Morgan, though she'd wanted to talk to me about the Co-op's medical-insurance policy mostly. Frank had organized a collection from the block and with it he'd bought all kinds of stuff, like books and flowers and a couple of new pairs of pyjamas. That was nice. Mrs Xhiu had given me a Bible and told me that I was in her prayers. Ben and Mandy had come without Billy because babies weren't allowed in the ward. Mandy's mother was finally in town looking after him. Apparently he had hair now. They showed me a picture. I managed not to cry. Anna-lise was much stronger. Henry was begging her back but she wasn't having him. And Mike just got promoted, though Juan didn't know to what. He just liked the sexy new uniform.

'I like being a super,' I said. 'I get to live with all these people and look after them and do simple things for them and just make sure they're all OK. I like helping them out. They're my family now.'

'As long as you're happy, Joe, that's what counts.'

It was only when she said that that I realized I was happy and that maybe it was because I hadn't heard the signal in a long while, not since coming to hospital, not since leaving 444. That made sense. Out of range, out of mind, so to speak. In fact, I'd pretty much forgotten about it up to that point, and that made me wonder what that might mean. I was definitely glad I couldn't hear it, that I was free of it. It meant there was more space in my head for my own thoughts, my own memories, my own feelings. I almost felt like myself again, or at least, the person I used to be.

How long would my freedom last?

Frank watched Mack talking to himself from a distance. He hadn't meant to spy on him. Things had just worked out that way because the nurse at the ward desk – who reminded Frank of a stage seamstress he used to know (perhaps it was the half-moon glasses and petite exactness of her gestures) – had told him to wait while she printed out the release forms, before disappearing behind a door for half an hour.

Not wanting to miss her when she got back and then get forgotten, Frank hovered outside the ward, looking through the windows in the doors to make sure that Mack was ready to go. He was in a hurry.

Mack was dressed and was sitting upright in a wheelchair looking out of the window, the words PROPERTY OF ST MARTIN'S painted crudely in white on the back of the leather. His bed was tightly made up and his bag was packed and sitting on a table beside him. At first Frank didn't notice anything odd about his behaviour as he peered through the latticed window and he was about to turn back to trill the bell on the desk to hurry things along when he saw Mack throw his head back and laugh.

'Leave the building? I can't do that!' he half-shouted, laughing some more.

Frank couldn't remember the last time he'd seen Mack laugh like that, if ever. For some reason, it worried him. He moved to the other window in the door to his right to get a better view and saw that Mack was grinning and his jaw was jumping. He opened the ward door slowly and stepped inside.

'I'm only safe in the basement,' he said softly now.

He paused, as if in conversation.

'But there's so much more to talk about. What about the message? What about the collective?'

Frank took a step closer, wanting to see his face.

'I'm not ready. I'm scared they're still going to make me.'

He moved another quiet step, feeling himself intrude.

'Don't go, please, Joan, I . . . '

Mack fell suddenly still. He didn't give an indication, but Frank sensed that Mack knew he was there. Frank wanted to say hello but something held him back. He scanned the rest of the ward. One man was asleep in the corner. There was another man reading a book. No one seemed to see him or be taking any notice of Mack's strange behaviour. Everything was quiet. Mack was motionless. He almost felt as if he had imagined the episode. Very quietly, very slowly, he stepped backwards and out of the ward.

'Mind!' the nurse said loudly behind him as he stepped through the door.

Frank jumped on the volume and threw a hand to his chest.

'You scared me!'

'Here are the papers for you to sign,' the nurse said through thin lips. Frank noticed a shadow of blonde hair on her cheeks.

'Thank you.'

'I'll send someone up to wheel him down. Then he can go.'

'No,' Frank said too quickly. The nurse's eyes widened. 'I mean, don't worry about that, we'll manage.'

The nurse shook her head and turned away to a telephone on the desk. 'Hospital regulations.'

Frank mouthed a curse before catching his breath and moving to the desk to sign the release forms.

'So he's gonna be OK, then?' Frank started. 'He's ready to come home?'

'That's what the doctor says.'

'And work? When can he start work?'

'Not for another month.'

Frank grimaced. 'He's not going to like that much. Sitting around all day, I mean.'

'Yeah, well, that's what you get when someone stabs you in the chest with a four-inch knife.'

'So everything's definitely all right? It's just that I was watching him a moment ago and he seemed a little . . . disorientated.'

The nurse turned and glanced sharply up at Frank over her glasses, her eyes a dull grey.

'How so?'

'He seemed to be talking to himself.'

The nurse squinted at Frank, sharpening her look. 'I thought you were a relative.'

'Me?' Frank replied. 'No, I'm not a relative. He's the super in our building.'

'Are you authorized to collect him?'

'Of course. I'm on the Board. He lives with us. As far as I know, Mack doesn't have any relatives.'

'I see,' the nurse said, turning away to step around to the back of the desk. 'Well, I'm surprised you don't already know about his condition.'

'Condition?'

'He sleep-talks. Doesn't stop. He's been keeping the whole hospital awake with his midnight speeches, daytime ones too.'

'Sleep-talks?'

'You can have an entire conversation with him if you can make any sense of it. Get him going and you'll have hours of entertainment talking about the message and something he keeps calling "the collective".'

'Wow. I never knew Mack slept-talked.'

'Yeah, well. I shouldn't read too much into it.'

'OK, then, I won't. Thanks.'

'I'll tell you one thing, though.'

'What?'

'You're wrong about him not having any relatives,' the nurse said. 'He's got a wife. Her name is Catherine.'

'Are you sure? I've never heard him mention her.'

'He talks about her a lot.'

'Wow, that's really weird. I never knew he was married.'

'He's wearing a ring.'

'Is he?'

'On his right hand.'

'But . . . '

'It's a Claddagh ring, a traditional Celtic wedding band. Some people wear them on their right hand with the crown facing out like that. It means his heart is pledged.'

'Wow. You think you know someone . . . '

'I guess,' the nurse replied before turning away.

When Frank stepped back into the ward again Mack had turned himself in the wheelchair to face him.

'Hey there, Soup. How you feeling? Ready to get out of this place?'

Despite his injury, Mack looked better than usual, but that might have been because he was wearing a new shirt Mrs Xhiu had brought for him and the staff had taken the trouble to shave him. Frank was used to seeing a field of burnt stubble across his face and neck.

'Are you going to an audition?' he asked.

Frank looked down at himself, down the length of his body, and noticed his crisply ironed white shirt, jeans and smart dark shoes.

'That obvious, huh?'

The super nodded.

'I've got to be there in an hour. It's a small production on the Lower East Side. Two nights a week, nothing major, just two nights.'

'You'll get the part,' he said.

'That's what you always say.'

'This time it's true.'

Even though I'd readied myself, I still wasn't prepared for the flood of sound as the electric doors of the hospital slid open and we moved out into the street. The world was much louder than I remembered it. Maybe it was just that I'd always been careful to go out only during the tender times of day, dawn or late dusk, for example. As a rule, I definitely never ventured outside during rush hour.

The effect of the volume was disorientating. The sights of the street swam before my eyes in syncopated rhythm with their own violent issues, off-kilter. I saw a yellow taxi lurching on its suspension and a light changing. I heard the anger in someone's shouting before the bleeping of the traffic signal leapt like a morning alarm. I caught sight of an ambulance firing up its lights and knew then what was about to happen. But before I had the chance to say anything, the yell of the taxi's horn arrived and I found myself pinned into the wheelchair.

A wave of nausea came over me and I was glad that I was sitting down. I might have collapsed otherwise. I watched as Frank bent down towards me and I saw his mouth moving but I couldn't make out the words because my hearing was off, the range in volume was too vast.

I watched as the driver opened the taxi door and I felt myself being lifted by two sets of arms. I thought that I was going to make it OK but then the ambulance siren shrieked and I found the air catch in my throat and close itself over my heart like a hand, squeezing. For a moment it felt like my life was shuddering to a halt.

I can't recall exactly what happened next but they must have lowered me into the taxi because the next thing I knew the door was slamming in my ear and the whole world became suddenly and wonderfully muted. The discomfort and nausea fell simply and instantly away, the heavenly way you wish it to in the height of distress.

For a while I was so happy with relief that I even found myself able to enjoy the beginning of the journey home. At least, I wasn't afraid to look as we travelled and I found myself catching sight of a city I had deliberately not laid eyes on for nearly twenty-eight years. Hank's, three blocks south of VanVanVane Street, was the furthest I usually went.

On the Upper East Side, travelling from St Martin's, I was pleased to see that a lot of things hadn't changed. There weren't many new buildings I didn't recognize and the area had the same feel of elegant and established wealth I remembered it for. I think it had something to do with the billiard-felt green in the turreted roofs and the large blocks of iron-grey stone they used to hang the grand entrances with. Of course, I noticed some new stores with new names selling new things but I saw them for what they were, facades that rarely remained.

Closer to Central Park I started to see some differences; like the sidewalks. They looked cleaner, but that might just have been the cold. There was still a chill in the air even though spring had started. I saw that a magnolia tree had lost its blossom to a late frost, its magnificent cream tulips now brown husks perched precariously between eye-shaped leaves.

We took the road across the park and I remember vaguely wishing it had snowed as I looked at the Day-Glo-dressed rollerbladers and earphoned joggers making their rounds. I watched dogs walk their people. There was a man sitting on a bench under a tree reading the *New York Times*, which he'd folded into quarters. Turning the page was a matter of origami.

At the lights, an old joker in red, white and blue rolled past on a bicycle adorned with plastic windmills and tinsel. There was a tinny boom box strapped to the back sounding out the

Rocky theme tune too slow. It gave the impression that he needed to pedal faster.

We exited at 66th and Eighth and the traffic on the West Side was worse, which gave me more time to take things in but made Frank anxious about making it to his audition on time. I saw that a lot of people were smoking. Women in officewear wore sneakers. I noticed that certain shops came in rows, as if they'd been stencilled on block by block: Manhattan Health World, Pharmafree, Latte and Lights, Bank Corp. There were a lot of cranes, especially in former car parks. The city seemed to be an erection of scaffolding and excavated red holes.

At 57th and Ninth there was gridlock. I saw three black kids banging on old plaster buckets with drumsticks while people stood and watched. I saw an ad of a man hanging upside down, which covered an entire building. In his lowest shirt button I could see a window with the light on and the silhouette of someone moving inside.

Frank was very anxious now. He asked the driver how long it would take to get to the meat-packing district. The taxi man said it would be OK once we reached the West Side Highway. Frank then asked how long it would take to reach the Lower East Side. The driver couldn't say. Frank turned to face me.

'I'm going to miss my audition,' he said, grim-faced.

I looked at him carefully. There was something very fine about him. He had a presence, a stage confidence, as if he knew his own character and could say the lines well. I told him we could go straight there if he wanted.

'What will you do, Mack? I might be a while.'

After several minutes of my reassuring him, he finally agreed. The driver turned east on 57th and then south on Broadway, the ancient Native American trail snaking itself through the branches of the grid system.

It wasn't long before we reached Times Square.

Neon lights fluttered and flashed like cards in a croupier's hands. I spotted hearts, the jack of clubs, an ace of spades. Electronic ticker tapes trilled our score in the sky as we thundered and lurched and bounced against the round, pinging mushrooms on the pinball slide. I watched orange words race up block-length straights and melt on the corners as they took them at the same, reckless, G-force speed. A stock fraction lapped itself. I saw that King Kong had been stripped down and waxed and was now glued to the side of a building chicane wearing tight underwear. Women with small breasts stared acidly at their camera lenses, while some of them even danced on steel stilts like cardboard cut-out can-can girls at the rodeo. Below, in the throng, there was a naked man in a cowboy hat and cowboy boots playing a guitar. Televisions watched us through their pixel-pointed rectangular spectacles, which somehow lent them an air of academic authority. The gleam of metallic chrome was everywhere, mirrored and round and reflecting everything in distorted circus-images, the arcade game on constant multi-ball function. Cartoon characters with their eyeballs on springs tried at several points to chop my tail off, all the time laughing with manic hilarity. I saw the letters WB hanging in the sky like a tablet – a drug, or a stone bearing the Holy Commandments.

There seemed no logic to this tangle of fairground themes other than a loose idea of entertainment. I don't know how long we were trapped in there. It seemed like an hallucinatory eternity, a cosmic instant. I lost the memory of New York I had worked so hard over all the years to preserve. This was the reason I had never gone out. I had never wanted to see all this. This was not the Times Square I remembered. I had never been here, this wasn't a city I had been to, I didn't live *here*. I lived somewhere else. I lived in a different New York, *we* lived in a different New York.

And now I couldn't pretend any more. Not even vaguely. I had opened my eyes completely this time. Catherine was gone.

Gone. Just like the New York I'd known. I should never have agreed to this journey.

I hid my despair by pressing my face against the taxi window, hiding my silence. I did not want Frank to see how sad I felt. He had his own problems. I wasn't going to tell him my sentimental story. I could already see the sympathy and I didn't want it. So I kept my head turned away.

I saw now: the Empire State Building without Catherine and me on top of it, just swimming with people; the Korean district, which was quieter, a small oasis of secret chefs; the Flatiron Building, with its confluence of city winds; Union Square and the Farmers' Market smelling of hens, a long line of numbers speeding above it like a countdown or a machine estimating the national deficit (it was actually a piece of art, I heard Frank tell the driver); over 14th Street and down into Greenwich Village, beautiful people starting to emerge like ants at the edge of their nest; into Soho and the smaller streets, the men turning to look at women, the women turning to look at strollers; left into Little Italy just before hitting the cheap watch and Chinese chaos of Canal Street, past the rooftops designed for getaways in classic gangster movies; and finally, into Alphabet City, between the breezeblock Projects and into the big wind coming off the Williamsburg Bridge blowing Hassids in from Brooklyn on wide-brimmed hats and overcoat tails the size of sails.

The taxi stopped.

I watched Frank get out and step across the street to a small hidden theatre in the side of an old tenement block. He turned to face me before going inside.

'Wish me luck!' he shouted.

*S*he is *fucking beautiful*, the taxi driver thought in a matter-of fact Russian accent, staring at a passer-by. *I would like very much to fuck her. What, old man? What are you fucking looking at? Just because you are too old for fucking beautiful women, my friend. Me? I fuck beautiful women all of the time. There are so many lonely women in this city. They get into the back of my taxi and they talk to me. They tell me how sad they are. How hard it is to find love in this city. Anyone who falls in love here does it in spite of New York, they do it against the odds, that's what everyone says. No one falls in love here. They just fuck and then find something better. That time a woman asked me to stop the taxi so I could fuck her in the back of the car. I did that on Riverside Drive. Three women have asked me in the last month to come up to their apartment. One of them I fucked in the ass. I have had sex with two women at the same time. I have had sex with three women. I have fucked all of them. I don't like doing it all the time. I don't want to fuck all of these women. But they ask me. And this job. It gives me stress. There are so many assholes in New York City. Everybody is an asshole in New York City. They are all walking upside down with their assholes up in the sky. Talking shit. And the days are too long. Last week I worked more than one hundred hours. What kind of life is that? It will be better when I get my own medallion. I have saved thirty-four thousand dollars. Soon I'll have enough to go to the bank for that loan. Fucking medallions, three hundred and fifty thousand dollars, can you believe that? Harry told me that in his time they used to cost a couple of thousand dollars maximum. Now they cost more than his house. Fucking crazy life. Still, it is better than my last job. Air-traffic control. Now that was a stressful job. I would rather be a taxi driver. At least I fuck all of these beautiful women. And . . . oh yes, here comes another one now. Look at this bitch. Look at those tits. I would like to suck them. I wonder* *who this freak in the back is. Why does he keep looking in the rear-view mirror for my eyes. I don't like him. Maybe he knows I want to fuck this bitch. Maybe he knows I'm going to fuck this slut. Maybe he wants to watch me do it. Want to watch me fuck this little girl, is that it, old man? Is that what you want? I bet she is a nasty little whore.*

'Touch her and I'll cut out your throat.'

I watched the taxi driver's shoulders tense inside his shirt. He threw his eyes at me in the rear-view mirror like a bottle against a wall. Miraculously, nothing shattered.

'What?' he said.

'You heard me.'

The taxi driver turned in his seat and thrust his head through the rectangular opening in the divider.

'You are threatening me?'

'Yes.'

The driver fumbled with one hand for his small leather purse on the passenger seat.

'Why?'

'If you don't stop raping women I'm going to tell the police. I know your name, I know your medallion number.'

The driver managed to squeeze two fingers through an opening in the zipper. He could feel the butt of his small gun. Using his fingers like scissors, he prised the zipper open.

'You are crazy, old man.'

'I can hear what you're thinking. I know who you are. I know what you've been doing.'

The driver managed to get a good grip on his gun. He started to shake the purse away. He fingered for the safety.

'Stop now,' I warned. 'Then Harry doesn't need to know.'

The driver froze.

'What?'

'Remember everything he's done for you. He was the one that recommended you to the taxi company, found you a place to stay, helped you get settled. I know everything. If you stop now, I won't tell him. He doesn't have to know about what you've been doing.'

The driver was shaking. His face had lost its blood. There was sweat in the air. I could see his heart leap-frogging across his chest. He didn't know where to put his eyes. He was still pawing at the gun but it was just a drowning man's straw now. All he could feel was the wet. That, and the strange light between us. I'd seen all this before. My hearing often affected people this way.

The taxi door opened.

'That's it, I'm done.'

The taxi driver jerked and looked at Frank as he fell into the back of the cab.

'How did it go?' I asked.

He shrugged. 'Hard to say.'

That was the first time in a long time I'd picked up such a strong signal. What was happening to me? First the city and now this! I found it hard to believe it was all just a coincidence. What were the chances of picking a cab driver with a mind on fire? OK, maybe they weren't that slim. There had to be lots of crazy people in New York, lots of rapists, lots of loud signals I needed to avoid.

After all, wasn't that the *real* reason for my not going out? I'd go crazy just walking down the street, hearing all the screams and the ranting and the raving going on inside each person's head, each time I passed or came into contact or the close vicinity.

Seeing the things inside that man's mind terrified the living hell out of me. I could see now very clearly why I kept indoors, why I tried to avoid contact with people I didn't know. There was too much depravity in this world. You can't even imagine what it was like to look at it, to actually see it from the thinking. It was real-life hell.

I promised myself to not go out again. It was too dangerous out here in the world. I'd lose my mind. I just couldn't get over the strength of that taxi driver's signal, how loud and clear it had come through. Was it him or was it me? I'd seen black minds like his before but never in such detail, never with such vicious clarity.

What had happened to me since taking the job as the super, what had happened since I'd started listening to everyone in the building, recording their stories?

It seemed possible that I'd heightened my abilities, honed my senses and now I was even more alert than when I'd started. Maybe that was how I'd come to see them in places beyond the building. Maybe it was *because* I'd learnt how to follow them outside. Tracking them that way had developed my sense. And to think that things had been getting out of control before.

What was I going to do? I felt trapped. I couldn't leave 444 even if I wanted. I couldn't be out here, I couldn't survive in this outside world. Not with all this insanity. Maybe I could get myself to the countryside. Somewhere quiet, somewhere secluded. Would I even be able to make the journey without my head exploding?

I considered suicide again. It had been years since I had last done that. The thought of it made me fear that it was me who was mad, not the world, just like the doctors at the asylum had said.

But I dismissed those thoughts quickly. I knew the truth. Too much had happened for me in one day, that was all. I couldn't cope with all this. It was too much. Life was beating me today, the way it can happen to anyone. I felt tired. I had to get home. I needed to be where I was familiar, where I had things organized the way I like them, not too loud, not too quiet. Just right.

I looked out of the window and decided to focus only on the things that hadn't changed. I needed the reassurance, the stability, a moment of calm. I picked out all the scenes I recognized, the ones that made me feel like I'd been here before, that I'd seen all this, that nothing had really changed, that everything would be OK.

I watched the steaming manholes, the thumping vibration of the cars as they rolled. I looked at the guy with the metal trolley and the umbrella who was selling hot dogs and pretzels and coffee in *I ♥ NY* paper cups. I turned to the white sky that vaulted over the skyscrapers. I looked at the way everyone shuffled and jostled together on the sidewalk. I looked at the lights. I followed the hobos pushing shopping carts full of cans. I counted the vending machines filled with newspapers. I stared at people's faces. I concentrated on churches. I spotted signs for the subway. I absorbed the green in the dollar bills Frank took out of his wallet.

And then I saw the scaffolding. It was mounted like a terrifying work of medical science, surgical pins all over the face of my building. I must have gasped because Frank said:

'I know. It looks like a robot, doesn't it?'

Mandy noticed the pale light in the room. The days were lengthening.

She gazed down at his softly resting eyes, the portals to his perfect sleep. His eyelashes stepped like spider's legs. His skin was flawless. She stroked a cheek with the edge of one finger – softer than velvet. His mouth was shaped and gently open, like the entrance to a wonderful cave. She wanted to shrink herself and captain an expedition over the ridge of that flushed red, lower lip and venture inside that toothless place.

He was the most beautiful thing she had ever seen – a work of art. Mandy wondered whether everyone could see it – they might have just been saying so.

She suspected that her marvel was merely the product of hormones. She could feel them coursing through her system, making her love her child with heart-crushing intensity. She wondered if, without their spell, she'd even care. Parenting was so hard, it was such a sacrifice. Maybe she'd just throw the baby away. Without the love, there wouldn't be a good reason to keep it.

It seemed a clever trick of nature – the addition of this love potion, the casting of beauty into the eye of the parent – because it was in feeling the beauty that the baby became hers.

Mandy wasn't truly responsible for Billy's beauty – she knew that.

But she felt as if she was. She felt responsible. She felt the pride of someone bestowed a great honour, one that exceeds them, like someone taking high office.

Mandy was a mother. No one could take that from her now.

And in motherhood, she had fulfilled herself, the meaning of her being. She was humbled by that. She questioned if she truly deserved it. It seemed as if she had done so little to earn it. It had just been given to her.

'The monthly report if you will, please, Mr Treasurer,' Morgan said, beaming. She couldn't help herself. She was in a playful mood.

'Yes,' Ben started, noticing for the first time something different in Morgan's appearance. She seemed somehow . . . brighter. Then it clicked. It was her teeth. They were dazzlingly white. 'As most of you know, we've spent the last few weeks putting the company accounts into Quicken,' Ben continued, shifting his gaze away from the sunshine of Morgan's mouth, which was incandescent now against her dark skin. 'It hasn't been as straightforward as we would have liked but now there's a clear and easy way to manage the building finances. Each month,' he handed Mrs Xhiu a small pile of papers, 'I'll be giving out print-outs of our asset/liability profile, the current account, interest accrual on CDs, so on and so forth, so we don't have to go through the details during Board meetings. You can look at them in your spare time and, if you have any questions, you can come see Morgan or me, and we'll be happy to help.'

'Excellent, excellent,' Morgan said as she received the papers from Garry.

'Which means we have more time to discuss important things . . . like my going to the bank!'

'Yes, how did that go, Ben?' Morgan said gleefully. 'Do tell.'

Frank opened his mouth at Anna-lise, stuck his tongue out and moved two fingers into the back of his throat.

'Well, the good news is we're all set for the loan. The money should be in our account any minute now.'

'Good. I've started to get calls from Aaron,' Morgan said. 'He wants the next payment before they start work on the extension frame.'

'Already?' Mike asked. 'That was quick.'

'I know,' Morgan replied. 'The work is proceeding much faster than I had imagined. Aaron's now saying he expects to be finished by July.'

'Amazing,' Mike said.

'They must be worried about the penalty clauses I put into the contract,' Morgan said.

'Yeah,' Mike agreed. 'That was good thinking.'

Anna-lise, Garry and Frank all looked at one another.

'Please, Ben, carry on,' Morgan said.

'Well, there's really only one thing left for me to report and it's bad news, I'm afraid. I've crunched the numbers and come up with what I think is a suitable maintenance increase.'

People looked down at the things they were holding between their fingers – pens, paperclips, air – and fiddled.

'In order to service the loan and raise enough cash over the long term to repay the debt completely, I feel that maintenance rates have to be doubled.'

Anna-lise giggled. Frank looked as if he were looking out over a wide-open space. Mrs Xhiu took hold of Mike's hand. Someone sneezed.

'Stop playing games, Ben,' Garry said.

'I'm not playing, Garry.'

'How can you expect people to pay double maintenance?'

'Well, maintenance rates here are already very low, half, in fact, compared to the city average.'

'Yes,' Garry said. 'But that's because this is an Assisted Housing building. That means housing for the poor. That's the whole point of the place. That's why the maintenance is low. So that poor people can afford to live here.'

'Well, the thing is, Garry,' Ben tried, 'it's not a building for poor people any more.'

'Excuse me?' Garry replied, sneering.

'A lot of the original tenants have moved out.'

'Mrs Xhiu?' Garry said, turning to face her.

'Yes.'

'When did you move in?'

'Nineteen seventy-eight.'

'Are you an original tenant, then?'

'I paid two hundred dollars for my apartment. Same as everyone else.'

'And Diva?'

'She bought the week before me, the exact same day as Daniel, in fact.'

'And what will happen to you if the maintenance gets doubled, Mrs Xhiu? What will you do? Where will you go?' Garry started to sound shrill.

'All right, Garry, thank you very much. You've made your point,' Morgan intercepted.

'I'm not sure I have, actually, Morgan,' Garry replied, managing to look at her. 'This place was never meant for yuppies. It's a state organization, a charity, something designed to help people who can't help themselves. It was never meant to be a business. Maintenance rates here can't be compared to "city averages" and other bullshit. This whole asset/liability shareholder corporate capitalist thing has gone way too far. Totally out of hand. I veto your proposal, Ben,' Garry said, standing up now and driving a finger into the air. 'All those with me say aye!'

'AYE!' Mrs Xhiu said, almost throwing the hand that was holding Mike's into the air but not quite making it under the weight of his muscle. It fell limply back onto his thigh. He smiled gently at her.

'Garry—' Morgan started.

'No, it's OK, Morgan,' Ben interrupted. 'I can answer Garry's question.'

'I'm not sure I asked one,' Garry replied, slowly sitting back down.

'I accept your point about the roots of the building and how it started but you have to realize that the building finances have not been managed that way for nearly two decades now. This building has been a commercial entity for some time and the people that made it that way were the original tenants, not me. If they had run it according to the rules laid down by the City then we wouldn't be in this position. In fact, most of us wouldn't even be living here.'

'I don't understand,' Garry said.

'When the City sold the building – gave it, really – to the tenants, there were rules. For example, no one was allowed to sublet. And a flip-tax was introduced to prevent people from selling.'

'We still have a flip-tax,' Anna-lise offered. 'Fifteen per cent of the profit from the sale of G1 to you and Mandy went back into the building, the remainder into Daniel's estate.'

'I know, Anna-lise, and we should be thankful for that otherwise the building would be in even more difficulty than it is now,' Ben replied. 'But the flip-tax used to be a hundred per cent, then it was ninety, then seventy, fifty, forty and now just fifteen. I imagine, one day, it will go altogether.'

'Really, a hundred per cent? I never knew that,' Anna-lise replied. 'I can see how that would stop people from selling.'

'The City, which was financially on its knees at the time, sold buildings like these to tenants so that it wouldn't have to subsidize their maintenance. But it didn't want the people who were benefiting from low-cost housing to sell their apartments on for profit. That's why they introduced the flip-tax. Over time, though, property laws in the City changed, allowing tenants to relax the tax. And quite a few people did sell, taking a large chunk of money with them. At the same time, no one took steps to increase maintenance rates to compensate for the corresponding decrease in building revenue – at least, not by enough.'

No one said anything.

'I guess what I'm trying to tell you is this,' Ben continued. 'Most of us aren't meant to be here. We were never meant to be living in 444, we should never have even had the opportunity to buy. If the original flip-tax rule had remained in place, then the original tenants wouldn't have sold. I don't blame the tenants. Who wouldn't sell an apartment worth five hundred thousand dollars that only cost them two hundred dollars? If anyone deserved to benefit from New York's property boom, it was the people who had to live in this neighbourhood in the seventies and eighties. It can't have been pleasant. Diva was telling me the other day about how the community set up nightly patrol groups to get the pimps and the pushers and the crack addicts off this street. It was the beginning of Community Service.'

Mrs Xhiu nodded.

On a roll, Ben continued, 'I don't even blame the City. Life in New York is very different compared to thirty years ago. Back then no one could have imagined that the city might become what it is today. People were talking about Boston or Philadelphia becoming the major eastern seaboard centre, not New York. The City couldn't even afford to collect its own trash. Now look at it. Much as you may hate it, Garry, Manhattan has become a city for those that can afford it. Low-cost housing and programmes for the poor can't exist here because there isn't even room for those who do have money. This is an island and the only thing that matters now is space – space, and the amount of money people are prepared to pay for it. I don't know about you, but when I first moved to New York I imagined myself in a loft. As it is, I can barely afford an apartment bigger than a cigarette box. You shouldn't feel too sorry for Mrs Xhiu or Diva. They're the lucky ones, they're the ones who are sitting on a goldmine.'

'Garry's right. It's corporate America all over again,' Frank said.

'They've privatized low-cost housing,' Anna-lise murmured.

'Even Project apartments are going for millions,' Mrs Xhiu added.

'Well, gee, thanks for the fascinating history lesson, Ben,' Garry said. 'We really appreciate it. But you still haven't answered my question.'

'I thought you weren't asking one.' Morgan sighed, inspecting her fingernails.

'What will Mrs Xhiu and Diva do if maintenance rates double?' Garry said, ignoring her.

'Well,' Ben breathed. 'If they can't afford to keep up the payments, then . . . '

'Say it,' Garry started. 'I dare you to say it.'

'Then they'll have to sell,' Morgan said.

Mrs Xhiu gasped. 'But where will I go? This has been my home for as long as I can remember.'

'Honey, on the amount of money you'll make selling your place you could live like a queen in the Bahamas,' Morgan said, not unkindly.

'But I don't want to live in the Bahamas. I don't want the money. I just want my home. I don't know where else to go. What do I do? I'm too old to move. Where will I go, Morgan? Please, tell me. Where will I go?'

Morgan shrugged her shoulders at her. 'Well, then you're going to have to find a way to pay the new maintenance rates. I suggest you mortgage your apartment like the rest of us.'

'Mortgage my apartment?'

'With your apartment as collateral, the bank would lend you at least a hundred thousand dollars, Mrs Xhiu,' Ben said.

'A hundred thousand dollars?'

'At least,' Morgan said.

'A hundred thousand dollars?' Mrs Xhiu repeated in a daze. 'How will I pay it back?'

'I could help set it up for you, if you like,' Ben offered, not answering her concern.

Mrs Xhiu nodded slowly.

Mike raised a hand. 'I've got a question.'

'Yes, Mike,' Morgan replied.

'Are there any plans to remove the flip-tax altogether?'

'Why do you ask?'

'It's just that Ben said he imagined it would go one day.'

'I suppose it will.'

'But we don't know when?'

'No. It won't be for a while, that's for sure.'

'Why?' Frank asked.

'Because in the event that someone did decide to sell, the building would need the revenue,' Morgan replied. 'The flip-tax raises more money more quickly than maintenance ever could.'

'So what you're saying is it's in your . . . I'm sorry . . . it's in the interests of the building for someone to sell,' Frank said.

'It always has been, Frank, you know that.'

'But it would be better for the building if, say, Mrs Xhiu sold than somebody like Ben, for example.'

Morgan levelled her look at him. 'Obviously the profit from the sale of Mrs Xhiu's would be more than Ben's. What's your point?'

'Oh, nothing. It's just interesting, that's all.'

Mike raised his hand again.

'Yes, Mike.' Morgan sighed, before adding, 'It's not school, you know.'

'Sorry. I just wanted to know, if someone were to sell tomorrow, would there still be a need to increase maintenance?'

'I think Ben's done a pretty good job of explaining why the building needs to increase maintenance.'

Ben nodded. 'Yes, but maybe not as dramatically as this. It would depend on who sold and how much flip-tax profit was made. I've made my calculations based on the assumption that no one will sell their apartment in the immediate future.'

'So, in a way, it all comes down to who sells their apartment next, then?' Mike said.

'Quite,' Morgan replied.

Everyone in the room looked at one another, waiting to see who blinked.

I woke up at 5.30 a.m. to the sound of two transsexual hookers on the corner of VanVanVane Street and Eighteenth Avenue competing to give a guy in a car a blowjob. One of them offered to do it for twenty bucks, but he decided on the other for more. The cheaper one screamed disgusting abuse at the world for four minutes after they left.

Billy cried for one minute at 5.50 and then suckled before falling back to sleep.

Morgan's alarm clock went off at 6.00.

At 6.40 the trash truck arrived, beeping, the guys talking dirty to one another. One of them commented that there were too many tins in one bag. He issued the building with a ticket.

At 6.54 parking attendants and tow trucks arrived, working fast and in tandem.

I ate breakfast at 7.15: a single piece of toast with bitter marmalade.

At 7.35 the workmen arrived. The scaffolding tubes filled with pings and the long sound of trapped metal echoes. It was like listening out for U-boats in the groaning deep.

At 7.43 a street-cleaner vehicle passed, its brushes picking up debris and removing tartar from the edge of the sidewalk.

At 7.45 a drill squealed in pain. Billy did his best to imitate it. There was a thrum of sleepy complaint throughout the building. After ten minutes, Garry shouted out of his window that if he couldn't listen to his music at night, there was no way the workmen could wake him up with a drill at seven 'each and every frickin' morning'. A workman told Garry to come down and talk like that to his face. Garry said sorry. The drilling continued.

With the exception of Diva, everyone got up between 7.45

and 8.00 and the sounds of their morning routines danced for the following hour to the cacophony of construction work: a coffee percolator bubbled as a cement mixer churned; a shower rushed while a circular saw screamed; a workman barked orders to the jingle for NY1; a labourer puffed and wheezed as the running machine started; the elevator mechanics whirred, a pulley squeaked; footsteps marched, a nail gun fired; a hammer banged, a front door slammed; a toaster popped, something heavy was dropped.

It was almost orchestral.

But I'd already decided to stick to just the facts. Just the facts.

At 9.30 there was a lull. The building had emptied and the workmen were taking their first break. It might have been the initial rush of activity that made this period seem so utterly silent. I could barely hear the workmen as they talked to one another. Their chatter evaporated in coffee-cup steam and they smothered their sentences in pastries.

Only Diva was audible, her soft, slow footsteps padding across the carpet. Focusing in on them, I was drawn back to sleep.

I woke up just after 11.30 to the squeak of the postman's trolley and the jangle of keys as he let himself into the building. He let the aluminium mailbox slam open on its own weight before jamming magazines and fat stock-market-company reports into the cubbyholes. Slim letters slid between them like waitresses between tables. The mailbox slammed again as the postman threw his own substantial weight against it and there was another jangle of keys as he secured the lock.

The workmen were taking their lunch break. Henry was tapping on his computer. Mrs Xhiu had returned from church and was listening to Reverend Jeremy on the television. Diva was turning the leaves of a novel at magazine speed.

I listened to the radio for half an hour but turned it off when I heard Mandy step out from her front door and come down to the basement.

She filled the laundry and dropped her coins and started the machine and then knocked on my door. She asked me if I was ready for lunch and presented me with an Italian from the deli. It contained three types of salami, pepper, spicy and plain; two types of ham, Parma and prosciutto; Italian sausage; two cheeses, provolone and mozzarella; rocket; sun-dried tomatoes; balsamic vinegar; olive oil; roasted peppers. She must have gone out and bought it while I was sleeping. The ingredients melted on my tongue in salty textures. I drank a glass of water with it and noticed something pleasantly metallic in the taste.

As I ate and the laundry cycle completed itself, Mandy and I talked. She asked me if I was OK and if I had everything I needed. She told me that Billy was trying to roll on his side now. He was asleep. She would take him out to Central Park later because it had stopped raining. She commiserated with me for being holed up in the basement, especially with all the noise from the workmen. She said that the job was starting to get under everyone's skin. After the initial fast progress, work seemed to be slowing. There were half as many workmen compared to the beginning and they seemed to take three times the number of breaks. Even Morgan was expressing frustration. The main worry on everyone's mind was the escalation in costs. The job had been contracted but still the price tag went up. Morgan's latest proposal was to use the future funds from the Water Board compensation package to cover the extra expense. The laundry machine buzzed. She told me to call out for her if I needed anything.

She could hear me?

At 2.30, work started again. A truck bearing a large amount of timber arrived and there was the sound of a crane hoisting it onto the scaffold platform that had been built over the sidewalk. The workmen shouted at one another.

Helmut returned to the building just after 3.00 and hurried from his apartment down into his storage area in the basement, back up to his apartment, down again, up again and then down. He seemed to be packing boxes and moving them.

At 4.00 the workmen tidied up and left.

At 4.30 Nicolette arrived and I was surprised when she stopped by my place before going up to clean Morgan's. She had heard about my accident. She had been praying for me. She said it was a shame I hadn't been able to give the police a more detailed description of my attacker. Kids like that should be put away, she said. From a large paper bag she pulled out a colourful bedcover that she'd knitted herself. Looking at my reaction she got very embarrassed and said that it hadn't been that much trouble and it was something she liked to do in her spare time and she felt especially bad seeing as she hadn't made it to the hospital to visit. She then went into a long explanation about it being spring so I probably wouldn't need it but that it might brighten up my place, which I admitted still looked sparse after the flood. She left, saying she had work to do. She promised to stop by again soon.

Someone in 443 Hanover Street started playing reggae music.

At 5.05, I heard Juan return to the building from work, five and a half hours earlier than usual. At quarter past the hour the intercom buzzed and I heard someone announce: 'It's Jay from Little Angels!'

Over the course of the following hour, food-delivery flyers arrived under the door at printing-press speed. One guy managed to get buzzed into the building by Mrs Xhiu but was caught throwing dragon-green leaflets in the corridors by Henry, who threatened to call the police if he didn't leave.

Frank and Morgan arrived home just after 7.00 and were forced to take the elevator together. Frank positioned himself at the back even though he'd have to get out first. As the doors closed I saw Frank making faces at the back of Morgan's head.

I watched Morgan catch his reflection in the elevator circuit and swivel quickly to face him. Frank composed himself but

Morgan stared at him until he felt uncomfortable enough to shrug. The elevator arrived at Frank's floor and he had to squeeze his way past. When the elevator closed, I watched Morgan take out a mobile phone from her pocket and punch the numbers.

Between 7.00 and 9.00 the building shuffled sounds like suits in a deck of cards: televisions flashed, the gym flickered to life, take-out food arrived, the laundry cycle turned. There wasn't much conversation. People seemed to just miss one another.

I ate at 9.30: a chicken jalfrezi from Kunda's Curry House that tore the roof off my mouth like a tropical storm. Afterwards, I took a shower and, for several minutes, stared in the mirror at the raw scar in my chest. Somehow, I thought it made me look younger: battle-scarred and vital.

The night exodus began at 10.00 with Mike, followed by Anna-lise, Frank, Henry and then Morgan. Helmut was the last to leave at 11.00. Ben and Mandy went to bed at 11.15. Garry got back from work at an unusually early 11.20. Mrs Xhiu went to midnight mass. Diva hadn't moved from her apartment all day.

I waited into the night for it but it didn't come.

I fell asleep around 3.00.

H enry woke up. He didn't know why, he didn't know how. It was dark. But he could hear her.

'*Wake up, Henry. It's me.*'

'Anna-lise?' he murmured, the weight of sleep still pulling on him.

'*At last!*'

'What?' he said, startling at the surface. 'Where? What time is it?'

'*Come talk to me.*'

'Where are you?'

'*In the heating pipe. The one next to your bed.*'

Henry sat up. He was a little freaked out to consider that this might just be his imagination, that he was hearing voices. He peered through the purple darkness at the pipe, suspiciously.

'Anna-lise, is that really you?'

'*Jesus, man, you sleep like a log. I've been calling and banging on this pipe for ten minutes already.*'

'Sorry,' he said, rubbing his eyes.

'*I want to talk to you.*'

'OK,' Henry said, pressing the back of his neck. 'Come down and . . . '

'*Not face to face!*'

'Oh yeah, not face to face. You don't want to see me ever again. I forgot.'

'*Shut up, Henry.*'

'I can see that this is going to be a great conversation.'

'*Will you listen for one minute?*'

'Aren't you worried that someone might hear?'

'*It's three o'clock in the morning. No one's gonna hear us, OK?*'

'I still don't see why you can't just come down. Tell you what, how 'bout I come up?'

'*NO!*'

'I'll be there in five seconds.'

'*Just stay where you are! Please, Henry, promise me you won't come up.*'

'Why?'

'*Because . . .*'

'What is it, Anna-lise?'

'*I'm drunk.*'

'So?'

'*I'm scared that if I see you I'll want to make love.*'

Henry smiled. 'And that's a bad thing?'

'*I don't want to make love to you, Henry.*'

Henry stopped smiling. 'You don't?'

'*No. Yes. I don't know.*'

'I'm glad we've sorted that out.'

'*I don't want things to go wrong again.*'

Henry let his head fall against the pipe in a mixture of exhaustion and tenderness.

'Me neither.'

There was a moment of silence. He thought he could hear her breathing.

'*Henry?*'

'Yes?'

'*You do still love me, don't you?*'

Henry sighed. 'Yes.'

'*I'm sorry I haven't been very nice to you lately. I just . . . where did we go wrong?*'

'It's my fault. I'm the one who messed up.'

'*Yes! It is your fault! You're a bastard, Henry. Do you know that? You're a real bastard.*'

'I know. I'm sorry.'

'*You should be.*'

'Will you forgive me?'

'*It depends.*'

'On what?'

'*On you.*'

'What about me?'

'*I don't think I can go through breaking up again.*'

'You won't have to, Anna-lise.'

'*How do you know?*'

'Because I know this time.'

'*How do you know? How do you know now what you didn't know before? What's changed?*'

'I don't know. I just know.'

'*You nearly killed me the last time.*'

'I want to be with you, Anna-lise. I won't screw up again, I swear.'

'*Come what may?*'

'I'm ready for anything, Anna-lise.'

'*Anything?*'

'Anything.'

There was a long pause.

'*OK, then.*'

'OK, then?'

Silence.

'Anna-lise?'

Silence.

'Are you still there? What do you mean, "OK, then"? Does that mean you want to get back together? Anna-lise? Don't pass out on me now.'

There was the sound of the key in his lock. Light from the corridor arced on the floor and then folded in on itself like a concertina breathing a note. Henry could hear footsteps. He felt the sheets move. The mattress shifted.

And then she was there. After all these weeks, she was simply there again. Like a light switched on, she was suddenly beside him. She moved in. He reached out and felt for her waist. It dipped and tensed. He pulled on her softly, using the tips of his fingers. She slid closer and her lips were in the night, soft and tender and melting on his.

Henry's hand travelled up her back, over shallow plains, skirting the epic ridge of her spine, over the sheer face of her shoulder blades. Anna-lise squeezed him, fighting. He strangled the back of her neck. They rolled and there was the sound of something falling to the floor.

She was on top of him, their sexes pressed together like hard, hot bones. Henry had his eyes closed. He thought he could see patterns like sunlight coming through the leaves of trees, blurry and ill defined. He reached out for her breasts and found he was seizing her buttocks and gripping the backs and insides of her thighs – he wanted as much of her as he could have. There was a moment of clothing before he entered her. He cried out inside himself. What was this place?

They morphed and mutated, his hand in hers, their fingers growing into one another like banyan branches finding roots. She looked through the darkness into his eyes. They fell into a reflection of themselves. Their groins disappeared into a single, deep gorge. Their breathing was simultaneous. Henry could feel their hearts bouncing against one another like perfectly timed strikes, the sweet spot in a volley.

And, somewhere in the midst of their convulsion, Henry bled his being. Any final, lingering sense of individual shape or form between them slowly melted into a long, liquid stream. There were no borders, no boundaries to define them here. They were lost in one another. They had become one. They were warm.

We bought the rings in London. It was the one time Catherine and I went abroad. The company sent me so I added some holiday time and we made a vacation out of it.

Catherine wanted to go to St Paul's Cathedral. We climbed up to the Whispering Gallery. There were a lot of boys in school uniforms running around. Catherine thought they looked like miniature men.

'*Can you hear me?*'

'Yes, Catherine. I can hear you.'

She was wearing a long charcoal overcoat that still shone from the rain. Her hair fell in rivulets. I watched her place a hand in blessing on one young boy as he tore past. She smiled and looked at him as he slowed down to glance back over his shoulder at her. He smiled back and then ran on.

Catherine turned and cupped her mouth close to the wall.

'*Is this what it feels like?*'

'What?'

'*You know . . .*'

'Sort of.'

'*It's freaky.*'

'Hmm.'

'*And to think, it's all just acoustics.*'

'I know.'

Outside, a fine mist hung in the air and painted our faces. We managed to find a cafe with steamed-up windows and walls the colour of over-brewed tea. I ate a boiled-egg sandwich in wet bread. Catherine drank a weak coffee. As we stood by a counter near the window, playing with a tabloid newspaper, Catherine spied a sign for an antiques market. We left to follow its arrow.

A lot of the stalls were closed. Forbidding iron curtains were slammed down and chained with thick brass padlocks. Some of the shops had been left unmanned – bright lights shining hotly on cheap china and ornamental art.

We lost one another and I wandered aimlessly, browsing the stalls with the curiosity of someone not buying. The stall owners eyed me suspiciously.

I found her again in one corner, huddled over a rickety display case filled with old gypsy rings and silver lockets. The man behind the stall was smoking a pipe and sipping a cup of tea (with brandy in it too, no doubt). A damp blanket around his shoulders steamed. There was an old brass lamp at one end of his counter. I wanted to ask him for our three wishes.

'How much for those?' Catherine said, peering intensely and pointing, not wanting to look up in case she lost the treasure she'd found.

'Fifty quid for the pair,' the stall owner replied without moving.

'Can we try them?'

The man slid from his stool, set his tea and pipe aside, and pulled out a puzzle of keys from a pinstriped trouser pocket. He selected one blindly and opened the case.

Reaching for the rings he said, 'Cast in cuttle-bone, these are original pieces from Galway dating back to the early eighteenth century. The mark here,' he pointed with a fat finger, 'indicates that the jeweller is unknown but originates from the birthplace of the Claddagh.'

He poured them into Catherine's palm. She pulled them into her, with her elbow pressed tightly to her ribs, cradling them.

'They're beautiful,' she said.

'Are you getting married?' the man asked.

'We're married already,' I said.

'We never got rings, though,' Catherine said, smiling.

'I thought you didn't believe in them,' I said.

'I don't,' she replied, looking at me. 'But these are different. They symbolize more than marriage.'

'Friendship, loyalty and love,' the stall owner said. 'The cupped hands over the heart with a crown.'

'I thought you said that rings were a chain,' I said to Catherine. 'That no one should feel bound by a piece of jewellery.'

'We could wear them on our right hands.'

'Why don't you try them?' the owner said.

Catherine passed me mine and started to slide hers on.

'Not that way, miss,' the stall owner said. 'It means your heart's still available.'

'Damn!' Catherine said, grinning and turning the ring around. 'Nearly got away with it.'

Hers fit perfectly. Mine was too small.

'I can have that enlarged for you, sir. It will only take a couple of hours.'

I looked at Catherine.

'Please,' she looked at me. 'I think these are right for us.'

'It would be my pleasure,' the woman said with an enormous, toothpaste-white smile.

The sight of all those teeth made Mrs Xhiu feel nervous. They were as big as tombstones. And her hands were huge. In fact, everything inside the bank looked enormous. The ceiling soared, the cashier counters loomed, the desks seemed to stretch like banquet tables.

Mrs Xhiu shrank into the office chair and tried to hide.

'Thank you, Steffanie,' Ben said, turning to face Mrs Xhiu. 'OK, Steffanie is going to take things from here. She'll help set up the loan and answer any questions you might have. I'm going to do a few things and be back to pick you up in half an hour, all right?'

Mrs Xhiu managed to nod.

'OK, then!' Steffanie said as Ben got up and left. 'Let's see what we can do for you today, Mrs Chew.'

'Mrs Xhiu,' Mrs Xhiu whispered.

'I'm sorry, I didn't catch that,' Steffanie said, her smile spreading so far Mrs Xhiu wondered if her face was about to crack.

'It doesn't matter.'

'OK, then! First, we'll have to fill out some forms.'

'OK.'

'Great! This'll only take a few minutes,' Steffanie said.

Mrs Xhiu did her best to answer all the questions. Some of them were easy. Some of them she didn't know the answers to. Steffanie tried to reassure her with a lot of 'OK thens!' and 'We don't need to worry about thats', but somehow the bank just kept on getting bigger and bigger.

'So,' Steffanie said, once all the formalities had been completed. 'How much would you like to borrow?'

Mrs Xhiu stared at her. 'I don't know. How much can I have?'

'Well,' Steffanie sighed, looking down at the application, 'I'm afraid that without any guaranteed form of income, a lack of credit, and the fact that your apartment is in an Assisted Housing block, which we don't normally like as security, I would have to say that I can't see the bank offering a loan in excess of three hundred thousand dollars.'

Mrs Xhiu gasped. 'Three hundred thousand?'

'OK then, if you really push us maybe we could take things up to three fifty.'

'Three fifty,' Mrs Xhiu repeated slowly.

'But I have to tell you, Mrs Xhiu,' Steffanie said, enunciating her name carefully now, looking down at the spelling on the application, 'given the risks associated with this loan, the bank will have to charge two percentage points over LIBOR.'

Mrs Xhiu nodded in total incomprehension.

'Which will make your repayment amount come to . . . ' Steffanie punched a calculator as if it were an automatic weapon. ' . . . eight hundred and forty thousand dollars.'

'Eight hundred . . . '

' . . . and forty thousand dollars, that's correct,' Steffanie said with a stern, official look. 'We won't be compounding the interest.'

'I have a question,' Mrs Xhiu said.

'Go right ahead,' Steffanie replied.

'I just want to make sure I understand.'

'Of course.'

'You are going to give me three hundred and fifty thousand dollars.'

'The bank will.'

'And I will pay eight hundred and forty thousand dollars back to you?'

'We'll set up an account for you here, if you like.'

'And when will I have to do that?'

'At maturity,' Steffanie said before reading Mrs Xhiu's blank expression. 'In twenty years' time,' she added.

Mrs Xhiu nodded, trying not to smile. 'So the bank doesn't want its money back for twenty years?'

'Since you don't have a regular income the bank will not be giving you a mortgage. Instead, we'll be giving you an equity-release loan. That way, you won't have to worry about making any monthly interest payments.'

'And if I needed, I could sell my apartment to pay the bank back.'

'Yes.'

'And what if I didn't want to do that?'

'The bank will foreclose on the loan and repossess the apartment for sale at auction.'

'But not for another twenty years.'

'That is correct.'

'And what happens if I die?'

'In the event of your death, God forbid, Mrs Xhiu, whoever inherits your apartment will take on responsibility for the loan.'

'What if I don't leave a will?'

'The bank will sell the apartment to recoup its funds.'

'I see.'

'Hi there,' Ben said breezily from behind. Mrs Xhiu turned and threw him an enormous smile. 'How are you getting on?'

'Fine,' Mrs Xhiu said happily.

'Great!' Ben replied. 'Are you finished?'

'Yup,' replied Steffanie. 'I think we have everything we need. We should be able to get this application off today and have the funds in Mrs Xhiu's new account by the end of the month.'

'That's great news,' Ben said smiling. Mrs Xhiu beamed back at him. 'Isn't it?'

'Yes, thank you, Ben.'

'Are you ready for me to take you home?' he asked.

'I've just got one more question for Steffanie.'

'Fire away,' Steffanie said.

'That credit card you mentioned. The one that goes up to twenty thousand.'

'Yes.'

'Can I have one of those as well?'

M organ decided to skip lunch so she could go take a look at the apartment.

She had to keep up regular checks because everything – and this really did mean everything, from the smallest light fixture to the structure of the staircase – had gone wrong.

It was as if the project were cursed, the coincidence of catastrophes was uncanny. How was it that nothing, not one single thing, could go right?

Even so, as she approached the building and saw a busy throng of activity on the roof – a good sign – she couldn't help getting excited. They were mounting the frame for the extension today. A whole new room! She could only imagine what it might look like.

Seeing her approach, a workman waved down. Morgan was about to wave enthusiastically back but then the guy turned and shouted ominously to his companions.

On the way up in the elevator, Morgan's anticipation turned to nerves. Doubt started to creep in. She tried to tell herself she was being paranoid but that workman had looked so *guilty*.

She closed her eyes and took five yogic breaths. When the elevator doors slid open, she gasped. It was so bright. The apartment looked incredible. Morgan looked up. A beautiful spring sky was pouring in from above like water. It took Morgan a few seconds to realize that the roof had gone. It had been there in the morning. And now it was gone.

Where was it?

Morgan stood, stunned. Her mind stepped timidly closer to observe the detail. Piece by piece she took in the chaos and destruction. She saw the mangled remains of her ceiling. Hunks of plaster hung from snapped wood furring like shredded flesh on broken bones. Expensive fixtures had been ripped from their fittings and spotlights hung by wires like torn-out eyes. Pregnant dust clouds drifted through the apartment, threatening rain. The rafters were the only things still remaining, but stripped this way even they looked fragile and weak, like anorexic legs.

Morgan thought she was going to be sick.

A recognizable boot stepped sure-footedly onto the top rung of a ladder that was leaning against one of the roof supports.

'Ms Honeysuckle!' she heard Aaron saying before he reached the bottom of the ladder. Then, as he turned to face her, beaming. 'You should have told us you were coming.'

Morgan could feel herself hyperventilating.

'Do you smoke?' was all she could manage.

'No,' Aaron said, frowning.

'I need a cigarette, Aaron. Who has a cigarette?'

'Are you OK, Ms Honeysuckle? You're sweating.'

Morgan just stared.

'Yeah, well,' Aaron said with a philosophical wince that had the threat of hard truth in it. 'You can't build Rome without breaking a few eggs.'

'What?' Morgan said, confused. She thought that maybe her hearing was off. She was in a state of shock.

'Don't worry, Ms Honeysuckle, we had to make a few adjustments to the drawings but I promise you, we've got everything under control.'

Just then a workman's Timberland boot plunged through the ceiling above Aaron and a large chunk of plaster shaped like a piece of cake fell and landed perfectly on his yarmulke.

'Lavi, you fucker!' Aaron shouted to the sole of the boot. 'Sorry about dat, Ms Honeysuckle. We'll get that fixed up right away.'

'Yes,' Morgan said quietly. 'Tell me what's going on, Aaron. I'm feeling . . . apprehensive.'

'Well,' Aaron started heavily.

The following moments passed in a blur for Morgan. She noticed how the workmen all seemed to have stopped what they were doing as Aaron delivered the news. She couldn't tell if this was out of consideration – they needed a quiet moment to talk – or if they were just using Morgan's frozen state of shock as an excuse to stop working.

One thing Morgan did know: she didn't like their looks of considerate worry. It was disconcerting to solicit pity from a group of men she knew hated her guts, especially this way, with them above her, like gods in heaven.

It only got worse when Aaron started with his insights on life. They reminded Morgan of the time her stockbroker had taken her out to dinner after the dotcom crash. For an hour and a half, blissfully unaware, Morgan had listened to the man's relaxed, lyrical treatises on youth, challenge and the texture of life's surprises. They had sat until midnight, quaffing espressos and liqueurs and marvelling at the retro decor of the place.

And when the broker had offered to pay, Morgan got a warm, fuzzy feeling inside. She didn't even question why the guy might have called her up, out of the blue, to take her out. It had simply seemed like a perfect and wonderful way to spend an evening. Morgan had even dared to believe that she might have found a new friend.

Three days later, the statement had arrived. Ever since then, Morgan had understood: if a professional ever got philosophical, it meant trouble.

'Just give it to me straight, Aaron,' she managed to interrupt.

'OK. Your architect messed up. He measured the clearance for the extension from your ceiling, not the roof.'

'So?'

'Your ceiling sags, Ms Honeysuckle.'

'Yes.'

'But we have to build from the roof.'

'I don't see the problem.'

'If we build from the roof, you won't be able to stand up in your extension. You'll be like this.' Aaron cocked his head to one side like a confused robot.

There were one or two sniggers from the vultures circling.

'I don't think you want to walk around in your extension like this the whole time.' Aaron threw his head the other way. 'Do you?' There was more sniggering. Aaron threw his head the other way again. 'Ms Honeysuckle, hmm?' Naked laughter now accompanied Aaron's attempts to snap his own neck. Morgan was very tempted to help.

'Why don't you build the extension higher?' Morgan asked.

Aaron and the laughter stopped abruptly and Aaron was about to answer the question when Morgan managed to do so herself.

'Planning regulations.'

'That's right, Ms H. We have to maintain the roof line, remember.'

'Yes,' replied Morgan. 'I remember. So what does this mean?'

'We have to lower your roof.'

'Lower it? By how much?'

'A foot . . . a foot and a half.'

'Which is it, a foot or a foot and a half?'

Aaron cocked his arm and reached for a tape measure off his belt like a man drawing a gun from his holster. He issued a length and held it in front of him.

'Eighteen inches,' he said, spirit-levelling his look.

Morgan gulped.

'But . . . is that even possible?'

'Sure. I mean, it's gonna take time and, you know it means that there's gonna be a lot more work, but, yeah, sure it's possible. And the best thing is, we can get rid of these old wood beams for you and put in nice new steel ones, triple the strength.'

'You're going to remove my exposed, solid-oak beams?'

'We have to.'

Morgan felt very sorry for herself all of a sudden.

'Look, don't worry, Ms. H. Things look bad right now but I guarantee you, one hundred per cent guarantee to you, that we'll get this sorted out. Your architect made a real mess of things. The good news is, I'm here to put things right.'

'For some reason, Aaron,' Morgan said. 'I don't find that even remotely reassuring.'

Aaron's eyes darkened. Morgan stood for a moment, banging her teeth together. Aaron looked at her, impatiently. He seemed to think the conversation was over. He wanted to get back to work. If only construction workers were as enthusiastic about building things as they were about destroying them, Morgan thought to herself. It had taken weeks for them to build the staircase and yet they'd managed to demolish her apartment in a single morning. The guy couldn't wait to get back to it.

'Sink the floor,' Morgan said, without knowing precisely what she was saying.

'What?' Aaron said.

The thought came into focus.

'Use the roof as the base for the extension and sink the floor into the gap so that it meets my ceiling level and gives me the head height in the extension I need.'

A look of enormous exhaustion fell across Aaron's face.

'You want us to sink the floor?'

'Is it possible?'

Aaron sucked air in between his teeth long and low and with such consideration it was as if Morgan had just asked him if he truly loved his wife.

After an interminable length of time, he conceded.

'Yeah, Ms Honeysuckle, it's possible.'

One of Morgan's new sunshine smiles spread across her face. 'I knew you could do it, Aaron.'

'Hang on there a second, Ms Honeysuckle.'

Morgan noticed that the looks of divine compassion on the workmen's faces had fallen away now and several were turning and muttering obscenities. This, on consideration, made Morgan feel three hundred times better about things.

'Go on,' Morgan said.

'We'll have to use hanging struts for the joist work.'

'OK.'

'The floor's gotta be able to take your weight.'

'Yup.'

'We're gonna have to get the structural engineer down to do some calculations.'

'Bring him.'

'He might not make it till next week.'

'I'll call him. He'll be here tomorrow.'

'This is gonna cost you, Ms Honeysuckle.'

'How much?'

'Hard to say.'

'More than lowering the roof?'

'No,' Aaron conceded. 'But it's still gonna push you way over budget.'

'Let me worry about that.'

'You're the boss.'

Like drones on central command, the workmen all turned at this statement to gather their tools.

'Where are you going?' Morgan asked.

Aaron cast his arms to his sides. 'Not much we can do here, Ms H, till the engineer comes.'

'Sure there is, Aaron. You can rebuild my ceiling. Remember? The one you destroyed without consulting me first.'

It was Aaron's turn to gulp.

'Hey, Ms Honeysuckle, I was just doing what I thought was best.'

'I'm not paying you to think, Aaron, I'm paying you to do

what I say. Now I want you to start putting my ceiling back or I'm going to implement another penalty clause from the contract.'

'Yes, Ms Honeysuckle,' Aaron said with empty eyes.

'You should be grateful I'm not docking the costs of damage from your fee.'

Aaron didn't say anything.

'Just make sure you put it back to the way it was before,' Morgan said, stepping onto the elevator.

'*Timtzots li et haboolbool kalba,*' Aaron said.

'I'm sorry?' Morgan said, turning quickly.

'It means "Peace be with you".'

'Oh. Right. Well, you have yourself a nice day too, Aaron.'

The elevator doors breathed.

Juan skipped out of work to get lunch at his favourite salad bar. He had only five minutes before bad impressions. This was life in fashion: no pay, long hours.

'We do it for the love, sweetie, for the love,' the black-shirted afashionada editor – a real fashion fascist, if ever there was one – had screamed as he left.

He was such a bitch.

First stop: the ATM at Flatiron. The three winds that shaped the building bundled Juan into the hall of booths. There was a Latin American unarmed guard looking lost in a corner. Two people raced each other to fill out deposit slips on a razor-thin counter, which had only two working biros. Several chains without pens hung limply over the edge. Juan couldn't bear the public-relations-red trim they'd used to decorate the place. He found an empty machine almost immediately, just as an operatic reprise of hallelujahs started appropriately on his MP3 player.

Juan sang along silently and slipped his card into the slot. The machine ate it. Juan punched his PIN and chose Fast Cash. Juan liked the sound of that as he read it so he started mouthing the phrase and jigging his hips to a snappy, happy, new tune that had just come on. (Mike must have hired Garry's music-consultation service, he didn't have taste as good as this.)

'Fast cash, gimme some fast cash, I want fast cash, yeah!'

The display screen flashed a message:

I'm working on it.

Juan sang silently.

'I'm working on it, working on it, workin' on that fast cash.'

Another message from the bank:

That's it, I'm done. Have a Nice Day!

Juan waited. Nothing happened. He waited some more. The machine seemed to have frozen. Nothing was happening. This had to be the slowest fast cash ever.

Juan turned around and saw a queue of four people stabbing at his back with eyes shaped like scissors. What was *their* problem?

A man with a waistline that ate genitals, his stomach sticking out with cartoon simplicity onto fat thighs, mouthed something at him. Juan decided he'd better take out his earphones. The music faded and cut to:

' . . . Nice Day!'

Juan gave a plain vanilla smile. 'Excuse me?'

The queue broke out in unison: 'You gotta say, Have a Nice Day!'

'What?'

'Before the machine gets upset,' one woman wearing a grey pinstripe suit pleaded.

'It'll shut down otherwise,' said a good-looking adolescent with a foolish haircut.

'You've got to be kidding,' Juan said, turning around to look into the ATM. A camera stared at him like HAL. The display suddenly went as blank as space. 'What . . . '

'That's it,' Juan heard someone say behind him. 'You were too slow. That machine's out for the rest of the day. You broke it.'

'Thanks a lot, buddy,' Fat Man added.

'That can't be right. What about my Fast Cash? What about my card?' Juan said, bending down to peer into the dead machine.

'Gone,' said the woman. 'You'll have to apply for a new one.'

'What!' Juan shrieked, turning.

'Have a Nice Day!' a man in the next ATM said, unable to resist turning with a smile in Juan's direction as he took his money.

'But I need that card.'

'It'll take days for you to get a new one,' Fat Man wobbled as he approached the free machine. 'Serves you right.'

'I didn't know,' Juan replied. 'I was listening to my music. I didn't hear.'

'The machine did flash the message,' the woman said. 'You coulda used your eyes.'

'Since when have we gotta start talking to machines?' Juan asked. 'This can't be happening. Please.' Juan turned to the machine and started shouting: 'Have a Nice Day! Have a Nice Day!'

'Too late, buddy,' Fat Man muttered. 'You blew it, big time.'

'Hello?' Garry said.
'Yes?' Mandy said.
'Who is it?' Helmut answered.
'Hello?' Garry said again.
'Helmut?' Mandy asked.
'No, this is Juan.'
'What?' Garry said.
'I'm sorry, I didn't get you,' Mandy said.
'This had better be good,' Diva said.
'What?' Garry said again.
'I was sleeping,' Diva said.
'Is that you, Diva?' Juan said.
'No, it's Garry.'
'Garry?' Henry said.
'Who is this?' Diva said.
'Anna-lise.'
'Have you lost your key?'
'No more menus!' Morgan said.
'Come in,' Frank said.
'If you think I'm gonna buzz you in at this hour . . . ' Diva said.
'I'm not interested, sorry,' Mrs Xhiu said.
'Who the hell is this?' Henry said.
'Henry?' Anna-lise said.
'Come back tomorrow,' Mrs Xhiu said.
'Anna-lise, what are you doing outside?'
'That's not me.'
'What?' Garry said.
'I'm going back to bed,' Diva said.
'I'll call the police,' Morgan said.
'I'm calling the police,' Juan said. 'Michael! Come here.'

'This is ridiculous,' Mandy said.

'That's it, I've had enough,' Henry said.

'Henry?' Anna-lise said.

'Fuck you, whoever you are,' Garry said.

'I said, come in,' Frank said.

'Will you please stop buzzing my bell?' Henry said.

'What in the hell is wrong with this thing?' Helmut said.

'I can't see anyone,' Morgan said.

'Damn kids,' Mike said.

It came to me again in my sleep, the one place I had thought was safe. Maybe that was how it found me, because my guard was down. Or maybe it was me who found it. I was still looking. I just wouldn't admit that to myself.

I was dreaming that I was sleeping. I was lying in bed, my eyes darting under my eyelids, trying to find a way out. There was a small opening, like a crack in a doorway. Light was coming in. My eyeballs were trying to prise the opening. But they couldn't get a hold.

There was someone with me. I could feel them. They were very near. They were lying down next to me. I could hear their breathing. They were saying something to me. But I couldn't make out the words. I wanted to see who it was. I tried to turn my head but it was so heavy. I'd lift it an inch and find myself pinned to the pillow.

I managed to turn a little to one side. I strained to look out of the corner of one eye. I could just make out a silhouette, a shadow of something, but the harder I focused the darker things got.

And then I heard it.

It wasn't faint like before. It was as if it had been there all this time, all around me, at full pitch, but I hadn't heard it up to now because I'd lost the signal. That didn't mean it wasn't there. It didn't mean it hadn't been getting stronger. It had. I just hadn't been listening.

And the message was getting clearer.

It was in the pipes, making the intercom system malfunction, disrupting cable TV transmissions, distorting radio waves, making the elevator control panel fuse, flashing up strange words on the running-machine display.

As I lay there I could feel the vibrations. The building hummed. Everything was shaking, getting louder, getting stronger. It was like a force, a sonic pitch that portended natural disaster. The birds were in flight. The dogs were howling. Everything knew.

Joe?

'Catherine?'

Joe, it's me.

'Catherine. I've missed you so much.'

Let me in.

'Where are you?'

I'm right here.

'Where?'

Wake up, Joe.

'I can't.'

Joe. Get up.

'I can't. I'm tied down. Help me.'

I felt her hands on my face. She cradled my head like a precious egg. She pressed my cheeks. I could smell her. She was so near now. I could feel her. I had to see her, I had to.

'Joe? Wake up. It's me, Mandy.'

Mandy smiled anxiously at the workman.

'He's not normally asleep at this hour,' she explained.

The workman nodded like he was keeping time.

Mandy knocked on the door, loudly.

'Let me in.'

'Where are you?' the super said, his voice coming through the wall slowly, as if it were being smothered in a blanket.

'I'm right here.'

'Where?'

'Wake up, Joe!'

'I can't.'

'Joe!' Mandy said strictly. 'Get up!'

'I can't. I'm tied down. Help me.'

Mandy looked at the workman who was looking at her in a worried way, as if she were somehow responsible for this bizarre behaviour, a party to it. She felt an inexplicable rush of guilt.

'What do you mean?' Mandy said, embarrassed. 'Come on, Joe, stop playing games and open this do—'

The door swung quickly open and Joe, dressed in his dusty blue overalls, stood in front of them.

'Oh, Joe. Hi. I'm sorry. I hope I wasn't disturbing you.'

Joe shook his head.

'Lavi needs access to the junction box.'

Joe glanced at Lavi. Lavi smiled back. Joe looked at Mandy.

'They need to turn the power off,' she added. 'It will only be for a couple of hours. Right, Lavi?'

'Right.'

'They've promised,' Mandy said.

Joe didn't say anything.

'Are you all right, Joe?'

'Just gimme a minute,' he said, turning back into the apartment.

DUE TO CONSTRUCTION, THERE WILL BE NO WATER BETWEEN THE HOURS OF 10 A.M. AND 4 P.M., MONDAY TO FRIDAY, FOR THE NEXT TWO WEEKS.

M

Garry had Memorial weekend all figured out. He was on his way out to La Guardia to pick up the rental car. The out-of-town deals were half the price of any in the city.

When he finally got to the airport – the shuttle bus had taken two and a half hours – he was greeted by an enormous queue. All the planes were coming in. Garry waited.

At one-thirty, a woman finally called him up to the rental-car counter. She didn't bother giving him her plastic grin and he didn't bother complaining. They'd both gone far, far beyond that.

She pointed on the form, he signed, she gave him the keys and told him where to get the car. Garry sleepwalked himself away from the counter making an effort not to thank her.

The following morning, Garry woke up with a start. A gentle breeze was swinging the blinds so morning sunlight stabbed at his eyes.

'What?' he said, sitting upright, trying to gather his bearings. 'What time is it?'

He looked across at the alarm clock. Ten to ten.

'Shit! The car,' he said, rolling himself out of bed and into jeans.

It took him several seconds of outside air to fully register that the car wasn't where he'd parked it.

He went to check the parking rules.

Memorial Day and Labor Day weekend restrictions apply. Every second year, street-cleaning restrictions will reverse, unless on a Leap Year. Triple fines apply for Holiday offenders.

'Every second year?' Garry said out loud to himself. 'What does that mean?'

'It means you got towed, my friend,' a voice said behind him.

Garry swung around to see a lean man in a dark uniform with matching turban staring at him.

'I've been waiting for you,' the parking attendant said, handing Garry a ticket.

Garry looked down at it.

'Five hundred bucks!'

'And another five hundred to get it released from the pound,' the attendant said sternly.

'I don't believe this.'

'You'd better start.'

Garry didn't know where the pound was and nor did the taxi driver, who was another turbaned man. There were stickers pasted all over the inside of his cab saying:

God bless America!

I love the U.S. of A.

I'm a Sikh not a Muslim, there's a difference.

After driving all the way to the East side and back again, they found the pound just two blocks west of VanVanVane Street, up the West Side Highway.

The fare came to twenty bucks. Garry didn't tip. He got out of the cab and climbed over a chain loosely guarding the driveway.

'Hey!'

Garry vaguely heard the shout but chose to ignore it.

'Hey! I'm talking to Jew!'

Garry carried on walking.

'Stop or I shoot.'

Garry froze.

'That's it, asshole. Now turn around.'

Garry put his hands in the air and did as he was told.

A man with arms the size of Garry's legs and a chest the width of a car was perched on the edge of a tow-truck seat, the industrial springs visibly straining underneath him. Garry saw he didn't really have a gun. He put his hands back down.

'You scared me,' Garry said.

'What didju say?' the tree trunk said, sliding down from the truck with an earth-crunching thud. 'Did you just call me a fuckin' asshole?'

'No.'

'I'm gonna whup you, boy. This ma pound. Joo mess with me in ma pound, I'm gonna whup ya.'

'What have I done?'

'Didn't you see the No Entry sign posted?'

He didn't wait for Garry to answer.

'It means no entry, faggot.'

He stared with rage at Garry for a few red seconds.

'Walk back.'

'What?' Garry said.

'You heard. Walk back and come around the appropriate route.'

The tow-truck thug indicated with a cigar-thick finger at the vehicle entranceway.

'What difference does it make?' Garry asked quietly. 'That sign is for cars.'

The man took five quick steps towards Garry, blasting hot air at him.

'NOW!'

Garry jogged out of the pound the way he'd come, along the ten-metre stretch of sidewalk to the entranceway and headed quickly for the office without making eye contact.

The office was a temporary set-up, a Portakabin processing centre for the parking criminal. There were public-information posters on the walls and a ticket counter. Thick, iron-mesh service windows compensated for the fibreglass counters, which looked weak enough to kick a hole through.

To Garry's surprise, there wasn't any shouting or fighting or objections going on. The rectangular, uniformed women who sat behind the service counters carried a relaxed air of authority and everyone on the wooden waiting bench seemed correspondingly resigned to their fate. One man was stretched out asleep.

Garry overheard a pinstriped Wall Streeter boast to his impressed neighbour that the fine was weak, he'd rather pay it than bother wasting the time looking for a decent parking space. All the old parking lots in his area had been developed and now the nearest one to his home was three blocks away. He was damned if he was going to walk three blocks.

When it finally came to his turn to pay, Garry took his lead from everyone else and silently handed over his credit card. He didn't want to threaten his chances of getting the car returned quickly and then losing the whole weekend. As it was, he could still hope to set off by three and be in Montreal for dinner.

The women bounced Garry between a number of counters armed with different-coloured forms and tags. He watched his car keys make the same journey on the other side of the iron grilles, trapped in a parallel universe.

Eventually Garry got his keys and graduated to the pound itself, with its ramshackle ranks of vehicles. He needed to find the officer on duty so that he could be escorted to his vehicle.

'Jew again.'

Garry pursed his lips and handed over his forms. The officer inspected them carefully.

'Incomplete,' he said, handing them back.

'What?'

'Don't tell me I gotta teach you rules again, boy. Go back to the service counter. These forms are incomplete.'

'In what way?'

'Not my place to say.'

Garry took the long walk back to the Portakabin and tried to approach a window directly. He was made to take another ticket and wait.

Fifteen minutes later, Garry got called to the counter and the problem – a tick in a box – was resolved.

'Here,' he said, handing the form to the thug.

'Follow me.'

Garry wasn't surprised to find the windscreen of the car smashed in.

'You shouldn't have put the handbrake on. If you think that's gonna stop us towing your car you got another thing comin'. Cheap tricks like that don't work.'

Garry didn't bother to explain that he always put the handbrake on.

'Why the windscreen?'

'Most people have windscreen insurance.'

Garry remembered he'd said no to that option.

'How am I meant to see?'

'Go slow.'

Satisfied, the officer left Garry to sweep diamonds away from the seat with bare hands. He climbed into the car, the glass crunching beneath his shoes, and called the rental company.

'OK, sir, well, that's gonna come to one hundred and ninety-eight dollars for the damage to the car.'

'Fine,' Garry huffed, throwing an ineffectual middle finger out of the window as he exited the pound.

'And because you took the special weekend rate from La Guardia, you'll have to return the vehicle there before getting a replacement.'

'You're kidding.'

'No, sir, I'm afraid I'm not.'

'Shit,' Garry said, hanging up.

WATCH TEAM USA VS GERMANY IN THE WORLD
CUP IN APT G1 THIS SUNDAY (6/6). 2 P.M. SHARP!

ALL WELCOME! (Bring beer)

Ben

Henry, Anna-lise, Helmut, Garry, Mike and Frank all showed up. Ben was having a great time hosting, making sure everyone had a drink, teasing Helmut (who knew much more about soccer than him), generally enjoying the anticipation. He was glad he'd asked everyone to come early – this way they could all enjoy the build-up to the game together.

The only annoying thing was that he still had to finish the laundry money. Mandy had reminded him just before she'd left. While making sure everyone was happy and served, Ben was also having to stand by the kitchen counter carefully slipping flimsy sheaths of card over ten-dollar stacks of quarters, so they could be deposited at the bank.

'Shit,' he said, as another cardboard sheath caught an edge and tore.

Frank laughed at him and told him to come sit down, forget about it, enjoy himself. But Ben had finished only thirty dollars' worth, three lousy rolls. There were four hundred dollars from the laundry for the month. It was going to take him the whole afternoon. There had to be a more efficient way of doing this, he thought to himself. Here the world was, in a modern era of finance, and the only way to sort quarters was with this stupid plastic tube and a bunch of cardboard condoms.

He tried again, biting his lower lip in concentration, listening with a little irritation to everyone else chat excitedly over the TV volume that was deliberately set too high. It wasn't just the laundry money that was getting on his nerves. Monday was also on his mind. His probation period at Largent was over. His review was at eight. He thought he'd had a pretty good run. At least, he hadn't lost the firm any money, even made them a little. He didn't know if they'd put him on a full salary yet. There was still that issue with M&M at the back of his mind but he was fairly confident he was in the clear there, as long as Morgan hadn't totally screwed things up for him.

Looking back on it, Ben still couldn't believe the way Morgan had blackmailed him into doing the Treasury job. Mandy had had a lot of fun reminding Ben that it had been his own fault.

'If you hadn't pressed Record instead of Play on the answer machine then you wouldn't be in this position.'

Served him right, he supposed. He'd certainly embarrassed himself in front of enough of their friends. Even Mandy's mother had heard the message, said she couldn't believe the way he talked to her daughter. Said that he'd better start treating his wife with more respect blah, blah, blah . . .

She'd never liked him, anyway.

The important thing was that Susannah hadn't heard it. The important thing was that he'd got the job at Largent. The important thing was that he could pay the mortgage. The important thing was that they still had a home. And now they had voicemail too. He wasn't going to let himself in for those shenanigans ever again.

'Christ!'

Ben threw away another torn card and glanced up at Garry, who was getting himself a beer.

'This is a nightmare,' Ben said.

Garry shook his head at him. 'Can't it wait?'

The answer was no, definitely no. Mandy had already set him straight on that score, reminding him several times in the space of three minutes that he wouldn't find any other time to do it, that he couldn't afford to leave it till later.

Somehow, her taking Billy out to a first-birthday party in Brooklyn so he could have the apartment to 'himself' had gotten tied in with a chore. The afternoon had been meant as a first step in a new arrangement to give each other more space, give time to one another so they could do things purely for themselves.

Yet, on this, his first afternoon of independence, he still had something to do, he wasn't actually free at all. It was hard not to resent her for it, even though he knew it wasn't her fault. He knew he'd fight with her about it later. Everything ended up in a fight these days. They were bickering all the time. Stupid, petty arguments over who did what or whose turn it was to do something. Ben knew when they were doing it. His wedding band got tighter. At least it felt like that because his fingers swelled up hotly whenever he got mad.

It was because they were both shattered. Billy was turning out to be stubbornly nocturnal. No adult human being could survive on his three-hour shifts of sleep. It essentially meant no sleep, because there wasn't enough time for the body to reach deep sleep, the nourishing part of sleep.

Ben was still trying to convince Mandy to give up breast-feeding. He believed the heavy formula milk would help Billy sleep longer. All the books said he should be sleeping through by now. Ben had even suggested they try furthering him, but Mandy wasn't having any of it.

If he was totally honest with himself, Ben was worried about Mandy. Each night when he got home, she gave him a blow-by-blow account of the workmen and their movements. She'd even developed a theory that they worked only when Billy went to sleep. She said the knack of a hammer banging or a drill firing at the exact moment she got the baby to bed was uncanny.

And when there wasn't any noise she could hear the echoes and the workmen talking in her head. And if it wasn't work-men, she heard voices coming through the walls from the other apartments in the building. She said it was like there were no walls at all sometimes. She said she could hear people so clearly it was as if she were standing in the room with them.

Occasionally, while they were watching TV or having dinner, she'd say: 'There! Didn't you hear that?'

All in all, the claustrophobia of her situation was getting to both of them. Some nights Ben dreaded returning home from work. The stuffy tension from Mandy and Billy's constant presence in the apartment was palpable. Driving her out of the house to Brooklyn for the afternoon was as much for her benefit as it was for his.

'Come on, Ben,' Anna-lise called out over the noise. 'They're playing the national anthem.'

'OK!'

Ben told himself he could join them if he succeeded with this stack just as the cardboard found its track and slipped beautifully over the coins. He knew it was cheating but he couldn't miss the game. That wasn't a realistic option, even if it was the right one. He folded down the ends neatly and threw the completed roll down (four rolls, just four – ugh, it didn't bear thinking about) and grabbed his beer.

'U.S.A, U.S.A,' he chanted as he joined the others in the living room. They all sang with him, even Helmut, until the electric strains of the Star-Spangled Banner began and they all relaxed into a respectful, thrilled silence.

Ben could feel a small knot of happiness beginning inside, like a salt crystal forming on piece of string, as the camera panned its way past the players. The World Cup was starting!

He recognized a couple of experienced hands but otherwise they were all fresh, young faces. The team was under the guidance of a new coach. They'd shown guts in the previous tournament but they had to do better this time, they just had to. The orchestra wrapped up the anthem and a speaker-rattling roar erupted from the television. Anna-lise cheered and hugged Henry.

'Come on, America,' she yelled.

There was an irritating commercial break, a trip to the bathroom for Frank, two more beers from the cooler for Helmut and Mike, and then the two teams were standing opposite one another.

The referee, in bright yellow and black, stood over the ball. Germany were to kick off. Ben watched as the whistle was raised. It touched the referee's lips. He could almost see him taking in a huge draw of air. He waited for the shrill alarm.

Then the power went.

There was a long, loud knock on the door. Ben went to answer it, half hoping in his fury to discover an explanation on the other side. Everyone was jeering and yelling at the TV. Ben needed somebody to shout at – all his emotions were coiled up inside the pit of his stomach.

He was stunned to discover Morgan on the other side. She was the last person he'd expected to come for the match.

'Morgan. Hi. How's it going?' he stammered.

'It's going, I suppose,' Morgan said, walking past him into the apartment. She was wearing a pair of dark linen pants too high so her torso looked disproportionately short compared to her legs, and a tucked-in cream satin polo neck. She also had on a pair of two-tone golfing shoes with white leather tassels dangling brightly. 'What took you so long? I've been knocking for ages.'

'Have you? Sorry, I didn't hear,' Ben said. 'Come in. Sit down. The power just went. We're going crazy in here. Can you believe it? I could kill Electrocert.'

Morgan glanced round the kitchen wall to survey the scene and winced weakly.

'Oh,' she said. 'I forgot you'd asked people around. I'm sorry, Ben.'

Ben frowned, not understanding.

'I told the guys upstairs it would be OK to turn off the power.'

'What?'

'They're re-doing the wiring.'

'No.'

'Excuse me?' Morgan said, levelling a look.

'I mean they can't. It's Sunday. And the game – it's just start-ing. Everyone is here. We've got to watch it. I thought you'd come to watch it. You can't turn off the power now.'

'I'm really sorry, Ben,' Morgan said with sincere finality. 'They didn't do it right last time. I've asked them to do it again. It'll only be for a couple of hours.'

She might just as well have slapped him in the face. Ben didn't know where to look. He was too stunned for a moment to protest. Morgan took the chance to explain herself.

'Anyway, I just came down because I have to talk urgently with you about something.'

'What?' Ben replied, still trying to digest the news, wondering how to handle the situation, telling himself to not get angry.

'I've noticed in the financial reports that the laundry revenue seems to be going down these past few months,' Morgan said, ignoring the waves of conversation coming from the living room. 'Ever since you took over as Treasurer, actually.'

Ben's body flushed with heat. The truth was, Ben hadn't bothered sorting the coins till now, he'd just estimated the total and transferred the money from his bank account, keeping the change. He figured Mandy needed it for the machines. The only reason he was bothering this month was because they now had more loose change than a Las Vegas one-arm bandit.

'What are you saying?' Ben replied a little too defensively.

'I'm saying that the laundry revenues are going down. Can you tell me why?'

'Nope.'

They looked at each other.

'Maybe the building should have bought its own laundry machines instead of allowing the rental company to replace the ones we had after the flood,' Morgan mused. 'That's still a possibility, isn't it?'

'Look, Morgan, this isn't fair,' Ben said, recovering. 'It's Sunday. You can't turn the electricity off. We're all trying to watch the soccer.'

'I know. You said. And I'm sorry. I really am. But there's

nothing I can do about it now. They've started the work. They can't reconnect the power until they've finished. It won't take more than two hours, they've promised.'

'But the game will be finished in two hours.'

The pink at the edge of Morgan's nostrils flared as she drew in air. She stretched her long spine upwards, making her neck elongate. Then she exhaled so heavily, Ben could feel her breath. It was as if she was sucking up his protest and regurgitating it into his face.

'Do I really have to make the point, Ben, that this construction work is of vital importance to the building? I think it takes a little more priority than a soccer match.' Morgan looked at him for a moment, waiting for his agreement, but Ben found he felt too sick to respond so Morgan simply continued: 'Besides, I think now would be a good time to reconcile the building accounts.'

'You've gotta be kidding me,' Ben muttered, being too afraid to look her in the eye.

'We have to do it before the Board meeting on Tuesday.'

Ben realized he wasn't getting anywhere this way and that it was time to tell the others.

'Will you excuse me a second, Morgan?' he said, sliding past her. As soon as he was out of her glare, he discovered a previous confidence. He found himself striding into the living room. 'Well, guys, we were wrong about one thing,' he said as he approached the group, who were now chatting among themselves quite casually. They didn't seem nearly as anxious as he was that vital LIVE-viewing minutes were slipping through the neck of the ninety-minute glass and turning into dead sand. 'Electrocert aren't to blame. The construction guys upstairs have cut off the power.'

Morgan walked slowly in behind Ben. The group looked up at her. Sometimes, she could look so tall.

'What?' Garry said.

'They've started a re-wiring job and, *apparently*, they can't reconnect the supply until they've finished,' Ben explained.

'When will that be?' Henry asked.

'Not for two hours,' Ben huffed.

'I'm sorry, guys,' Morgan stepped in. 'I really didn't think it would be a problem. If I'd known . . . '

'I did put a message up on the blackboard,' Ben said, without turning to face her.

Morgan took the objection quietly but there was no contrition in it. It felt more like a refusal to apologize for a fourth time. Everyone looked at each other, waiting for – they didn't know exactly what. Ben realized that he was expecting a riot or, at the very least, a vote. Surely they could band together to make Morgan turn the power back on? He didn't believe for one second that the workmen couldn't do the work another day. But no one seemed that outraged. Ben couldn't understand what was happening.

Eventually it was Mike who got up and said: 'OK then, well, that's a shame. I guess I've got a couple of things I should be getting on with anyway.'

'Yeah,' Henry confirmed. 'So do we, Anna-lise.'

'What?' Ben said. 'No! Come on, guys. We brought beers. I got snacks. We've been planning this.'

Helmut, Frank and Garry all shrugged their shoulders and wore sad looks on their faces.

'It's not a big deal, Ben,' Helmut said.

'I've got some things I need to do as well,' Frank said.

'I don't really like soccer that much,' Garry offered.

'And you've got the laundry money still to do, Ben,' Anna-lise tried.

'Thanks for reminding me,' Ben said, too bitterly. This felt like a betrayal. 'Listen. Why don't we all go down to the Four Leaf Clover instead? They're bound to be showing the game in there.'

No one looked convinced. They started to pick themselves up and make expressions in the direction of the door. Ben couldn't believe how quickly things had flipped. One minute they were all getting excited to watch the World Cup, the next everyone was tripping over themselves to get back to their dark apartments. How was this possible?

'Morgan,' Ben said, finally turning to face her. 'You should tell the workers to put the power back on. You shouldn't have told them it was OK to switch the power off on a Sunday.'

Morgan pursed her lips, knowing she'd already won and why. 'I would if I could, Ben. Honestly.'

Ben stared at her, unable to ignore the deflating silence of everyone starting to leave. All the air was going from his sails. Anna-lise squeezed his arm gently as she passed.

'Fine,' Ben said loudly to the room. 'I'm going even if no one else is.'

He grabbed his house keys from the kitchen counter in a final act of defiance. But it didn't stop anyone. There were just more sorry smiles and quiet words of thanks before the front door was opened and the tenants drained out of G1 and into the building corridor.

Ben was left alone with Morgan. He felt his inner engine winding down with a droning whir, as if she was somehow sucking the juice out of his bones.

'We really should reconcile the accounts this afternoon, Ben,' Morgan said, almost with a caring kind of concern.

Ben briefly considered a big, loud speech but then, to his surprise, he just caved – his shoulders visibly slumping.

After all, who was he kidding? He already knew the score. There simply wasn't any such thing as an afternoon off at home with a few friends to watch soccer. These kinds of moments didn't exist for him any more. If it wasn't Morgan, it was the laundry quarters, or an errand for Mandy, or a diaper change for Billy, or work, or something for nothing. There was no way for

Ben to even imagine having things his way. Life was on full alert and admin had just gone to Defcon 5. There would always be some mundane, shitty thing left for him to do. This was his life now. Free time was not an option. He'd lost that privilege a long time ago, along with the war. There was no point in bleating about it now.

'I'll just go get the file,' he said quietly, dropping his keys back on the counter just as the last person left and the front door swung to with a quiet bang.

'Good,' Morgan said softly, smiling. 'Very good.'

' . . . *In my twenty-five years of sports reporting, I have never witnessed a spectacle like it. Truly magnificent. Team USA are playing like the possessed. To come back from three–nil at half-time to three–two against World Cup winners Germany, it's just incredible. There's a real belief now that they can do it. The noise from the crowd is fantastic. They're right behind their players, willing them on. And here comes Davis again, straight into the heart of the midfield. He sends it wide, finds McDonald. McDonald's first touch is a good one, the crowd is going berserk, there're just two minutes left of added stoppage time. McDonald crosses, Davis has made a fantastic run into the six-yard box, the ball goes long, look at the hang time on that, it finds Harvey at the far post, he heads it, Benz is forced to make the save, he parries, it falls to Davis, he strikes . . . GOAAAAAALLLLLLLL!*'*

I listened to the radio roar, hoping Ben might somehow still be able to hear it up through the floorboards or in a heating pipe, though I doubted it.

'*Incredible, Mike! Just incredible! Look at the players, look at the fans. What will this mean for soccer in the USA? This has to be one of the world's greatest comebacks. Talk about the underdog. And now the players salute the fans who helped make it happen. Fantastic stuff.*'

'*Something special happened out there, Jerry. The crowd, the team, I'm not sure what it was, but somehow that ball just seemed to fall for Team USA when they needed it to the most. And now we go into a nail-biting extra time. Boy, it has been one hell of a ride.*'

'*There's a real sense that Team USA can go on and win this game now, Mike. The Germans are dropping their heads. Things just haven't happened for them in this second half. They've lost faith somehow, which isn't like them.*'

'I think they were caught in the headlights there, Jerry. Team USA want this more. They came back at half-time believing they could do it. And when they scored that first goal and the crowd started to believe as well, it became a reality.'

'The power of faith, hey, Mike.'

'You said it, Jerry. When everyone believes that ball will fall, the impossible becomes possible, anything can happen, anything at all. It's what makes sport so special.'

CODE OF ETHICS

For consideration by the Board of 444 VanVanVane Street, New York, NY 10111 on this day 8 June 2010.

Dear Board,

In the interests of good governance, civil courtesy and societal welfare, I would like to propose an ethics code and guide to good conduct, a quasi-constitution if you will, to be adhered to by tenants.

They follow (in no particular order):

1. A building-wide ban on smoking.
2. The building should attempt to reflect the ethnic diversity of the city.
3. An affirmative-action programme to fulfil point 2 should be implemented.
4. Mandatory, random drug testing for tenants.
5. Tenants should fit into the national weight bracket to reduce building-insurance liability.
6. No cussing or blasphemy of any religious order will be tolerated.
7. There should be a balance of left-handed and right-handed people in the building.
8. To reduce the risk of sexual harassment, physical contact between tenants should be restricted to hand shaking

only. Prolonged eye contact should be avoided. Mutually consenting sexual liaisons should occur outside the building.

9. Tenants should be tested annually on their general moral fibre.

10. Paedophiles and pornographers will be severely prosecuted.

11. A formal dress code for weekdays should be observed. Smart casual wear may be worn on Fridays. Tenants are free to dress (within reason) as they please on weekends and holidays.

12. Tenants who have outstanding obligations to the running of the building should dedicate sufficient free time, including weekends and holidays, to fulfilling them. Business before pleasure, folks!

13. The following styles of hair are acceptable (see Appendix A).

14. If you have any thoughts that you suspect are in violation of the corporate code, a counsellor can be made available for one-on-one sessions each evening after office hours at a rate of two hundred dollars/hour. Check with your insurance carrier for coverage.

15. Everyone in the building should endeavour to get a good night's sleep. Anyone found yawning in communal areas will be fined.

16. We at 444 believe in the business of ideas. Any inspired thought that develops the essence of the corporation and maximizes shareholder value will be rewarded. But please remember, thinking out of the box is good, radicalism is not. Be free-thinking insofar as it is controlled.

17. Tenants must report tenants they believe to be in violation of this code. Failure to adhere to the code of ethics may lead to fines, additional work duties or eviction.

Further suggestions/amendments to this document will be most
welcome.

Yours truly,

Morgan H. Honeysuckle
President

When Diva found out about the rising cost of construction and the new timetable for maintenance increases approved by the June Board meeting she knew what she had to do.

She wasn't upset or angry or scared or excited – at least not in any conscious fashion. Subconsciously, she was probably really pissed. This would be the first time she'd had to pick up the phone and work in years, let alone the small matter that she was about to break her oath to never do hard drugs again.

But she'd smoked too much to know that she cared or to have any kind of dramatic reaction. In some ways this was just an understanding that returned to her, something she knew had never left, would never really leave. There wasn't even resignation. Ultimately, everything returned to the same point. The gaps in between were just time.

She rang Jonathan who confirmed in code on the phone what her cut would be, the supply, and the meeting points for the drops. Just before he hung up, he told her she wouldn't regret it.

Diva turned the fortune cookie in her fingers for a few minutes before breaking it open. Tan baked dough crumbled into her lap, the pill fell into the palm of her hand.

It certainly looked harmless enough, no bigger than an aspirin.

She ate the cookie and then washed the pill down with a Coke and sat in her La-Z-Boy waiting for the drug to take effect. It was a bit like waiting to die, she thought to herself before remembering Jonathan's comment about DMT being released by the brain just before we pass.

She decided she didn't like that idea so she got up to choose a book. She selected blindly, not minding what she read, simply knowing that she wanted something to take her thoughts away while she came up.

As she turned from the bookcase, she heard something, a thick shushing sound, like a card being selected from a deck. There was a flutter of paper wings and then a thud. She looked at her feet. A book had fallen. Somehow, she must have caught its spine when she drew her first choice.

She bent down to pick it up. It was L. Frank Baum's *The Wonderful Wizard of Oz*, an old favourite. If there was one thing in life Diva could really appreciate, it was that the Wizard was nothing more than a humbug. She pressed the other book back, leant against the wall and started to read.

She was instantly transported to the desolate plains of Kansas, to life with the dour Aunt Em and Uncle Henry, and then quickly into the eye of the tornado.

She read the words: 'And then a strange thing happened.'

And then a strange thing did happen. A word peeled off the page and floated slowly into the air. Diva stared at it. From the corner of her eye, she sensed another lifting, being teased from the paper as if caught on a magician's invisible thread. There was another. And another.

Before Diva knew what was happening, she was caught in a twisting maelstrom of words, sentences wrapping around her like a string of Matisse dancers. Some went this way, some went that. The letters swam through the air in 3D, she could see their shadows. They looked tangible enough to touch. And they were getting faster.

'What the hell . . . ' Diva said and watched, in horror, as the words came out of her mouth and took shape in front of her, briefly, before being sucked into the walls of the word vortex.

Books started falling from the shelves, their flecked white wings flapping and emptying yet more words into the flow. A section of the room to her right was pulled loose and was drawn, tumbling, towards the eddy, which was now swirling around her quite quickly.

She watched another section prise free and nearly hit her. Diva threw her hands over her head and crouched down to the floor. The whole room started dissolving. Words were no longer themselves. Everything was getting lost in a twisting, turning mire.

Diva even started to lose sense of her own physical being. She felt herself, until now safe in the eye of the storm, coming apart and being pulled in towards it. She felt as if she were just a letter herself, and she was getting lost in the current.

Time bent and twisted in on itself. Diva started to pass out. She couldn't tell if she was upright. She felt nothing more than a loose collection of molecules. The stuff that bound the world was disappearing.

She located a thought in what would have been the crook of her arm but which was now the first angle of the letter Z. A chequerboard spiralled out from it and flew through the air like an enormous sheet unfurling, laying out its black and white tiles on a ferocious wind.

Her apartment was gone. She was in a blank new world, standing on a chequerboard floor. An eternity passed. The floor created itself on the horizon, seemingly more slowly but clearly still with great speed as it reached new faraway distances in short spaces of time. She looked up at the abstract white sky, into an abyss as empty as the now blank pages of her beloved books.

Where was she?

Click, click, click.

What was she?

Click and click and click.

And what was that noise?

Don't listen, Diva.

Clickety, click.

Don't tune into it.

She recognized that voice.

Run, Diva, run.

Something had changed.

Diva suddenly saw herself falling and breaking two milk teeth.

She saw herself chasing her brother in the garden on a bright day, around and around and around, laughing.

She saw herself making it to a platform on Plough Lilly Lake.

She saw Mother crying in the mirror as they got dressed for Daddy's funeral.

She saw herself arriving for her first day at Helena High.

She saw that bird dying on the road.

She saw Johnny, her first crush, walking across the grass.

She saw herself graduating *summa cum laude*.

She watched Donald make love to her and then propose.

She saw their apartment in Sausalito.

She watched Donald climb on stage at Altamont and take off his clothes.

She stared down at Lisa breastfeeding.

She saw Carlos teaching Donald how to cook cocaine.

She watched Donald chase after Lisa riding on her bike.

She saw Donald, the vomit frozen across his mouth.

She saw them taking Lisa away.

She saw the man who beat her.

She saw the hospital.

She saw herself writing.

She saw herself going to work.

She saw the hospital again.

She watched Lisa, a woman, from afar, running across a road.

She saw her apartment in 444 VanVanVane Street.

She saw herself in the mirror, the way she'd aged.

She saw Jonathan.

She saw herself on the phone.
She saw the fortune cookie.
She saw the can of Coke.
And she sobbed.

Frank was babysitting for Ben and Mandy, rehearsing lines for the play, half-watching a faint, ghost transmission on cable, when a cold sweat came over him.

For no apparent reason, he was suddenly finding it hard to breathe. A spasm fired across his ribs and the words HEART ATTACK flashed through his mind like a road warning in the night.

He thought he was going to be sick. He clamped a hand over his mouth to stop the vomit. Another spasm across his chest sent terrifying shock waves through his nervous system. His mind spiralled. He was paralysed with a fear that told him he was in real physical danger.

He felt a mild subsidence. Not enough to get a grip on, not enough to feel confident with, but enough for him to at least see what was ahead, enough for him to get his bearings. He caught a reflection of himself in the window. The blood had drained from his cheeks, leaving an empty whiteness behind.

He managed to stand, leaning heavily on the edge of the sofa, his legs shaking. He moved towards the kitchen. He kept saying to himself: 'Nice and easy, nice and easy.'

He reached the refrigerator. He opened it. There was a carton of milk in a brown-paper bag. He took the bag out and placed it over his mouth, half-wondering how he knew about this.

Slowly, gradually, he felt better. He stepped to one of the stools by the breakfast bar and perched himself. He breathed.

'I think there's something wrong with our babysitter,' Mandy said, looking into the mobile.

'What?' Ben replied.

'Take a look.'

Mandy handed Ben the phone and took another long suck on her margarita – it tasted so damn good.

'Jesus,' Ben said.

'Is he OK?'

'It doesn't look like it.'

Ben looked down into the phone and mumbled something about the Webcam and bytes per minute and the fact they'd OKed a man to do the job. Mandy took the chance to look away. The restaurant sloshed around in an orange liquid light. There was a TV hanging over a bar, showing basketball. There were signed pictures on the wall of famous people and disembowelled *piñatas* hanging from the ceiling. Waitresses moved between the tables gripping pitchers of margaritas by their chests, like barbells. She watched lovers gorge themselves on tepid beans and half-melted cheese.

'Maybe we should go home,' she heard him say.

'But we only just got here.'

'I know,' Ben sighed.

'Why don't we give him a call, see if he's OK?'

'Wait a second. I can't see him now. I think he's gone to the bathroom.'

'Give him a few minutes, I'm shurr he'll be fine.'

Ben looked up at her. 'Are you drunk?'

'No.'

'You've nearly finished that already!'

Looking out of the tops of her eyes naughtily at him,

Mandy took a long slurp on the straw till the glass gurgled and burped.

'Correction,' she said, putting it down. 'I have finished it.'

'Mandy,' Ben said sternly. 'You always peak too early and then pass out. I don't want to have to carry you home.'

'You won't have to, I swear,' Mandy managed to reply without slurring this time.

'Hmm,' Ben frowned.

'How about a toast!' Mandy restarted, grabbing the pitcher and refilling their glasses. Sour-sweet green slush slopped out in dollops. 'My darling husband.'

'My beautiful wife.'

They chinked.

'Bastard.'

'Bitch.'

They laughed.

'Did you hear that?' Mandy said, her expression suddenly shifting.

'What?'

'I thought I heard Billy.'

'Billy?'

'Check the phone.'

Ben picked up the mobile.

'That's weird.'

'Is he OK?'

'Frank's giving him the bottle.'

'Look,' Mandy said, glancing at her chest. 'I'm leaking.'

'Christ, Mandy,' Ben said, looking around anxiously while his wife reached for napkins and stuffed them into her bra.

'What else do you want me to do?'

'I dunno,' he replied, realizing he wasn't equipped to answer the question. 'I'm sorry.'

'It's your fault. If you hadn't insisted on giving him formula this wouldn't be happening.'

'I'm sorry,' Ben said again. 'Look on the bright side. Maybe he'll sleep through.'

'I'll believe that when I see it.'

A waitress arrived and took their order.

'Did you really hear Billy crying just now?' Ben asked after she left.

'Yeah,' Mandy said, taking another sip of her drink. 'It happens all the time.'

'Really?'

'I think the pregnancy did something to me. I hear all kinds of things.'

'Not people in their apartments again?'

'Not just that.'

'What, then?'

'It's hard to say.'

'Try.'

'It's mostly a jumble,' Mandy said, looking at him with alcoholic lucidity. 'You remember that video installation we saw at the MoMA with all the voices going in and out and over-lacing one another? It's kind of like that.'

'When did this start?' Ben said, looking worried.

'Couple of months ago.'

'A couple of months!'

'Don't freak out, Ben. It's no big deal.'

'No big deal? Don't you think it's kind of weird for you to be hearing voices? I mean, why don't I hear them?'

'Maybe you're not tuned in.'

'Tuned in?'

'I think they're ghosts.'

'You think 444's haunted?' Ben said.

Mandy nodded earnestly. Ben did one of his looks, which combined rolling his eyes, looking away into a distance, vaguely shaking his head, jutting his jaw forward and frowning, all at the same time. It was a pretty irritating expression.

'I was looking the building up on the Internet the other day,' Mandy said, managing to ignore him. 'Did you know, it used to be a tenement block for Irish immigrants? Our apartment had a family of fifteen people living in it. There was an outhouse in the corridor, that's what all the disused cupboards on the landings are, old outhouses. Can you imagine what it must have been like . . . '

'No.'

'The disease, the poverty, the death . . . '

'I can't.'

'I wonder what they were like.'

'Mandy.'

'I think they lost a child.'

'Mandy.'

'I hear it crying sometimes. I thought it was Billy at first, but then . . . '

'Mandy!'

She stopped and looked at him, a milky glaze in her eyes slowly clearing. 'It's all right, Ben. I don't think they want to hurt us.'

Ben didn't reply.

'You think I'm mad, don't you?'

He still didn't say anything.

'Maybe you're right,' Mandy said, suddenly looking worried.

'You don't seriously believe in ghosts, do you?' Ben tried. 'I mean, you've always been like me on those sorts of things, so . . . level-headed.'

'I know.'

'It's probably just your hormones, or something. Maybe you should go see Dr Weiman.'

'Yeah. Maybe.'

She was pregnant. Of course, she was. Anna-lise let out a short laugh at the bitter sweetness of it. She sat, straddled on the toilet, her cream satin-nightdress falling away from her body, and stared into the result.

Pregnant.

At what point did I grow up to become a moron? she wondered to herself. It was her mother's rhetorical voice working inside her brain, a voice that echoed from her past each time she did something wrong.

Maybe this was why she had shot that scene with Helmut in Morgan's place. Not because she wanted revenge, not even because she enjoyed it (even though she had), but because she knew it would come back and bite her right on the ass. It had to, for it to make sense. That was the whole point of recording it – to get caught, to fuck up.

But she hadn't counted on getting pregnant, nor on getting back together with Henry for that matter. She'd tried not to, she'd tried to protect herself, but what could she do? She loved him.

And now she had set herself up for real damage because somehow, in her brilliance, Anna-lise had managed to get exactly what she wanted at the very instant of her own, self-made demise.

And it would make things much harder, it would make the fall that much further, an unbearable additional distance, in fact. She had been counting on a simple ruin. How would she cope with this extra dimension to her tragedy?

Because if the pregnancy didn't scare him off, the video definitely would.

Anna-lise stood up, threw the pregnancy test into the small plastic bin under the basin, flushed the toilet and stepped outside. Henry was in the living room with his back turned, looking at the work she'd recently framed and hung on the wall, drinking coffee.

'I'm trying to decide which one I like best,' he said.

'Why?' Anna-lise said, sliding her arms around him and pressing herself into his back.

'I want to give one to my father. It's his birthday next week.'

'I thought you two didn't talk.'

'We started again.'

'Really? When did that happen?'

'After I got back from Thailand. I went to see him because I wanted to tell him something.'

'Yeah?'

Henry paused and rubbed Anna-lise's hands, which were clasped together across his stomach.

'I wanted to tell him I'd met a girl I liked.'

'Has she got bigger breasts than me?'

Henry broke her clasp gently, as if he were undoing a valuable necklace, and turned to face her.

'Anna-lise, there's something I need to tell you.'

'Me too.'

'It's important.'

'So's this.'

Henry looked at her sternly. 'It's about my father ... I ... He ... The thing is we ... how do I put this?'

'I'm pregnant.'

Henry stared at her exactly as she imagined he would. A small part of her felt proud. That's how you tell someone something, Henry, she thought to herself. You just come right out and say it.

'Pregnant?'

'Yup,' she said, popping the P with expectant indignation.

'Are you sure?'

'The test is ninety per cent certain and I've done it three times so I'm two hundred and seventy per cent sure.'

Henry laughed.

'I'm being serious.'

'I know,' Henry said, grinning.

'Why are you smiling? Are you freaking out?'

'No,' Henry replied. 'I'm happy.'

'Happy?'

'Aren't you?'

'No.' Anna-lise stopped. 'I don't think so.'

'I thought you wanted babies.'

'I do.'

'Well, then, let's have one.'

'You're kidding, right?'

'Why would I be?'

'Isn't it a bit soon? We've only been back together six weeks. Are you sure you know what you're saying?'

'Listen to me, Anna-lise,' Henry said, finally looking serious. 'This is the reason I asked you to have me back. This is where we've come to. We've been together long enough to know we should be together. So let's just be together. Let's be together and have babies. It's what we both want. I'm not scared any more. I want to be with you.'

'Is that a proposal?'

'Yes.'

'Jesus Christ, Henry, you could have said something, you could have warned me.'

'I only just realized myself.'

Anna-lise threw her hands to her mouth.

'Well,' Henry said. 'Will you?'

'You know I will! Yes. Oh my God.'

Anna-lise tried to throw herself into Henry but he stopped her.

'Wait. I still haven't told you my thing. You need to know.'

Anna-lise stared at Henry and waited.

'Go on, then,' she said.

Frank stepped into the shadow of the green awning and smiled as the elderly doorman, who was dressed in a grey-green uniform with brass buttons and cap to match, opened the door with a small bow. He felt the doorman follow him down the shallow marbled corridor into the art-deco lobby with its brass-fronted elevators and tin mailboxes. There was a wooden desk in one corner.

'Visiting?' he said, stepping behind the desk.

'Goldstein. Elena Goldstein.'

'P14.'

'That's right.'

'And you are?'

'Frank Mellie.'

'I'll let her know you're here.'

'Thank you,' Frank replied and watched as the doorman punched numbers on a telephone, turned and mumbled discreetly into the receiver.

'Dr Goldstein will see you in just a few minutes,' he said, turning back around brightly, replacing the phone and motioning towards a chair at the far wall. 'Will you take a seat?'

Frank smiled at him and did as he was told. He waited, resisting the urge to tap his toes against the cold floor. He watched the doorman busy himself with nothing – arranging letters, marking a large book that lay open on the desk, sliding a key onto a key ring.

'When I was a kid,' the doorman started without looking up, 'I used to love people with names like yours. My brother and I, we'd go through the telephone directory and call up S. Mellie asking: "Hello, are you Smelly, are you Smelly?" and when they said yes we'd roar with laughter, then hang up.' He momentarily caught himself and glanced up at Frank. 'No offence, mind.'

'None taken.' Frank smiled.

Frank noticed a skeletal woman in white fur approach the building. Three dogs, their shaven stick legs trotting under flying white coats, yapped at her heels. The doorman rushed to open the door.

'Good morning, Mrs Land!' he said.

'Morning, Harry!' she replied.

'Good morning, ladies!' the doorman said, bending down.

'Don't be nice to them, Harry,' Mrs Land replied. 'They're on probation.'

'Oh dear,' the doorman replied. 'No treats today, then?'

'Absolutely not!'

Thick curtains of cosmetic powder hung from cheekbone rails, drawn into the hollows of her face as if caught on a through draught. Her terrifying red lipstick was poorly applied, so too the rainbows of peacock-blue mascara. Somehow the misapplication gave Frank the impression that Mrs Land was a drunk. She looked to be a hundred years old.

Studying her more carefully, Frank figured she was probably a beauty of the 1920s. She was a living relic, as classic to New York as the art-deco lobby they were in. In one hand, she held a transparent bag filled with dog shit.

'I'll just get your mail,' Harry said as Mrs Land waited for an elevator. The dogs sniffed Frank's air. 'Here you go.' He handed her a pile of bills bound together with an elastic band, just as the elevators chimed.

'Thank you,' she replied, taking them and disappearing into the wall like a ghost.

A buzzer went. Harry stepped towards the intercom behind his desk and pressed a button. He glanced at Frank with a gentle look.

'Dr Goldstein will see you now, Mr Mellie,' he said.

'Thanks,' he replied, getting up.

'Fourteenth floor.'

'Yes,' he replied, pressing the call button.

In the elevator, Frank took the opportunity to gather his thoughts. He took several deep breaths and wondered where he might begin the session. He'd had so many thoughts since the panic attack.

He found himself in front of Dr Goldstein's door. He pressed the buzzer. There was the sound of movement within and then the door opened to reveal a corridor, some houseplants, another door, a thin shaft of light – but no Dr Goldstein.

Frank remembered to look down.

Dr Goldstein smiled up at him, large round glasses encircling her face like a Venn diagram, an elaborate green clasp holding up bark-coloured hair.

'Hello, Frank,' she said in a helium voice, holding out a tiny hand. 'Nice to see you again. It's been a while.'

'Hello, Dr Goldstein,' Frank replied, taking the hand in his without gripping or shaking. It was too small a hand for that. Instead, they pawed each other for a moment, a handshake's equivalent of an air kiss.

The doctor turned and padded gently down the corridor. She was dressed in a long flowery skirt and deep-red satin blouse. She was wearing a thick gold necklace over the blouse. It clashed with Catholic boldness. Her broad hips jolted from left to right as she walked, as if the balls of her thighs were snagging on her hip sockets.

Frank followed her into a room that probably had a view of Central Park if the blinds were drawn. There were more potted plants on the sill.

'Take a seat,' Dr Goldstein squeaked.

'Thank you.'

The experience of arriving for the session – starting in the lobby, which acclimatized Frank from the frenetic pace of the street to a calmer, gentler way in the building; then on to the elevator with its sense of enclosure and composure; then walking down the long corridor of the fourteenth floor as if travelling on a conveyor belt to a different world; and finally stepping into the apartment with its subdued lighting and the surreal presence of Dr Goldstein herself – was meditative. Frank found himself breathing deeply, calmly. Already he had found some sense of inner peace.

'Thank you for seeing me at such short notice.'

'That's all right,' Dr Goldstein replied.

'I needed to see you urgently.'

'Yes.'

'I've had a panic attack. At least, I think it was a panic attack. I've never had one until now.'

'When someone has a panic attack they usually know,' Dr Goldstein said reassuringly. 'So chances are, it was a panic attack.'

Frank breathed a sigh of relief. At least one answer had presented itself quickly.

'I thought I was going to die.'

The psychiatrist nodded. 'Can you tell me,' she said, 'what you were doing at the time, just before the attack came on?'

'Just watching TV and rehearsing lines for a play.'

'What were you watching?'

'*Big Brother*.'

'And what play are you rehearsing lines for?'

'*One Flew Over the Cuckoo's Nest*.'

'And what thoughts, as best as you can remember, immediately preceded the attack?'

'I was thinking about finding a new tenant to share.'

'Do you think the prospect of getting a new tenant made you have the attack?'

'Maybe. People are so crazy in New York.'

'Some people can be.'

'I feel like I'm living in an episode of *Big Brother* myself.'

'How do you mean?'

'Just that New York is like reality TV. We're living in a game show.'

The psychiatrist looked at him with a blank expression.

'Oh, I don't know.' Frank sighed. 'Maybe it's just my building. We've got a lot of construction going on – we're doing the roof. The noise never stops and the water and electricity keep getting cut off. The costs keep going up. Everyone's really stressed out about it.'

'I see.'

'The worst thing is, we're only doing it because our Co-op President, Morgan, needed an excuse to extend her apartment.'

Dr Goldstein nodded.

'I feel like we're coins in an arcade game; you know, the kind with the shelves that drive piles of dimes. Ultimately, some of us have to fall over the edge. The more coins that get added to the machine, the more we get piled on top of one another, the closer we all get. Maybe some of us will never fall. Maybe fifty of us will fall at the same time. There's no rhyme or reason to who goes or how, but we're all a part of it, we're all in the same game, and the chasm is just there, right there, for any one of us to fall into.'

'You're scared that the city is too crowded?'

'We're all cooped up on this island. The place feels like an oversized lunatic asylum. Everyone is mad in one way or another. We call them neurotic but, really, it's much worse than that. I know I kill someone in my thoughts nearly every single day on my way to work.'

'Go on.'

'Come on, Doc, you gotta admit everyone in New York is a latent sociopath. Everyone I know has a shrink. Most people are on medication.'

'It can be stressful living in the city.'

'It's 'cos they got us all wound up so tight.'

'Who does?'

'The government, the police, the corporations, Morgan . . . everyone. It's a massive conspiracy. They're all working together to keep the noose tight. Zero-tolerance, corporate policing, news propaganda; anything and everything to make sure no one steps out of line, that we all act right, think right. It's driving me nuts. It's driving everyone nuts. They've got us in this box with their insane rules, making sure we keep the machine working. They don't let anyone express themselves any more, be who they really are. They're only interested in control and power and making money. We're living in a fascist democracy. The notion that we have any real say, any individual will, is a joke. If they don't like the numbers, they just change the answer. We don't have the ability to change things, be ourselves. We're just pawns. But one day something's got to give. It has to. The pressure is too much.'

There was a pause as a soft breeze moved through the window and caressed the plants.

'You know, in the old days, the seventies, when there was bad crime and stuff, people were allowed to go mad, you know, like Charles Bronson in *Death Wish*,' Frank tried, 'I think that was better in a way. The people that were prone to insanity were the ones that went over the edge. The instances were more isolated. This plastic Disneyland they've got us living in today is scarier than that world because there's a facade of control, an image of sanity. But the madness hasn't gone away. It's just been suppressed. And now we're all living in a pressure cooker where no one freaks out. And all that really means is that any one of us could, even the straightest, sanest, most normal person. Maybe all of us will go crazy. Maybe that's what I'm scared of. I'm scared that, one day, the whole city is going to tip over the edge. When summer gets going, people are going to snap. When it gets to a hundred degrees and a hundred per cent humidity, the collars on all those suits are going to get real tight. I'm telling you, Doctor, everything you see right now, people walking calmly down the street, it's all an illusion. They're trying to stay calm, they're trying to look as cool as possible, but it's not real. People are seething in their normalcy. There's only so much we can take. People are going to go over the edge. One day, one day soon, there's going to be an episode of violence.'

'Violence? What kind of violence?'

'The killing kind.'

Dr Goldstein took a long look at Frank. Frank stared back at her, breathing heavily, not sure about the way the session was going. He hadn't expected to say that last bit. It had just come out. It wasn't that he regretted saying it, he just hadn't known it was there, inside him – until now.

'Do you remember, Frank, when you came to see me for a few weeks – right after the September 11th attacks?' Dr Goldstein eventually restarted.

Frank nodded.

'Do you remember how angry you were then?'

Frank looked at her.

'I mentioned to you that in times of collective social trauma, people tend to respond by reliving their own personal traumas, they have the same emotional response. Do you remember that?'

'Yes,' Frank replied. 'You said that I was angry after September 11th because anger was my emotional response to the time Dad left me on the mountain and I got lost in the dark. You said it was the emotional tool I relied on to cope. It helped me to survive that night, just as it helps me to survive in life. But after a while, it can be self-destructive and I have to know when to stop being angry in order to survive.'

'That's right. But for the purposes of today's discussion I want to focus you on the idea that not everyone has the same emotional response to trauma as you. Some people cry. Some people become withdrawn. Some people flip out. It all depends. People react differently.'

'OK.'

'So what I'm saying to you is this: you don't need to be scared that everyone else is feeling the same way you are. You don't need to fear that the whole city is going to sink into a violent killing spree just because you imagine that that is what you might do. There may be a collective trauma of sorts occurring in your building right now but that doesn't mean everyone is going to react to it in the exact same way.'

'What do you mean, collective trauma in my building?'

'Isn't that what you've been saying, Frank?'

'I was talking about New York.'

'No, Frank, you've been talking about Morgan and the construction work and the people in your building.'

'Have I?'

'Haven't you?'

Frank stopped and thought.

'In order to stop these panic attacks from recurring,' Dr Goldstein continued, 'I want you to stop worrying about everyone else. I want you to forget about them entirely. As I explained to you before, dealing with mass trauma on a collective scale is a near-impossible task because it means you have to deal with everyone's individual traumas. It's like trying to undo an enormous ball of knotted string. You literally have to go through the whole mess and undo each individual knot one by one to solve the problem.'

'Which is what makes the whole world such a depressing place,' Frank said. 'The kid in Syria whose parents get killed by an American tank, he's gonna grow up furious with the world and when the next war happens a thousand miles away he's gonna become a suicide bomber, right?'

'Possibly.'

'And so the whole thing just goes on and on and on and the whole world becomes a fucked-up mess and all that's ever going to happen is war and violence and death and suffering. Now try and tell me that the world isn't crazy. Tell me I don't have to worry about everyone going simultaneously insane.'

Dr Goldstein opened her palms submissively at Frank.

'This is just what I'm trying to tell you not to do, Frank. You can't drive yourself into a corner trying to solve the world's problems. All you'll achieve is more panic attacks. What you need to focus on is your emotional response to the stress you're facing right now, especially with this new development you've mentioned.'

'What new development?'

'These thoughts of violence.'

Frank huffed. 'You're taking that out of context. I was talking about everyone, I was talking about everyone turning violent, not just me.'

'Are you saying you don't harbour fantasies about killing Morgan?'

'What? No. I mean, not specifically. At least, I don't think so.'

'OK, then. Well, why don't you think about it and we can discuss it more next week? Would the same time suit?'

'I guess,' Frank replied, looking at his fingers. He didn't like the way things had ended. He felt very dissatisfied.

'Good,' Dr Goldstein said, marking her diary. 'Next week, then.'

'Sure.'

EXTRA BOARD MEETING:

APARTMENT P1, THIS TUESDAY 7.30 SHARP!

M

(Aka The Wicked Witch of the West)

M ike was on duty for an anti-globalization protest. He was posted at 59th and Fifth. It was his job to ferry human traffic north and as circuitously around Central Park as possible, without actually preventing the protesters from reaching the Global Bank meeting in the Ferrari-Roche Hotel if they really, really wanted to get there.

The City had pulled every blue uniform for this determined effort in crowd aggravation. There must have been a cop for every two protesters.

And we have guns, he thought to himself.

There were cops on foot, cops on horses, cops on motor-bikes, cops on scooters, cops on Razors, cops in cars, cop dogs, cop cats – it was Cop World.

Even so, everything was proceeding with miraculous calm. So far.

'Jumping H. Christmas, did you get a look at that one?' said Johnny Columbus, the Long Island jockstrap Mike had been assigned to. He'd recently promised to his dying Catholic mother never again to blaspheme. 'She had more metal in her face than a fucking car.'

Mike didn't see the point in encouraging him.

'I thought tongue studs were meant for better head but that's taking it too far,' Columbus continued. 'I'd rather stick my dick in a meat grinder.'

Mike gazed up into the cleansing depths of the denim-blue sky. He noticed a new ad plastered on the side of Gotham Tower. Molly Turrentine, an androgynous sitcom actor, was sticking her non-existent ass into the camera with a look of supremely smug serenity.

'Step back onto the sidewalk, please, sir,' Mike heard Columbus drill at someone robotically.

A well-dressed couple with a stroller had come to a stop at their junction, waiting for the WALK signal. Cars thundered past. The two front wheels of the buggy were on the road but were shielded from the traffic by a large drain.

'Excuse me, sir,' Columbus said with emphasis. 'You'll have to step away from the kerb.'

'Why?' the man replied sharply.

'Because I said so,' Columbus said, moving forward.

'Just do as he says, Adam,' the woman offered.

'No,' the man said, turning on her. 'I'm not breaking any law.'

'You're endangering the life of your child,' Columbus started.

'I think I know how to look after my own son,' the man replied.

'Please, honey,' the woman beseeched her husband, tugging at his elbow. 'Just do as he says.'

'People are unbelievable,' Columbus said, turning to Mike. 'Can't even trust them to raise a child.' He turned back to the man. 'Step away from the road, sir. Please.'

'No,' the man said flatly, levelling his gaze at him. 'No,' the man said again, turning to his wife. 'We've had to walk thirteen extra blocks just to get to the Park because of these police barriers and I'm not about to take shit from some stupid cop just because he can't see that I'm perfectly capable of taking care of my own kid.'

Mike watched Columbus take a large, forbidding step towards the man, placing him firmly in his Barney-shaped shadow.

'Would you care to repeat that, sir?'

'Jesus, Adam,' the wife added.

'Anyone can see that these barriers have been set up to make the whole city walk in circles. If the hippies want to waste their day walking the length and breadth of the island that's their problem but the rest of us have got better things to do. It's driving me nuts.'

Mike could see that Columbus was having to breathe deeply to control himself. His fingers were twitching at his holster. It was time for Mike to intervene.

'I'm sorry, sir,' he started (good cop). 'These barriers have been prearranged as part of the city mandate for efficient crowd control. If you have a complaint, please take it to City Hall. My colleague and I are just doing our jobs.'

The WALK signal fired and the pool of people that had gathered around them at the kerb began seeping past into the street. Mike, Columbus and the small family remained trapped in their eddy, caught on the end of this pointless barb.

'Who the hell is this guy?' the man said, looking at Columbus. 'Your lover?'

Mike now realized he'd have to arrest the man before Columbus shot him. Somehow he managed to squeeze himself between the two men.

'Sir, you're under arrest,' Mike said.

The woman screamed, 'Ohmygawd!'

'What for?' the man replied.

'Disturbing the peace, reckless endangerment, insulting an officer of the law . . . '

'And resisting arrest,' Columbus added.

'Resisting arr—'

'That's right,' Columbus said, now managing to shoulder past Mike and forcing the man to the ground in two swift moves that also upended the stroller.

'My baby!' the woman yelled as the infant nearly spilled out into the road.

Mike instinctively jumped for the child and scooped him up in his arms. The man yelped into the concrete in pain. Columbus screamed at Mike for help.

But Mike wasn't there. A strangely familiar, yet alien, urge – like some long-forgotten instinct to protect and to serve – was flushing through him. He was lost in the child. He marvelled at its tiny features. He found himself making cootchie-cootchie-coo faces while Columbus did his best to kill its parents.

He only snapped out of it when the walkie-talkie crackled:

'Attention all units! Attention all units! All units needed urgently at 52nd and Fourth. Massive civic unrest. Assistance required immediately!'

Mike glanced up to see police helicopters whirlybird-waltzing with the press.

'Get your asses down here fast! There's a goddamned riot going on.'

'Come on, Columbus,' Mike said dreamily, handing the baby back to its distraught mother. 'We gotta go.'

Columbus jumped up, reaching for his truncheon. 'It's about goddamn . . . Damn, I keep doing it.' He made the sign of the cross and looked heavenward before turning back to Mike. 'OK, then, let's go kick the shit out of some freaks. I'm all warmed up.'

It started with the chanting. The vibration of sound within and between bodies pressed tightly up against one another, finding frequency, broadcasting harmony, was a powerful force that drew the protesters into a single collective mass.

They methodically and meditatively rolled through the slogans, turning over angry mantras with rhythmic monotony, working themselves up with deliberate purpose, brainwashing themselves into a crescendo of emotion, so they could finally and cataclysmically roar out horrible truths to the rest of the world.

One or two bricks in the black wall of police riot shields shivered each time the crowd reached a cathartic climax – the men behind them wondering if the levee was going to break this time, if they had to brace themselves for a sudden rush of violence.

And then it would start again, on the cue of a megaphone, low and steady – different words, different message, same intensity, same ferocious feeling.

Garry was there, amongst it. He was lost in the crowd. He wasn't aware of himself, his own physical being. He was a part of something else, a larger human body. He couldn't see the details of people immediately around him, they were too close for focus, but he knew their features – their smells, their hair colours, their shapes – as if they were his own.

They sounded as one. They swayed together. They threw their fists into the air on one arm, the muscled kind depicted in revolutionary art. Something was happening here, something was happening. And Garry was a part of it.

He didn't know how the riot started. He didn't see the catalyst, if indeed there was one. It could easily have all been prearranged and orchestrated. Not that Garry cared. By the time he was in the crowd, by the time he started shouting, he knew he wanted a fight. That was what he was there for. That was why he had come. He just hadn't known it till now.

They were in the middle of a very long, low, bass-heavy protest. It had been rolling and rolling and rolling – in and up and over and through the crowd for what had seemed like hours, somehow finding new strength each time the call threatened to wane. A determined new voice always rose up from within to spur the rest of them, keep them going on and on, keep them driving at the enemy with relentless, militant intent.

And then, somewhere in the midst of the chanting – still a long way from climax but in a place where the words weren't, a place where the hoarse shouts were just a feeling, where people knew the phrases intuitively – came the release.

The revolution arrived in two stages, like the issue of thunder after lightning. First, a sonic pulse surged from behind and broke the wall of people in front. A few seconds' delay, and then came the roar.

They charged as one. They attacked with direction. They knew what to do, where to go, and how to get there. They concentrated on the spot and drove themselves towards it with the intensity of an arrowhead.

But then, as they hit resistance, they broke apart easily, and what had just been a solid, single mass became a random chaos of colour and clothes and hair. Garry found himself still amongst it but alone now, an individual in a collective madness, thrashing around within limbs like a snapped spasm.

It was too late for him to get out. He had to fight now, if only for survival. He found himself bandying with a small group that took on the police with a more cautious kind of frenzy.

Suddenly, from nowhere, there was blood and truncheons

and a smashed nose. Someone lashed out blindly and a blade flashed.

Where had that come from? Garry thought to himself with real fear. Who were these people? What was he doing here with them? He could just as well have been holding the knife himself. He felt guilty by association.

When the police concentrated their attack on one woman, Garry made his escape. As he broke away he came face to face with a young policeman. Garry kicked him as hard as he could and ran away blindly.

He went against the crowd, trying to find an exit. Pools of violence swirled. He weaved between them, kicking and punching at the fray – protester or policeman, it didn't matter now. He just had to get out.

Somehow, miraculously, like a time portal that would imminently close, a clear path with light and tarmac and road signs spread itself before him. Garry could see the way. He ran for it, ducking and shimmying between bodies – fighting and pushing and pressing – until he found himself close enough to a building to hold on to.

He smeared himself along the edge of it, inching himself away from the madness by using the straight wall as a guide, until finally, breathlessly, he found a sharp corner and turned. He found himself in an empty street, the roar of the riot coming through the concrete behind him.

At the end of the street, he could see policemen gathering and pointing. He looked up and saw a helicopter jerking a bright, judicial light. There was the whoop of sirens, the pop of tear gas, a rush of boots, the slow reassembly of order.

Adrenalin-charged, he tried to figure how to get himself away without being arrested. He scanned for buildings to duck into but there were none – just grand, glassed, mega-corporation lobbies with obviously locked revolving doors. He was in skyscraper territory.

There was only one thing for it – he'd just have to hope for the best. Policemen were coming towards him. He straightened his clothes, stiffened his spine, took a breath, turned on his heels, looked straight ahead and started to walk home.

Diva was watching the news at eleven, waiting for the *Star Trek* rerun – the first in the Borg series – to start.

'Sushi, the legendary front man for Austrian rock sensation Schadenfreude, was today pelted with eggs and vegetable missiles by anti-globalization demonstrators just moments after receiving a standing ovation from world leaders in Manhattan's Ferrari-Roche Hotel for his impassioned speech on space-programme development for the Third World.'

Diva cheered quietly at footage of the man, who was dressed in a leather Star-Spangled Banner outfit, being pelted and booed by crowds.

'More than two hundred protesters, who police say could have links with al-Qa'eda, were arrested under the nation's homeland security laws, without bail.'

She hissed at the footage of students being dragged through the streets by their hair.

'Gerrard Hitzlersperger, head of Global Space Enterprises Inc. and sponsor of the conference, condemned the attack: "Sushi has striven tirelessly for this worthy cause that might one day lead to comprehensive space programmes in developing countries. Accusations of oppression and exploitation are wholly unfounded. We are all working towards the same goal: to see Africans in space. At the end of the day, that's what everyone wants."

'Sushi had this to say: "If people buy my latest album and actually take the time to listen to the lyrics, they'll see that I've always believed that change can only come by working with the system. We've all got to work together, that's the meaning of my protest, that's my revolution. Throwing eggs isn't going to help Harry Soloudo, Tanzania's top astronaut. If it wasn't for me, Haiti, Ghana and Nepal wouldn't even have their own space-station

programmes. I'm not here to just make politicians look good."'

Diva booed. She remembered the days when she'd liked to listen to Schadenfreude.

'In spite of the attack, Sushi still managed to go on and later wow crowds at the Yankee Stadium in an impromptu performance of his number-one hit, "I Wanna Be An American", before setting off on a three-month whirlwind tour of the country to promote his new album, "Space Is Black".'

Diva watched with horror as the ageing Sushi strutted on a stage. Red, white and blue fireworks erupted around him while cheerleaders, with the word *Schadenfreude* stitched on their underpants, flew through the air.

'What a guy!' the plastic anchorman said, as the guitar strains faded. *'Isn't it a shame that a few rotten eggs have to go and spoil the party for everyone else?'*

'Some people have no respect,' added the peroxide-haired sex toy beside him. *'Didn't they see the suit he was wearing?'*

'He's got my vote,' the anchorman said.

'Mine too,' said the newswoman. *'I think he's just dreamy.'*

'And the album's great,' the anchorman continued. *'Go out and buy it, people. It's truly an American masterpiece.'*

'Coming up next in World News; a look at the train labour dispute in Philadelphia. Right after these messages.'

It was the clicking, insect sound people were hearing first. That was the way it came across initially, that was the way the transmission sounded, before the message made itself clear. I could see how that worked now.

One by one, the tenants in the building were all starting to tune in, opening their minds to the power of the collective. Mandy was the most receptive, cooped up in her apartment and still so tenderly receptive to the universal in the months after Billy's birth. And, of course, she was so much like Catherine – that helped her.

And to varying degrees, through different exposures, there were others as well. With the assistance of drugs, Diva had glimpsed it. Garry had beamed his experience of the riot to me very loudly – I could tell he was overwhelmed by the ecstasy of that particular collective experience, though it wasn't related to what was happening in 444.

Anna-lise and Henry were stepping into a beatific singularity each time they made love, which was a lot. I think that was what was keeping them safe up to that point, powerfully deaf to the malevolence. Frank's panic attacks were a direct result of his not being able to handle the violence that was so intrinsic and overbearing in the building. By contrast, Anna-lise and Henry had founded their own mini-collective, a bubble of love, which was protecting them – for the time being.

Who would be next, I wondered.

The transmission was becoming so strong now that the message was making its way out into the open, forming thoughts and words and shaping deeds.

I don't know who wrote *The Wicked Witch of the West* under Morgan's name on the blackboard – somehow that fell under my radar. Maybe I was asleep or tuning into something else at the time. I know it wasn't me. I was the one who rubbed it out so she wouldn't see. But it was clear that others were falling into the trance of it, if they were compelled to vent the truth that way.

It was a very frightening knowledge but there was no escaping. People were tuning in and the message was getting louder. It was only a matter of time before something actually happened.

Garry locked one headphone to his ear using his shoulder and cued the record with his forefinger. He checked the crowd. He released the vinyl. The beats banged together clumsily. He used his finger to slow the second record down and bring it in time. He turned up the headphone volume on the mixer and closed his eyes, trying to concentrate.

He felt a tap on his shoulder. He ignored it at first, still trying to get the beats in time. He felt it again. He glanced around. A half-naked, muscle-pumped, sweat machine with orange hair and red, hairless skin, grinned at him, rocking his head in double time to the music. Garry raised his eyebrows.

'Got any gangsta rap?' the man said, chewing on gum manically.

'No,' Garry said, trying to keep cool.

'Oh, come on, man, just give us a little bit of Brazen X.'

Garry smiled at him. 'OK.'

'And make it fast,' the red-head said before leaving.

'Sure,' Garry said, still smiling. He turned back to the turntables and mumbled, 'Asshole.'

He was running out of time on the first track. He lifted the stylus on the new record and took it back to the beginning of the beat, fine cuing with his index finger again. Then he released the record.

Thud, dud, thud, bud, dud, thud, dud.

The beats just weren't coming together. He flirted with the idea of another track. He looked at the record that was playing. He had only twenty or so seconds left. He tried not to panic. He concentrated, unable to enjoy the music for the work of getting the mix right.

He felt another tap. He threw a STOP signal over his shoulder. This guy was really getting on his nerves.

'Come on,' he mouthed to the mixer.

Suddenly, they were there. They were there! He'd have to keep making small adjustments but the beats were close enough to travel. He brought the new track in, gently. It wasn't a strong enough mix for him to flick the cross-fader back and forth, but it would do.

Another tap. Garry glanced around now. The red man had turned into an African supermodel. She was six foot, svelte and with hips. She was smiling brilliantly at him. Garry edged the cross-fader a few centimetres and stood up straight to smile back at her. He hoped that mixing the two tracks without looking might impress.

'Hey,' Garry said.

'Have you got any gangsta rap?' she asked.

Garry slid the cross-fader to centre. He could hear the first track fading out naturally. Everyone was bumping. They didn't seem to even notice that he'd changed records. The set was going well.

'Now tell me honestly,' he said, leaning close enough to brush his lips against her ear. 'You don't really want to hear that shit, do you?'

'I hate house,' the model replied, leaning away.

'Well,' Garry said, reaching around her waist and spreading a free arm over the crowd as they rose with the horn section, some of them calling out and whistling. 'You're in the minority, then.'

The model huffed like a spoilt child. 'No one wants to hear any more of this,' she said. 'Everyone wants gangsta rap. They're all talking about it.'

'Sure,' Garry replied.

'Look,' she said, reaching for his CD case. 'I'll show you.'

'Uh-uh!' Garry said sharply. 'I don't think so.'

Just then the red man swam into view beneath the DJ booth, mouthing words, holding two righteous fingers in the air.

'What's the matter?' the model said, turning so that her face was very close to Garry's. 'Don't you trust me?'

'It's not that,' Garry said.

'What then?' the model said, reaching again for the CD case. This time Garry let her take it.

'Where are you from?' he asked, watching her turn the plastic pages.

'I grew up on the West Coast but my parents are from Senegal.'

'Cool,' Garry said, glancing at the record. He still had time.

'Here,' she said, pulling out a CD. 'Put this on.'

Garry looked at it.

'Everyone will go crazy, I swear,' the model said.

'Sure they will.'

'If you don't put it on, my friends and I are gonna leave,' the model said, pointing at a miniskirted cluster in the crowd.

Garry looked at her. 'What's your name?'

'Chantal.'

'I'm Garry,' he said, holding out his hand.

'Pleased to meet you,' she replied, holding his hand like it was dirty linen.

Garry looked at her breasts for a second and weighed them up against the happiness of the crowd.

'Listen,' he said. 'I'll make you a deal.'

She eyed him suspiciously.

'I'll put this CD on, if you give me your number.'

'I've got a boyfriend,' she replied quickly.

'And I've got a girlfriend,' Garry shot back even though it wasn't true.

She shifted on her feet. 'I dunno,' she said.

'No number, no gangsta rap.'

The model tutted. 'OK, then. Have you got a pen?'

'I'll put it in my cell,' Garry replied.

After they were done, Chantal stepped gingerly down from the DJ booth, her long calves shaking in high heels. Garry felt a small, helpless feeling in his stomach as he watched her hips.

He turned back to the decks and opened the CD player. He considered the best way to bring the song in but decided there was no point in pretending. He was about to trash a perfectly decent set – he might as well get it over and done with.

He pressed play and flicked the cross-fader across. The room froze for a second. Time stopped. Eyes flashed. Garry was on stage, naked before them all. What had he done?

Then, from nowhere, everyone roared. Garry watched with horror as the place exploded with new energy and excitement. Shit, Garry thought to himself, they really did want gangsta rap. He saw Chantal in the crowd. She was dancing erotically with a girlfriend under the enormous Fake! sponsorship banner. The red man caught his look and threw him a thumb. Garry threw one back. People pumped their fists at him. He was the Man. Garry basked in the glory, unable to resist taking credit.

But then he realized – there was a problem.

He quickly searched his CD case. He scrambled through his records. Now he was in trouble. He didn't have any more gangsta rap with him. And he couldn't segue back into house. And time was running out. He tried to find something that might mix, even remotely, but there was nothing.

Ten seconds left on the track. He picked the first record he could find. He slapped it on the turntable, cued it up. The rap tune started to fade. People slowed down. They waited for the new beat, the next tune, to rock their bodies.

Garry brought it in.

He watched them listening, frowning, visibly sighing. People streamed off the dance floor like there was a fire. The red man walked past the DJ booth and booed. Chantal was nowhere to be seen.

Garry felt himself come over in a hot flush. He suddenly hated the record he'd put on. He wanted desperately for it to end. He wanted people to come back and dance. He wanted to turn back time.

But it was too late. They were gone. Only three or four people remained. In the space of a few seconds, Garry had successfully emptied the dance floor. He ducked behind the deck desk to hide, flicking through his records half in hope that he might find something to turn things around, half doing it to look busy, like there was some sort of game plan to all of this.

The booth shook when Wolf, the party organizer, jumped up. 'Garry . . . '

'It's cool, everything's cool,' Garry tried. 'Trust me.'

'No, it isn't cool. You're off. Max is coming on next. You've got one tune left.'

Garry nodded. He didn't even want it. He just wanted to get as far away as possible. And the worst was still to come: the walk of shame, the one where he left the party with his records slung heavily over his shoulder, everyone looking at him, knowing he was the DJ that had emptied the place, the Loser.

'And if you think I'm gonna pay you for a full set you got another thing coming, bud.'

'Hey,' Garry cried, looking at him. 'You can't do that.'

'We agreed two hours, you've played for forty-five minutes. I'll pay you half minus whatever you've had from the bar.'

'Wolf, don't do this to me, man. I got major money problems. My maintenance has gone way up and gigs are tight at the moment with the crackdown – you know how it is.'

'Yeah, I do. Which is exactly why I can't afford fuck-ups like this,' Wolf said. 'Take what I give and be grateful. Maybe I won't tell people what happened here.'

As Wolf left, Garry realized that he didn't want to be a DJ any more. He had been humiliated. No one even cared about the music anyway, not like he did. They didn't want to hear anything good. They just wanted to hear whatever was being sold, mass market, on CDs. Whatever the multinational music-company marketing departments had decided was the new Big, that was what people wanted to hear. They wanted to be led. They wanted to be told what to listen to. People were sheep. They were all sheep.

Their lack of interest made Garry hate his passion. It seemed futile to invest so much in something no one else appreciated. Garry resented the music. He hated it. It was as if it hadn't fulfilled its end of the bargain. It hadn't delivered the glory on him that he had bestowed upon it. It had betrayed him.

He'd lost his dream. Grief rushed over him. It was as if a dear friend had died. He couldn't hear the music any more. He couldn't feel it. It was gone.

He chose his last record, the slowest, most melancholy one he could find, partly out of spite (he wanted to screw things up for Max's set as much as was humanly possible).

He chose 'Everybody's Got to Learn Sometimes' by the Korgis.

He put it on the turntable. He pressed play. The last of the dance floor turned and left as the cheesy synthesizer bleeped out the dying melody.

He was alone. The drumbeat dropped like plodding feet. Garry pumped up the volume. He stared out into the disco lights that were flashing slowly as the chorus rang. It was over. He'd decided. The next day, he'd put his record collection up for sale on eBay.

The Carlyle Garden started after a disused tenement block four blocks north of 444 collapsed in the night. I remember the sound of it, the instant of something crucial resonating, like a bone dislocating from its socket, or the sound of ground giving way. Then there was a sigh, followed by a crashing rattle of bricks that seemed to go on and on. It finally ended with a long, muted wheezing of air being drawn powerfully through a thick blanket of debris.

The following morning people had congregated at the wreckage and work soon started to turn it into a garden. It was back in the days when we knew the City wouldn't care, much less be able, to do anything about it. So we took account of it by ourselves.

We went down on weekends and all laboured at it together – all kinds of people from the neighbourhood. It took three months to remove the bricks and mortar, with only the brief assistance of an industrial digger to remove the final, embedded sections of concrete.

The south-eastern section was divided into allotments. Anyone who wanted to grow vegetables put their names down on a board and the winners got drawn from a hat. There was the erection of a steel fence and gate with a padlock to keep the drug dealers and hookers out. Keys were given to people who could prove tenancy in the vicinity and were prepared to make a donation.

Turf was laid. Because the whole block had gone, there was plenty of sunlight and we ensured good drainage by mixing fifteen tons of sand with fine earth as a base. Ericaceous soil in the beds meant that rhododendrons, camellias, azaleas and Japanese maples all flourished. We also managed to grow tree peonies, birds of paradise, lilies, sunflowers, roses and irises. I helped plant the magnolia tulip tree. An apple tree was planted in a northern corner.

Careful consideration went into the landscaping so that every day of spring and summer delivered a flash of new colour or scent. Long varieties of clematis, climbing roses, honeysuckle, morning glory, wisteria and jasmine were trained through the fence to make it look less forbidding. In the shady areas we grew ferns. There was a bed for herbs – rosemary, basil, thyme, coriander, oregano. Anyone who wanted could help themselves. Lavender was placed strategically to waft thick soap smells. And plenty of annuals were sown into the beds to pick up the perennials – busy Lizzies were my favourite. A pergola was built out of deeply veined rosewood and a grape vine was planted so that the fruit hung down in thick clusters over a shaded, flint-stone seating area. There was even a beehive. Each October jars of honey were sold.

I loved going to that garden. Working in it gave me the same, simple, meditative satisfaction I got from my superintendent maintenance work. Life was simple when it was boiled down to digging a hole or watering a flowerbed. In some ways, I enjoyed the gardening more. It thrilled me to see something I had planted grow. Some mornings I used to go down first thing just to see what had happened overnight. And when a plant blossomed, it put a song in my heart; quite different to the prosaic satisfaction I got from seeing something I'd fixed working again. There was godliness to it, a spark of magic, a flash that reminded me of little Jimmy.

In fact, working in the Carlyle Garden was probably the closest I got to life again after Jimmy. Though I kept myself to myself, I still met people from the area who came to work. I wasn't allowed to live in a bubble in there; I had to help out where I was needed, or speak when I was spoken to, and generally do as I was told for the sake of getting a job done.

It was a community effort and I was required to cooperate. No one took charge; no one claimed a right they didn't have. Sure, there was the occasional gripe about who'd done what or who'd done more, but it never lasted, it never amounted to anything. Like me, people were only there because they enjoyed the work, they weren't trying to own anything.

Mrs Xhiu had one of the best seats in the stadium, fifteen rows from the front, centre stage. God bless Bank Corp, she could afford it now.

And heavens, she'd never seen such a spectacle. Newspapers had reported that this was expected to be the single largest crowd in the forty-three-year history of the stadium, but never in her dreams could she have imagined this.

People filled every available space. Additional seats were set up in the aisles. The stage had been set back to make more rows. The crowd rose high in the open-air arena, people's faces a sea of colourful dots, a pointillist painting of humanity. Energy vibrated off the canvas.

It had been a long day for Mrs Xhiu, travelling all the way to the borough, shuffling with the madding crowds to her seat, setting herself up, taking a light lunch, working through the afternoon prayer sessions, glorifying in the Gospels, celebrating in the sermons by some of the lesser-known, supporting evangelists, and, of course, singing with all her heart every chance she got.

And now, as the climax neared, the stiflingly humid summer air heating up in the night, Mrs Xhiu started to feel overwhelmed. She fanned a dead breeze with her song sheet, trying to fend off giddiness. Her underarms were drenched in a nervous sweat as she waited fearfully for her hero, the saviour of the New World, her beloved Reverend Jeremy. Her head felt terrifyingly light.

But just when she thought she might have to sit down, the incandescent spotlights that had been burning the stage went black. Darkness jumped out at the crowd alarmingly. A thrilled hush tolled. Mrs Xhiu closed her eyes and felt out for the hands of her neighbours. Then she heard him. His words came to them – gently at first, deep and resonant through the PA.

'People, let us call on God.'

Everyone bowed their heads. Reverend Jeremy started humming in a low bass. It rumbled from deep within and vibrated out through the speakers. Mrs Xhiu could feel it in her body. She responded. They all responded. The stadium shook with a deep meditation.

It went on. On and on and on.

Mrs Xhiu started to lose her sense of balance. A strange, disorientating pitch began in her ears. And then lights exploded.

Reverend Jeremy boomed: 'LET HIM COME! LET HIM COME!'

People threw their hands into the air.

'JESUS! JESUS! JESUS!' they chanted.

Spasms seared violently through Mrs Xhiu's body. It was as if she were being torn from her clothes, out of herself, into the terrifying glare of magnificent Light. People took a hold of her arms and lifted her, above them. She convulsed in their grip. In the madness, she could hear Reverend Jeremy calling:

'CAN YOU HEAR IT? CAN YOU HEAR THE MESSAGE?'

People leapt. They fell. They threw themselves to their knees. They embraced one another and collapsed in heaps. They rent their hair. They roared in a hot, bodily mass, wringing their hands and praising the Lord.

And then they were gone.

Mrs Xhiu squinted in a new darkness. She tried to see. She could hear a faint, clicking, insect sound. A dim light started to glow from the back of the stage. She could just make out shapes. She could see white squares. There was a figure in the distance.

'Reverend Jeremy?'

The message, Mrs Xhiu. Do you hear the message?

'Yes,' Mrs Xhiu cried. 'Yes, I can.'
Can you bear it?
'You know I can. Thank you, Reverend Jeremy. Thank you.'
I'm not Reverend Jeremy.

Hamburger and hot-dog smells mingled with the aroma of sharp cheeses. Someone sold a selection of olives from large stained pine tubs. Teenage Hispanic girls paraded themselves in sequinned bikini tops and tight hot pants. Three black kids hung in a doorway with their shirts rolled up, their designer vests showing. When Ben walked past them pushing the stroller, one of them muttered: 'Pussy.'

Cops wearing comic-book utility belts stood in self-conscious repose by a sky-blue cordon as a cavalry of police horses clicked their way past with clipped respect, crapping heavily. No one said anything to them about poop bags. A woman organized children into turns at a water-balloon stall. Sunlight caught the veins in a blood-red rose at a flower stall and made its colour course magnificently. Mike bought a bag of hard candy from the stall next door for Juan and put it in his pocket to get sticky in the heat.

Bubbles as big as boulders rolled through the air. A man sneezed seven times in quick succession and cursed the pollen. Coffee swam in the smell of honey. A three-piece band played ragtime favourites. They were dressed appropriately in stars and stripes for the July 4 weekend. Frank stopped to watch them for a few minutes before heading into the video store.

Tomato sauce dripped between the fingers of a very fat man as he tried to eat a meatball sandwich from a family-run pizza store. He had to lean forward to keep it from going on his shirt. A dog sniffed the wheel of a moped before cocking his leg to pee. A young man walked into a corner store to buy cigarettes. An old man in a trench coat walked out holding a bottle of beer in a brown-paper bag. Garry lugged another box of records to the subway, on his way to the Rare Record Center.

A pigeon made an emergency landing, narrowly missing a young girl's hat and stopping with a skid by a trashcan that was oozing litter into the street like lava from a volcano. There was the sound of two women laughing freely, enjoying a joke. Gum snapped in someone's mouth. A man called out about his New Zealand wool moccasins. There was a smell of eggs. An advert for sunglasses beamed down from the side of a shop awning. Anna-lise enquired about the price of a lamp before a man seized it from her, thrusting a twenty-dollar bill into the stall owner's hand. When Anna-lise protested, the thief said, 'Possession is nine-tenths of the law, lady,' and walked off.

A woman in high heels stepped with disgust over the steaming contents of a burrito, mistaking it for human vomit. Two dogs in matching green coats sniffed one another, while their owners made conversation. Three kids in basketball shorts walked quickly, talking quickly. The sun pitched light into a doorway, soaking a potted plant on the edge of bloom. Henry found Anna-lise and asked her what the matter was.

Baseball caps hung from a tall stall of hooks in primary colours. An argument broke out between two men with camp accents over an ad in the real-estate section of a newspaper. 'You shut up.' 'No, you shut up.' 'No, you shut up.' 'No, you.' A young girl stepped slowly through the street fair smiling with wonder at everything and everyone she saw. A black guy sucked his lips as a Caribbean woman walked past, showing off her thick thighs in a tight grey leotard. The smell of marijuana surfaced and then was gone. A long queue lined up outside the entrance to a fast-food restaurant. A public telephone rang. Morgan stopped for a moment in the street to make an entry in her personal organizer.

There was the sound of a truck reversing in the distance. A man tripped on one of the street-stall poles, nearly bringing it down. An old woman pushed a plaid shopping trolley in front of her, leaning on it heavily, as if it had a dead body inside. A young couple leant out from a window on the third floor of a brownstone and watched life in the street fair pass by below. A drunk stumbled from out of the dimness of O'Reilley's, squinting in the daylight. A black guy in a suit set up a tripod and took pictures with an old camera. A single white cloud appeared from nowhere and smudged the sun, its shadow moving up the side of a building. Mrs Xhiu got back from the key cutter with new heels on her shoes.

The sidewalk rumbled as a subway train passed underneath. A young boy with a knapsack and a red cycle helmet paddled past on a chrome Razor. There was the smell of bleach as an Indian man scrubbed the doorway of a store selling picture frames. A mini ticker-tape display flashed the winning Lottery numbers in the window of a photocopying shop. A man stepped out of the hairdresser's and paused momentarily under the twisting lollipop sign to brush hair from his shoulders. Helmut sailed past him, rubbing his beard.

A slim middle-aged woman paid twenty dollars for a denim jacket at a vintage-clothing stall. A man in rectangular white-bone glasses came out of the photocopier's holding a long cardboard roll. Cigarette smoke poured out of the pool hall as four girls walked in, in pairs, arm in arm. There was the wheeze of a police siren in the distance. Two men shouted at one another as they tried to get a trolley filled with crated bottles through a doorway. Diva walked slowly past them, smiling.

I took a few more moments. I breathed in more old smells. I looked out for what few, new clues I could find. I tried to familiarize myself as best I could. It was important that I practise being outside. This was the furthest I had ventured on my own in years. I had to do this if I was going to leave. I was glad to see that some things hadn't changed. The community hadn't disappeared entirely. Maybe things would be all right.

'Ben, would you stay behind, please? I have something I'd like to discuss with you.'

The rest of the Board were standing up to leave. Anna-lise glanced at Ben, teasing him with the suggestive lift of one eyebrow, puckering her lips into an exaggerated smooch: Teacher's Pet.

Funny thing was, Ben didn't mind. He was even starting to enjoy his special privilege as Morgan's favourite. He was getting used to her compulsive need for control and he couldn't exactly say that he didn't like her. She *could* be charming – when she wanted to be. Even reconciling the monthly statements together was sometimes fun – bouncing the occasional flirtatious humour between the income statement and the bank ledger. In a funny way, it was flattering that she paid him so much attention. He'd even managed to forgive her for ruining his World Cup opener. Besides, the USA were through to the quarter-finals now. There'd been plenty of other matches to enjoy.

Ben was just happy that he was getting along with everyone in the building. He really felt as if they'd settled in now – as a family. He and Mandy belonged here. It was a good feeling – to be a part of something. The fact that he and Morgan got along was a testament to that. And the fact that no one else resented him for being Morgan's second-in-command was a bonus. If anything, they seemed grateful to him for taking on the mantle.

Morgan marched them out – Mike, Frank, Garry, Anna-lise all taking the stairs, Mrs Xhiu the elevator. Ben got his paperwork – the minutes, the Treasury report, the construction-progress report – into his file and into his bag.

He scanned Morgan's apartment and found he didn't envy the woman. The construction looked a nightmare. Clear plastic dustsheets were taped to the walls and tables, even over the cooker in the kitchen. Each time she made herself a cup of coffee or toasted a piece of bread she'd have to unwrap and then re-wrap the necessary appliance. And if the sheets stopped dust from damaging her furniture, they didn't stop it from getting into her food, her clothes, her hair. It looked to be an oppressive experience.

And her beautiful apartment had been ruined. The cracks in the ceiling had turned into crevasses. The ceiling even sagged now in one section, like old underwear. Some of the polished-chrome light fixtures had been badly scratched and bent. The cornice work in the kitchen was very damaged. The solid-wood flooring had pockmarks where bits of grit and dust had been stamped in by heavy workmen's boots. There was a large yellow stain, like urine, streaking down one wall. In the bathroom, the basin had been removed from the wall and the plumbing taken apart because someone had poured grout down the drain and blocked it. The spiral staircase looked skewed. Ben wondered if it had been designed right.

She'll deserve the extension after all this, Ben thought to himself.

Morgan returned. Ben smiled at her. Morgan didn't smile back. Ben felt as if he was about to be taken into Morgan's confidence. Maybe she needed a shoulder to cry on – the poor lady.

'Is everything OK, Morgan?' Ben said when Morgan failed to start the conversation.

Morgan looked at Ben, breathing through her nostrils, like a bull. She took a short, sharp inhalation and said, 'Not really, Ben, no.'

'What's wrong?' Ben asked gently, genuinely concerned. Maybe there'd been a death in the family. Love problems? She seemed really upset.

'Well,' Morgan started with a very heavy sigh. 'I'll start by saying I never expected it from you.'

Ben sat up. He realized he wasn't here as Morgan's favourite. Quite the opposite – he'd been called in to see the Principal. He was quickly nervous.

'What do you mean?' he asked, genuinely bemused.

'I was down at the bank the other day.'

'Oh yeah?'

A very vague sliver of understanding dawned on the horizon, like first light. It wasn't enough to clear the dark, it wasn't enough for Ben to know with certainty where this was going, but it was an indication, a dim, grey glow. He felt the first twinges of guilt.

'Yes,' Morgan replied.

They looked at one another. Seconds turned into minutes turned into hours turned into days. At least it felt that way. Ben wasn't sure how long the silence lasted. He felt himself readying a denial but he couldn't be sure what for. Was it something to do with the laundry money? He couldn't think.

'I went because one of the maintenance cheques bounced,' Morgan said eventually.

'Really? Whose?'

'Guess.'

'Frank's.' Ben sighed.

'Got it in one.'

Ben tutted in sympathy with Morgan. Was this the problem? If so, he should show solidarity. Frank would have to be punished. Not so much because he cared about the offence, but because he wanted to deflect Morgan's anger onto the real culprit.

'The bank contacted me because I'm still listed as Treasurer for the Board,' Morgan explained.

'Oh, I'm sorry about that, Morgan. I've told them three times already to change the records.'

'That's not the point,' she restarted. 'The point is that when they gave the cheque back to me, I noticed the date.'

Sunlight reared its ugly face. Ben could see. He gulped.

'Yes,' Morgan said, watching the change in his expression. 'That's right, Ben. And I've been over the financial reports for the last five months. I notice you haven't been depositing maintenance cheques until well after the mid-month deadline. I can only assume, therefore, that Frank has been late on his payments every month since you took over as Treasurer.'

'No,' Ben replied. 'That's not right.'

'Do you expect me to believe that?'

'It's the truth. It was just that one time. I told him that he couldn't be late again. He promised he wouldn't be.'

'Are you quite sure about that, Ben?'

Ben had to wear his best poker face.

'Yes,' he tried.

Morgan reached into a file and pulled out the cheques. She dealt them on the coffee table between them, one by one, like cards. How on earth did she get a hold of those? Did it matter? Ben had gone bust.

'I, I . . . didn't think it was that big of a deal,' he started.

'Oh?' Morgan said with an unusually – given the situation – feminine tone. 'Well, I'm afraid it is a big deal, Ben. It's a very big deal.'

'Look, I'll sort things out with Frank, OK?'

'No, Ben,' Morgan replied. 'I'm afraid you won't.'

'What do you mean?'

'You have assisted in defrauding the corporation. If you take a look at the shareholders' agreement you'll find that that is grounds for eviction.'

Ben laughed. 'You're joking, right?'

Morgan didn't say anything.

'Look.' Ben smiled. 'How about I pay the fines, yeah? We both know that Frank can't afford it. If it's the money you're worried about, I'll take care of it. I can see why you're upset. I only did it because he was doing us a favour on the babysitting rates and I figured that a few days here or there didn't matter. I was wrong. I'm sorry. At a time like this, the building needs money. He should have been fined. I'll make up the loss. OK?'

Morgan grunted as she impaled her matador, breathing in the smell of blood with lust.

'It isn't the money.'

Ben noticed that his leg was shaking. He tried to make it stop. But he couldn't.

'I trusted you with a senior responsibility in the building,' Morgan continued. 'You have betrayed that trust. The fact that you did it to save money on babysitting charges only makes it worse. I find your admission of guilt very disturbing.'

'You trusted me with this?' Ben said, getting angry. 'You *made* me do this. I didn't want to do it. Mandy and I invited you into our home, cooked you dinner, welcomed you and then you blackmailed me into doing the Treasury job. You made me do it because nobody else would. Don't give me that trash about trusting me. You've never trusted me, Morgan.'

'You're right, Ben,' Morgan said. 'I'm sorry. It was a mistake giving you the job. I should have known that you couldn't be trusted, knowing how you lied to your employer, covering up your dismissal from M&M. I still don't know how you managed to get away with that.'

'Fuck you.'

The shutters went down behind Morgan's eyes, slowly and completely, as if on a mechanism.

'Goodnight, Ben.'

'I'll fight it,' Ben said, standing up to leave, stamping his way towards the elevator. 'You'll never win,' he called as he punched the call button repeatedly with a finger. 'No one in this building will support you in the motion to evict us.'

'We'll see,' Morgan called out.

Ben got into the elevator. He wanted so desperately to slam a door. He needed the last word, the last something; he was so burning with fury.

But the doors just whispered and closed with a tormenting kiss.

'But first, let's check out the five-day forecast with our weatherman, Flash Nebula . . . '

'Hey there, folks! Temperatures in the city are gonna touch a tough 105 today, dipping to 90 overnight. Humidity levels will be 100 per cent, with a light north-easterly breeze. Things don't get any easier over the rest of the week. Electrical storms on Tuesday and Wednesday are expected to interrupt the power grid. Citizens are advised to prepare themselves with flashlights and necessary supplies. A city advisory has also been issued to drink plenty of water, at least five quarts a day. We don't want people overheating out there, OK? Temperatures will be well over the 100 mark for the next four days. Humidity will remain at 100 per cent for the rest of the week, with winds variable. For more details please visit our website at www.weatherworld.com . . . Back to you, John.'

Helmut was busy organizing boxes, taking some from his storage area up into his apartment, moving others down. He'd taken his top off and was actively dressed in a pair of black nylon running shorts, socks and running shoes.

Mandy watched him from the corner of her eye as she folded Ben's underwear and Billy's Babygros. He strode over to her, the sweat defining his pectorals and making his light-brown chest hair glisten. She never knew Helmut had such an athletic physique. Something fell in place, a piece of a puzzle, unlocking a picture she hadn't seen until now.

'Are you using this?' he asked, pointing at the shopping trolley that had somehow, one day, randomly made its way into the basement and now spent most of its life waltzing aimlessly in the laundry area with tenants who pushed and pirouetted it out of their various ways. Morgan let it remain because it had its uses – like moving stuff between storage bins.

Mandy glanced at it. 'No, go right ahead.'

'Thanks,' Helmut said, reaching for the handle.

'You seem very busy,' Mandy said, turning her back to him and reaching inside the dryer for a statically lost sock.

'Ya,' Helmut said. 'I'm organizing a party this weekend. Everything is crazy.'

'A party. Is it your birthday?'

'No, it is an event. A launch party in a studio downtown.'

'What are you launching?' Mandy said, folding the socks in on themselves and balancing them on top of the pile of clothes.

'My new film.'

'You've made a film?' Mandy said, genuinely interested. She pawed the pile of clothes and noticed they were still damp, despite having been in the dryer for over an hour. There was no escaping the humidity these days, least of all down in the basement, which sucked moisture from the earth around it like a cave.

'It just got back from production. That's why I'm moving all these boxes. I have to make space for stock.'

'I never knew you made films.'

'Ya, sure.'

'Will there be a screening at the launch?'

'Of course. And live performances, food, music, all kinds of things.'

'Sounds great.'

'Do you want to come?' Helmut said, his chest expanding.

'I'd love to. Where is it?'

'I'll put an invite under your door.'

'Great, thanks. Can we bring Billy?'

'Ya, sure, why not?'

'Or will it be too noisy for him?'

'Hmm, ya, on second thoughts, maybe.'

'Shame. I don't know if I'll be able to get a babysitter in time.'

'Why doesn't Ben babysit? Then you come? Anna-lise will be there. You could come together.'

Mandy paused and thought for a moment. She was sure that Ben wouldn't mind her going out on her own for one night. After all, he'd been out plenty of times without her. She deserved it. It would be good for her. He kept saying how she needed to get out. She wanted to go.

'OK,' Mandy smiled warmly. 'That would be nice. I'll ask him.'

'Great,' Helmut grinned. 'See you Saturday.'

'Yeah,' Mandy replied, drawing the pile of laundry and cradling it into her chest as Helmut turned the trolley. 'Saturday.'

She stole one last look as he wheeled it with a clatter over the concrete floor.

Nice back!

Mike reached for Juan's hand beneath the table. Why was he nervous? Juan gave him one of his 'stop being ridiculous' squeezes.

The restaurant throbbed with gloriously fashionable New Yorkers. All the wannabe-but-probably-won't-bes were there. Juan had secured the reservation through the magazine. The week before they'd done a shoot entitled *Iconic Iron*, at the bar using wigless mannequins, so they'd gotten a good table.

So far, they'd spotted Jane Trimble, Alan Grade and Tate Bruppard. Models were fastened to chairs like safety pins; loose summer dresses hung from their coat-hanger shoulders, empty, sexless breasts showing at the sides.

At one end, there was a long dark bar, which looked like it had been carved in the previous century. It had propped up everyone from Hemmingway to Picasso at some time or another – or so it seemed. It housed a number of European beers on tap. Row upon row of glass shelving at the back stocked vodkas, whiskey and liqueurs from around the globe.

On the walls there were stencilled signs saying TABAC and DEFENSE DE FUMER; and prints of people from the 1930s skiing in the Alps wearing baggy tweeds. There were pillars plastered in green-glass rectangular tiles and mirrors with the menu specials written in red lipstick across them. The floor was a mosaic of pastel browns depicting various Roman numerals. The lights had been designed to look like Parisian street lamps.

And there were babies – so many babies. Maybe it was just that Mike was noticing them more these days, but everyone seemed to have one. It was almost as if having a baby was a fashion statement in itself here.

While they had waited their turn to be seated, a young

couple with a stroller had announced they didn't have a booking. Mike had held his breath, waiting for the painful rejection, the cumbersome exit, the red faces. But he'd been amazed when the maître d' had whispered in the welcome girl's ear and ushered them quickly to an invisible spot right in the middle of the throng.

Morgan reckoned the management was just worried about getting sued. She claimed it was the latest in affirmative action. There was a backlash because the neighbourhood had become too gay. She wasn't able to hide her fear as they themselves were led to their own seats, looking at another family's child at a nearby table as if it were radioactive waste.

She was talking now. Mike was watching her mouth move.

'So they're in court.'

'That's horrible,' Mike heard Juan replying. 'Isn't it, Mike?'

'Horrible,' Mike repeated.

'Can Larry prove that Zach gave the dog cancer?' Juan said.

'Second-hand smoke, he's saying.'

'And the suit is for how much?'

'A hundred million, plus custody.'

'My God,' Juan said. 'Smoking is so expensive these days.'

'So's owning a dog,' Morgan replied.

'Hmm,' Juan said slowly.

There was an uncomfortable pause. Their mimosas stood untouched on the table, like elegant ladies waiting. Juan gave Mike another squeeze, this time not a reassuring one.

'Morgan,' Mike started. 'Juan and I have something we'd like to say.'

'Don't tell me,' Morgan replied with an exhausted roll of the eyes. 'You're getting married.'

Juan blushed.

'Nearly.' Mike smiled.

'Oh no, you're not getting a dog.'

'Better than that.'

'Well, if it's a cat I'm still not sure. You know what the building rules are on pets. If a tenant . . . '

'No, Morgan.'

' . . . wants to apply for permission . . . '

'It isn't a pet.'

' . . . then a detailed submission—'

Morgan stopped.

Juan seized the chance. 'We're having a baby.'

'What?' Morgan said.

'We're having a baby,' Mike repeated.

'Am I missing something?' Morgan asked, genuinely bemused.

'Mike's ex-wife has agreed to surrogate,' Juan said.

'Interesting.'

'Oh, don't worry,' Juan said quickly. 'We're using my sperm.'

A waitress delivered their food. They'd ordered eggs Benedict, except for Morgan who'd taken things one step further with eggs Royale. She stared down at her plate, watching the Hollandaise sauce oozing over slices of smoked salmon.

'I think I'm going to vomit,' she said, as the white-shirted waitress reached for a phallic pepper grinder from under her arm.

'Is something the matter?' she asked.

'No,' Morgan said, pushing the plate away. 'I've just lost my appetite is all.'

Mike and Juan looked at her sadly.

'Would you like something else?' the waitress asked. 'Would you like me to take this away for you?'

'Yes,' Morgan replied. 'Nothing more for me. Just a cup of coffee.'

'Sure.'

'But you never drink coffee after twelve,' Juan observed, as the waitress gathered her plate and turned.

'I need waking up,' Morgan replied. 'I'm having a bad dream.'

'Oh, come on, Morgan,' Mike said. 'You could be a little bit happy for us. Or at least pretend.'

'I'm sorry, Mike. You've caught me by surprise. The thought of your ex-wife injecting herself with a syringe full of Juan's sperm isn't something I would have normally considered over Sunday brunch.'

'There's no need to be disgusting,' Mike replied.

'I'm not the one being disgusting, Mike.'

'And we are? Why? Because we want to be parents?'

Morgan didn't reply.

'I knew she'd be this way,' Mike said, turning to Juan. 'I told you she'd do this.' He wanted to add that Morgan was starting to live up to the nickname that person had written on the blackboard, but he didn't.

Juan reached across for Morgan's hand that was resting on the table between them. Mike realized that Juan was now holding hands with both of them. He didn't like that.

'You don't really mean it, do you, Morgan?'

Morgan looked at Juan and then around the restaurant, pinpointing the infants with her glare.

'I just don't get it,' Morgan said. 'What do you want a baby for? They ruin lives. The only men who have babies are the ones who make mistakes or get bullied into it by females raging with hormones.'

'Plenty of men get broody too,' Juan said gently.

'I find it hard to see how,' Morgan said.

Juan sighed. 'Oh, Morgan.' He paused. 'Look. Can I tell you something? When my mother found out I was gay she cried. I thought I'd broken her heart. Later she told me she was just sad for me. She said I would never know what it was to be a father. She wanted me to experience that. I've never forgotten her telling me that I would always be lonely as a gay man, that I'd never find real happiness.'

'How clichéd,' Morgan replied, pulling her hand away.

'Maybe. Or maybe it was just true.'

'So now you're getting the best of both worlds, is that it?'

'You may say so,' Juan said quietly.

Mike pulled his hand out of Juan's grip and put his arm around the back of his chair instead, as a gesture of protection.

'All I can say is don't come crying to me when it goes wrong,' Morgan said. 'I'm warning you now, as your friend, not to put yourselves through the humiliation.'

The baby at the nearby table started to wail. Juan dropped his head. Mike stared at Morgan. Time inched across an oversized clock on the wall. Morgan's coffee arrived. Juan and Mike started slowly eating.

'So,' Morgan restarted after a very long time. 'When are we going to see Frank's play?'

Anna-lise was doing her taxes. She was late – again. It was undoubtedly her least favourite way of spending a weekend. Here she was, on a Saturday night, adding up receipts, when she should have been going out, having a good time.

To make things worse, she was coming to the horrible realization that she'd underpaid for the year. She couldn't see how. She'd earned less and deliberately spent more.

But they'd introduced a whole bunch of new rules for the self-employed. On top of Federal, State, City, there was now a self-employment tax as well. Deductions for the home office had to be itemized. Medical-insurance costs were no longer deductible.

It was as if the government wanted no free-thinkers in the city – they were deliberately making life too expensive for the self-employed. All the artists had been driven out to Williamsburg. It was like Frank said. There were only two ways to get by nowadays – either get a mind-numbing office job with benefits, or leave. The city was losing its creatives, its edge. It was becoming just like the rest of America; a shopping mall financed by brainwashed consumer drones and tourists. A day in the Village was enough to see that.

Thank God she was getting married to a multimillionaire.

There was a knock on the door. Anna-lise smiled to herself, thinking that the timing had to be telepathic. She skipped to answer it, ready to plant a big kiss on Henry's lips and thank him for giving her the excuse to quit.

'Oh,' Anna-lise said, as she swung the door open. 'Hi, Mandy.' Mandy was dressed in a tight black number that showed off her figure. Not bad for a new mom, Anna-lise thought to herself. Maybe she should fish for tips on how she managed it – be prepared and all. 'What's going on?'

'Hi, Anna-lise!' Mandy said, smiling brightly. 'I was just wondering if you were coming to Helmut's launch party.'

Anna-lise double-took. 'He invited you?'

'Sure,' Mandy said with innocent excitement. 'Is something wrong?'

Anna-lise peered over Mandy's shoulder to check the corridor.

When she saw that the coast was clear, she said: 'Do you want to come in?'

The inside of Anna-lise's space was a wreck. Underpants, socks, dirty shirts, old take-out trays, cigarette ends in coffee cups – she didn't bother trying to tidy up. Things were too far gone for that. She was planning on a clear-out for Sunday. Yes, this was the brilliant weekend she had arranged for herself – taxes and cleaning the apartment.

'Sorry about the mess,' she said.

'You should see ours,' Mandy reassured her. 'At least you don't have diapers to contend with.'

Anna-lise blushed with panic as she realized that, in the not too distant future, she would have diapers to contend with and they wouldn't sit till the weekend.

'How *do* you cope with all the poop?' Anna-lise said, trying not to sound too interested. This was the start of Mothering 101 as far as she was concerned.

'We have a wonderful invention called the Diaper Genie. It seals Billy's accidents in little baggies and stores them in a container till we're ready to throw out the trash. Ben calls it the Shit-Eater.'

'That sounds totally gross.'

'You should have been there the time the baggies split and all the old diapers rolled out. *That* was gross.'

'Eugh.'

There was an uncomfortable pause as the two women considered how best to go on from here. Mandy berated herself for being out of touch socially – she couldn't even carry a conversation for five minutes without the subject of Billy's bowels coming up. Meanwhile, Anna-lise fretted that someone else in the building might be about to see her 'performance' in Helmut's video.

'So,' Mandy said eventually. 'Are you gonna come? I'm pretty excited. It's my first night out in months. We were all going to go but I convinced Ben to babysit.'

'You were all going to go?' Anna-lise said, reaching her refrigerator. 'Beer?'

Mandy grinned and nodded eagerly. 'I decided to have some time for myself.'

Anna-lise cracked open a can and passed it to Mandy. She got herself a soda and was glad when Mandy didn't ask her why she wasn't drinking. 'Does Ben know what Helmut's got planned?'

'Cheers,' Mandy said as the two women clinked. 'Sure . . . well, sort of.'

'And he doesn't mind?'

'No,' Mandy said, taking a swig. 'He says it will be good for me. I need some freedom for the sake of our relationship. It will help me to appreciate him more.'

'I never knew you guys were so liberated.'

'What else am I meant to do? Stay at home and feed the baby while he has all the fun?'

'No, of course not. It's just, well . . . I didn't have you two down as swingers.'

'Swingers? You mean dancing? I've done it once or twice but I'm no good. Is that the kind of music they'll be playing tonight – fifties stuff?'

'What? No. Er, Mandy, what kind of a party do you think Helmut's throwing?'

'Same as any, I guess. He said there'd be music and food and stuff.'

'And stuff is exactly what.'

'What?' Mandy said.

'I can't believe he said you could take the baby.'

'Why not? Will it be really crowded?'

'Mandy, there's something you should know.'

'OK.'

'How do I put this?' Anna-lise remembered how she told Henry she was pregnant. It was best to just come straight out with these things. 'Mandy, Helmut's a pornographer.'

'A what?'

'He shoots pornos, in this building mainly.'

'You mean sex?'

'Yes.'

Anna-lise could see Mandy's mind turning behind her eyes.

'And that's the film he's made? He's screening a porno tonight?'

'And a lot more besides.'

'What do you mean?'

'He told me there was going to be an orgy, plenty of S&M. You get the picture.'

'Jeez, Louise,' Mandy whistled. 'I never would have guessed.'

'Well, now you know.'

After a couple of minutes, Mandy asked, 'Are ... are you going to go?'

'No way! I'm not into that sort of stuff.'

'Me either,' Mandy said, frowning. 'Wow. I'm in shock. Thank God I stopped by your place first. I very nearly went on my own. He said you were going.'

'He's wicked. I told him a snowball had a better chance in hell than me showing up for one of his gang-bangs.'

'I wonder why he invited me.'

'It wouldn't take a mathematician to figure that one out. He's making up the numbers. Besides, you're an attractive woman. I love your outfit, by the way.'

'Thanks,' Mandy said, looking down at herself self-consciously.

'Look at me. All dressed up with nowhere to go. Ben's going to have a good laugh at me about this when I go downstairs. Christ! How could I have been so naive?'

Anna-lise looked at her for a second. 'Don't go down, then. Stay here. We can have a couple of drinks and a chat.'

'You sure? I'm not disturbing you or anything, am I?'

'The opposite. You're just the distraction I've been looking for.' Anna-lise paused. 'Besides, I want to pick your brains.'

'What about?'

'Oh,' Anna-lise sighed, 'not much, just marriage and babies and stuff.'

'I see,' Mandy smiled. 'Well, that might take a while.'

'I'll get you another beer, then.'

Mandy beamed. 'Great. That will be just great.'

Morgan was waiting in line at the Video Bar, getting very frustrated. The idiot in front *still* hadn't run his membership card through. Morgan had tsk'd twice already – loudly – but to no effect.

She managed to kill three seconds watching two teenagers wearing red polka-dot bandannas under baseball caps enter the store, the sliding electronic doors breathing carbon monoxide down the Horror aisle while they cased the place.

Morgan knew not to look for too long. She found herself drawn painfully, like a fish on a hook, back to the man in front who still (can you imagine?) hadn't swiped his card.

Morgan's bones ached with video-store fatigue – it had set in after just fifteen minutes of unsuccessful browsing. She needed a movie now just to recover. She watched the fat, purple attendant behind the counter slowly locating the man's selections, and had to tut again, really loudly this time.

The man finally glanced over his shoulder. Encouraged, Morgan turned to the queue behind her and grimaced. She managed to make eye contact with an elderly woman three people down the line but there were no signs of solidarity. To make matters worse, the membership card still sat on the counter untouched.

Morgan let out a long, loud, laboured sigh.

'Is there a problem?' the man said, turning.

'I'm sorry, what?' Morgan replied, looking up with a slow expression, mimicking her neighbour's mental agility.

'You seem upset about something.'

Morgan noticed he had a foreign accent, British. He probably thought that entitled him to something, special treatment of some kind. As if anyone cared! This wasn't Ohio, you know.

Morgan turned towards her audience and half-laughed. 'You're taking a long time.'

'I'm sorry,' the man replied disarmingly.

Morgan shook her head. 'Well, why don't you swipe your membership?'

'What?'

Morgan pointed at the card lying infuriatingly on the counter.

'It would save a lot of time.'

The man smiled. 'Oh, I thought I had to wait until—'

Unable to bear a moment more of this excruciating ignorance Morgan reached across and did it herself. 'Look. See. Obserrrrrve,' she drawled.

'Oh,' the man replied slowly.

Did they have brains, these English?

The Oompa-Loompa returned, thin gold-plated earring chains swinging lazily from her Mexican ear lobes. She pushed the video cassettes across the counter between long sparkle-encrusted, rainbow-painted nails.

The top one read:

HELMUT PINK presents: PENTHOUSE

Morgan shrieked and seized the tape.

'Excuse me!' the Englishman said.

'I have to rent this,' Morgan said, clutching it.

'What? No. It's mine.'

'You don't understand.'

The Englishman tried to grab it. 'Let go,' he said.

Morgan held on. The man's face flushed. He finally relinquished.

'Don't get worked up,' the Englishman said quietly. 'There's plenty more at the back.'

'You're kidding.'

'Take a look for yourself.'

Morgan looked at the rental attendant. She shrugged her shoulders at her. Morgan threw the tape down on the counter and strode towards the Adult section of the store.

'Save my place,' she called out as she weaved her way through the aisles towards the dirty French shutters.

Long moans from a row of blood-red booths at one end of a corridor filled the air. A South Asian man with boiled skin was perched on top of a stepladder peering down into the booths, on the lookout for things Morgan didn't want to imagine. A man in a corner dressed in a raincoat threw her a soliciting look. Three other men browsed garish titles single-mindedly, one of them with his kid asleep in a stroller.

There wasn't a trace of femininity to the place – odd, given the rolling sound of female orgasms and repetitive flash of breasts from video covers. Even the attempt to keep the area clean had an overbearing maleness to it, the chemical aroma of disinfectant smothering vile, frat-house sins with clinical indifference.

Morgan started to browse the titles. Shaved genitalia flashed pinkly at her, the glare of featured studio spotlights leaping from the pictures. Morgan saw cocks in mouths, cocks in pussies, cocks in asses, cocks in more mouths, cocks in more asses, plastic cocks, black cocks, gay cocks, socks on cocks, until finally Morgan didn't even know what she was looking at. Gay, straight, she-male – it all became a blur.

In the end she had to ask.

The man led her to a section, ominously titled 'Specialist'.

She found Helmut's video. There was a picture of 444 on the cover, with some cheaply photocopied colour Polaroids of people she didn't recognize. She turned the box over.

Morgan read.

Welcome to the latest instalment of Helmut Pink Productions. In this selection we offer you more kinky, down and dirty, genuine New

York City sluts. There's Tyra taking it in the boiler room and Tyra in the gym with Helmut and friend. There's even a special bonus scene with Harvey the Hellraiser being hung out to dry. You've gotta see it to believe it. And, as usual, we've got plenty of prick and pussy abuse, this time with Tina and Lucinda and a hilariously reluctant friend they found at a party. But the pièce de résistance has got to be newcomer, Anna. She manages to humiliate her sworn enemy of the building in the filthiest of styles. She sure is naughty! Order this special-edition video on 1-800-HELMUTPINK or online at helmut-pink.com immediately. You won't regret it.

M organ raced straight to Mike and Juan's.
      'You're never gonna believe this,' Morgan said, striding straight into the apartment as the elevator door opened.

'What?' Juan said, too intrigued to object. 'What's happened?'

'I think I've just found one of Helmut's videos down at the store.'

'You're joking,' Juan said.

'What's going on?' Mike called from the kitchen.

'I've finally got him, Mike,' Morgan said. 'I've finally got proof.'

'What? Who? What are you talking about?'

They gathered in the sitting room, the TV standing like an anxious guest in one corner, knowing it was about to be introduced.

Morgan handed the tape to Mike.

'He's even put a picture of the building on it.'

'Jesus,' Mike said, scanning the blurb.

'Let me see,' Juan said, taking it. 'Oooh, this looks good!'

'What are you going to do?' Mike said.

'We've got to watch it.'

'Goody,' Juan said. 'I love porn.'

'Don't get too excited,' Mike said. 'It's straight.'

'I don't care, as long as the guys are hot.'

Morgan took the tape back, moved towards the video player and squatted, balancing expertly in her heels.

'This is going to be fun,' Juan said, curling up on the sofa, winking at Mike as he sat down slowly beside him.

The screen blinked. Morgan stepped back, punching the volume on the remote control. There was a quick, clumsy, drunken swing of a spotlight and then an immediate close-up of Anna-lise's face that shone too brightly.

Juan screamed.

Morgan sank blindly into a chair, her mouth falling open.

Mike felt himself tensing.

'Is it on?' Anna-lise said to the camera.

The picture nodded and panned down to Anna-lise's ass as she turned, her hips shifting seductively as she walked, the slinky cream silk dressing gown flashing. The camera followed her.

'Oh my God,' Juan said. 'Morgan, that's your apartment. Isn't it?'

Morgan didn't move.

They all watched Anna-lise stride into Morgan's kitchen.

'First up, folks,' Anna-lise said, draping her arms along the counter theatrically, *'this state-of-the-art kitchen. Premium fixtures and fittings only, of course.'*

They watched Anna-lise open a drawer and pull out a silver serving spoon. She looked at the camera and licked it with a long, slow tongue.

'Delicious cutlery,' she said before throwing it back into the drawer with a crash and a slam.

They all jumped. Anna-lise waltzed into the dining room.

'And here's my favourite dining table,' she said, sliding herself up onto it, writhing erotically. She smeared herself along the length of it, before swinging her legs over one end and straddling the back of a chair. *'Wouldn't you just love to eat me on a table like this!'*

'Oh sweetheart!' Juan said.

'Morgan—' Mike started, before Anna-lise interrupted.

'I think we'll come back to the living room,' she said breezily, walking off screen. *'I want to show you boys good grooming.'*

The camera followed her into the bathroom.

'See!' she said, swinging open the vanity cabinet, the reflection

of the camera equipment flashing briefly in the mirror. *'Just have a look at all this product, guys. This is how to keep your ladies clean. After all,'* she said, wagging a finger, *'we wouldn't want to catch any nasty smells from all our hot romping, would we now?'*

She beamed at them.

'Shall we go to the bedroom?' she asked. *'Yes, I think so. Come with me, big boy. There's something in there I really want to show you.'*

The camera followed her like an eager dog, the light shifting as they left the bathroom, passed through the corridor and went into Morgan's bedroom.

'She wouldn't dare,' Morgan murmured.

'Now, people, this is what I call a bed,' Anna-lise started.

'She wouldn't dare,' she said again.

'Just look at it,' she said, lacing herself around one of the posts, letting the dressing gown slip from a thigh. *'Now this is the kind of bed I'd like to fuck in, wouldn't you?'*

Morgan gasped as Anna-lise stepped slowly over to her pillows, hitched up her dressing gown and slid herself down. She pressed herself onto them, rubbing slowly at first but building quickly to a moan. Juan couldn't help giggling as she came fakely. Mike flashed him a stern look. They both watched Morgan. She'd gone a deathly grey.

'I think we've seen enough,' Mike said, getting up.

'Don't move!' Morgan snapped, flashing him a stop signal with her hand. Mike froze. Juan pulled Mike gently back down onto the sofa.

'Hmm, that's better,' Anna-lise said, after she was done. *'Now, what next?'*

There was the muffled sound of a man's distant voice from behind the camera while Anna-lise looked.

'Are you sure?' she replied.

The camera nodded.

'OK,' she said.

There was an edit and Anna-lise was back in Morgan's living room. She was taking the place in, coolly eyeing the furniture and Morgan's other possessions. Her hands hung loosely at her sides. She looked fierce.

Her glare finally rested on the leather sofa. She moved towards it. Resting one hand on her thigh, she rotated slowly, her body curling in the shape of a sexy S, and sank down into it, in the middle, the crevasse between two cushions cutting between her legs. One edge of the dressing gown slipped from her knee. She let it stay.

There was a long pause as Anna-lise looked into the camera while the picture lowered to her level. They could see the inner edges of her breasts. She was sitting up straight. She had a sullen look, cast in half-moon eyelids.

'I have a dog, guys,' Anna-lise started after a while, seemingly from nowhere, looking straight into the lens. 'His name is Ulysses.'

She stopped and parted her legs. Wide.

Juan gasped and made the sign of the cross.

'Now poor Ulysses can't always control himself. He finds it hard to hold on.'

The camera zoomed in slowly, edging Anna-lise's face and feet out of the frame until there was just a view of her torso and inner thighs. They could make out a swirling pattern on her underpants.

'And now I find I'm having trouble too.'

There was a change in the light.

'Oh my,' Anna-lise said with sudden, silly, Marilyn Monroe surprise.

The view of Anna-lise's darkening groin grew.

'What is she . . . ' Mike started.

'She . . . ' Morgan added.

'Oh. My. God,' Juan said.

'Look,' Anna-lise said, as urine spurted through the thin fabric of her underpants. 'Now see what I've done.'

Juan and Mike both screamed and had to clamp hands over each other's mouths to muffle them. Juan started giggling in Mike's grip. Morgan was shaking both her legs uncontrollably. Mike was having to grit his teeth.

They were glued to the screen as pee flooded from between Anna-lise's legs, making a puddle on the sofa. It dripped down between the cushions and rolled over the edge, down her calves, onto the floor. It went on for a long time, with intermittent strength, in waves, almost like an orgasm.

When it was finally over, the camera panned back, revealing Anna-lise in sections: her thighs, stomach, breasts, calves, face, feet. She was breathing steadily, smiling brightly.

She sighed blissfully. *'Gosh,'* she said. *'I really needed that.'*

With her hands still resting on her knees, she closed her legs with very final purpose, like someone closing a book they've just enjoyed. Helmut even managed a neat little amateur effect to echo the sentiment, drawing a black fade-out over the picture in the shape of a fan closing.

The words THE END shimmered into focus, written in yellow liquid.

No one moved a muscle.

B en was sweating in his suit. It stuck to him roughly, the cheap polyester sealing in the heat, rubbing coarsely against his thighs as he ran. He could feel wet collecting in the small of his back.

He dodged between people who were walking fast. He clipped their shoulders and invited quick tempers. He nearly had a head-on collision with a female cobra carrying coffee. She drew in her chest and stuck her elbows out in a hood to shield the cup, jumping up onto the tips of her toes and hissing at him.

He reached the subway stairs and leapt down them, three, four at a time. He stumbled on the final jump, his ankle giving way underneath very easily, like a weak twig. Surprisingly, he didn't hurt himself. He trotted out of the fall and made for the turnstile, reaching for his wallet from his back pocket as he ran, pulling on his Travelcard.

He swiped just as a silver train – with the all-important, green-circled Sesame Street F on it – flashed and squealed into the station. Hot, stale wind blasted into people's eyes and hair, pressing city silt into their pores, smashing dead smells into the fibres of their clothing.

They shuffled themselves towards the edge, waiting to board the ferry between graves. Ben tried to bundle his way through the turnstile but his thigh cracked against a locked iron leg. He looked down.

CARD NOT READ

He tried again, this time with the right tempo, trying to stay calm.

INSUFFICIENT FARE

He briefly considered jumping over the barrier but sensed he was being watched. There were plainclothes transport police at these stations on the lookout for desperadoes like him so he turned back just as the train doors opened with a *p'sht* and the station thundered with heels.

He approached the ticket console and slid his Travelcard and a twenty-dollar bill through the shallow chrome basin without saying anything, still breathing heavily from his sprint. The woman behind the counter took the card and the money, punched some keys on a keyboard, stashed the money in a till, pushed his card through the computer and passed it back without making eye contact.

By the time Ben returned to the turnstile, the platform had emptied and the disembarking passengers from the previous train were melting on the platform in patterns. Once more, Ben slid his card through the scanning device and read the credit. She'd given him only ten bucks' worth.

'Great,' he sighed, before turning back to the console.

'Excuse me, miss, excuse me.' The woman looked up sleepily at him. 'I gave you a twenty but you gave me only ten dollars' credit.'

She motioned at him to hand back the card, which he did. She slid it through the machine and started shaking her head.

'You gave me ten.'

'No, I gave you twenty.'

'No,' she said, firmly, looking at him finally. 'You gave me ten.'

The sound of another approaching train grumbled in the tunnels like indigestible food. Ben quickly realized he didn't have time for a fight.

'Oh, forget about it, then,' he said.

The lady reached under her desk with a wince and produced a long form with different-coloured pages.

'Fill this out,' she said, stuffing it through the basin.

'No,' Ben said. 'I don't have time. Just gimme back my card.'

The woman looked at him with exhausted rage.

'But this is the procedure for complaints.'

'Yes, but I don't have time. I'm late for work.'

Wind whistled as the train pulled in.

'It's too late for that,' she said.

'What?' Ben said, glancing over his shoulder. He had to make this train.

'Please, just give me my card.'

'I can't do that.'

'Why not?'

'You've made a serious allegation. There will be an investigation. This card is evidence.'

'Listen, lady,' Ben said in a way that made the woman widen her eyes, 'I really don't have time for this.'

'Are you withdrawing your complaint?'

'Yeah, sure, whatever.'

The woman turned and looked over into a far, dark corner of the station.

'Charlie!' she yelled.

Ben turned to see who she was calling for. He saw a man in a suit watching the arriving train, oblivious.

'Charlie,' the ticket attendant called out, rapping on the Perspex window.

'What's going on?' Ben asked.

'Charlie will know what to do with you.'

'What?'

'Charlie!' The woman leant forward off her chair to shout through the air holes. 'CHARLIE! Get over here.'

The train doors yawned, momentarily resuscitating the zombies with thin, second-hand air, just long enough for them to see if this was their stop.

Ben looked over at Charlie, who was still unaware of the muted screams of the ticket attendant, then at the train, then at Charlie again.

He decided to make a run for it. As he turned, he told himself he had to hurdle the turnstile cleanly. There wasn't room for mistakes or self-doubt. He just had to do it.

But as he took seven bounding steps and the barrier loomed, he quickly lost confidence. People seemed to be swarming from the other side. He feared he might collide with someone. He could sense himself coming into Charlie's peripheral vision. At the last second he backed out and had to do a small dance to stop himself from crashing into the barrier.

'Need to make this one?' a voice said beside him.

Ben turned to see a suited man in his mid-forties running his card through the scanner.

'I'll swipe you, if you want,' he said as he pushed himself through. 'Here.'

The comrade leant back and did it. Ben stammered his appreciation.

'Forget about it,' the man said, looking him in the eye. 'It's no big deal.'

The words stung. Ben felt as if he'd been seen arguing at the console and with one fell swipe, his benevolent observer had belittled the situation to the size that it was. Why was Ben fussing over ten bucks when he had so little time? He was becoming as bad as Morgan.

He squeezed himself through the turnstile only to get caught briefly in the oncoming crowd. The heat of bodies was like the heat of the station. It was a pressing, stifling, inner heat that didn't know how to escape. All it could do was sit and wait for something to give so it could release itself, very slowly, like heat off a cooling kiln, or off a sidewalk slab in summer.

A man with black gloves, black goggles, a black cap and a dark-blue uniform was peering down the length of the train, waiting to close the doors.

Ben managed to throw a shoulder into the carriage adjacent to the operator just as the doors were closing with a hydraulic sigh. He got caught between them. He waited for the operator to open the doors so he could get in but, instead, an announcement came over the Tannoy.

'Keep clear of the doors. This train will not leave until the doors are cleared.'

Ben, who still had his head outside the train, tried to make eye contact with the operator who was just two or three metres up the carriage. With surreal theatricality the operator deliberately avoided Ben's look, acting as if he were waiting for some invisible obstruction further down the line to clear.

'Hey!' Ben called out. 'Lemme on!'

The operator continued to ignore him. Ben got the sense that this was some sort of game. The operator seemed to be betting that the other passengers, in their frustration to get going, would rally against Ben and harass him out of the carriage, scoring an important moral victory in his long-running war with late arrivals.

Ben glanced at his fellow passengers, who were all staring at him. He gave them a beseeching look.

Sensing victory, the operator opened and closed the doors quickly, trying to squeeze Ben off. Instead, Ben threw himself the other way, further into the train, and managed to get his head inside. The doors slammed into his chest and back.

This was enough to turn the crowd, either because Ben's head now made him officially 'on the train', or because they felt sorry for him as he stood there being pummelled by the irate, punching door. Three passengers took hold of his arm and managed to haul him on.

The doors closed with a final, betrayed *hurrumph* and the train got slowly going.

'Thank you,' Ben said to the people around him.

They stared back without replying, their eyes drawing back into hollows. Ben swayed with them over the tracks. He tried to make out the graffiti that had been scratched angrily on the

Perspex windows and on the inside of the metal carriage, trying to figure out if it actually said something or if it was just someone marking out their territory. It seemed like a very violent form of self-expression.

Three stations later and the carriage momentarily emptied for a popular stop.

Ben took the chance to move further up the train, so he could look through the front window and watch the tracks weave and dance in the sallow headlights, maybe catch sight of a mythical subway dweller. For some reason, looking out into this dim, post-apocalyptic world comforted him. There was something soothing in it, though he didn't know what. A hot breeze came through the blades of a ventilation grille.

Ben got off at Traughley Street and tried to find the adrenalin that had got him out of bed and on the train in the first place to skip himself up the stairs and into his office with purpose. He took deep breaths and glanced up at the mirrored skyscrapers to remind himself that he was among giants.

He made it to his building by a quarter past the hour, just in time. He smiled his way into the elevator and looked up at the numbers as they travelled. He got off at the twenty-first floor and sailed through glass doors, down a corridor, hanging a hard left, another corridor, then through the back-office chicane and finally into the fixed-income department, the trill of trading already hanging from the drop-down ceiling struts like curling telephone cord.

He marched himself to his seat, toe/heel, toe/heel, toe/heel, feeling the soles of his new shoes sliding over the cheap carpet hair like skis. Susannah was there waiting for him with a security guard, her arms folded.

'Good morning, Ben,' she started. 'I'm sorry to inform you that your position here has been terminated. Please clear your personal effects and leave within half an hour.'

Seating was on a first-come, first-served basis so we didn't all sit together. Anna-lise, Henry, Garry, Mrs Xhiu and I were in the fifth row from the front. Helmut, his daughter and Diva were in the row behind us. Mandy and Ben were somewhere in the aisle to the left. Morgan, Mike and Juan arrived late so they were ushered to the back.

The theatre wasn't large, big enough for eighty or so people. It wasn't really a theatre, more of a 'space'. The stage was temporary. I noticed that the seating struts were collapsible. They must have hired the unit especially. It shook slightly whenever someone took their place.

Carpet the colour of grapes was rolled down the aisles. Large yellow spotlights breathing heat were bracketed to black tubes that hung on steel threads. The place smelled of damp clothes. The walls were painted a mottled dark brown. There were signs on easels saying QUIET PLEASE. Fire-exit signs glowed like embers.

It was muggy, the heat pressing down with the weight of water. Warmth from people's bodies and breath made things misty. People fanned themselves with their programmes.

I was very uncomfortable in the suit Ben had lent me. The tie felt tight. Anna-lise had to stop me from scratching inside the collar.

'Sit still,' she whispered, resting a hand on my arm and leaving it there. It was the first time I'd noticed the engagement ring.

The lights went down. There was a moment of darkness. Someone coughed. And then there was a broad hum as the stage ignited. It faded slowly into the distance as the sight of people wearing loud make-up and talking in big voices took over.

Morgan shifted in her seat, her knees kicking the man in front. The bald silhouette, which was reclining heavily, rocked gently each time Morgan moved, the mechanics squeaking.

'Are you all right?' Juan whispered.

'I can't get comfortable,' Morgan replied in a normal voice, which sounded very loud amid the audience hush.

An ice-cream cone of frozen, frizzy hair next to the bald man turned around.

'Will you please stop kicking my husband?'

'These seats don't recline,' Morgan replied. 'I need an aisle.'

'You should have come earlier,' the woman whispered urgently.

Somebody hushed them.

'Can't you tell him to sit up?'

The woman turned back to the play.

'Trust me to get a whale.' Morgan sighed.

The man started to turn. The woman reached for his arm.

'Morgan!' Juan said.

'Well,' Morgan cried innocently, 'why can't he sit up?'

'You're going to get us into trouble.'

Someone hissed, like a broken valve, from another part of the darkness.

'I don't care,' Morgan replied.

'He might have a gun,' Juan said between his teeth.

'Don't be ridiculous,' Morgan exclaimed. 'No one has guns in Manhattan any more.'

Juan told himself for the third time: This is the last time. He hadn't wanted a scene. He didn't do drama. But this was definitely it. They wouldn't be going out with Morgan any more.

Juan was still seething about the things Morgan had said at the restaurant but he knew that things were better this way. Better to keep this date as planned and then coolly, quietly, steadily write the woman out of their lives – for ever.

Besides, Juan had more important things to spend his energy on now. He was about to be a parent. He needed to keep serene for the sake of the child, for the sake of their new life. Morgan simply wasn't worth the effort. All he had to do was get through one more night, just one more night.

Helmut was having trouble getting over how grown-up Christie was now. Maybe it had been the way she towered by comparison to Mandy in her high heels. Perhaps it was the way she'd grown her burnt-redwood hair so that it draped in lush folds over her shoulders, like a theatre curtain. Or maybe it was the dress she'd bought with her birthday money, the elfish hemline zigzagging across her thighs.

If he wasn't careful she'd be a woman the next time he looked. It made him feel proud and confused and sad all at the same time. When they had taken their seats beside one another, he had found himself searching for her hand as if to catch hold before she sped off without him.

At least her small grip felt the same. If he closed his eyes it would be just like when she was a kid. Maybe it was time they started seeing more of each other, so these gaps didn't spring any more surprises on him, so he could adjust himself to the idea that he was about to be left again, for a second time, by the love of his life.

He didn't want to be alone.

Diva needed air. She hadn't been sleeping well. The dope was over. Her body was having to readjust to a forgotten life without drugs. It was hard.

But she couldn't bring herself to telephone Jonathan for a score. More importantly, she was terrified that the dope might trigger a flashback. She didn't want to go through *that* trip again. If only she'd known they were selling hell. Super-consciousness indeed.

She was enjoying the play, though. She thought that Frank, especially, was very good. He was one of the few actors absorbing enough to make Diva forgive the fact that she could see the backs of props, that there was something mechanical in their movements, that she was watching a stage. Frank made her feel like a fly on the wall in a room where things were really happening.

Someone broke the spell by sneezing and Diva's eyes shot to the left instinctively, still sensitive to anything startling. She caught an oblique view of Mack, sitting four seats along in the row in front. A strange noise hummed loudly in her head, and there was the taste of something metallic in her mouth. Pins and needles thundered in her face and an odd light came about, blurring colours and distorting shapes.

She turned quickly back to the play. The moment passed. She tried not to look at him again.

Ben couldn't concentrate on the show for more than a minute. The payment warning had arrived that morning with unfathomable speed. It was as if Susannah had telephoned the loans department herself.

It wouldn't have surprised him. She had done a good job of making sure everyone else knew about his indiscretions. His reputation was ruined now. No one was going to give him a job. His career was over.

'Nothing is as ever as bad as it seems, nor is it ever as good,' Jeff Kincaid, his lawyer, had told him earlier that afternoon. 'Some days you're gonna think you're out of the woods but you won't be, other days you'll think you're going down, but it won't happen. The truth will be somewhere in the middle.'

Ben wasn't reassured, mainly because Jeff had declined to take him on contingency, which was a bad sign considering he wore a cowboy hat.

So now he feared. It was a kind of fear he hadn't experienced before. It was a fear for his family. Enemies were out there, in the night, trying to get them while they slept. Billy made them all so vulnerable. Ben was sick with anxiety.

Would he be able to protect them?

G arry watched Frank.

He was doing a brilliant job of playing Chief Bromden. The play had been produced along the lines of the book, not the film. It was a much better version of things, making the dumb Indian the narrator.

It allowed for the ambiguity between Bromden's madness and his genius to be sewn into the storyline, something the film missed by focusing so exclusively on McMurphy and his war with Nurse Ratched. It made Garry appreciate how Chief Bromden – the quiet one – was the real hero of the story, not McMurphy.

It was funny to think that they had a Mack in their building. And watching the group-therapy sessions – they were just like their Board meetings. Morgan could so easily be Nurse Ratched – a more robotic and calculating and evil Nurse Ratched, if that was possible.

Garry found himself wondering: if 444 was a ward in the insane asylum that was New York what was he – an Acute or a Chronic?

It was a scary thing to think about.

It was impossible for Mandy not to absorb Ben's fears. She wanted to be strong but she couldn't help it. He overwhelmed her with it all.

The worst part was her blaming Billy for their problems. Their days before him seemed so sun-kissed in her memory; they had a golden magic to them, like a nostalgic flashback in a TV soap.

She tried to watch the play, not squander the freedom they'd paid for. She knew she'd only take it out on Billy later if she didn't appreciate this now.

And she had to admit – Frank was *really* good. Mandy wished she could do something like acting, she wished she had a talent. Now that she was a mom, the future seemed so sepia – there wasn't much on the horizon to define it.

Another wave of sickness washed over Anna-lise, her face flushing with heat. She felt like a red light, shining out in the darkness.

She hated the idea that she might have to get up and disturb the play. She tried to be angry with herself for not sitting in an aisle seat, in the hope that it might give her the strength to ride the nausea.

But it didn't work. The sickness came in another rolling wave, bigger this time, mounting and riding on top of the previous one that was still there.

Henry leant towards her and steadied her as she stood. She smiled an apology and stumbled her way through a thicket of limbs.

She hoped she wouldn't hurl in this woman's lap.

Mrs Xhiu felt numb. The glass of wine she'd drunk to get herself out of the apartment had walked off with her legs. Twice she'd giggled when she wasn't meant to. The play was funny. She grinned at her neighbours in search of agreement. They didn't seem to take much notice.

It was very hot. The handsome man next to her felt soft. She started sinking into her seat. She could feel the springs pressing into her behind. The thought of them made her giggle again.

Her eyes started to glaze over. She couldn't keep them open. Her head started to nod. Her neck collapsed and then she was gone, snoring loudly.

Henry wanted to get up and go with Anna-lise but Mrs Xhiu had him pinned. He tried to say as much with his eyes as she slid past but she didn't make eye contact. He watched her shuffling down the row and hoped she'd be OK.

He turned back to the play and found himself wondering if he'd ever write anything like Kesey. He felt very lost with his work. He genuinely had no idea if it was any good. He didn't know if he believed any more.

Now that he was considering Dad's offer, he wondered if it had all been for nothing.

Mike watched Anna-lise walking up the aisle. It didn't seem right. He'd complained that his personal involvement could prejudice the investigation but the chief was adamant. Some bullshit to do with resources.

He was to bring her downtown the next day. They said it like it was going to be easy. They made it sound like a routine arrest. He fingered his programme nervously.

Frank hadn't dared look out beyond the wall of lights but it was hard to avoid when it came to the electrotherapy scene. The director had had the idea of reversing things, sinking the stage into darkness before blinding the audience with spotlights each time they turned up the juice.

They came into focus one by one, blinking, as if being drawn out of relief on a string. He saw them, sitting, watching him, from a stage of their own. He heard a strange clicking noise in his ears and a cold fist tighten inside his chest.

For a moment he thought he was about to have a panic attack but then, just as he felt himself starting to lose control, the lights went quickly down signalling his final scene. He realized ecstatically that his role in the show was nearly over. He'd made it.

A shuttle bus took us from the theatre down to the South Ferry pier. It was funny watching the way people on the street looked at us as we travelled, all dressed up that way and together without 444 there to necessarily make the connection. They eyed us with suspicion, as if we were escaped convicts or something. For some reason, that made me feel kind of proud.

It was the same down at the dock where a big man checked our faces against names on a list. He scrutinized us as if it wasn't possible for us to be invited, we were a far cry from the thespian types already on board the boat, until the mention of Frank's name unlocked something in his mind as simply as a key. His body swung to slowly, like a big wooden door.

It was only as we set sail that I noticed Morgan hadn't made it. I saw that she wasn't on the bus but I had assumed, like Mike and Juan, that she must have somehow gone from the melee outside the theatre straight into a cab to the after-party.

The fact that she wasn't there before us meant she'd either gotten lost, gone home or not been invited, all of which made the happy sense of escape between us grow. There were several smiles shared when the horn finally blew and black water stretched gently between us and the island.

I spent most of the trip up on the deck of the ferry, glancing at Manhattan in silent awe and watching the tenants settle into things, sharing conversations and laughter, and drinking with people they didn't know. It was oddly reassuring to see them this way, exercising their independence, and I made an effort to do the same.

I think I did OK, all things considered. I was pretty amazed that I'd made it this far. Six months ago I could barely leave the building. Now I was taking a trip off the city. I experienced a surge of hope that things might be moving in the right direction. I watched Ben and Mandy, Mike and Juan, and Anna-lise and Henry all love one another and share their affection freely. Things really did seem as if they might turn out OK.

After making the turn at the Statue of Liberty, nearing Ellis Island on the return leg, the director of the play proposed a toast.

People stopped dancing and eating and chatting and gathered round to drink to the success of the show. With the warm, homing lights of skyscrapers behind him, the director singled out Frank for his performance and everyone from 444 gave a hearty cheer, which made him shed a couple of happy tears. I felt proud of him and said so when I got the chance. He gave me a tight hug.

'Where would we be without you, Mack?' he whispered in my ear and, even though I suspected he was a little drunk, I'll admit it moved me.

So too, when he called out for me to squeeze into the picture he asked someone to take of all the people in the building. He grabbed my arm and pulled me in tightly, standing close to the middle next to Mandy and Helmut. Someone called out 'Cheese!' and we all yelled it, the salty winds of the Atlantic and the sweet smells of the continent in our hair.

The good feelings continued all the way back to the docks and onto the pier and back into the shuttle bus waiting to take us home.

I listened with joy to the way everyone's words and sentences intermingled and danced and sang – just like a real group of friends should. There was no clashing cacophony of unsaid misgivings between them cluttering up my mind; no click, click, click of malevolent collective will. There was simple happiness and satisfaction and gentle shared inebriation.

It was only as the strange skeletal silhouette of the scaffolding loomed that I sensed a snap in the harmony. It rang out as brightly as the window-framed sections of light that were standing like sentinels high up on the top floor.

The moment was gone. As the bus pulled up there was a frightened silence to soberly commemorate our arrival back at 444, followed by a sad sigh of resignation as everyone gathered their purses and got themselves up to go inside.

And even though we made a determined effort to collapse through the entrance way as raucously and jubilantly as possible – heralding our return home with epic triumph – the sight of those stern, brooding lights staring down at us like angry, accusing eyes was enough to break our happiness.

Invitations to carry on the party were unconvincingly enthusiastic and there were only half-hearted protests when people said they were going to bed. One by one, the tenants accepted the fate of their new surroundings and made their excuses. Quietly, they filed, very separately, into their own apartments, into their own homes.

M ike stepped into the elevator. He took a minute to look at the call buttons and heard Juan's words again in his head.

Ees your job, honey.

Yes, it was.

He leant forward and pushed the button for the second floor, still not really accepting the task, just going through the motions. The doors closed and the elevator fell slowly, as if through water, and then jerked to a halt just one floor below.

Mike forced a smile as the doors opened. Garry nodded back sombrely.

'How's it going?' he said, stepping in.

'Not bad. You?'

'I'm on my way to a job interview,' Garry replied, taking his position next to Mike, turning to face the direction of the door.

'DJ-ing?'

'No.' Garry sighed and said without sarcasm, 'A real job.'

Mike smiled at him gently. 'Good luck with that.'

'Thanks,' Garry replied quietly.

The elevator came to a second stop at the second floor.

'You getting off here?' Garry asked.

Mike panicked. 'Er, no. I punched the wrong button by mistake.'

Garry snorted and leant across Mike's body to hit the button for the ground floor. There was an agonizing wait as the doors remained open and the two men stared out onto the corridor, waiting for something to happen. Mike prayed that Anna-lise hadn't heard the chime. He didn't think he could bear it if Garry watched him arrest her. He could just imagine the fuss he'd make.

Mike stabbed the close-door button with a stiff finger, several fast times.

'Easy there, tiger,' Garry said. 'You don't wanna break it, pal.'

Mike smiled meekly. Eventually, after three interminable seconds, the doors finally closed.

'You've been working out too much,' Garry teased as the elevator sailed again.

Mike laughed quietly.

'You OK?' Garry asked, after a pause.

'Sure,' Mike said quickly, turning. 'Why wouldn't I be?'

'I dunno,' Garry replied with a quizzical look. 'You seem quiet.'

'Juan and I just had a bit of a fight,' Mike lied. Taking Garry into a false confidence was the only way he could think of to ward him off the scent.

'Oh,' Garry replied.

Mike nodded, bowing his head slightly.

'Well, those things happen,' Garry said.

'Yeah.'

'If you ever want someone to talk to, you know, just come by.'

Mike nearly choked. Garry wasn't homophobic, but he wasn't exactly a fan either.

'Thanks, Garry. That's sweet of you.'

Mike looked up and found Garry looking at him. Their eyes met briefly and they exchanged a frown of manly resolve, solidarity in the face of marital hardship, which was ironic considering neither of them was hitched. Still, the sentiment was there.

Just when Mike was sure Garry was about to hug him, the elevator bell chimed and the doors opened with a keen sigh of relief.

'Oh damn,' Mike managed, thinking fast now. 'I've forgotten my keys. I'm gonna have to go back up.'

'Cool,' Garry said, not hearing the lie, stepping outside. 'Catch you later, then.'

'Yeah,' Mike said, waiting till he was out of sight to press the button for the second floor again. 'Later.'

Helmut was in a strange dream watching Leticia have sex with some guy in a Halloween goblin costume when he realized that the banging sound wasn't her head hitting the headboard of his bed but someone knocking on his front door.

'What?' he exclaimed, sitting up.

His world suddenly surrounded him. Bed, sheets, book, lamp, kitchen, clothes, television – only the daylight was new, streaming in through the window and into his closing thoughts of the previous night, making them seem different.

It had to be late.

'Open up, Helmut.' Mike's voice came through the wall like paper soaking.

Helmut rolled out of bed and into a towel. He rubbed his eyes and caught a glimpse of himself in the mirror. He winced. He'd go to the gym today. He swore it to himself. There was another bang on the door.

'Coming,' Helmut said and shuffled sleepily. He turned the knob and stretched the door open wide, enough to crucify himself on the frame. Mike was in uniform. Another officer stood behind him, one hand resting near his gun.

'Hey,' Mike said, visibly relaxing. 'Did we wake you?'

'No,' Helmut yawned. 'It's cool. What's up?'

Mike tensed, making his short-sleeved shirt smile on the shoulders. Helmut admired his triceps. He really did have to get to the gym.

'Helmut,' Mike started gloomily. 'I'm afraid there's been a complaint.'

Helmut released himself from the doorway and rubbed the

side of his face, enjoying the sensation of his stubble scratching the palm of his hand.

'Yeah?' Helmut replied. 'What about?'

'Your sick film,' the police officer behind Mike blurted, his fingers craning for the butt of his gun like leeches reaching for blood.

'My sick film?' Helmut said slowly, genuinely not comprehending for a moment. He didn't have any 'sick films'.

'*Penthouse*?' Mike said.

Helmut's eyes made two, slow 'Oh' shapes.

'I can't believe you've been letting this pervert get away with it for so long, Mike.'

'I said I'd handle this, Columbus,' Mike hissed. He took a moment to recover himself.

'A lot of people think my film is very beautiful,' Helmut tried.

'You should be locked up,' Columbus sneered.

'You admit you made the film, Helmut?' Mike asked.

'Sure.'

'That's it, Mike,' Columbus snapped. 'Cuff him.'

'Helmut,' Mike said gently, trying to maintain control, 'I'm gonna have to ask you to come down the station.'

'You're arresting me?' Helmut said. 'What for? It's freedom of expression. It's in the Constitution. It's my right.'

'Freedom to be a freako ain't in our Constitution,' Columbus said.

'I'm not arresting you. I just want to ask you a few questions.'

'What about?'

'We've got Anna-lise downtown,' Mike added. 'She's admitted you filmed her in Morgan's apartment. Morgan's pretty mad about it. She's pressing charges against Anna-lise for vandalism. You're a witness. I'm sorry.'

'What the hell are you saying sorry to him for, Mike?' Columbus yelled, trying to press past. 'Cuff him already, for

Christ's sakes. Shit! I keep doing it!' He added, crossing himself quickly.

'Will you come with us, Helmut?' Mike asked gently.

'Can I put some pants on first?' Helmut said.

Mrs Xhiu was celebrating. At least, that was what she told herself as she opened the bottle of Southern Comfort. She took a whiff, not knowing what it might taste like – she only bought it because she liked the name. A seam of alcohol kicked her away but then an aroma of boiled syrup lured her back in. Her nose swam in the golden sunset colours.

'Hmm,' she murmured appreciatively.

She poured herself a shot, toasted Jesus on the wall with a wry wink and threw the alcohol down her throat. A cold burn dripped down before the drink mellowed, nestling in the bed of her belly like breathing embers.

'Hmm-hmm,' she said.

She poured herself a tumblerful and went to switch on the TV. The God Channel flickered automatically to life as she sat down in her armchair.

She fingered quickly between the cushions for the remote, anxious to change over. She couldn't bear to watch this now, not since the Reverend Jeremy meet. God was gone from her life. She'd lost Him, suddenly, completely, like a person with amnesia loses their memory.

She finally found it, covered in fuzz, and pressed a button blindly. The signal changed with a cathode-tube sucking pop.

' . . . *electrical outages. Heavy rain as well as thunder and lightning will hit the city again Thursday, with temperatures well over the 100 mark for the third week in a row, breaking a 178-year-old mean temperature record for July. It's 9.20 a.m. here on Channel QRT-SPZYWLK. Coming up: a look at the Caribbean island of St Christopher . . . '*

Mrs Xhiu turned to her pile of junk mail. This was her new enterprise in place of faith, her new way of spending the day.

Ever since the bank loan, she'd been startled to discover just how much got given away in the world. All she had to do was take it. It was easy, like picking fruit from a tree. After forty years in New York, Mrs Xhiu had finally figured out how to pick the Big Apple; she'd uncovered this city of original sin, she'd discovered greed.

She dedicated herself to the task, rifling through the bogus Lotto offers with their expensive 1-800 call-ins and the lofty-casino-cruise-ship investment schemes for the simple, but lucrative, no-fee credit-card offers and subscription-service cash give-aways.

She'd become very good at filling out the forms.

And she was rich now, richer than she had ever been. As long as she never spent too much, as long as she never fell for the unwritten covenant that in order to receive one had to give, she always won.

So, the day she received her microwave, she took the three hundred dollars straight out of the Super Saver Account. As soon as the cheque for her personal profile arrived, she changed her phone number. When they gave her a free mobile, she scrutinized the small print for ways to exit the contract.

That way, they always came back to her with more free offers.

Mrs Xhiu opened her bank statement and sipped on her drink proudly. It had taken the Bank Corp loan, fifty-three credit cards and two more equity-release loans to achieve it but it was finally official. She was now a millionaire.

The show about the Caribbean island started up on the television. Mrs Xhiu found herself watching it. It jogged something within her, a vague memory, like the memory of herself laughing as a kid.

'*Honey, on the amount of money you'll make you could live like a queen in the Bahamas.*'

Mrs Xhiu watched the pictures of cobalt-blue oceans tugging at blinking diamond shores. She looked at the lush folds in the green jungle canopies as they tumbled down the sides of creased volcanoes. She matched up the colours of the sky with the bright local dresses.

Hers was a one-way ticket, she knew that. By the time they came to collect their money, she'd be dead. After all, wasn't that her trick? The Reverend Jeremy session had shown her that much.

'Hmm,' she murmured, looking between the drink and the TV. 'I could do with some of that Southern Comfort.'

Seeing as they weren't meeting Morgan for brunch, Mike and Juan thought it might be nice to have breakfast in bed for a change. Mike was so thrilled to have Morgan out of their weekend, he'd even offered to make it, which sealed the deal for Juan.

'*Voilà*,' Mike said, shuffling into the bedroom with a tray so laden with treasures it could only mean disaster in the kitchen.

Freshly squeezed orange juice, poached eggs on rye, a large thermos of coffee . . . he'd even got out the silver salt and pepper shakers and the cloth napkins.

'Wow,' Juan said, shaking his tail into the mattress and pressing himself up into pillows.

Mike balanced the tray on the end of the bed and went to raise the blinds. He threw open the window to let the high summer light that was pouring through the airshaft breathe on their bare-brick bedroom wall. Juan reached for the newspaper that was folded and squeezed tightly into a heavy-duty toast holder.

'You even got the paper?' Juan said. 'I didn't hear you go out.'

'I thought we could take a look at the Classifieds.'

'Serious?' Juan said, unfolding the paper in his palms like the Good Book. Mike grabbed a corner of an inner section and tugged, sending Gospels across the sheets: Fashion & Living, Money & You, Finance, Real-estate, the Magazine, the Review, Science & Technology, Jobs, Arts & Entertainment, TV Guide, Cable Guide, Eating Out, Eating In, Home Interiors . . . there were a lot of loose-leaf ads for a computer-sale bonanza with shampoo-sample sachets stuck to them as well.

'Very,' Mike said, unfurling the Real-estate section with a

maître d's flair into Juan's lap. He walked round the bed to serve coffee.

'You're so romantic,' Juan said, opening the pages. 'Where shall we look?'

'Brooklyn?'

'Too expensive.'

'Williamsburg?'

'We want a house, Mike, not a warehouse.'

'Do you really think we'll be able to afford one?'

'Depends how far out of the city we go. Thanks,' Juan said, taking the Alice-in-Wonderland cup and saucer from Mike as he reached over.

'And you think that's what we need?'

'If we're to be a family, yes. The baby will need space.'

'Ben and Mandy manage.'

'Do they?'

Mike paused briefly. 'True.'

'I think our best bet is New Jersey.'

Mike grimaced. 'Ugh, America. You really want to live there?'

'Good schools, reasonable commute, fair prices,' Juan said in a public-service-announcement voice.

Mike frowned as he dropped four sugars into his coffee. 'And you don't think we're jumping the gun.' He climbed back into his side of the bed, stirring.

'It's better we get things the right way around, be prepared.'

Mike nodded. 'So long as you're sure.'

He watched Juan reach for a pen on the bedside table and start attacking a corner of the paper with circles.

'I just hope it's not because you're still upset with Morgan.'

'Hmm?' Juan murmured, not listening. 'What?'

'Are you still upset with Morgan?'

Juan stopped marking and leant forward for his plate of eggs.

'Yes,' he said, stretching. 'Of course I am.'

'Is that why you want to move? Because, you know, we're

onto a good thing with this apartment. We've had a lot of good years here.'

'I know that,' Juan said. 'But things are different now, aren't they?'

As if to make the point, a circular saw carved the air above them in a neat, straight shriek.

'You have got to be kidding me,' Mike said. 'On a Sunday?'

Juan looked at the bedside clock. It read two minutes past ten. 'She's only doing it to get at us. She can't think who else to blame.'

They listened to the screaming for a few minutes in still silence.

'That's it!' Mike said, throwing the sheet into the breakfast tray. 'I've had as much as I can take.'

'Where are you going?'

'To give you-know-who a piece of my mind,' Mike said, looking for a pair of jeans to jump into.

'Don't you dare, Mike!'

'Why shouldn't I?'

'It will only make things worse.'

'I'm not scared of her.'

'Well, you should be,' Juan said. 'Now come back here and eat your breakfast.'

'No,' Mike said, staring defiantly as he pulled on a T-shirt. 'This noise has got to stop. It's driving me nuts.'

'Fine, don't listen. Whatever you do, though, make sure you don't tell her we're moving out.'

'I'm not a complete idiot, Juan.'

'You could have fooled me,' Morgan's voice ricocheted down the airshaft.

Of all the real-estate brokers, this one took the prize – radioactive red hair, purple eyeshadow, plastic bangles, a green tent dress, custard-yellow pumps – Lord!

'Oh, I love what you've done in here,' she lied.

Morgan had never considered that getting an appraisal for her apartment could be so much fun. It wasn't that she was planning to sell. She just wanted to know how much money it was worth. It was actually a very good way to spend a day.

'Thank you,' Morgan said, leading her away from the walk-in closet. 'I designed it myself.'

'Really!' Marion said, pressing a palm to her chest with such theatrical sincerity it hurt Morgan to watch her do it. 'That's so amazing.'

'I know.'

Morgan found that she didn't too much mind all the point-less tittle-tattle and personal detail these characters spouted. She was probably just a little bored without Mike and Juan around to entertain her. But she also understood that the self-obsession these real-estate brokers exhibited had somehow become an integral part of their sales pitch. These people gen-uinely seemed to believe that she cared. She just had to get past it if she was going to get to the juicy stuff.

Marion was a painter. And she was a lot less reticent than the others.

'It's as if some brokers have got nothing else in their lives,' she enthused. 'They come out of the exam brainwashed, actu-ally believing they're performing some kind of life-saving service. Can you believe that?'

'How boring.'

For some reason, Marion found this comment hysterical and begged Morgan to say it again.

'No.'

'Oh, go on, please,' she said, beaming, daring to believe she could charm her. 'I love your accent.'

'I'm not a performing monkey, Marion.'

'Jeez, sorry, Ms Honeysuckle. I didn't mean to offend you.'

'Shall we go upstairs to the extension?'

She led her up the spiral staircase to the roof. They entered the half-plastered, fibreglass-filled frame. All the major electric, plumbing and roof work had been completed. The Welsh slate had finally set. The Italian tiles were ninety per cent done. The stone sinks were in place, even the titanium taps were on. The oak flooring had been weathered and was ready for laying. The spotlights sparkled like diamonds. The project was at last on the final straight.

'This will be the master bedroom,' Morgan said, sweeping an arm.

'Wow! This is incredible,' Marion squealed, running to the newly installed French windows. 'And look at that view.'

Morgan watched her swish them open, walk out to the edge of the roof and lean over the scaffolding to look down. Now she saw the reason for the tent skirt – Marion had a seriously huge ass.

Marion turned and walked back towards Morgan smiling, a not insubstantial breeze powerless to move her NASA-designed shock of locks. Morgan noticed how scuffed and frayed her shoes were and realized for the first time that this was something the brokers all shared – old, worn shoes. It made them seem hungry – like sharks.

'I haven't had the China-silk blinds put up yet,' Morgan said. 'But hopefully you get the picture.'

'More than,' Marion said. 'You really have done an amazing job.'

'You've seen enough, then?' she asked.

'Yes, I think so,' Marion replied.

'Well?' Morgan said, tapping her foot, impatient now for the number.

'Should we go downstairs so I can run you through our services?'

'That won't be necessary.'

'Don't you want to know how we plan to market the property?'

'Not really.'

Marion feebly attempted to use this sleight to her advantage.

'I'm not sure it's worth me giving you my estimate of the property, Ms Honeysuckle, if you can't appreciate our strategy. I think it's important for you to understand the market we think you should be targeting for an apartment of this quality and the kind of aggressive campaign we'd like to employ to make sure of a successful sale.'

'Marion,' Morgan said sternly.

'Yes.'

'You're starting to sound brainwashed.'

Marion winced.

'I'm sorry,' she replied.

'I know what you're going to do,' Morgan continued. 'I know that you're going to put an ad in the newspaper. I know that you'll put a picture of the apartment on your website. And I know that for this minimum amount of effort, your firm will make tens of thousands of dollars. So let's not waste any more of my time. If you want to give me a number, I'd be obliged. Otherwise, I'd like to get on with the rest of my day.'

Marion looked at her.

'OK,' she started. 'I'd say that, given that this is an up-and-coming area, the unique view that this incredibly stylish extension offers, the excellent light, the wonderful interior design, the private elevator, laundry, storage . . . '

'Just the number, Marion. If you please.'

Marion shuffled in her pumps, muttering her sums to herself: 'Three-bedroom, two-bath duplex, self-managed, super . . . '

'Marion!'

Marion dropped her head and closed her eyes, like a robot going into shutdown, before finally lifting her gaze and saying, 'One point nine.'

Morgan stared at her. Even if she reduced her target by thirty per cent to keep things more realistic, it was still well above expectations.

'Once everything's finished, of course,' Marion clarified.

Morgan gulped. 'Are you sure?'

Marion nodded confidently. 'The thing is, Ms Honeysuckle, our firm specializes in high-net-worth clients. We normally focus on the more traditional areas of the city. But there is demand now for more Bohemian properties like yours. This area is very cutting edge.'

'Marion,' Morgan started.

'Yes, Ms Honeysuckle.'

'I owe you an apology.'

Marion eyed Morgan suspiciously.

'What for?'

'I underestimated you. I didn't think you'd manage it. I was wrong. I'm very impressed.'

Marion's body visibly relaxed. She even allowed herself to smile. 'Does that mean you want to hire AOK Realty on an exclusive basis?'

'No,' Morgan replied. 'It doesn't.'

The smile curled off her face like a stamp losing glue. Morgan turned to walk back down the stairs. Marion chased after her, the heels of her shoes clicking on the wood.

'Of course, we'd be happy to act in association with other brokerage firms but I'm afraid we won't be able to offer the same discounted rate we give our exclusive clients.'

'I'll let you know,' Morgan said, striding through the apartment.

'I'm leaving you with our corporate literature so you can get a good handle on our premium services. Inside, you'll find my card. When you've reached a decision, please, just give us a call.'

Morgan reached the elevator and pressed the call button. She held out her hand. Marion took it.

'I've put it on your coffee table,' she said.

'Thank you.'

'You'll be sure to give us a call?'

Morgan nodded.

'Our office hours are . . . '

'Brainwash!' Morgan said, cupping her hands over her ears.

Marion responded with a strange, resigned smile. She paused, as if considering whether to say something. The elevator doors breathed. Morgan threw a hand in to keep them open. She tried to usher her in with a grin. But it didn't work. Marion just stood there, looking at her.

'Can I help you with something?' Morgan asked.

'No,' she said finally. 'It's OK. I was just thinking to myself what a lonely woman you've become.'

Morgan tried to frown but somehow the smile stuck to her face so she just ended up looking like she needed the bathroom.

'You don't remember me, do you?' Marion said.

The frown finally fell.

'I'm Marion Sweffle, Morgan.'

Morgan shook her head, then stopped. She stared at her. 'Marion?'

Marion stepped into the elevator and turned. Their brief confrontation seemed to give her a hitherto unseen resilience. It was as if she was somehow stronger than Morgan now. Or maybe she just didn't have to pretend any more.

'What happened to you?' Marion asked, looking at her. 'You used to be nice. I guess it's funny how people change, huh? I'm sorry for you, Morgan. I really am.'

Morgan let her hand fall. The doors closed. She found herself faced with her reflection in the sheer chrome doors. She turned away, unable to look.

It was everywhere now. Just like after Jimmy died. There was no escaping. It didn't hurt but it was shining out, reaching. We were all tuning in.

This was where all things led. And I had transcended the pain, I'd passed through that barrier. I had been a mother of sorts, conceiving the transmission the day Ben and Mandy arrived nearly nine months before. And now labour was over. The message had birthed. It no longer relied solely upon me for survival. It was outside of me. Others could share the mother load.

Everyone in the building heard it these days, in some shape or form, in some stage of evolution. It wasn't an abstract, the same way an unborn child is an abstract to everyone but its mother. It was upon us. They would all see eventually. It wouldn't be long now.

Perhaps this was why I could go outside again. As they tuned in, I was being set free. I was being allowed to leave. They were taking over. That was why their narratives were becoming more prevalent, while mine was receding. As the collective message got stronger, I was getting smaller. The 'I' was being replaced by the 'they'.

Eventually I would disappear entirely. My role was nearly at an end. Soon they wouldn't need me. I wouldn't be a part of this story any more. I accepted my departure now. I understood why it had to happen. The only thing I wished was for something good to come out of it all – something well and healthy and beautiful, like Anna-lise and Henry's connection or the Carlyle Garden – if that was in any way possible.

I didn't blame myself for the fact that it was a bad resonance. I wasn't responsible for that. The only thing that counted was that it would be. It had to be, just as a child has to be born, whatever its nature. It was inevitable.

Outsiders would say it couldn't be right. They would blame me, say I acted alone, that I was mad, just like they said after Jimmy died.

But, in time, they would understand, just like the tenants of 444 were starting to understand. They would come to know the truth. They would see that I was merely an agent, an operative in the co-operative.

Besides, this was just a path – one single path. Good could still come of it. Just because it started out this way, it didn't mean good couldn't happen, eventually.

I believed in 444. I believed the tenants would one day create something well. It could be like the Carlyle Garden. Even though it started with something negative, something beautiful could still come of it. You have to break something to make something. Before creation must come destruction.

I believe that very much.

Henry strode into the roof-garden bar and scanned.

There were palm trees in enormous terracotta pots. The floor was under-lit like a seventies disco, with big squares that flashed different colours as people walked across it. Storey-tall mirror balls were scattered randomly like marbles lost by a giant. There were opulent purple sofas with brass brocades. Low glass tables, catwalk-waif flutes and silver ice buckets all sweated champagne. There was the chemical smell of cocaine in the air. Stale dance music bumped.

He caught sight of Morgan flapping a wrist at him.

'Sorry I'm late,' he said, walking over.

'That's all right,' Morgan said, quickly getting up to greet him with a kiss near the lips. Henry instinctively kissed her back.

'Great place.'

'I'm glad you like it,' Morgan said, sitting down. 'I went to extraordinary lengths to get a reservation. Extra. Ordinary.'

Henry saw that she was dressed in an elegant long black dress with a plunging décolletage. It made her look very athletic. She was also wearing make-up – some rouge and pink lipstick tentatively applied. There was a thin line of sweat along her top lip. 'I like your dress.'

'Thank you,' Morgan said, visibly thrilled. 'There's a sale on at Yarko's. I'll take you.'

A pretty waitress came over. 'Good evening,' she said with an English accent. 'Would you care for a drink before we seat you?'

'Yes,' Morgan said happily. 'A bottle of champagne, two glasses.'

'Certainly,' the waitress said, before stooping confidentially. 'Can I just mention to you now, madam, that you will be required to settle the bar tab before moving to your table?'

'Fine.'

'And service is not included.'

Morgan nodded, anxious for her to go away.

'Champagne, Morgan?' Henry said. 'That's very extravagant.'

'Well, we are celebrating.'

'Are we?'

'The extension is finally finished.'

'You're kidding.'

'More or less. There're a few snags that need to be ironed out but it's there.'

'That is reason to celebrate. You must be pleased.'

'Relieved, actually. I can safely say the entire project has been one of the biggest nightmares of my life. Everything went wrong. Everything. I don't know how I coped.'

The waitress plus friend arrived with the champagne and glasses. Henry watched them pour. The waitress had a very recognizable face – she was like an English rose you might see in the movies. After pouring their drinks she pressed the bill with unsubtle urgency onto the table and only half-left, hovering between nearby tables like a bee waiting to land.

'Cheers,' Henry said, raising his glass.

Stars sparkled in the golden liquid. There was a warm, soft summer breeze. The city glowed around them, like northern lights.

'Cheers,' Morgan replied and they chinked.

'So what'll you do with the extra space?' Henry asked, wanting to keep the attention on Morgan for now, biding his time carefully before bringing up the delicate matter of Anna-lise's arrest.

'I'll move my bedroom,' Morgan replied, crossing her legs so they brushed Henry's. 'The view is wonderful. You should see it.'

'I'm sure I will,' Henry flirted, figuring it couldn't hurt. 'Sometime soon.'

Morgan visibly fizzed as she took another sip of her champagne.

Things up until then had been going well. Henry was sending out all the right signals. Morgan wasn't surprised. The poor man had to be devastated after Anna-lise's shocking behaviour.

Morgan was only too happy to be the alternative. They'd always shared a connection. She supposed it would have happened one way or the other, sooner or later. As it was, it was going to be this way and sooner.

Anna-lise had only herself to blame for that.

But then that moronic waitress, with her irritating accent and her over-educated arrogance that presumed the world owed her something, came running after them and ruined everything.

'Madam, madam,' she called out, as they walked to their table.

Morgan did her best to ignore her, hoping she might go away. She knew what she wanted but she was damned if she was going to tip on top of champagne at those prices. 'Excuse me. I'm talking to you. Stop!' she barked.

It was Henry who stopped, forcing Morgan to follow suit.

'Yes,' she said, turning slowly.

'I'm sorry,' the waitress panted, trying a smile. 'It's just that I explained to you before, service isn't included.'

'Yes,' Morgan replied.

'But,' she said, opening the book, crassly exposing Morgan's money to the air. 'You haven't left me a tip.'

'I know.'

Morgan could feel people watching them. She hated it. But she was determined to not let this girl win.

'Was something wrong?' the waitress asked, her face reddening.

Morgan shrugged. 'No. Everything was satisfactory, I suppose.'

'Because if there was something wrong with my service then I'd be only to happy to get the manager so you can explain to him why you haven't left me a tip,' she continued melodramatically.

'That won't be necessary.'

'Then can I have my tip, please,' she said with stone-grey eyes. 'Madam,' she added insolently.

It was the final 'madam' that did it. Morgan might have been embarrassed into obliging up to that point. Now she was just being rude.

'No,' Morgan said. 'I don't think so.'

'Why not?'

'It's OK,' Henry stepped in, reaching for his wallet. 'I'll get it, Morgan.'

Morgan pressed a palm on his chest and shook her head. 'No, you won't, Henry.'

'You have to give me twenty per cent,' the waitress said. 'Everyone does.'

'There's no law that says I have to tip you.'

'Why would I serve you for free? They don't pay us enough to live in this city. You have to tip.'

'You're wrong. I don't have to do anything. If you're unhappy with the pay, I suggest you find yourself another job.'

'You think I want to do this lousy gig?' the waitress shrieked. 'I'm an actress!'

Morgan beamed when she said it, seeing her chance.

'No, darling, you're a waitress, and not a very good one at that. Now leave us alone before I change my mind and take you up on your suggestion to complain to the manager.'

The waitress crumbled like a petal. Morgan moved quickly to avoid the tears, grabbing Henry's arm and turning him.

'Come on,' she hissed. 'I'm hungry.'

The victory soon proved to be pyrrhic, however.

At the table, service, and the evening as a whole, took a diabolical turn. The waitress didn't even try to disguise her conspiratorial conversations with her colleagues. She was clearly determined to ruin Morgan's night. It seemed a very unladylike thing to do.

'Excuse me! Excuse me!' Morgan called for the fifth time to their waiter. She had to physically grab him by the arm to stop him. 'I'm sorry, but we ordered our fish an hour ago.'

The gorgeous boy rubbed the back of an immaculate white sleeve across raw nostrils.

'Certainly, madam, I'm sorry. I'll just check up on it.'

'You said that last time.'

'Yes, madam, right away,' he said, leaving quickly.

'That kid is fried,' Morgan said to Henry as if he cared.

Henry nodded in slow agreement. Morgan looked around the place to soak up another uncomfortable silence. Plump PR girls with Kiki Kookie stilettos drilled into their heels stumbled to the bathroom. Men tied up in Windsor knots stooped over candlelit tables in earnest one-way conversations. Morgan zoned in on two English lawyers (what was it with this city and its English?) at the table behind them.

'Jesus Christ, look at her.'

'We Have Arrived.'

'This place rocks.'

'I love this city, I love it.'

'Oh my God. Here she comes again.'

'We Have Arrived.'

'I'm not going back to London.'

'I bet I'm reincarnated. I feel like I've been here before.'

'This joint only opened last week.'

'I swear, though.'

'You are the man.'

'No. You are the man.'

'No. You are the man.'

'We Have Arrived.'

'The Eagle has landed.'

'Come to Daddy.'

'I'm off to the Jimmy.'

'Me too.'

'No, wait here. I'll rack them up. You go in after.'

'Good thinking.'

'Be back in a min.'

'Nice.'

Henry pulled Morgan away from the agony of her overhearing.

'Morgan,' he started. 'Would you mind if we talked about Anna-lise?'

Morgan could have kissed Henry with relief. She hadn't wanted to bring it up for fear that it was too sensitive a subject. Now, at last, they had something they could actually talk about.

'Of course we can!' she said, hiccupping inwardly. 'Let me just start by saying how sorry I am.'

Henry's eyes shone with surprise. 'You are?'

'Yes,' Morgan continued. 'The whole thing is wretched. Utterly wretched.'

'Morgan, I'm so glad . . . '

'I mean, I never really liked Anna-lise but I never imagined her to be a vile individual. What she did was truly repulsive, abusing my trust the way that she did just so she could perform her sick sexual fantasies.'

Henry kept smiling but his eyes dulled, like metal without its sheen. 'Oh, come on. It wasn't *that* bad.'

'What?' Morgan replied, shocked. 'Darling, the girl isn't well.'

'No,' Henry tried. 'You've got it all wrong.'

Morgan frowned.

'I was hoping that maybe, well, I know she did bad but – ' Henry sighed heavily – 'it would be really great if you could be big enough to drop the charges, see the funny side of things. She didn't mean to hurt you. She was just upset with me. We were going through a rough patch at the time. She was angry. It was only a joke. That's no justification for her behaviour, I know. But, well, it would mean a lot to us if you could see it in your heart to forgive her. She's truly sorry, Morgan. Truly, truly sorry.'

Morgan was too stunned to speak.

'You could consider it your gift to us, if you like. Anna-lise is pregnant. I've asked her to marry me. We're going to be a family.'

The fish – an enormous beast bloated with floating gases, bulging alive eyes and lime-green skin – arrived in a heavy, sloppy, swimming soup. Soy sauce splashed everywhere, sending up salty, Asian fusion smells. The waiter hurled cutlery at them before attacking the meat, smashing the bones into the flesh so they could discover them in their mouths later, like hidden needles.

'We're not eating that,' Morgan said. The waiter swung a fierce look at her. 'It's cold,' Morgan said, touching it.

'I'll heat it up for you, madam.'

'Good,' Morgan replied.

The waiter left. It would have been better if he had stayed.

'You're not being serious, are you, Henry?'

'I am. We're going to get married. I'm going to be a father. Isn't it great?'

'No.'

'Excuse me?'

'You can't seriously expect me to drop the charges.'

'But, Morgan, Anna-lise is pregnant. You can't put her through this.'

'Put her through what?' Morgan said with a grunt. 'The woman urinated on my sofa. It's all on tape, for the whole world to enjoy. I'm not putting her through anything.'

'We'll pay for a new sofa.'

'Henry, I think maybe you've had too much to drink,' Morgan said.

'Everyone said I was wasting my time with you. I should have listened to them. I thought you were better than this.'

'Sorry to disappoint,' Morgan replied.

'Anna-lise was right. You did deserve it. It's no wonder everyone calls you a witch.'

The fish returned with disconcerting and miraculous speed, piping hot and steaming saliva. Morgan admired it for a moment before putting her hand up to stop the waiter from grinding into it again.

'The maître d', please.'

The boy threw the serving spoon and fork into the fish. 'Certainly, madam,' he spat.

'Henry, I'm afraid I have to tell you that the Board has decided not to renew your lease.'

'You mean you've decided.'

'If you want to put things that way, then yes.'

'You'll have to get it voted in first,' Henry replied.

'The building needs the funds from an apartment sale. Otherwise, there will be another maintenance increase. I'm sure I can convince the other members.'

'Maybe,' Henry replied.

'Oh, I think maybe definitely.'

The maître d' arrived. He was very tall and very buff and dressed in black tie. 'Yes?'

'The service in this restaurant is unlike anything I've ever experienced,' Morgan said.

'I'm sorry to hear you think so, madam.'

'I want to settle the bill.'

'Certainly.'

Morgan gave him her credit card. Henry stood up.

'Leaving?' Morgan said.

Henry didn't reply. He just walked out. Morgan instantly felt a tap on her shoulder. She turned.

'Sorry, babe,' one of the English lawyers started. He had dark rings under his eyes. 'I couldn't help overhearing.'

'Yes?'

'It's just that I reckon maybe you need to chill.'

'Excuse me?'

'Your friend. He seemed a bit upset.'

Morgan didn't reply.

'Maybe you should have congratulated him.'

'On what?'

'He's having a baby. He's getting married.'

'Yes, thank you, I heard.'

'Don't you think that's cause for celebration?'

Morgan stared. The muscles in her jaw started to spasm. For the first time in as long as she could remember, she felt like she might lose control. She could feel something building inside her, something very strong and intense. A vision suddenly flashed before her eyes. She couldn't make out the detail, but she felt instantly and violently terrified.

She turned slowly back in her chair and looked out numbly into a blurred mid-distance. The voice of the man continued to buzz behind her but she couldn't make out the words. She could see all the waiters laughing. The room started to spin. There were too many people laughing. Everything was very loud. She felt faint. There was a strange sound in her head. Her face throbbed hotly. She thought she was going to be sick.

The maître d' returned and thrust the bill onto the table in front of her.

'I'm sorry, madam,' he said with a restrained grin. 'But this credit card has been declined.'

Helmut listened to the rings in the receiver cut to a distorted recording of the new Sweet Nachos number-one hit. He was disturbed to discover how much he liked it. He was definitely getting old.

'*Hiya. Me. Leave a message.*'

Helmut waited a moment, squeezing his forehead tightly between his fingers, his elbows pinching the table.

'Hi, Chris. It's Daddy. Listen, baby, bad news. I can't visit this weekend. I know I promised. But something's come up. The distributors have made a mess of things and, well, I'm not going to bore you with the details.'

He took a deep breath.

'I'm going out of town for a few days. I'm sorry. I'll make it up to you when I get back. Please don't be mad.'

He paused and felt the phone between his fingers.

'I love you . . . '

Slowly, he replaced the receiver and looked up.

'That wasn't very successful,' the fat social-services lady in the tight grey outfit sang.

'I got a machine.'

'She'll only hear it from us now,' said the fat lady's stick-thin male opposite. He was wearing a matching grey suit.

'Please don't do this,' Helmut beseeched. 'She's all I have.'

'You should have thought about that before you started filming porn,' the man said. 'You're not exactly role-model material, are you?'

Helmut looked up at his lawyer, who shrugged weakly at him. The interview room looked like the inside of an old classroom Helmut remembered from his childhood. It was ironic.

They thrust the document in front of him. It was covered in

red warnings and exclamation marks and arrows marking where to sign. He stared at it and at the pen, which lay on the table like an offending weapon, something that would be used as evidence against him later.

'And if I don't?' Helmut tried one last time.

'You'll lose all visitation rights,' the man said.

'You'll not see your daughter for a very long time, Mr Pink.'

'Trust us, Mr Pink. This is the best thing for Christie. You need to think about her now.'

Helmut breathed, picked up the pen, and signed – here, here, here and here – and then watched them file out of the room, one by one, saying things to one another. Helmut stood up to leave, sat down again, tried to stand, collapsed and very finally, wept.

Diva was packing.

She'd had another one of her nightmares. She'd tried to tell herself it was a side effect of her not smoking, that it was a good thing. Her mind was becoming more alert, it was waking up to itself again after years of being dulled. It was just a stage.

But the dreams were getting more and more horrific. And they had a prescient quality to them, charting the mundane and familiar with specific detail before revealing some ghastly turn – they almost *had* to be premonitions.

Things like: walking out of the front door of the building on a glorious summer day and seeing Frank waving and smiling at her as he crossed the street, before an enormous juggernaut appeared from out of nowhere and smashed him to small pieces.

Or going down to do her laundry, sorting her clothes into whites and darks, delicates and cottons, sifting through her purse for quarters before opening the machine only to find Ulysses inside, floating upside down, like a wig in the water.

Or the one she'd had last night, the worst of them all, where everyone was sitting in Morgan's apartment for an AGM. Halfway through reading out the minutes, Morgan had proposed a motion that they 'get rid of Mack' so they all went down into the basement and tore him apart with their bare hands and threw his dismembered limbs into a fire that was somehow raging in the airshaft.

She felt a tremendous urge to get out of the building now. She had to get away. She needed the misty breezes and dramatic cliff views of the west coast to clear her mind. She needed to see her daughter, see if they could mend their broken relationship.

If only she hadn't taken that DMT, she thought to herself as she pressed a pair of jeans into the case.

There was a knock at the door. Diva hesitated before answering. It came again, at the same, patient speed. She walked towards the door and pressed her eye onto the spyhole. It was the super, his features distorted and exaggerated through the fish-eye lens.

Diva's hand hovered at the doorknob. She wasn't sure whether to answer. Something inside told her not to, but then a strange sense of guilt came over her, as if she owed him something for her part in the dream she'd had the previous night.

'Yes, Mack,' she started as casually as she could, propping herself tightly inside the doorway.

He smiled gently. 'I found these,' he said, holding out her set of storage-bin keys. 'You left them in the lock.'

Diva took them. 'Thanks.'

'It's easy to forget little things when you've other things on your mind.'

Diva nodded.

'But the little things are still important,' he continued.

Diva humoured him with a big, apologetic smile.

'I won't take up any more of your time,' he finished.

'OK, thanks a lot,' Diva said, as he turned away.

'Have a safe trip,' he said.

Diva found herself instinctively calling out, like a wounded animal. 'Mack!' He stopped and turned back to face her. 'How did you know I was going away?'

They looked at each other for a moment.

'Your suitcase was gone from the basement. I figured.'

'Oh,' she replied with relief. 'Oh.'

'When's your flight?'

'Tomorrow night,' Diva replied easily.

'You'll miss the party, then.'

'Party?'

'After the Board meeting. It's on the building blackboard. Morgan's apartment.'

'Oh,' Diva said without remorse. 'That's a shame.'

The superintendent nodded, turned and walked away.

' . . . *emergency services on full alert. Long flight delays and power outages are expected. Citizens are advised to stay indoors. Meanwhile, as the rest of the city battens down the hatches, surfers are ignoring the hurricane warnings and heading for the coast in their hundreds, making the most of the huge waves . . .* '

Anna-lise found herself living life on a new plateau. There was a calmness to her demeanour, a philosophical detachment, that she'd never before experienced.

It was as if nothing really mattered – nothing outside of her, in any case. She wasn't angry with Helmut any more. Not even the criminal charges weighed too heavily.

The only thing she cared about was the baby. Just knowing it was inside gave her a strength that elevated her above the relatively mundane considerations of normal life – like going to jail.

Her body was a temple, a house for something holy. And with that knowledge came a certain Buddha-like serenity, an understanding that her actions were vital.

She was taking things extra slow these days, dealing with life one step at a time. Coming here, to the gynaecologist in downtown Chinatown, had been the perfect example of that.

She hadn't gotten stressed by the crowds and the spitting hawkers. She'd waited calmly for each WALK signal. She'd managed to breathe her way through the nausea as she'd passed the smelly market and the sights of strangely scaled, dying fish in small fish tanks.

The only time she ran was when she stepped off the elevator needing to pee. Somehow, there wasn't any warning any more, her bladder simply and instantly filled. Given this, and her performance in Helmut's video, she was a little worried she was about to earn herself a very undesirable reputation.

'The doctor will see you now,' the teenaged Chinese girl behind reception said inaudibly.

Anna-lise looked up from the celebrity-gossip magazine she was reading and bit her lip.

'But my fiancé isn't here yet.'

The teenager looked very serious for a moment before muttering anxiously into the phone.

'OK no problem, please weigh yourself,' she said incomprehensibly. Anna-lise filled in the words, using the girl's gesture towards the scales.

On the wall were pictures of all the babies the doctor had delivered. Most of them were fat Chinese dumplings with bloated, bursting cheeks that made them look like they'd just vomited into their own mouths.

But Jesus, they were cute!

'Sorry I'm late,' Henry whispered behind her, wrapping an arm around her waist and kissing her neck.

'Hi,' Anna-lise said, quietly turning. She smiled at the girl apologetically. 'My fiancé.'

'Go, go,' the girl said, or so Anna-lise guessed. She was waving her hands in the direction of the doctor's door.

'Come on,' Anna-lise said, leading Henry by the hand.

They stepped inside and saw Dr On sitting at her desk, smiling up at them. If Anna-lise had discovered serenity in her pregnancy, Dr On seemed to have discovered it in her choice of career. A small, handsome woman, she was the very embodiment of calm. Nothing seemed to faze her, which was the reason Anna-lise liked her so much.

With Dr On around, Anna-lise felt nothing could go wrong.

They talked about the delivery Dr On had done the previous night. They talked about her five kids (five!). Dr On flirted with Henry by telling Anna-lise how good-looking her baby was going to be, which made him blush.

There were some physical questions and then, before they had time to take in what was happening, Anna-lise was up on a bed in one corner, her skirt pulled down, jelly all over her belly, and a microphone pulsing out the echo of a heartbeat. A blue-green image popped and grew and melted like bubble-gum bubbles on a monitor as Dr On skated the ultrasound imaging stick over Anna-lise's stomach.

'There's the head, legs, spine,' she said.

Anna-lise and Henry squinted, trying to make out the shapes.

'A hand!' Henry exclaimed. 'I saw a hand!'

Dr On paused just long enough for them both to enjoy it.

'Would you like to know if you are having a boy or a girl?' Dr On asked.

'We're having a boy.' Henry beamed.

'That's right,' Dr On said. 'You saw.'

Anna-lise looked up and saw Henry's look. She felt a tremendous love swell inside of her and swallow all of them in its glow – Henry, the baby, Dr On. It was the happiest she'd ever felt in her life.

Afterwards, outside, in the wind, Henry told her the news.

'But what about your writing?' she asked anxiously. She couldn't bear the idea of Henry sacrificing himself for her. She was terrified he might hate her for it later.

'I'm ready now,' Henry said. 'I want to.'

'Are you sure?'

'More than sure,' he replied.

'And you're not just doing it to get me out of trouble?'

'No,' he said gently. 'I'd pretty much decided already. I want to spend some time with Dad.'

'But what will it mean?' Anna-lise cried. 'For us?'

Henry looked deeply at her and held her in his arms.

'Don't be frightened,' Henry said. 'This will mean we can be together. For ever.'

'I'm leaving you, Ben.'

Ben stared at his wife, at the suitcases.

'I'm taking Billy and we're going to my mom's for a few months, till I figure out what to do.'

There was a humming sound in his ears from all the blood rushing to his head. His heart was thumping at every extremity. He could feel it in the ends of his fingers, the tips of his ears . . . his elbows? He couldn't talk. His throat was dry and tight. He couldn't move. All he could do was watch as this train wreck that was his marriage and his life came hurtling towards him.

It was one of those moments of paralysing terror. Somehow, he knew that this was it. They were finally breaking up. After everything they'd been through together, all the years they'd shared, they were at an end. Their dying romance flashed before his eyes quickly before questions like *What will I do?* started spinning loudly around in his head. He found he wanted to cry but he was still in too much of a state of shock. The impact hadn't happened quite yet, the level of damage was unknown. He had plenty of time for tears.

'Oh, darling,' Mandy cried, seeing the anguish darting in his eyes. 'Can't you see that ever since we moved here things between us have gotten bad?'

Ben managed to nod numbly.

'I just can't take it any more. I can't take being cooped up in this place. I just think we've had so much bad luck what with your jobs and now the foreclosure. It's as if this wasn't meant to be, none of this was meant to happen. It's all been a mistake.'

'What about the baby?' Ben managed to murmur. 'Was he a mistake?'

Mandy looked at Ben sadly. 'I don't know any more.'

A tear did fall then, he couldn't help it.

'I still love you,' she whispered.

'Then stay,' he said. 'Walking away is the easy option. We've got to try and make this work.'

'Don't you get it? I can't live here like this, waiting to be thrown out, not knowing where we're going to go, when you might get a job again, if ever. I still love you, Ben, but I find I'm starting to blame you. If I stay I'm scared I might end up hating you.'

'That's so unfair.'

'I know.' Mandy sighed, dropping her head. 'But it's the way I feel.'

Ben felt a surge of anger then. Did he act on every emotion? Did he do whatever he 'felt' like? Why were women allowed to do so much in the name of feelings, while men were constrained to their responsibilities?

'I see,' he managed to reply tersely. Even though he wanted to scream and shout, he knew it wouldn't help. And Billy was asleep just next door. He didn't want his son to hear this, any of it. 'When are you going?'

'Tomorrow morning, first thing.'

'How are you getting there?'

'We're taking the train from Grand Central.'

'What about the storm? They say it's going to disrupt services.'

'We'll have to see.'

'You'll miss Morgan's party,' Ben said, realizing that he was falling from one weak excuse to the next now, stalling for time, delaying the inevitable impact, the beginning of his pain.

'I'll live,' Mandy said.

'Don't you want to see the extension?'

'To be perfectly honest with you, Ben, I don't. I really, really don't.'

Seemed to me we were losing babies. Ben and Mandy, Mike and Juan, Henry and Anna-lise – all the people with kids were leaving. Helmut's daughter wouldn't be allowed to come around any more. I was going to miss her. And even though Diva was rediscovering her daughter in her heart, the fact that she was leaving 444 to realize their relationship again felt like a loss. There wouldn't be any youth here.

It made me think of Jimmy and how losing him broke Catherine and me. And I remembered swearing to myself after leaving the asylum how I would always look out for folks with families – I knew how vital kids were to the equation. No collective can survive without them.

The people who say society can, who claim there isn't a place for children, are just scum, the lowest of the low, if you asked me. I didn't care how exclusive they thought their situation was. They needed to remember that they used to be children themselves – once, long ago, in a faraway, joyful place.

Look at what was happening here. Look at the state I'd allowed this co-operative to fall into. I was so ashamed of myself. I'd allowed this to happen. After everything I believed in and cherished, I'd let the building fall into this chronic condition. Now it was all dislocated and dysfunctional and full of misery.

I wasn't going to let it go on. I couldn't, not like this. This was one malfunction that had to be fixed – at any cost.

B en sat on Morgan's new sofa, the notice of foreclosure in his
hands. Mike sat cross-legged on the floor, by an empty
chair. Frank and Garry sat next to each other, on dining chairs.
Mrs Xhiu was pouring herself a drink in the kitchen. Anna-lise
was doing some last-minute revision on Henry's lease to see
about the return of his deposit, but to no avail. Ulysses lay dole-
fully in his bed in the corner.

Outside the wind screamed.

They all turned to the sound of Morgan stepping down the
circular stairs. She walked steadily and slowly. They saw her
ruby shoes with thick heels, the beginnings of dark pantyhose.
A tight knee-length black skirt cut into her waist. She wore a
sharply ironed white shirt with oversized collars and exaggerated French cuffs pinned at the wrist with fat, rectangular gold
cufflinks. The skin on the back of her hands shone with mois-
turizer. She stopped before her head came into sight, shielded
by the extension, as if waiting for something.

There was a dramatic flash of lightning and the near instantaneous roar of thunder.

She continued down the stairs without making eye contact,
the stairs turning her to everyone but Mrs Xhiu, who was too
preoccupied with the icemaker on the refrigerator to notice.

In one arm she held a heavy stack of files, her shoulder-line
tipping slightly with the weight of them. She placed them carefully on a small table by the wall, under a lamp with pictures of
Japanese cherry blossom painted on the shade. She turned and
stepped to the middle of the room.

Rain smattered against the windows like small stones.

Morgan put her hands behind her back, thought better of it,
pulled them out and pressed them in prayer in front of her

chest. She tilted her head and rubbed her forefingers together with a sigh. She stayed like that for a moment, before raising her head and dropping her hands back to her sides.

The lights in the apartment momentarily brightened on an electricity surge, flickered and then dimmed.

'I have an announcement,' Morgan said in the half-yellow. No one moved. Morgan sucked in air. 'I wish to stand down as President of the Board.'

Only Ulysses shifted slightly. Morgan looked at them.

'Who will volunteer as my replacement?'

Still, no one said anything.

'Frank?' Morgan started, turning to him.

He shook his head slowly. Morgan continued to look at him, waiting for a proper answer.

'I'm sorry, Morgan. I can't.'

'Why not?'

'I just . . . don't want to.'

Morgan huffed. 'That's hardly a reason. Besides, I thought you wanted the job.'

'I've changed my mind,' Frank replied. 'I'm committed to my acting right now.'

Morgan didn't press. She was sure there would be other willing candidates.

'What about somebody else, then?'

'Well, I can't do it,' Mike said.

Morgan turned to face him.

'We're leaving the building,' Mike explained. 'But then you knew that already.'

'Me too,' Ben said, holding up the foreclosure notice with its big red words. 'Though not by choice.'

'Henry and I have decided we need a bigger place,' Anna-lise said diplomatically. She still couldn't look Morgan in the eye.

'Don't ask me,' Mrs Xhiu announced, stepping in from the kitchen. 'I'm going on a long vacation. Like you suggested.'

'Garry?' Morgan said, turning to look at him.

Garry shrugged. 'No, I don't think I want to do it either.'

Morgan frowned. 'Interesting. So you're *all* saying no?'

'Isn't that what you want?' Frank said.

'What makes you say that?'

Everyone laughed. Except for Morgan, who stared at them with an utterly bewildered expression. It made her look unusually young.

'What's so funny?' she asked.

The laughter built until all Morgan could see was the backs of teeth, their mouths widening. Even Ulysses was laughing. It reminded her of being in the restaurant she took Henry to. She felt dizzy.

'Stop it!' she called out. 'Stop that at once.'

But it didn't stop. Their laughter rolled at her angrily. The wind joined in, and soon it was a mess of screaming sounds, people panting hard to get the hilarity out, wheezing with forced amusement, hateful in their glee.

'Please,' Morgan tried.

The power outage stopped them, throwing darkness fearfully in their faces with a purple-black flash. Moments passed before the lights came on again, making everyone blink as if waking up from a dream.

Morgan remained standing in the centre of the room, stunned.

'Are you going to call the meeting to order, Morgan?' Frank said.

'What?' Morgan said slowly.

'The Board meeting.'

'Yes,' she murmured. 'All right.'

She fingered for the edge of her armchair and sank slowly into it. Mrs Xhiu stirred her vodka with a finger as she took her place on the chair beside Mike. Ulysses did a ninety-degree turn and curled his back to the room with professional disinterest.

'The minutes from the last meeting, please, Frank,' Morgan said robotically.

'Oh,' Frank replied, as if suddenly remembering something. 'I forgot to do them. Sorry.'

Morgan realized her left leg was shaking. She turned to Ben. 'Mr Treasurer?' she tried.

'The rising cost of the extension has driven building accounts into the red,' Ben said flatly. 'We are no longer able to service the loan. But I've explained to the bank about our expected future flip-tax income so they've granted us a three-month extension. If we fail to make our payments after that, however, the corporation will have to file for Chapter Eleven.'

Morgan gulped and nodded simply. 'Thank you.' She paused for a moment. 'Is there any old business to discuss?'

'You need to give us an update on the building works. When will the scaffolding be coming down?' Mike asked.

Wind shrieked in the pipes.

'Next week,' Morgan replied, turning towards him, wanting to deliver this good answer directly.

'Good,' Mike replied, cold to the affection. 'It will make selling our apartment easier.'

Morgan's eyes fell.

'So it's finally finished?' Mrs Xhiu asked.

'Yes,' Morgan said.

'Can we see it?'

'Yes,' Morgan answered.

'When?'

Morgan looked at her watch. 'How about now? I don't think we're in the mood for a Board meeting. We may as well just start the party.'

The walls were sweating. The rafters were screaming. It was damp and musty and steamy. The tenants could smell themselves, their vinegary pungent funk, mixing with the smell of new wood. The air stuck to them like second skin, making them want to undress.

Rain lashed at the windows in random spurts, with menacing inconsistency. Lightning flashed lilac light, the colour of illuminated night, revealing the bellies of storm clouds. Thunderclaps snapped like trees. There was a vibration in the floor. Darkness loomed outside in the intermissions, as if hiding something, or someone.

Only a few lights of nearby buildings were faintly visible through the streaked foggy blur of the French windows, but they were just enough for the tenants to know that they were safe, that they were still docked in harbour.

They made intimate conversation in pockets, while Morgan to-ed and fro-ed from the kitchen and the living room and then upstairs again with refreshments and news of the hurricane.

In the bathroom, three rivets behind the basin stand shook with supersonic intensity and then popped loose, like bullets being fired from a gun.

It was the pipes, it had always been the pipes. We were su
rounded now by it. The scaffolding, the heating system, the
whole building rang, just as I had foreseen. It began on the top
floor, where they were congregating like water in an impression,
and then resonated its way through the entire structure.

They swam together: Mike and Juan, Frank and Garry, Anna-
lise and Diva, Mrs Xhiu and Henry, Ben and Mandy and Billy,
Helmut . . . even Morgan.

Because she was a part of it now. Overwhelmed perhaps by
the rest of the Co-op, she had finally succumbed. She seemed to
want it too, such was her self-loathing.

They still thought it was just the wind. They thought it was
the hurricane whistling and whinnying and clicking like that.
Even after everything, they still didn't understand how powerful it was, collecting that way in the extension, the focus of all
their anger, frustration, envy, suspicion, hatred.

But downstairs, in the dim, cold light of the basement, their
collective will was transforming me. I was powerless to stop it.
I was helpless in the night. Close as I had come to leaving the
building, far as I had managed to walk away – I was being
sucked back, further in than I had ever gone before, deeper into
the hard rock core of the island.

And it had to be released. The pressure had been steadily
building and now it had to be purged. The pipes couldn't contain it any more. The brackets were breaking. The metal was
cracking. Everything was shaking. Steam was screaming.
Something had to give, a valve had to be opened. It had to be
unleashed, before everything exploded and everyone was lost.

M organ's mind rang with increasing velocity, like a spinning
top being primed on a drill of angry voices.

HELMUT: *They say I can't be Christie's dad any more.*

MIKE: *Juan just felt sorry for you. That was all it ever was.*

MRS XHIU: *Living with debt is like guilt. The more you owe, the more you have to pay.*

DIVA: *My flight was cancelled because of the hurricane.*

MANDY: *So was my train. I was leaving Ben to go stay with my mom.*

FRANK: *I'm tired of fighting with you, Morgan.*

HENRY: *We're going to counter-sue. Do you know who my father is?*

BEN: *Admit that it was you who told Susannah. I just want to hear you say it.*

Ulysses yapped incessantly at her heels, chasing her each time she tried to escape.

There seemed no way out. It was much hotter in the extension than she had anticipated. She was sweating heavily. She wondered why the air-conditioning wasn't helping. She was worried that the glass in the windows was going to crack. The storm was showing no signs of letting up.

She felt alone and terrified, blinded by everyone's glare. She could literally *feel* them hating her. She wondered why they had come. Was it for this – to make her suffer this way?

It just kept coming at her, like relentless nausea. She was adrift. The rain lashed from all sides. She felt a tremendous urge to go outside, onto the deck. The new smells of the extension reminded her of being down below, in an airless cabin. There was no horizon to focus on, to help her gather her bearings and her sense of balance. She could feel herself going.

And then the power went for a third time. The city was plunged into a darkness that made people gasp. There was the groaning sound of power and air-conditioning systems winding down. The extension moaned and creaked melodic strains, like a sinking ship meeting the deep.

In the hot blackness, Morgan considered how they'd built too many buildings in the city, how they'd allowed too many storeys. And the weight had become too much now. The hard rock that everyone had counted on for so long had finally given way. Maybe it was her fault. Maybe her extension had tipped the balance. Hers was the straw that had broken the camel's back. The whole island was sinking. She knew it.

As I waited, I saw Catherine again – one last time.

I was travelling on the escalator and watching her, waiting on the concourse, beneath the four-faced clock. Her arms were folded, but not crossed, across her chest. She looked to the north, as if she wanted me to admire her profile. Standing in the empty station like that, dressed that way in a waist-length coat and long, dark skirt, her hair cut short again now, like when we first met. It looked strange this time for some reason, maybe because the fashion had changed. She could have been posing for a photograph.

She didn't know anyone was looking but the Gods of the Zodiac were watching. Drawn between spotlight stars in dot-to-dot, they gazed down from the vaults of the evening-blue ceiling, the light trace of their magnificent figures hanging as if on gossamer thread.

The clocks jolted forward another one minute.

It was all a question of time.

We had been determined.

She noticed me just as I reached the bottom of the whirring escalator, moments before I stepped off. I must have touched the edge of her line of sight. She didn't smile at me. She just looked as if she wasn't sure if she recognized me, lost in wondering. There was a moment when I thought she might look away. I feared she might have forgotten.

I waved the notion away with the champagne bottle and grinned. My snowy heels clapped against the floor, shaking rain from my shoes. She smiled back. I walked briskly, the wet hems of my trousers clinging to my calves before coming unstuck and flapping heavily. She ran towards me. There wasn't much time.

We threw ourselves into one another, and breathed. I could smell wet hair and wool. I could smell her perfume. I could smell her skin. Through the clothes, my lips somehow found her neck.

'You're late,' she broke.

'The crowds were terrible.'

We looked at the clocks. They ticked.

'Open the champagne.'

I tore the wire wrapping away and put the bottle between my knees, aiming it like a cannon. I pressed my thumbs and fired the cork. She cheered. The foam poured out onto the floor. We guzzled from it stickily. I felt it dripping down my chin, making my scarf wetter.

In the distance we could hear people shouting a count-down.

'When do you leave?' I asked.

'Tomorrow.'

There was a roar, muted by walls.

'You mean today.'

She looked over her shoulder at the quiet clocks and turned back to me with a smile.

'Happy New Year, my darling.'

'Happy New Year,' I said.

She moved to kiss me but stopped in my arms.

'We won't see each other again,' she said.

'How long?'

'A month, maybe more. I'm not sure.'

'Nothing is certain.'

'It never is.'

'Will you wait?'

'Only if you look for me.'

I looked into her eyes, into the cracks of colour.

'You know I will.'

She smiled.

'Don't forget.'

'I won't.'

We kissed finally. She pulled me in. The Gods watched us.

I won't.

It was a long walk down to the basement. The flashlight showed the way. Down and round and down. Morgan was going all the way. Corners loomed large on walls, arcing up and over, pressing her down.

It had been her place to volunteer when Garry pointed out that everyone else's power had come back, except theirs. Morgan had been happy to get away. It had been so hot up in the extension she thought she was going to faint. She'd left them to light candles. They were among shadows now.

At the basement door she stopped. She could hear her heart beating. She could hear the howl of the wind tearing down the street outside like a mad dog. She told herself to hurry up but still she waited – for what, she wasn't sure. Something reassuring. There wasn't anything. Just the night.

She pulled on the doorknob and the hinge creaked with the amplified horror of the dark. Morgan tried to tell herself it was funny, it was just funny. But she was forced to admit to herself for the first time that she was scared.

'Mr McMurphy?' she called out. 'Are you down there?'

She swung the flashlight down the stairs but it wouldn't do what she wanted, it wouldn't turn corners, it wouldn't illuminate. It only showed her how dark it was. Dark and dank and quiet. She hated going down into the basement.

'Mr McMurphy?' she tried again, meekly.

She tipped a toe tentatively, as if testing the water, onto the first step. She found ground and pressed her heel down. She followed with the other foot, tottering slightly. It had started. She took another step, reassured, until the basement door swung to behind her, the hinges miraculously silent, with a crash.

She jumped, sighed and rested a hand on her heart. Her ribs

were pulsing. Convinced that she had been revealed, she called out again, this time with more determination.

'Mr McMurphy!'

But there was nothing – just the wind.

Morgan decided the super couldn't be here, though where he would be on a night like this Morgan had no clue. It was a more comforting explanation than the idea that he might not be answering. That wasn't a thought that Morgan really wanted to consider.

She started to march. The stairs clapped beneath her feet, helping keep time. One, two, three, four. One, two, three, four. She reached the small landing with its little curtained window looking straight out onto an obtusely angled brick wall. She about-faced and continued her efficient walk, all the way down, onto the concrete basement floor. The brave noise of her feet fell away instantly as she struck.

She could hear something – something faint. It sounded like a fly trapped against a windowpane, or something plastic scratching the floor. It was an annoying sound, a sound that she couldn't hope to identify in the darkness.

But she wanted to. She wanted to stop it. She wanted to scratch it out. It was making her bones ache. It was in her fingernails. It had climbed into the back of her teeth. She knew that if she didn't find it, it would go on. She might convince herself she was just imagining it. But she knew. It was the kind of noise that could drive someone insane.

Morgan swung her flashlight in one direction.

'Mr McMurphy, is that you?'

The sound disappeared but somehow Morgan knew that it was about to return. She hadn't found the source so it would go on. It was just resting. The fly was walking on the glass. It was only a matter of time.

Morgan swung the flashlight left, right, up, down. She saw jigsaw pieces of pipes and chicken wire and two-by-four and the concrete floor and the filing cabinet and a hanging bicycle and the boiler-room door and the laundry machines and the airshaft door and empty naked bulbs and dog tags and the security screens and Mr McMurphy's apartment and, finally, the wall of electricity meters. They hung like clocks showing times of the world, but they weren't ticking.

She moved towards them. She heard the strange chattering, insect noise again. She stopped. She squinted. It stopped. She walked some more. The wind was a din. It was so black down here. She heard it again. She tried to ignore it. She marched on. She approached the wall with the circuit breaker. She was going to make it.

But then she heard the door to the airshaft swing slowly open behind her. She turned.

'What in the . . . '

'   ell was that?' Garry said.
...   **H**   The tenants of 444 VanVanVane Street froze. They
searched for reassurance in each other's faces but found only
wide, wild eyes among the flickering shadows of candlelight.

'It came from the bathroom,' Mike said.

They all turned and stared. They could see the bathroom
door rattling violently in its frame. There was the rippled reflection of a flame at the bottom of the door.

'Maybe it was a pipe,' Mike added.

'I don't think so,' Helmut said.

'Where's all that water coming from?'

Garry stepped towards the bathroom door and rested a hand
on the shaking door handle. It tugged at him. He squeezed on
it, as if pulling a trigger.

'Garry, don't!' Frank called out.

But it was too late. The door tore itself out of his hand. There
was a massive explosion of wind, overwhelming the sound of
their screams. It nearly knocked Mrs Xhiu over. Garry had to
grab hold of the doorframe to steady himself. Everyone
crouched, instinctively, to the floor.

The bathroom door slammed randomly between walls of
wind before quickly coming loose, like the rest of the bathroom, and flying away high into the night, spinning lethally.

Remnants of what had just been – sharp sections of porce-
lain, ripped pieces of wall – danced in large puddles on the roof
deck. Half the bathroom ceiling hung down like hair. The world
was a black hole. And they were about to get sucked into it.

'EVERYBODY DOWNSTAIRS!' Garry screamed over his
shoulder. 'NOW!'

Juan and Mrs Xhiu had already started, smearing the rain

that had blasted into the room like shrapnel away from their faces, battling against the howling elements for the circular stairwell. Henry and Anna-lise followed. Diva and Helmut were next.

'GARRY!' Frank yelled.

'GO!'

Somehow Mike managed to grab hold of Garry's arm to pull him away. They shared a look that Mike needed. He still didn't know if Garry had forgiven him. He didn't know if he had forgiven himself. But there wasn't time for that now. Together they grabbed Frank and ran.

They all fell down, one after the other, down the circular stairs like it was a slide, ignoring the blows to their elbows and knees. At the bottom Mrs Xhiu fell with a squeal and sprained her wrist. Juan pulled her away to safety.

Moments later, they all watched as the roof of the extension peeled away like someone fanning through a deck of cards. Debris rained down through the stairwell opening. A piece of glass kissed Henry's forehead, leaving a lipstick mark. Anna-lise pressed down on it tightly with the edge of her sleeve.

There was a final, tremendous, heaving groan. They looked up again. There was a loud flash, a snap of lightning, and then they saw; the thing had simply gone.

Morgan stepped up stairs and through the fire-escape hatch. She walked into the airshaft. It was strangely calm inside. She could still hear the wind howling on the other side of walls and she could see the clouds swirling like a whirlpool in the sky above but there wasn't much violence here. It was like being in the eye of the storm. She felt much more at ease.

Lights from 443 spilled into the area, revealing sections in soft golden rectangles, but it was still quite dark. Morgan had to squint to see properly. But seeing the way 443 was lit up made her remember her purpose. She wasn't about to hang around. She strode confidently on.

'Mr McMurphy, are you in here?' she called out impatiently.

Still, there was no reply.

'What does that stupid man think he is doing?' she muttered to herself. 'Mr McMurphy, can you tell me why we have no power? I'll have you know I'm trying to host a party upstairs. Mr McMurphy? Are you deaf? Mr McMurphy!'

Just then the doors to the fire-escape hatch slammed themselves shut. Morgan span round and stared. Were they supposed to do that? It seemed extremely dangerous. What if she'd been coming up the stairs at that precise moment? She could have been killed.

She felt a quick surge of anger push herself forward another step, into the perfect position. Then there was a rip of thunder directly above that made her jump. She looked up, half wondering why there'd been no lightning, just as the rooftop extension started hurtling down at her with bewildering speed and agility. Morgan could just make out the ends of the cornice work falling apart from one of the ripped walls and realized in an instant of irritation that it would have to be redone. Only then did it register that she was about to be crushed. By then it was too late.

'Interesting.'

The construction collapsed in an explosion of wood and plaster and tiles and mortar and dust. Morgan was killed instantly, her brain smashed by a slab of granite, her body squashed by rafters. The only part left untouched were her feet, which stuck out from under the wreckage, her Yarko Thomas Mary Janes still shining with glossy red polish.

One Year Later

N ext on the agenda, the sale of Apartment P1,' Frank said, pressing the clipboard into his lap.

He looked up at the rest of the Board, sucking on his lips. They looked back at him with the same lost smiles.

'Has it really been a year already?' Mrs Xhiu asked.

Frank nodded quietly. 'To the day,' he replied.

'I still find it hard to believe,' Mike said.

'Walking out into the airshaft on a night like that,' Ben said. 'I can't imagine what might have possessed her.'

'She must have finally got the message,' Garry said.

'Poor Morgan,' Anna-lise added.

They all dropped their looks in sober respect.

'Well,' Frank sighed, 'the enquiry is over. The authorities are satisfied. I spoke to them this morning. They've closed the case.'

'They never really opened it,' Mike said. 'Lots of people died that night. They blame it all on the freak weather.'

'Yeah, but you would have thought—' Garry stopped.

'What?' Anna-lise asked.

'I dunno, I just thought the City might want to prosecute somebody – the construction company, maybe.'

No one said anything.

'We're getting off the subject,' Frank resumed. 'What are we going to do about P1?'

'Henry says he'll buy it,' Anna-lise said.

Everyone smiled at her.

'Hasn't Henry done enough?' Frank asked.

Anna-lise shrugged.

'The money's not important. He doesn't want someone new coming into the building, someone we don't already know. He wants us to be a real co-operative from now on. His words, not mine.'

They all nodded in appreciation.

'The least we can do is sell it to him at a discounted rate,' Frank suggested. 'Morgan's estate will no longer have an interest.'

'What would you suggest?' Mike asked.

'I dunno,' Frank said. 'How are the books looking, Mr Treasurer?'

'Flush,' Ben replied. 'In fact, I was going to propose a motion to abolish maintenance. There seems little need for it now.'

'Are you sure that's wise?' Mrs Xhiu asked.

'I don't see why not. Thanks to the Water Board compensation package and Henry's generosity, the building has no debt. All major construction has been taken care of. Money is just sitting in the bank earning interest.'

'And what about the future?'

'As long as we stick to the hundred per cent flip-tax rule we reintroduced, there should be no need to worry. If anyone leaves, there'll be more than enough in the accounts. If we all stay, then we can work off the understanding that everyone chips in. It will be just like before, in the old days.'

'A real co-operative,' Anna-lise said.

'Exactly,' Frank added.

Everyone nodded, feeling good.

'OK, then,' Frank restarted. 'Why don't we set the price of P1 at a level where the accounts will be comfortable – shall we say a hundred thousand dollars?'

'That's too low!' Anna-lise said. 'Henry's prepared to pay a million for it.'

There was a grumble of benign disagreement, like Congressmen.

'What's the matter?' Anna-lise pressed. 'It's easily worth that much.'

The Board shook its head at her.

'At least let him pay half a million,' Anna-lise said.

Frank looked at her with Morgan-like severity. 'A quarter of a million and that's our final offer.'

Anna-lise groaned. 'Have it your way, then.'

'Thank you,' Frank said. 'And please tell your husband that we're very grateful. We don't get to see so much of him these days.'

'He's busy,' Anna-lise said, a little sadly. 'Taking the company public.'

'We understand,' Frank said quietly.

There was a pause.

'So will you move upstairs, then, Anna-lise?' Garry restarted. 'What will you do with it?'

'We've decided we like where we are,' Anna-lise said. 'Putting the staircase between our two apartments has made all the difference. It's like living in a house, same difference anyway. Better for the baby.'

'You could always rebuild Morgan's extension,' Mike said. 'You'd have tons of space then.'

Anna-lise smiled at him. 'I don't think that's such a good idea, do you? Not after what happened.'

'That was just shoddy work. You wouldn't have to cut corners like Morgan did.'

'Still,' Anna-lise said, wincing.

Mike looked at her. 'Maybe you're right,' he said.

'No,' Anna-lise continued. 'We've decided we'd like to give P1 to Mack.'

Everyone nodded with quick and happy approval, except for Frank.

'What?' Anna-lise said, looking at him.

'I'm sorry, everyone,' Frank said slowly. 'I've got some sad news. Mack's leaving us.'

There was a gasp.

'He told me last night.'

'But why?' Ben said.

'Did we do something wrong?' Mrs Xhiu said.

'I thought he was happy,' Mike added.

'Me too,' Garry said. 'What will happen to the airshaft garden?'

'He says it's our responsibility now,' Frank said. 'He wants us to look after it for him. He says he's taken care of the hard part. The soil is fertile.'

'Will he come back?' Anna-lise asked.

'I don't think so.'

'Where's he going?' Mrs Xhiu asked.

'I don't know,' Frank replied.

There was a long silence. They looked at one another like children being forced to grow up, uncertain as to whether or not they could fly.

'When?' Mike asked.

'Soon,' Frank replied.

'He always said he wanted to spend more time outside,' Mrs Xhiu said wistfully. 'Maybe get out of the city.'

'I can't believe he's going,' Garry said. 'After everything . . . '

They all looked at each other meaningfully.

'I know,' Frank said.

They all came to say goodbye. It was strange to see them together that way, without knowing what they were thinking, without being able to hear them any more.

My hearing started to fade the day after the hurricane. First, the noise in the pipes went. Then I couldn't hear them outside. Later I couldn't even see them in their apartments – know what they were thinking, doing, saying, feeling. I was just left to myself, to my own thoughts, as I should always have been.

Now they looked to me like people, just normal folks. I watched them from the window as the cab pulled away, standing proudly and happily on the doorstep to 444 VanVanVane Street, arm in arm, hand in hand, like one big happy family, waving me farewell.

I was proud of what they had managed to achieve in spite of me. I hoped that maybe, somehow, I had been of some assistance, however cock-eyed it may have been. I wasn't much in control, looking back on things.

I did get one last message from them, weeks later, from nowhere, in the night, like the last paragraph of a narrative, a final piece of the puzzle that they perhaps wanted me to see.

The airshaft garden throbbed. The tenants all busied themselves between colours. Sunlight rained. Mike was struggling to turf one corner. Ben and Helmut were cleaning the beehive stand. Anna-lise and Juan were upstairs in the new penthouse community nursery, with the kids. Frank told Mandy she should take a break from training the wisteria. Mandy held her back and wiped sweat from her brow and nodded at her belly in appreciation. Garry smiled at Frank warmly. Mrs Xhiu and Diva were tackling triangles of busy Lizzies with Carlo and Hazel from 443 Hanover Street. Carlo stabbed the dark, moist earth with a trowel, his face screwed up like spaghetti on a fork.

It was a good scene.

We live in Montauk.

She always said it was the closest we'd get to Ireland without actually going back.

We spend most our time looking out at the Atlantic from the headland, the tip of the American Pier. It feels like we're looking back over both our lives, our history ahead of us.

She hasn't changed, a few grey hairs. She has her hair long again, tied up in an ambassadorial bun, like a stateswoman for old age. Her face is as I always remembered but her teacher's eyes look young on her now.

I wish I could say the same for myself. All that time spent in the basement has made my skin a strange colour. There's a blue luminescence to it, like blind eyes.

And spending all that time in other people's minds has taken its toll on my features. Parts of myself look nothing like they used to. Even though it has released me, the collective has had a particularly bad influence on the size of my ears. They're enormous, though I claim it's just with old age.

Of course, it wouldn't let me go without saving one laugh for last. I always vaguely suspected it might happen, though I never knew why. Maybe it's just a way of making sure I don't ever go back. If so, I'm grateful for the gesture.

One thing is for sure: I wouldn't make much of a superintendent now. I wouldn't be able to understand a single instruction, let alone manage an entire co-op building. Catherine has a hard time just getting me to do the simplest of tasks, unless she manages to catch my eye. It's nice. After all these years, in my old age, I've finally found a quiet place I can relax in. I don't even have to try any more.

I've gone deaf.

Acknowledgements

I would like to thank the following people who have helped me, in many varied ways, and so share the credit for this work. Without your support none of this would have been possible. Thank you all.

In no particular order: Shai Hill, Tara Wigley, Suzanne Baboneau, Andrew Nurnberg, my wife Maria, Libby Vernon, Oriel Prizeman, Pari Grey, Brenda Gravelle, my parents and family, Rachael Horsewood, Jonty Woodhouse, Elisa Rivlin, Ian Hutton, Ian Chapman, Digby Halsby, Toby and Tanya McPherson, Emma Lo, Ben Ray, Mark Nicholls, Helen English, Pete and Georgia Raphael, Shan Millie, Vicky Mark, David Cahill, Melissa Weatherill, Annette Crossland, Sheila and Peter Cousins, David Hooper, Isobel Griffiths, Rivka Greenberg, Robin Strauss, Cindy Spiegel, Martin Evans, Nigel Stoneman, Adrienne Page, Dominic Powers, Pauline Read, Grandma.

Finally to friends who have passed: Mary, Neil and Dinah – you are missed and remembered.

Thanks also to Suhrkamp Verlag for use of the Herman Hesse quote, © Suhrkamp Verlag GmbH und Co. KG, and to EMI for use of the lyrics for 'What's Going On'. Words and music by Alfred Cleveland, Marvin Gaye and Renaldo Benson © 1970, Jobete Music Co Inc/Stone Agate Music, USA. Reproduced by permission of Jobete Music Co Inc/EMI Music Publishing Ltd, London WC2H 0QY.